Praise for Emma Miller and her novels

"There is warmth to the characters that will leave readers looking forward to seeing more."

—*RT Book Reviews* on *A Match for Addy*

"A captivating story."

—*RT Book Reviews* on *Miriam's Heart*

"[A] heart-warming romance."

—*RT Book Reviews* on *Courting Ruth*

Praise for Marta Perry and her novels

"Marta Perry's warm novel…is a well-written story."

—*RT Book Reviews* on *Hide in Plain Sight*

"While love is a powerful entity in this story, danger is never too far behind. Top Pick!"

—*RT Book Reviews* on *Season of Secrets*

"*A Christmas to Die For*…is an exceptionally written story in which danger and romance blend nicely."

—*RT Book Reviews*

Emma Miller lives quietly in her old farmhouse in rural Delaware. Fortunate enough to be born into a family of strong faith, she grew up on a dairy farm surrounded by loving parents, siblings, grandparents, aunts, uncles and cousins. Emma was educated in local schools and once taught in an Amish schoolhouse. When she's not caring for her large family, reading and writing are her favorite pastimes.

Marta Perry realized she wanted to be a writer at age eight, when she read her first Nancy Drew novel. A lifetime spent in rural Pennsylvania and her own Pennsylvania Dutch roots led Marta to the books she writes now about the Amish. When she's not writing, Marta is active in the life of her church and enjoys traveling and spending time with her three children and six beautiful grandchildren. Visit her online at martaperry.com.

EMMA MILLER

Leah's Choice

&

MARTA PERRY

Hide in Plain Sight

HARLEQUIN® LOVE INSPIRED®

Recycling programs for this product may not exist in your area.

ISBN-13: 978-0-373-83897-4

Leah's Choice and Hide in Plain Sight

This edition published by arrangement with Love Inspired Books.

www.Harlequin.com

Printed in U.S.A.

CONTENTS

LEAH'S CHOICE

Emma Miller

Do not press me to leave you
Or to turn back from following you!
Where you go, I will go;
Where you lodge, I will lodge;
Your people shall be my people.
And your God my God.
—*Ruth* 1:16

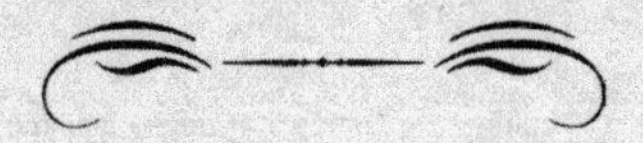

Chapter 1

Kent County, Delaware, Spring

More than forty people, Mennonite and Amish, waited in the old Grange building for the speaker's arrival. A long table covered with photographs and maps stood at the rear of the hall, and volunteers had arranged folding chairs in two sections, one on either side of a central aisle. Leah Yoder, three of her sisters, her brother-in-law, and nine giggling and whispering Amish teenagers from Seven Poplars filled the first two rows on the left.

It was rare for Old Order Amish to attend events hosted by other denominations, but tonight was an exception. Leah's older sister, Miriam, and her husband, Charley, had volunteered to chaperone the outing for their church's youth group, the Gleaners, and the bishop had given them special permission to do so. Leah, at twenty, was too old for the Gleaners, but she had been just as eager as her younger sisters, Rebecca and Susanna, to see the PowerPoint presentation and hear the Mennonite missionary share his experiences in spreading God's word outside the United States.

A young man in jeans and a raincoat, carrying a briefcase and a camera, wandered in from the offices in the back, and Leah thought that he might be the speaker, but it was only a reporter from a local newspaper. She hoped that he wouldn't attempt to take photos of the audience. Having pictures taken was against Amish beliefs, and if he tried to snap their picture, Charley and Miriam might decide that it was better to leave. To Leah's relief, the man found a seat near the front and didn't even look across the aisle at them.

The program had been scheduled to start at seven, but it was already twenty past the hour and Susanna was growing restless. Susanna had been born with Down syndrome, and although she was eighteen, in many ways, she would always be a child. Leah had convinced their mother to allow her to bring Susanna to the presentation this evening, so her sister was her responsibility.

Susanna wasn't the only one losing patience with the long wait. Herman Beachy, who could never sit still for long, was tugging at his sister Verna's bonnet strings and, by the expression on her face, she appeared ready to give him a sharp elbow in the ribs. Amish considered themselves nonviolent, but that didn't mean brothers and sisters didn't have their spats. Leah could see that the rest of the Gleaners were keyed up as well. If the youngsters became unruly, it would reflect badly on the entire Amish community, and that would put an end to any future outings of this kind.

Leah leaned forward, cleared her throat and threw Charley a meaningful look. *See what's keeping him,* she mouthed silently.

We'll just wait, he mouthed in return.

Leah rolled her eyes in exasperation. What was wrong with Charley? It had been his idea to bring the youth group, but now that they were here and things weren't going as smoothly as expected, her usually gregarious brother-in-law seemed unsure of himself. Even Miriam seemed out of her element.

Leah wished she and Rebecca had come alone, as she'd first planned when she'd seen the notice for Daniel Brown's talk. The sisters had recently returned to Delaware after spending a year in Ohio caring for their aging grandmother and great-aunt. The Amish church in *Grossmama*'s community had been more liberal than in Seven Poplars, and she and her sister had often gone to dinners, charity auctions and programs put on by the Mennonites. There, the two denominations mingled more regularly than in Seven Poplars.

Leah had never stopped to think that not all Old Order Amish were so at ease with the Mennonite community. And the same went for the Mennonites. She'd certainly seen it tonight when the Amish had all taken seats on one side of the aisle and the Mennonites on the other. And now, both Charley and Miriam, of all people, seemed nervous. Well, if they wouldn't go see what was going on, she'd have to.

"Stay here with Rebecca," she whispered to Susanna as she stood up.

Smiling, Susanna nodded and clasped Rebecca's hand.

Leah crossed the aisle to where a gray-haired woman

stood talking anxiously to a middle-aged man. Dinah was a cheerful woman who always wore a modest dress and a white crocheted head covering. She often stopped by the Yoder farm to purchase large quantities of eggs for her church bake sales. It was Dinah who'd made a special point of inviting the Seven Poplars Amish community to hear the speaker.

"It's an opportunity not to be missed," she'd said to Leah's mother, Hannah, a few weeks ago. "Daniel Brown faced down an angry Moroccan mob to rescue a homeless youth falsely accused of theft. If Daniel hadn't put his own life in danger to interfere, a tragedy could have occurred."

"An excellent role model for our children," Mam had agreed. She'd said no more about Daniel Brown, but Leah had seen her mother deep in conversation with their bishop after church the following Sunday. Both Leah and Miriam were convinced that it was due to Mam's powers of persuasion that Bishop Atlee had agreed that the Gleaners should accept the invitation to hear the young missionary speak.

But now they were here and anxious for the program to begin…and there was no Daniel Brown in sight.

"I apologize for the delay," Dinah said as Leah approached. "Daniel's on his way. He's usually very dependable, but he had some problem. Something about leaving his coat at a rest stop." Dinah chuckled. "Men. But, we're so pleased that so many from your church have come out to hear Daniel, especially the young people."

"We didn't want them to miss hearing Daniel's story," Leah said. "How often do we have a real hero in our midst?"

"Exactly," Dinah agreed. "Oh, Leah, do you know my eldest son, Raymond?" When Leah nodded, Dinah went on. "Raymond's been trying to reach Daniel on his cell phone to see how soon he expects to arrive, but he hasn't had any luck. We thought he'd be here by now."

"I'm sure it's just the storm." Leah offered a quick smile.

It was raining hard outside, and the wind was rattling the shutters. Earlier, as they'd driven here from the farm, they'd been caught in a sudden flurry of thunder and lightning so fierce that Leah had wondered if she should turn back, but that had passed, leaving just a steady downpour. Fortunately, there was a long, open shed with a good roof behind the Grange where they could shelter the horses and buggies.

"Daniel's driving up from Richmond," Dinah explained, "and I understand that Virginia's had bad weather all day."

The side door opened, and everyone glanced up expectantly. "Evening, Daniel," Dinah said. "Maude." The couple took seats on the Mennonite side in the last row, and Dinah turned back to Leah. "That's Daniel *Warner* and his wife." She dropped her voice to a whisper. "They're always late."

"I'd hoped that was the speaker," Leah said.

Dinah laughed. "We seem to have a lot of Daniels in our community. It's a popular name among us. One of my sons is also a Daniel. Named after my father-in-law. My husband always teased that perhaps we should give them nicknames to keep the Daniels straight." Another gust of wind shook the windowpanes and she grimaced. "If we'd realized that it would be such a nasty evening, we could have postponed until tomorrow night."

"I see that there are pictures and other material up front." Leah pointed. "I was wondering if it would be all right if the young people looked at them while we're waiting." She chuckled. "You know how impatient youngsters can get. They've been looking forward to tonight for weeks."

"Absolutely," Dinah said. "And we have a refreshment table. There's no reason we shouldn't all enjoy lemonade and cookies while—"

Abruptly, the heavy door at the front of the building banged open and a blast of wind blew through the hall sending photos and maps flying. Leah turned to see a tall, slim man about twenty-five years old standing in the doorway. Water dripped off his jean jacket and the bill of his ball cap, pooling on the floor. A gust tore at the door, threatening to wrench it out of his grasp, but he held it open until ten-year-old Abraham Beachy ducked into the hall.

Abraham was even wetter than the man in the jean jacket and ball cap. The Amish boy's face was pale and he looked frightened. The man said something to him that Leah couldn't hear, but Abraham just shuffled his feet and stared at the floor.

The newcomer looked up and cleared his throat. "Could I have your attention, please!" He nodded to Abraham who shook his head. "Go ahead," he urged.

Everyone in their chairs who hadn't turned around to look when they made their entrance, turned now.

Abraham swallowed hard and a deep flush rose from his throat to tint his face. "…Need help," he squeaked. "…Joey."

Charley stood up and hurried toward Abraham. "What's wrong?" he demanded.

Abraham, an undersized lad, burst into tears. Leah left Dinah and Raymond and walked down the aisle toward the Beachy boy.

"Abraham's parents—Norman and Lydia Beachy—have asked for help," the stranger said, speaking for Abraham. "It seems one of their children—"

"Joey!" Abraham wailed. "We can't...can't find... Joey."

"Their six-year-old son has gone missing," the man explained calmly, turning his attention to the Amish side of the aisle. "The family has asked if your youth group can come to their farm and help with the search."

Miriam walked up to the stranger. "Of course," she said. "We'll all help."

Chairs scraped against the worn floorboards. Everyone in the hall, Amish and Mennonite alike, stood.

"We have to look for Joey," Abraham managed. "It's all my fault. I... I lost him."

"It'll be all right." Miriam put an arm around Abraham. She was short, but Abraham's head barely reached her chin.

"Lost him where?" Leah asked. She couldn't imagine a six-year-old out in this weather. It didn't make sense. Maybe he was hiding somewhere in the rambling Beachy farmhouse or in the barn or outbuildings. With fourteen children under the age of sixteen, it was easy for Lydia to lose track of one little boy. That didn't mean that Joey was really lost.

Herman Beachy, Abraham's brother, hurried up to him. "What do you mean you *lost* him?" Herman demanded. Their sister, Verna, covered her face with her hands and sank back into her chair.

"How did you find out about the missing boy, Daniel?" A Mennonite girl only a little younger than Leah joined them. "Daniel's my cousin," she whispered to Leah. "I'm Caroline Steiner. I think you know some of my Steiner cousins in Ohio. From Hope Mennonite Church?"

"Sophie and Jeanine." Leah nodded.

"Hey, Caroline." Daniel offered a worried smile. "It's good to see you. Abraham's father flagged me down at the end of his lane," he explained. "He knew that some of the young people from their church were here with their group leaders and asked if I could bring Abraham to ask for help looking for the boy."

"You can count on us," Charley said.

He and Miriam went back to their group and began to organize them. Leah knew that some of the children were too young to join in. The girls' parents, especially, would want them safely delivered home. Luckily, they'd come in four buggies. Rebecca could be trusted to drive Susanna and some of the others home; Miriam could manage the rest.

As for Leah, she had no intention of going home. She'd always had a particular fondness for freckle-faced Joey. She would offer to take Verna, Abraham and Herman back to the Beachy farm, and once she was there, no one would object to her joining the search.

As the Amish moved toward the doors, the newcomer strode past Leah and called out to the Mennonites. "Michael? Gilbert? Who'll come with me to find the boy?"

"I'd be glad to," a stout man answered. "I've got a flashlight in the truck, but there are a lot of woods and fields around here, and I'm not familiar with the area."

"So we'll form groups," Daniel said, checking his pockets. "Someone can ride with me, if they like…soon as I find my keys." He looked up, extracting keys from a jacket pocket. "We'll make certain that there's someone in each group who does know their way." There was a chorus of agreement as men and women raised their hands and offered to help.

Leah knotted her bonnet strings and waved at Caroline just before dashing out into the rain. It made her feel good that Caroline's cousin had urged the others to join in the search.

She couldn't help but think how attractive the new Daniel was. He had a serious but handsome face, and nice hands that were never still when he was talking, even after he'd found his keys. As he'd walked past her in the aisle, Leah had noticed that his eyes were clear green—he had beautiful eyes. She couldn't remember ever meeting anyone with eyes that green before.

After telling the children to wait for her at the door, Leah made a run for the buggy. With so many more volunteers, she was certain they'd find Joey quickly. As Mam often said, most people had good hearts and were willing to do the right thing, if someone would just point them in the right direction.

Minutes later, Leah guided her horse up the muddy lane to the Beachy farmhouse. Buggies, SUVs and pickup trucks already filled the yard. Amish neighbors always came to help out in any emergency, but the Mennonites and Englishers were more than welcome. Norman, Joey's father, stood in the pouring rain, shaking hands with friends and strangers alike and thanking everyone for coming, but it was Samuel Mast, their church deacon, who appeared to be in charge.

One of the kids took Leah's horse and promised to

find the mare a dry stall in the barn. A red-eyed Lydia came to the back door and called for Leah to join the women in the kitchen. Leah hesitated, then went in, but kept her green rain slicker on. It wasn't Amish clothing, but Mam had bought everyone in the family one at an Englisher store years ago.

"I'm going right back out," Leah explained to the worried Lydia. "To help with the search."

As usual, Lydia's kitchen was complete chaos, with toddlers dashing about, a cat carrying kittens to a basket in the corner of the room, and Jesse, Joey's twin brother, climbing up on the counter to get something out of the cupboard.

Leah was surprised to see her Aunt Martha standing at the counter making coffee. Aunt Martha and Lydia didn't usually visit each other's homes, and Leah wondered how her aunt had heard the news about Joey and gotten here so fast, but then Leah's mother, Hannah, came from the hallway with Lydia's newest baby in her arms.

Samuel must have gone for Mam, Leah thought, leaving her sister Anna, his wife, home with their children. Samuel would have guessed that Lydia needed Hannah, Leah's mother. And somehow, Aunt Martha had included herself in the emergency.

"You're certain you want to go out with the men?" Aunt Martha asked. She had the misfortune to be born with a nasally voice that always came out sounding as if she was peeved at someone.

Leah nodded. "I am."

"I told you she would." Hannah handed the fussing baby to Lydia.

Aunt Martha wiped her hands on her apron, poured a

cup of steaming coffee and pressed it into Leah's hands. "Drink this," she ordered. "If you're determined to go out in this rain and catch your death, you'll need it."

"Thanks, Aunt Martha, but I couldn't drink a drop."

Her aunt frowned, and Leah knew she'd offended her again when she voiced a *thank you.* Most Amish considered *please* and *thank you* to be fancy words. *Showing off.* The service to one another and the thanks were assumed, and such words weren't bandied about, but that was another habit she'd picked up from her more worldly friends back in Ohio.

"I need to go." Leah gave the coffee to her mother. "The search parties are getting organized."

"I wouldn't stand for my Dorcas to be out in the dark with strangers. Not my daughter," Aunt Martha fussed. "That's a man's place, not a woman's, and certainly not a girl's." She threw a meaningful look at Mam. "This is what comes of her running wild out in Ohio, going to fairs with her Mennonite friends, eating ice cream at all hours and taking herself to every frolic in the county."

"Not every frolic, Aunt Martha," Leah defended. "Rebecca and I spent most of the time taking care of *Grossmama.*"

Aunt Martha scowled. "Not what I hear."

"All these years and all these blessed children, and I've lost nary a one before," Lydia fretted to no one in particular, rocking the baby. "Where can my Joey be?"

"*I'm* here, Mam," Jesse piped up.

"You hush," Lydia corrected. "And get down off that counter before I dust your bottom."

Jesse ignored her and kept digging in the cabinet. Aunt Martha scooped him up, deposited him on the floor and said. "You heard your mother. Shoo!"

Jesse shooed.

"Joey's just turned six and he's scared of the dark." Lydia glanced at the dark windows. "Where can he have got to?"

"We'll find him," Leah promised.

"Be glad you've got other children," Aunt Martha intoned as she cut herself a slice of chocolate cake. "Reuben and I were never so blessed."

Leah wished her aunt had stayed at home. Lydia didn't need to hear that. She was worried enough. "Have the kids searched the barns and the house?" Leah asked.

Lydia nodded. "Root cellar to attic. I've had the girls digging through the straw in the hayloft and looking under the chicken house. God help him, he's such a rascal to put us all through this."

Mam removed her blue headscarf and handed it to Leah. "Give me your *kapp* and bonnet," she said. "The woods at night are no place to be wearing your bonnet. And button up your slicker all the way. It will keep the rain off."

"Be quick about it," Aunt Martha said. "It's not seemly for either of you to go uncovered. With all these Englishers and Mennonites wandering about, no telling who might take it into his head to wander in the kitchen without knocking."

Leah quickly traded head coverings with her mother.

Seconds later, Charley opened the door and peered in. "Come on if you're coming, Leah. Samuel's assigning groups to search together."

"I've got to go, Mam." Leah gave the ends of the headscarf she tied beneath her chin a firm tug.

Fresh tears filled Lydia's eyes and rolled down her

cheeks. "You find my Joey," she murmured, rocking the baby against her.

"I'll do my best," Leah said.

Her mother put her arms around Leah and kissed her on the forehead. "You take care, daughter. I'd not have you come to harm out there in the dark."

"I'll be careful, I promise."

Mam as usual, was worrying unnecessarily. What could possibly happen to her if she wasn't stupid enough to fall into the pond or walk into a tree? It was Joey Leah was worried about. A lot of things could happen to a lost six-year-old on a night like this…none of them good.

Chapter 2

Twenty minutes after arriving at the Beachy farm, Daniel found himself trudging through a pasture in the rain with his cousins Caroline and Leslie, whom he would be staying with, and a young Amish woman, Leah Yoder. It was a strange turn of events. He'd expected to spend the evening giving his PowerPoint presentation, but this wasn't the first time that God had steered him in a new direction.

Daniel had learned to listen to his inner voice, and it had never failed him. No message had ever come stronger than the need to join in the hunt for little Joey Beachy and to enlist the Mennonite community in the search. His talk could be given another day. A child's life might be in danger, and Daniel couldn't stand by while others went out to find him.

Growing up, he'd often been rebellious. He loved his

parents and family, and he knew the importance of the missionary work that they did, but he'd never thought it was the life for him. When he'd left them in Morocco to go to college in the States, he'd insisted on a typical college experience. He hadn't even gone to the Mennonite Bible School that his parents and his older brother had attended. Instead, he'd gone to the University of Ohio to study nursing. He'd expected to work in a small community hospital in the Midwest when he graduated, but then, like now, God had other plans for him. In the end, he liked to think that his early rebellion against his parents' expectations had better prepared him for his life.

Daniel suddenly felt his foot slip in a water-filled hole and he threw his hands out to try to regain his balance. At the same moment, Leah grabbed his arm to steady him, keeping him from falling onto his bottom. "Thanks," he said as he righted himself, giving her a sheepish smile.

"Careful where you step," she cautioned. "You'll do Joey no good if you twist an ankle."

Leah's grip was strong. Being a farm girl, he supposed she must be used to lifting hay bales and chopping wood, but he still felt a little foolish. He should have been the one coming to *her* rescue.

Caroline giggled. "And watch out for the cow pies."

"Plenty of those out here too," Leah agreed, a hint of amusement in her voice.

"I'm good now." Daniel pulled away his hand, telling himself he shouldn't feel embarrassed. He'd have done the same for her, wouldn't he?

Daniel had been glad when Samuel Mast had picked Leah to accompany his group.

"She knows these woods and fields," Samuel had explained quietly to him. "We're glad for your help, but it's easy to get turned around out there if you don't know where you're going. You'll be all right with Leah. She's a sensible girl."

Watching Leah in the dark, Daniel thought that it was probably a good assessment. She was dressed for the downpour in boots and a rain slicker and she'd brought her own flashlight. She was keeping the strong beam steady to light their way.

In spite of the confusion at the Grange, Daniel had noticed red-haired Leah right away. Not only was she particularly attractive, but he'd been struck by how worldly she'd seemed for a young Amish woman. Her starched white *kapp* and modest blue dress and cape had looked exactly like those of her companions, but Leah Yoder stood out among them. She maintained a certain poise he didn't usually see in Amish women. It was immediately clear that she had a strong personality and was a take-charge type of person, all characteristics he admired.

Daniel remembered that when he was in Ohio recently, a cousin had talked at length about her Amish friend, Leah, from Delaware and the fun they'd had last summer at the county fair. He wondered if this could be the same Leah. It had to be. How many Amish Leahs could there be in Kent County, Delaware?

After all the search groups had been organized back in the barnyard, Samuel had suggested that each group choose a leader. Samuel had made a joke about Daniel not letting his girls get out of hand, and the other men had thought it funny.

Daniel ended up being the only man on an otherwise all-female team, but it didn't matter to him. He'd promised his Aunt Joyce, Caroline and Leslie's mother, that he'd look after them if they were allowed to help in the search. He had every intention of keeping his word, but once they'd left the barnyard, he suggested Leah take the leader's position in the group.

"You don't want to?" she'd asked. "I have to warn you, you might get some teasing from the men if they hear about it."

"I'm not a country boy," he'd explained. "It would be foolish for me to tell you where we should look for Joey. You know the area. Besides, I'd get us all lost in the dark, and search parties would have to come find us."

Caroline had chuckled. "He's right, Leah. Daniel's sense of direction isn't that great. He got lost at Hershey Park with his church group."

"I was only eight," Daniel had protested. "And the whole family has teased me about it ever since."

"Believe me," Caroline had said. "We're all safer if you lead the way, Leah."

"All right," Leah had agreed. "If you put it that way, but we may have to walk a long way and there will be fences to climb and briars to wade through."

"Lead on, Sacagawea," Daniel had said. "I promise not to wimp out."

And here they were now, in the dark, in the rain, mud sucking at Daniel's best leather shoes. His *only* pair of good shoes.

The pasture was huge. After they'd gone far enough that the house was only a small light in the distance, Caroline asked Leah if she knew how Joey had gotten lost in the first place.

Leah slowed her pace so that they could walk closer together. "Barbara—that's Joey's sister—told me that their mother had sent Abraham and Minnie to find their Jersey cow."

"The Beachys must have a large family," Leslie remarked.

"Fairly large." Leah flashed the light across a hole to be sure they all saw it. "Joey has thirteen brothers and sisters."

"So what happened in this hunt for the cow?" Caroline asked.

"Abraham and Minnie went out looking for Matilda," Leah continued, keeping the flashlight beam steady ahead of them. "Watch out for that briar." She pointed. "The spines are sharp enough to go through your clothes."

"Who's Matilda?"

"Matilda is the cow. Matilda hadn't come in to be milked with the rest of the herd. Apparently she's due to drop her calf in a few weeks, and Lydia was concerned about her. Pregnant cows sometimes wander off and hide, and a rainy April night is no place for a newborn calf."

"Too cold, I suppose," Daniel offered. He didn't know a thing about cows, even less about cows having calves, but it seemed logical.

"True," Leah agreed. "But more than that, there's a pack of dogs in the neighborhood. Englishers like to drop their unwanted pets near our farms. I guess they think that we can take in every stray, but we can't. It's a real problem for farmers or anyone with livestock." She sighed deeply. "There are four or five dogs in this particular pack. I doubt they were abandoned together, but they found each other. Left to fend for themselves, eventually even pets turn feral. They kill squirrels and deer and rabbits to live, but they find their way into barnyards. Penned animals are easier prey. My Uncle Reuben lost a milk goat to them this winter. I'm sure Lydia was afraid that if Matilda dropped her calf, the dogs would smell the blood and come after them."

"Almost like wolves." Leslie looked around fearfully.

"Could these dogs be a danger to a child?" Caroline asked.

"I hope not, but you never know." Leah continued forward, lowering her head against the driving rain. "Anyway, Joey must have followed the bigger kids. When Abraham saw him, he was already angry with him because Joey had seen him accidentally spilling a bucket of milk this morning, and Joey had told their mother. Abraham got in trouble and, naturally, he blamed Joey, instead of his own carelessness."

"Like my little brothers," Caroline said. "They're always getting into it. I never realized that Amish mothers had the same trouble."

Leah chuckled. "We aren't that different," she reminded. "We may offer our prayers in a different form and dress differently, but kids are kids."

"It's like that all over the world," Daniel put in. "But go on."

"Anyway," Leah continued. "It started to thunder, and Minnie got scared."

"How old is *she*?" Leslie wanted to know.

"Minnie's eight," Leah said. "She started crying to go back to the house. Annoyed because they hadn't found the cow and he still had chores to finish before dinner, Abraham told them both to go home. He told them he'd find Matilda himself."

"But if Joey was with his sister," Leslie said, "how did…"

"According to Minnie," Leah went on, "Joey had gone only a short distance with her when there was thunder again and he decided that he wanted Abraham. He left Minnie to run back to his brother, leaving Minnie to think he was with Abraham, and Abraham believing Minnie had taken him back to the house. Abraham eventually found the missing cow, and drove her back to the barn, but he never saw Joey."

"Was there a calf?" Caroline stopped to untangle herself from some tall weeds. The rain wasn't making it easier for any of them. Instead of letting up, it was coming down harder, and they were walking directly into it.

"No, Matilda was just being a cow." Leah slowed to wait for her. "They aren't as smart as horses or dogs, and they can be a little hardheaded. Anyway, no one missed Joey until his place was empty at the dinner table. By then he'd been missing for nearly two hours."

"Well, he's got to be out here somewhere." Leslie moved closer to Daniel. "There aren't any bulls in this pasture, are there?"

"The Beachys don't have a bull and the cows are all up at the barn." Leah made a small sound of distress. "I can't imagine being Joey's age and out here alone. Wherever he is, he must be terrified."

Across the field, Daniel could see flickering lights from other search parties' flashlights, but they were too far away to hear the volunteers. The only sounds besides their own footsteps and voices were the rain falling, the wind and the occasional rustle in the grass. Every so often, they stopped and Leah called the boy's name, but there was never an answer.

The house and barn were far behind them, and in the wet darkness, Daniel felt as though he was in a wilderness. He'd traveled all over the world, but he'd always lived in an urban environment. He was used to towns and teeming cities, airports and hospitals. He was at home in noisy bazaars and crowded neighborhoods where Arabic and Spanish and a dozen other languages were spoken. He'd learned to feel at ease on busy trains, buses and subways, but here he felt completely out of his element. How could they possibly find one small child in all this darkness? Joey could be anywhere.

It was no wonder the Beachy family had called for help. Daniel had been told that women from the Amish church were organizing a prayer vigil, and he knew that Dinah Rhinehart had asked the Mennonite women if they would do the same. Samuel Mast said that someone had notified the Delaware State Police. And in the farmyard, Daniel had heard talk of sending for search dogs.

"There are a lot of rumors flying around," Leah said when they stopped to catch their breath. "One of the Beachy girls said that Joey had told her that a man in a blue pickup offered him candy at their mailbox a few days ago."

Daniel and his cousins moved closer so that they could hear what she was saying.

"And Noodle Troyer told my brother-in-law, Charley, that Elmer, Joey's brother, found Joey's hat and one shoe in the mud beside a pond. But I don't put much stock in that story, since it's Noodle." She cocked her head to one side. "He's known for telling tall tales and making much out of nothing."

Rain was running down the back of Daniel's jean jacket, and his trousers were soaked. He wished he'd checked the weather report before heading north to Delaware from where he'd been speaking in Virginia—he could have used his raincoat right now. Leah was the only one who seemed to be properly dressed for a night like this. She had a hooded rain slicker that reached past her knees to her black rubber boots. Wide sleeves protected her arms and covered half her hands. Her flashlight was an expensive Maglite. His flashlight was a cheap one from the dollar store, and it wasn't as bright. It needed new batteries; he remembered that now. But he didn't always think ahead, a fault his father was quick to point out.

"Did you have time to stop home for your flashlight?" Daniel asked, giving his a tap.

"We always keep it in the buggy." Leah offered a quick smile. "Just to be safe. And it looked like rain, so I threw boots and the raincoat in the back before we headed to the Grange to hear the speaker. My mother always told us girls to be prepared for anything whenever we left home."

"She sounds wise, your mother," Daniel said.

"*Ya,* Mam is smart. She's the schoolteacher here in Seven Poplars. But she's got a lot of common sense, too."

"What else do you carry in case of emergencies?" Daniel asked. He was teasing her a little, but he was also curious. There were all sorts of things about Leah Yoder he wanted to know.

"I have flares in the buggy, too," she answered, "but I didn't see any need to bring those."

"You don't have a cell phone, do you?"

"Nah." Leah shook her head, sending droplets of water flying. "Our church doesn't permit them."

"Don't you have a phone, Daniel?" Caroline asked.

"I keep telling Mom that I need one just as much as Leslie does."

"I do have a cell," Daniel admitted, "but it's back in my truck. I forgot to charge it, so it wouldn't be much use to us. But if Leslie brought hers…"

"I've got it," Leslie assured him, patting the pocket of her coat. "And it's charged."

"We don't have electricity so a cell phone wouldn't do me much good," Leah explained. "There's a regular phone at the chair shop across the road from our house. We can use it to call the doctor or make important calls, but we aren't allowed to have personal phones."

Daniel liked Leah's voice. It was clear and sweet, yet she had no trouble making herself heard above the rain. Leah had a slight accent, not German, but almost Southern. Her grammar and vocabulary were very good. Hearing her, no one would guess that she'd never completed high school. The Delaware Amish, he knew, sent their children to private church schools that ended with eighth-grade graduation.

"There's a fence just ahead," Leah said. "I thought maybe we should search the woods, but I see lights there so I think some of the other groups are looking there. If we cross the fence line, we'll be on the Crawford sheep farm. The Crawfords are living in Dover while their house is being remodeled, and there's a long lane from the road to the buildings."

Using his little flashlight, Daniel located a fence post and three strands of barbed wire. "How do we climb over that?" he asked.

"We don't." Leah plucked at the top row. "But the wire isn't tight. If one of us holds up that bottom strand, the others can crawl under."

Daniel nodded, resigned to whatever it took to find the boy. He was already wet and cold, so what was a little mud? "I'll hold the wire until you get through, and then one of you can hold it for me."

The plan worked, but the ground was just as wet and uncomfortable as he thought it would be. He supposed that a six-year-old would have had an easier time getting under, if he'd come this way. But why would a child venture farther away from home rather than closer? He felt a sense of dread. What if the rumor about Joey's hat and shoe discovered by the pond was true? Or, God forbid, the story about a stranger offering the boy a treat? Tonight could end in more than discomfort. It could be a real tragedy for the Beachy family and the whole community.

"Please, God," he murmured under his breath as he wiggled the last few inches until he was clear of the barbed wire. "Be with this child. Hold him safe in the palm of your hand until we can get to him."

"Ouch!" Caroline cried.

Daniel got to his feet. "What's wrong? Did you hurt yourself?" He shone his flashlight on Caroline. She was holding her left hand out, and even through the rain, he could see that blood was oozing from a deep gash across her palm.

"Let me see," he said. On closer inspection, he saw that the cut was ragged and about two inches long.

"Does it hurt?" Leslie asked.

"It stings."

"That barbed wire is rusty." Leah came to stand with them. "I hope you're up-to-date on your tetanus shot."

"She was vaccinated when she was little," Leslie said. "Isn't that good enough?"

"I don't think so," Leah said. "Irwin—he's sort of my foster brother—stepped on a nail a couple of weeks ago and our doctor said he had to have a booster. She'll probably need to have one, too, but it's not an emergency. It can wait until tomorrow as long as she doesn't need stitches."

"I don't think it needs stitches." Daniel handed his cousin a handkerchief. "But Leah's right. You should check with your doctor to see when you were last vaccinated. I've actually seen cases of tetanus. It's not something to mess around with."

Caroline wrapped his handkerchief around her hand, but the cloth turned from white to pink. "I feel like such an idiot. I thought I had hold of the wire, but it slipped through my hand."

"I think you'd better go back to the house." Leslie rested her hand on Caroline's back. "Mom will want to have a look at this."

"But I wanted to help." Caroline's voice quivered. "And now, I've caused all of you a problem."

"Why don't the three of you go back?" Leah suggested. "I want to check some sheds on this farm, but I'll be fine. I know the way."

Daniel reached out and pressed his hand over Caroline's. "More pressure should stop the bleeding. Do you think you'll be all right to walk back with Leslie?"

"Sure," she answered. "It's a cut hand, not a broken leg."

"Leslie?" he asked. "You okay walking her back?"

"Sure. I'll go with her. I hate to leave you guys, but I agree she shouldn't go alone. What if she faints or something?"

Caroline made a sound of disbelief. "Have you ever

known me to faint in my life? Stop making such a fuss. I'll be fine. You stay and hunt for Joey with Daniel and Leah. I can go back myself."

"I don't think that's a good idea." Daniel adjusted his ball cap to try to keep some of the rain out of his eyes. "The two of you should go back together. No one should be out here alone. I'll go with Leah." He looked at Leah as it occurred to him what he was saying. Three girls and a guy was one thing. A guy and girl, in some cultures, was something entirely different. "Will you be in trouble if the two of us go on together alone? We're not breaking any Amish rules, are we?"

"Nah," Leah assured him. "It isn't encouraged, a boy and girl alone together, but it's not forbidden. We're looking for a lost child. It's not like we're dating or anything."

Caroline giggled.

Leah glanced at Caroline, then back at Daniel. "This kind of situation allows for exceptions to the rules. Besides, I haven't officially joined the Amish church, so I'm sort of *rumspringa*. This is my running around time. The rules aren't so strict for me."

"So you don't mind if I come with you?"

Leah shook her head. "I would be glad of your help. But we have to get going." She looked out over the dark field ahead. "I have a bad feeling about this," she said softly. "A really bad feeling."

Chapter 3

Daniel watched as Caroline and Leslie's flashlight beam grew smaller as they recrossed the big pasture beyond the barbed-wire fence. "I guess it's just the two of us," he said to Leah, raising his voice so that she could hear him above the sound of the rain and the booming thunder.

"Just the two of us," she repeated. "Come on. This way. It doesn't look as though this is going to let up."

Not only wasn't the downpour easing, it was getting worse. He glanced up as lightning zigzagged through the sky. It struck so close that he smelled the burnt grass when a bolt hit the ground. "Maybe we should think about looking for shelter," Daniel suggested, not so much worried for himself as for Leah. "Just until the worst of this passes."

"There's a shed in the pasture beyond these woods

where the farmer stores hay," Leah shouted. "We can duck in there." She began to walk faster, and he lengthened his stride to keep up with her.

Water was running down the inside of Daniel's jacket, and his pants were soaked and muddy to his knees. Leah was wearing a skirt, so he knew she had to be colder than he was, even wearing her rain slicker. He couldn't imagine any of his sisters out here in the dark and pouring rain with a strange man. The two still at home were both younger than he supposed Leah must be, but he doubted they would ever have the self-confidence that she seemed to have. Most girls, especially girls born with such outer beauty as Leah possessed, rarely showed the same strength of character.

A gust of wind shook the trees overhead and nearly knocked them off their feet. Daniel took Leah's arm to steady her, and she made no protest. *A night like this and a child lost in it? What must the boy's family be going through?*

Once, when his family was sightseeing in Barcelona, his younger brother, Matthew, had gotten separated from the rest of them during a festival. The streets were crowded, and eight-year-old Matthew spoke only a little Spanish. They'd notified the police and looked for Matthew for hours without finding a trace of him. Daniel remembered how pale his mother's face had been, and yet, she'd remained calm. "Have faith, but don't stop hunting for him," she'd said. "God expects us to do our fair share."

Their prayers had been answered. When his mother had returned to the bed-and-breakfast where they'd been staying, Matthew was sitting on the steps waiting. Earlier that morning, he had picked up a brochure in the hotel because it had red balloons on it. He'd stuck the folder in his coat pocket, and when he got lost, he'd asked a teenage girl for help. She'd studied English in school and was able to understand why Matthew was crying. Somehow, the girl had seen the brochure, read the address, and given his little brother a ride back to the B&B on the back of her bike.

"Lucky," the policeman had said, when Daniel's parents had reported Matthew as safe.

"Not lucky, but blessed," Mother had insisted.

Daniel hoped that Joey Beachy would be just as blessed. He was even younger than Matthew had been, and the family still talked about the incident. Daniel missed his family, but he missed his little brother most of all. This would have been Matthew's senior year in high school, but he'd moved to Canada with their mother, father and the three girls. Daniel hoped he'd have time to visit with them before he left for his new assignment.

Lightning flashed, closer this time, and Daniel felt a little better when they left the trees. The batteries in his flashlight were growing weaker, however, and the beam was a pale yellow light. "I think it's going out," he said to Leah, tapping the flashlight against his leg.

"Don't worry," she said. "Mine's good."

As if on cue, his flashlight went out. He smacked it against his leg, but it wouldn't come back on.

"It's okay. We're almost there." She pointed with her flashlight, and Daniel made out a dark outline of a wooden gate in the tall grass.

"I see it," he shouted, shoving his useless flashlight into his jacket pocket. He didn't have much hope that little Joey would be this far from the house, but once the worst of the storm passed, maybe they could double-back to continue their search.

They dashed the last few yards to the shelter. Leah shone her flashlight on the wooden gate and Daniel tugged it open. The first thing that he saw when he stepped into the shed was the pale frightened face of a small boy looking up at him.

"Joey!" Leah cried.

Little Joey Beachy sat on the ground with his arms around a shaggy brown-and-white goat. His eyes were red and swollen from crying; streaks trailed down his dirty cheeks. When he saw Leah, a cascade of fresh tears began to flow.

"Joey," Leah crooned, setting her flashlight on a bale of hay. She dropped to her knees and gathered the child into her arms. "What are you doing here?" she murmured. "Your mam is so worried. Everyone's been hunting for you."

Joey began to sob. Daniel couldn't understand what he was saying because the boy was speaking Pennsylvania Dutch. Leah switched to that language as well, leaving Daniel at a loss. He glanced around the low shed. It was too dark to see much, but the roof was sound, and it was a relief to be out of the downpour.

The goat got up and began bleating pitifully. Daniel didn't know much about goats, but this one sounded as if it was in distress. Daniel's wet coat clung to him. It was so soaked through that it gave little protection against the cold, so he took it off and draped it over a bale of hay. Then another sound, a feeble high-pitched squeak, caught his attention.

Leah must have heard the noise as well, because she turned her flashlight toward the source. Nestled in the hay was a baby goat. Daniel hadn't noticed it before because it was black and nearly hidden in the shadows. The larger goat nosed at the little one, looked back at her midsection and began to bleat again.

Daniel didn't need translation. As an RN, he'd had a rotation in maternity at Rutherford General Hospital. He hadn't seen any pregnant goats there, but he'd helped deliver a lot of babies. And now that he looked at the brown-and-white goat closely, he could see that her belly was still swollen. She'd just given birth to the little black kid but was obviously carrying a second one.

Leah hugged Joey and stood him on his feet, wiping under his eyes with her thumbs. "He said that he got separated from his brother and sister and a wolf chased him."

"A wolf?"

She shrugged, but her eyes twinkled. "He said he ran to the shelter to get away from the wolf and found the goat here."

Joey nodded and started talking again in Pennsylvania Dutch.

"English," Leah reminded him.

"The baby. I didn't want the wolf to get it," the boy said. "Then it was night and…and…" A rattle of Dutch followed.

"He was afraid of the storm," Leah finished. "And he couldn't leave the goats. The doe is having trouble."

Daniel nodded. "I think there's a second kid."

"Probably," she agreed.

Daniel picked up her flashlight and shone the beam around the shed, seeing that the roof slanted toward the back. Bales of sweet-smelling hay were stacked against the far wall, making the shelter feel snug and almost warm.

"So he stayed here all this time with the goats?" Daniel asked.

"He was afraid the wolves would kill them. It was probably the wild dogs I was telling you about." She rubbed the boy's arm, said something in Pennsylvania Dutch again, then continued speaking to Daniel in English. "A goat can usually drive off a single dog, but not a pack. Joey was smart to stay here where it was safe."

The mother goat began to paw the floor and bleat. Leah walked over to the goat and ran her hands over its belly. "I think the twin kid might be stuck," she said. "The first one is already dry. This one should have been born by now." She bit down on her lower lip. "I wish my sister Miriam was here. She'd know what to do." She looked up at Daniel. "She's really good with animals."

"Can you hold her?" Daniel asked, putting the flashlight back on the bale of hay. He dug into the deep pockets of his jacket and pulled out a pair of latex gloves he always carried. "If you can hold her still, I can examine her."

Joey said something in Pennsylvania Dutch.

"He wants to know if you know about goats."

"Not so much about goats," Daniel admitted. "But I'm a nurse. I know about babies. Goats can't be much different, can they?" He couldn't see Leah's face in the shadows, but he sensed that she was looking at him in a different way.

"You're a nurse?" she asked softly. "I thought nurses were women."

"Not all nurses." This shed wasn't the ideal spot for a delivery. He was used to the sterile conditions of a hospital. He put his hands on the goat and she squealed and tried to get away.

"Wait," Leah grabbed her flashlight off the bale of hay and handed it to the boy. "Hold it steady, Joey. I'll hold the doe." She slipped her arms around the goat's neck and pushed against its front legs with her knee. To Daniel's surprise, the doe's legs folded under her and she lay down on the hay-strewn floor.

With Leah holding the animal still, it was much easier for him to run his hands along its abdomen. "I think I see the problem," he said. "One of the kid's legs is twisted back, keeping it from being born."

"Is there anything you can do to help?" Leah asked softly.

Daniel liked the way she remained calm. He could imagine what the reaction of most girls would be, but she was different, more mature…sensible. He found he liked Leah Yoder more and more as the night wore on.

"If you can keep her still, I think I can wiggle that leg free and…yes, there it comes!"

The goat leaped to her feet and a moment later, another kid slipped out into the straw on the floor. The baby was still encased in the birth sac, a clear bubble; it wasn't moving. Daniel pulled the membrane away from the nose and mouth, and began to rub the tiny body.

"Is it dead?" Joey asked, holding on to Leah's raincoat.

The mother goat nosed the kid.

Daniel kept massaging the baby. Lifting the head, he scooped out the mouth and wiped the nose clean. "He's tired, poor little thing," Daniel explained softly. He picked up a handful of hay and began to rub the damp hide briskly. "Sometimes, all it takes is—"

The baby choked, coughed and let out a wail. The doe pushed past Daniel and began to lick her second newborn. In minutes, the tiny newborn was on its feet and jostling the older twin for a turn at the mother's teats.

"You saved them," Leah said, getting to her feet. "I didn't think..."

"Ya," Joey agreed, returning the flashlight to Leah. "You saved them." He knelt beside the little goats and petted first one and then the other.

"The mother might have been able to deliver it." Daniel didn't want to appear to take too much credit for doing what he'd been trained to do. But secretly, he was thrilled. He'd felt that way whenever he'd seen a new life come into the world. It never failed to strengthen his faith in God. How could anyone watch a newborn take a deep breath, look around and not see God's wonderful plan? He allowed himself a deep sigh of satisfaction and pulled off the gloves.

"I think the brunt of the storm has passed." Leah listened for a moment. "I think it's safe to go out again. We should get Joey home to his mother."

"But the goats," the boy protested. "The bad wolf might come and—"

"We'll lock the gate," Leah assured him. "The goats will be fine until the farmer comes tomorrow." She took Joey's hand. "Daniel?"

"It's still pretty nasty out there," he said, glancing into the dark as he grabbed his wet jacket. The rain was still coming down, though not as hard as before. "Maybe you and Joey should stay here while I go for—"

Leah laughed, her flashlight beam steady on the gate. "And do you remember the way back to the Beachy farm? Or will we have to send a search party out for you?"

He chuckled and looked down at his wet shoes. "You're probably right."

"I am. Now come on...we'll go together. All three of us."

"I guess we do make a pretty good team," Daniel dared. He liked the sound of her laughter. She was teasing him, but not in a mocking way. She was teasing as a friend might tease another friend. It gave him a good feeling; he'd made a good friend in Seven Poplars. He had a big family, but in their travels it hadn't always been easy to make friends and keep them. Leah was a special young woman, and he hoped he'd see her again after tonight.

The walk back to Joey's house didn't seem as far as it had on the way out. Another search party met up with them in the pasture. Joey's uncle was with them, and he'd whooped for joy and picked the boy up and carried him back to the house on his shoulders.

At the Beachy house, the adults and most of the children were still awake. Men stood on the porch and outside the back door drinking cups of steaming black coffee, and someone thrust a cup into Daniel's hand. Joey was hugged and fussed over and trundled off into the house by his mother and a gaggle of women. Leah was caught up in the crowd and vanished along with the boy.

"Good work for a city boy," Samuel Mast said as he slapped Daniel on the back. He was grinning. Everyone was.

"Leah Yoder deserves the credit," Daniel insisted. "She was the one who thought to go where the hay was stored. The weather had gotten so bad, I thought we should turn back."

"But if the boy wasn't hurt, why didn't he run home before it got dark?" A bearded Amish man stuck his hand out and Daniel shook it. "Roman Byler," he said. "I own the chair shop down the road."

Daniel began to explain about the dog that Joey thought was a wolf that had chased him and the pregnant goat. Before he knew it, Joey's mother was ushering Daniel into the house and waving him to a place at the table. Other men were already there, eating sandwiches and vegetable soup.

"To warm your insides," Joey's father said.

Daniel hadn't thought he was hungry, but after the first bite, he remembered that he hadn't eaten anything since he'd stopped for lunch on the interstate at about one o'clock. After the mishap at the rest stop, when he'd left his coat, he'd ended up running late and hadn't had time to stop and eat before he reached Seven Poplars. The ham sandwich was good, and the soup delicious. He hadn't had a better meal since he'd last sat at his mother's table.

The large kitchen was overflowing with men and women, most talking to each other in Pennsylvania Dutch, laughing and joking. Daniel was surprised by how at home he felt here among these people, even though he didn't speak their language. But the one person he kept looking for he didn't see. He'd wanted to tell Leah how much he appreciated her help and what a great job she'd done. Soon the sun would be coming up, and he was tired. He hated to leave without saying goodbye to Leah.

Finally, when the men began to take their leave, Daniel stood, thanked his host and hostess and made his way out to where he'd left his pickup truck. Buggies were rolling out of the farmyard, and men, hands in pockets, walked off into the soft darkness.

He was disappointed that he hadn't seen Leah, but he knew he should go. Even though his aunt knew where he was, she'd be worried about him. He put his hand on the driver's door handle and was about to get into his truck when Leah appeared from around the back of the pickup.

"A goodnight to you, Daniel Steiner," she said.

He looked up at her. "Excuse me?"

"I said goodnight to you, Daniel Steiner," she repeated.

"I'm not Daniel Steiner."

"You're not?" Leah sounded confused. "But I thought you were Caroline's cousin and—"

"Oh," he said, understanding the mixup. "Caroline is my cousin. She's a Steiner, but her mother is my aunt. I'm a Brown, Daniel Brown."

"Daniel Brown." Her pretty blue eyes widened. "*The* Daniel Brown…the speaker we were supposed to hear tonight?"

"That's me." Feeling awkward, he slipped his hands into his pockets. He really liked Leah, so much so that he didn't want to say goodbye. "We're going to reschedule for another night this coming week. I hope you…you and your friends can come back."

"*You're* the Daniel Brown—the hero who saved that boy from the mob?"

"Hardly a hero," Daniel protested.

"I didn't know…" She hesitated. "Now I feel foolish. I spent the whole night with you and I never asked you about your travels. I never…" She stopped and started again. "I really feel foolish."

"Don't. It was a natural mistake." He struggled to find the right thing to say. He didn't want her to walk away feeling embarrassed. "I'll be looking for you—at the presentation. I hope you aren't disappointed."

"Ne," Leah said. "You couldn't disappoint anyone, Daniel Brown. Least of all me."

"I'll see you there, then?"

"Leah?" a woman called from the porch. "Are you ready?"

"Ya," she answered. "Coming." She smiled at him. "I'm glad you were with me tonight."

"Me, too."

"What you said before," she murmured shyly. "I agree. We made a good team."

"We did," he concurred. And then she turned and hurried off, leaving him standing there staring after her and wishing she wasn't going.

Chapter 4

The following morning, as golden rays of April sun-light spilled through the bedroom window, Leah sighed and snuggled deeper beneath the crisp blue and white Bear's Paw quilt that had been her Christmas gift from her eldest sister, Johanna. Below Leah's window, from a perch on the top rail of the garden fence, a wayward rooster crowed. *Just a few more minutes,* Leah thought, burrowing under her pillow. *All I want is a few more...*

A high-pitched giggle pierced her groggy haze. "You a-wake, Leah? Mam made pancakes!"

Leah caught the scent of fresh coffee, felt the mat-tress bounce and groaned. It had been nearly daylight when she'd finally gotten to bed, and she couldn't have had more than three hours' sleep.

"An' bacon!" proclaimed the cheerful voice.

Leah opened one eye and smiled into the round,

red-cheeked face hovering only inches from her own. "Morning, Susanna-banana," she mumbled.

Her sister giggled again. "I'm not a banana. Get up, silly. I'm hungry." She pushed a mug of coffee under Leah's nose. "Brought you coffee." It came out sounding more like *toffee*, but Leah had no trouble understanding Susanna's sometimes childish speech.

"You're always hungry," Leah replied, but it was impossible to remain out of sorts with Susanna, even too early on a visiting Sunday when there was no church and they could sleep in. Her sister was such a sweet-natured soul that simply being near her made Leah smile. "Thanks for the coffee. Tell Mam I'll be downstairs in two shakes of a lamb's tail."

"'Kay." Susanna's mouth widened in a grin as she scooted off the bed, carefully sliding the brimming cup to the end of the nightstand. Then she trotted out of the bedroom and down the hall toward the stairs.

Leah stretched and rubbed her eyes before reaching for the coffee. As always, Susanna had sweetened it to her own taste and drowned it in heavy cream, but it was hot and bracing and washed some of the sleep out of Leah's brain. Yawning, she padded barefoot to the window and threw up the sash. The sun was already high, and the sky was a robin's-egg blue without a hint of clouds. Spread out before her were Mam's kitchen garden, rich farm fields and fruit trees in the first blossom of spring.

"Thank you, God," she murmured as she breathed in the sweet smell of newly turned soil and fresh-cut grass. "Thank you for keeping Joey safe through the stormy night and letting us find him." Closing her eyes, she offered a simple and silent prayer, asking His blessing on her family and community and for guidance through the coming day.

Almost instantly, a sense of contentment and pure joy washed over her. How was it possible that last night, an evening that had started so fearful, had turned out to be so wonderful?

Not only had Joey been returned to his family without harm, but she'd met a dynamic stranger and helped him deliver a new life into the world. Goose bumps rose on Leah's bare arms as she exhaled softly. Nothing like that ever happened in Seven Poplars, but it *had* happened last night, and she'd been part of it. She couldn't wait to tell her sisters about her adventure, especially Johanna. Of all of them, Johanna shared her sometimes rebellious spirit and would understand best how she felt.

Leah had loved coming home after almost a year in Ohio taking care of *Grossmama,* but things here had quickly fallen back into the ordinary. Not exactly boring… There were always chores to do and new challenges to face, especially now that Anna had married Samuel in a whirlwind romance, leaving only Susanna, Rebecca, Irwin and her at home to help Mam. But after the hustle and bustle of *Grossmama*'s more liberal Amish community, her new Mennonite friends, and the relative independence she and Rebecca had experienced in Ohio, it wasn't easy settling in under Mam's authority again. And she did have to admit to herself that sometimes Seven Poplar's conservative customs seemed a little old-fashioned.

So many changes, Leah thought wistfully. When she and Rebecca had left for Ohio last year, the house had been bursting with unmarried sisters, and when they'd returned, three had found husbands, and Mam had hired and then practically adopted Irwin, a thirteen-year-old orphaned boy who had lived with Joey Beachy's family. It all took a little getting used to.

Not that her beloved sisters were far away; Miriam and Ruth were just across the field in the little farmhouse with their new husbands, and Anna and Samuel's farm was next door. But they had their own families and households, and it wasn't the same as waking up every morning to a gaggle of giggling girls or having so many to share secrets and gossip with after the lights had been blown out at night. Plus, Grandmother Yoder, no longer able to live alone, and her sister, Aunt Jezebel, were now part of Mam's household.

Grossmama was going to live with Anna and Samuel this summer. Anna had wanted her to move in sooner, but Mam had been firm. She'd insisted that Anna needed a few months to adjust to being a wife and mother to Samuel's five children before taking on *Grossmama*, no matter how well the two of them got on together. That would leave Aunt Jezebel here, but compared to her sister, Aunt Jezzy was a dream.

"What's taking you so long?" Rebecca called from the doorway. "You aren't even dressed." She came in and plopped onto the unmade bed. "*Grossmama* won't be happy if her pancakes are cold."

Leah rolled her eyes and forced back a snappy response. "Sorry. I didn't expect anyone to wait breakfast on me this morning." She went to the corner where her clothing hung and took down a fresh shift and a lavender-colored dress.

"Mam said not to wear that," Rebecca said. "Wear your good blue one. Aunt Martha thinks that the lavender is too short, and she's bound to come visiting today.

She'll want to hear all about that Mennonite preacher you were running around with in the dark last night."

Leah wrinkled her nose. "Since when does Mam take Aunt Martha's advice on what we should wear?"

Rebecca shrugged. "I'm just telling you what Mam said. I think Mam thinks it's too short, too."

Leah's mouth puckered as she hung the lavender dress with its neat tailoring back on the hook and took down the dark blue one her mother had given her for her birthday. Leah liked the blue. It went well with her eyes and her dark auburn hair, but she was particularly fond of the lavender dress she and her Mennonite friend, Sophie Steiner, had cut and stitched. Sophie's mother had a new electric-powered Singer that practically sewed a garment for you. Maybe the lavender was a little shorter than the blue dress, but it covered her knees and the neckline and sleeves were modest enough to satisfy even the bishop.

"And your good *kapp*," Rebecca added. "No scarf today."

Leah sighed. She and Rebecca had spent so much time together in the last year that they should have been as close as Ruth and Miriam, but somehow, this sister always brought out the worst in her. She loved Rebecca dearly, but they were just too different to have the relationship she had with Johanna or dear Anna. Leah loved to be doing something with her hands: picking blueberries, making jam or selling vegetables to the English tourists at Spence's Auction. By contrast, Rebecca was happiest at home, drinking tea with Mam or Aunt Jezebel, reading a prayer book or writing a letter for publication in the *Budget*.

Rebecca never questioned the rules. She'd always been the good girl of the family, the serious one. She'd been baptized at age sixteen, before she'd even ventured into the outside world. It never occurred to Rebecca to be cross with Aunt Martha for her criticizing or bossy ways. In Leah's mind, Rebecca was simply too meek for her own good. And worse, Rebecca couldn't understand why Leah sometimes longed to kick out of the traces, and why, at almost twenty-one, she had yet to make the lifelong commitment to join the Amish Church.

Leah gathered her brush, *kapp* and her clean underclothes and started for the bathroom. "I'll be quick," she promised her sister. "Tell Mam, five minutes."

"What was he like?" Rebecca asked.

"Who?"

Rebecca raised an eyebrow. "You know who. The Mennonite preacher. Was he as fast as they say?"

Annoyed, Leah stopped short and glanced back over her shoulder. "As fast as *who* says? Who around here knows him well enough to say something like that? That he's fast?"

Her sister smiled. "It's what they say about all Mennonite boys, isn't it? People say that they're wild, that they try to take liberties with Amish girls."

"That's nonsense. And Daniel isn't a boy. He must be twenty-five, maybe older."

Rebecca snickered. "And it's just *Daniel* now, is it? But then you probably got to know him well out there in the woods. He didn't try to steal a kiss, did he?"

"No. He didn't. And Daniel Brown's not a preacher. He's a nurse, a good one."

"And you know that how?"

"Because he helped a baby goat to be born when we were out looking for Joey. It was stuck, a leg tangled.

The nanny would have died and the kid with her if Daniel hadn't known what to do."

"So he's not a preacher. But he is a missionary. He must have been lots of places, known lots of English girls. Fancy foreign girls, too."

"I suppose he has, but he was nice. *Is* nice. And when he gives his program, I'm going to be there to hear it."

"If Mam lets you go again."

Leah's brow creased as she tried to hide the annoyance she felt at Rebecca's words. "*Ne,* sister," she answered softly. "That's not what I said. I said I'm going to hear Daniel's talk and see the pictures of Spain and Morocco. I'll be twenty-one in a few weeks, and I'm an adult. I think I can decide for myself if I'm going to hear a missionary speak about his experiences in spreading God's word, *without* asking for my mother's permission."

Rebecca slid off the bed, moisture gleaming in her dark eyes. "I've made you angry."

Leah shook her head. "Not angry."

"Ya." A single tear blossomed on Rebecca's cheek. "I never say the right thing to you, Leah. I try, but it always comes out wrong. I worry about you."

Leah opened her arms and Rebecca came into them. Leah enveloped her in a hug. "Worry about me? Why? Because I hunted for a lost child last night—"

"Ne." Her sister switched from English to Pennsylvania Dutch. "You have a good heart. It was wrong of me to tease you about the Mennonite boy. I only did it because I'm frightened that we might lose you."

"Lose me?" Leah pulled away to look down into her sister's face. Rebecca was a small girl, like Miriam, not tall like Mam's side of the family. "How could you lose me?"

Rebecca clasped her hand and squeezed it hard. "You move too easily in the outside world. Since we were children, you always have. The English don't make you uncomfortable, as they do me."

"But why should that frighten you?"

"We're *Plain* folk—we're a people apart. Do you forget the martyrs who died that we might worship according to our beliefs?"

Leah leaned close and brushed a kiss on her sister's temple. "How could I forget? Being who I am—who we are—is bred into me, blood and bone. Surely, listening to a Mennonite tell about his mission work doesn't change that."

"It's not just that." Another tear followed the first. "It was the Mennonite friends you made out in Ohio. You went to their charity auctions, and you went to the fair with Jeanine and Sophie. And at least once, you helped out at their bake sale for their church."

"I did, but that was to raise money for a mission in the Ukraine. They wanted to send books and school supplies to orphans in a remote town. I wasn't attending worship services. And going to a fair to look at animals and eat cotton candy doesn't mean that I've forsaken my own faith," Leah protested. "I haven't."

Rebecca's chin quivered. "Everyone thought that you'd start classes for baptism this spring, but you didn't. Even Ruth is concerned about you. She and Aunt Jezzy were talking about it last week after church."

"And Mam? What does she say?"

Her sister sighed. "You know Mam. She just smiles and says, 'All in God's time.' But it's past time, Leah. You're the prettiest girl in Kent County, but you've never had a steady boyfriend, and you don't even let any boys drive you home from frolics and singings."

Leah wrinkled her nose again as she thought of Menno Swartzentruber, who'd tried to get her to ride home in his buggy last Sunday. "Maybe I haven't met the right boy. The ones around here seem too young and flighty." Menno was a hard worker, but his idea of a good joke was piling straw bales across the road to stop traffic in the dark or filling a paper bag with cow manure and leaving it on an Englisher's porch. No, she couldn't see herself dating Menno.

"And what about Jake King from the fourth district church? He's what? Twenty-eight or twenty-nine? He likes you, and you can't think Jake's too young."

"I like Jake—he's a good man. But his wife's only been dead six months. I wouldn't feel right walking out with Jake so soon after his loss."

"You see how you are." Rebecca stepped away and straightened her *kapp*, which had come loose when they'd hugged. "You always have a good excuse. But wearing that Ohio-style dress doesn't help. You know how people are—how they will talk. They start to wonder if you are drifting away from us."

"It sounds as though you've been talking to Aunt Martha," Leah said. "Or Dorcas."

"Aunt Martha has a sharp tongue," Rebecca admitted. "But she means well. She knows Dat would have been worried about you."

"You miss him a lot, don't you?" Leah murmured. Their father had been dead almost three years, but the hurt hadn't faded. Rebecca had taken the loss especially hard.

"I do."

"Me, too," she admitted softly.

"Leah! Leah!"

Both Leah and Rebecca turned toward the stairs as the clatter of footsteps echoed down the hallway.

"Leah! There's a man!" Susanna's eyes were wide, her cheeks red with excitement. "In a truck! In the kitchen!"

"A truck in Mam's kitchen?" Leah teased.

"Ne!" Susanna was breathless from running up the steps. "An Englisher man. He wants…" She inhaled deeply. "He wants you!"

Chapter 5

As Leah hurried down the front staircase, she suspected that she knew just which Englisher was waiting in the kitchen for her. It could only be Daniel Brown, and the thought that he'd come to her home so soon after leaving her at the Beachy farm a few hours ago made her pulse race.

What she wasn't expecting was to see Daniel seated at the head of the table in her father's chair, the one always ready to welcome guests. When she stepped through the doorway and Daniel saw her, he immediately rose to his feet. "Leah." His intense green-eyed gaze locked with hers, and her heart skipped a beat. "Good morning," he said with a smile.

Suddenly too shy to speak, she nodded and patted her *kapp.* She'd dressed so quickly that she wasn't entirely sure she was put together.

"I hope..." Daniel began.

"Yes?"

"You got some sleep?"

Leah nodded again. "Yes, I did." She didn't miss her grandmother's frown of disapproval. *Grossmama* didn't have to say a word. Her expression left no doubt as to what she was thinking. *Disgraceful!* A Mennonite boy come to seek out one of her unmarried granddaughters—more evidence of Leah's unorthodox behavior.

"The sun is shining," Daniel said, all in a rush. "After last night... I mean...after the rain."

"It is," Leah stammered. Behind her, she heard Rebecca stifle a giggle. "A beautiful morning," she added, feeling foolish. What was wrong with her that she was suddenly tongue-tied, unable to think of anything sensible to say? Daniel must think her a wooden head. "It happens a lot," she finished. "A beautiful sunny day after a storm."

"Yes, it seems that way," he answered.

"Sit, please," Leah said. Her stomach felt as though she'd swallowed a live moth. She clasped her hands together, and then smoothed her apron. When she'd first stepped out of the hall and seen Daniel at the table with her family, the kitchen had felt warm and welcoming, but *Grossmama*'s tight-lipped stare was quickly frosting the air.

Leah sucked in her breath, realizing that Daniel had displeased her grandmother even more by standing when Leah came into the room. It wasn't *Plain* behavior and went against the beliefs of the Old Order Amish.

Standing up when a woman joined them was what Leah had seen Englishers do in restaurants or on TV. Of course, television and movies were frowned upon by the church elders, but Leah was fascinated by glimpses of the outer world. Her Mennonite girlfriends had a television set in their family room, and Leah had watched Disney movies and some family shows with them on Saturday evenings when she was in Ohio. But she wasn't in Ohio now—she was in Kent County, Delaware, and Daniel's action had reminded everyone that he was an outsider.

"I didn't mean to intrude on your breakfast," Daniel said. "I wanted to invite you all to come back and…" He paused for breath and her mother finished the explanation.

"Daniel's program at the Grange will be this evening," Hannah said. "He wanted to make sure that we knew about it."

"He missed his breakfast this morning so he wouldn't be late for church," Aunt Jezzy put in. *Grossmama* glared at her, but Aunt Jezzy went on in her timid voice to say, "Hannah asked him to eat with us."

"I really didn't need to eat—" Daniel began.

Thirteen-year-old Irwin cut him off. "Don't just stand there, Leah. Come to the table before the pancakes get cold."

Susanna and Rebecca took their places, but Leah glanced at her mother. The only seat left was her usual one, and that was next to Daniel. Leah could feel those moth wings fluttering in the pit of her stomach. If she sat beside Daniel, *Grossmama* would assume she'd invited him here, and she'd never hear the end of it.

"Leah, sit." Her mother slid into her own chair at the foot of the table. "Let us have prayer, and then everyone can eat before the food is ruined. I've just put more scrapple on to fry. You can turn that and then pour the coffee." Mam wiped her hands on her apron and smiled at Daniel. "You eat scrapple, don't you?"

His pleasant face creased in a smile. "Yes, Mrs. Yoder, I do. I love it, but I never get it anywhere but Pennsylvania, Delaware, or Ohio."

"Mam made it," Susanna chimed in. "I helped."

"Ya." Now that his pancakes were only a prayer away, Irwin's attitude softened. "It's *goot*." He looked at Mam. "Can I go with Leah and the girls to see Daniel's show?"

Mam put her finger to her lips to signal silence. Everyone at the table, including Daniel, closed their eyes and offered silent thanks for the food and for the promise of the coming day. But when a moment had passed, Mam surprised them by saying, "Maybe our guest would like to say grace. I believe it is the Mennonite custom."

Leah looked at Daniel. He squirmed, cleared his throat and said, "Thank you, Lord, for family, community and new friends. And bless the hands that made this meal. Amen."

Grossmama grunted and reached for the syrup. "That was *goot*," she admitted. "A *goot* prayer."

"It was." Aunt Jezebel's eyes twinkled. "A *good* prayer. Thank you, Daniel."

Soon, everyone was too busy eating to talk or to stare at their visitor. Leah had been hungry when she'd awakened, but now, she found Mam's usually delicious pancakes tasted like dry fodder. She pushed a forkful around on her plate and sneaked a glance at Daniel, who was eating heartily.

"Leah," Mam reminded. "The scrapple?"

She leaped up, smelling the first whiff of something burning. "I forgot," she said, hurrying to the range to flip the crispy slabs. "Just in time." Using a hot mitt, she pushed the cast-iron frying pan back to a cooler section of the stovetop. It would soon be too warm to use the woodstove until fall, but Mam always said that the old stove cooked better than the modern gas one that stood beside it.

With something to do with her hands, it was easier for Leah to act as if a Mennonite boy came to breakfast every Sunday. What was wrong with her this morning? She was as giddy as a teenager. If she didn't gather her wits, Daniel would be sorry he'd come.

As Leah filled coffee cups around the table, she managed to get a good look at Daniel. She'd spent hours with him the night before, but in the dark, she really hadn't been able to see him clearly. He did look a little English in his white, button-up shirt and brown dress trousers, but there was something Dutch about him as well. Daniel had a pleasant face, good straight teeth that showed when he smiled and a fair complexion with ruddy cheeks. His thick brown hair was cut a little short for an Amish man, but what attracted her most were his unusually green eyes—even more striking than she remembered.

"Will you stop staring at him and give me some coffee?" *Grossmama* asked in the Amish dialect that the family usually spoke among themselves.

Mam's mouth firmed, and she looked directly at her mother-in-law. This was Mam's home and her kitchen, and she'd invited Daniel to eat with them. One of Mam's rules in this house was not to speak German in front of the English, because she felt it was rude.

Leah's insides clenched. Her grandmother had no call to embarrass her in front of Daniel—hopefully he didn't understand Pennsylvania Dutch. But Rebecca giggled, and Susanna's mouth dropped open as she stared at Leah.

"Why's Leah starin' at Daniel?" Susanna asked, also in Dutch.

"She wants to make sure he has enough to eat," Mam supplied. "Leah, bring Daniel some of that scrapple."

"Danke," he said. *"Wunderbar."*

Leah's eyes widened. "You speak Pennsylvania Dutch?"

"Not very well, I'm afraid." He shrugged. "My grandfather spoke it when I was a child. I think I've forgotten most of what he taught me."

Hannah smiled. "But you probably understand a great deal."

"Ya," he replied.

Leah glanced at *Grossmama*, who had suddenly taken a great interest in her breakfast, and then back at Daniel.

He laid his fork down, wiped his mouth with a napkin and looked up at her. "Can you come this evening? Do you think the young people can come back as well? I thought tonight might be too soon for people to make arrangements, but it's the only night the Grange is free until Wednesday."

"You'll have to ask my daughter and son-in-law," Mam said. "They're the sponsors for the Gleaners. And, of course, it's up to the parents."

"We already got permission from the bishop," Rebecca reminded her. "For the kids to come last night."

"Aunt Mildred said that this wasn't a church Sunday for you," Daniel continued. "I promise not to keep the Gleaners up late. I think they'd enjoy the PowerPoint part of the program. Most people love the pictures of the camels. I know tomorrow's a school day, so my aunt has volunteered to pick everyone up in her van."

Irwin held up his plate for scrapple. "School's out for the summer in a week," he said. "I can't wait." Leah put two slices on his plate, and he slid them into a mountain of homemade catsup. "Can I go, Hannah? Can I go with Leah?"

Hannah shook her head. "*Ne*, Irwin. You are not old enough to be a Gleaner. Next year, when you're fourteen. The bishop said, 'No children.' He only gave permission for the teenagers."

"But I'm thirteen," Irwin protested. "I should be—"

Hannah gave him a *look*. Irwin's face fell, but he held his tongue. Leah was glad. Irwin was a normal boy who sometimes got sassy, but she didn't want him to make Mam look bad by arguing with her when they had a stranger at the table. Irwin continued to eat in silence, but the fact that he didn't run from the table in tears proved that he was gaining a little maturity.

"Will you be leaving Seven Poplars tomorrow?" Mam asked Daniel.

He shook his head. "No, Mrs. Yoder. I'm staying on at my aunt's for a few weeks until I get my next assignment."

"Assignment?" Leah's curiosity got the best of her, and the question popped out before she'd thought better of it. Daniel had just come back to the United States. Was he leaving again so soon? Disappointment washed over her. Other than finding Joey safe and sound, meeting Daniel had been the most exciting thing that had happened to her since she'd come home, and she'd hoped to continue the new friendship.

He nodded. "My parents, younger brother and

younger sisters are living on an Indian reservation in Canada—my parents teach there. They've recently made the move from Spain, where I lived with them, but now I'm on my own."

"Do you get to pick where you go?" Mam asked.

"Sometimes," Daniel replied. "But I've asked to serve where I'm most needed."

"Could they send you back to Spain?" Leah asked.

"That's possible. At least I speak the language. But I could be assigned here in the States as well—anywhere from Appalachia to an inner-city community. Or they could send me as far away as Ukraine."

Leah put the serving plate back on the counter and returned to her seat at the table. "Won't you miss your family?" she asked him. "If you go far away?" She remembered how strange it had seemed at first when she'd gone to Ohio to tend to her grandmother. She'd been terribly homesick, and she'd had her sister Rebecca for company.

"I will," Daniel said, grimacing. "That's the hard part about serving at an overseas mission. You're so isolated from family and friends you care about most. But I feel that the Lord has called me to help people who need it. There are lots of places where there's a real need for medical services. I'm not a doctor, but I am a nurse, and I think I can make a difference."

"So, as a nurse, you get to see other places and customs while you're doing God's work." Mam nodded. "Many Mennonite families are called to go on mission, but it can be hard on the children."

"My eldest sister, Margie, would agree with you, Mrs. Yoder. She married a Methodist dentist and lives in a small town in Nebraska. She says she has no intentions of moving again—ever."

"Call me *Hannah*, please," Mam said gently. "We Amish don't use fancy titles."

"I'm sorry," Daniel said. "I didn't—"

"Ne," Grossmama interjected. "It is not the *Plain* way."

"Just *Hannah* will do fine," Mam said. "As to whether or not the young people may go to hear tonight's program, I think the best thing would be for you to go down to my son-in-law Charley's house. Leah can show you the way."

"I'll just help clear the table first," she said.

"*Ne*, no need." Mam sipped her coffee. "There are plenty of hands to make short work of the breakfast dishes. You go on with Daniel."

"Irwin can point out Miriam and Charley's house," *Grossmama* said. "It's just across the field."

"I don't mind." Leah rose, wiping her mouth with a paper napkin. "I wanted to take some of that scrapple to Miriam anyway. You know it's her favorite."

Taking the hint, Daniel murmured his thanks for breakfast, said his goodbyes while she made a plate of scrapple, and then followed her outside into the yard. His truck was parked in the driveway.

"Did you want to drive over or should we walk?" he asked.

Leah caught a glimpse of someone pulling aside a kitchen curtain and waved as Susanna's round little face appeared, pressed against the glass. Her sister waved furiously before abruptly disappearing. Probably Mam had seen her peeking out the window and pulled her away. One thing about having a big family—someone was always watching.

"Leah?" Daniel looked hesitant. "I'd be glad to drive you, if it isn't against the rules for you to ride with me."

She looked at him in disbelief. "Why wouldn't I be able to ride in your truck? I'm Amish, not Muslim."

His ruddy cheeks grew even redder. "I didn't know. I already did the wrong thing inside—by calling your mother Mrs. Yoder. I didn't want to get you into trouble." He reached over and opened the cab door.

Leah smiled at him. "Don't worry. I doubt if Mam was shocked. She used to be Mennonite, you know—before she married my father. She converted to Amish for him."

"Oh." Daniel walked around the front of the pickup and got behind the wheel. "So, what you're saying is that your mother isn't as strict?"

Leah chuckled, setting the plate covered with foil on her lap. "No, I didn't say that at all. Delaware Amish are very *Old Order*—very traditional—and my mother is a faithful member of the church. It's just that few people, other than my grandmother, would object to my riding down our lane to my sisters' house. We won't even have to go out on the blacktop road. It's not as though we were going to Ocean City, to the boardwalk." She stopped, suddenly feeling very silly. "Not that we would—that you would. I was…was just saying."

Daniel smiled at her. "I think that you are a unique young woman, Leah Yoder. And with me, you can say whatever you like."

Leah smiled back as her awkward moment slid away. It was hard to remain on edge around Daniel. He was just so…so nice. He made her feel happy, just being near him. "I wanted to hear your talk last night," she said. "And now that I know you a little better, I'm even more eager to hear about your experiences. It's something I've always admired, spreading God's word." She pointed. "Go that way, around the barn."

"I don't know if I've led anyone to the Lord," he answered as he turned the key and drove slowly out of the farmyard.

"What about that boy you saved from the mob in Morocco?"

"Mousa?" Daniel chuckled again. "That rascal? It turned out that he was innocent of the theft that almost got him killed, but I'm afraid that he's still…um…a work in progress."

"Mou-sa? His name is Mou-sa? What happened to him? He must have been grateful that you saved his life."

Daniel shrugged. "I'll explain it all during my program, or at least a shortened version of *life as Mousa sees it.*"

"But you kept him safe, didn't you?"

Daniel eased the truck around the barn and corncrib. "After I brought him home, it was impossible to reform him, and even more impossible to make a convert of him. When he claimed to be a homeless orphan, my father found a respectable foster family for him and paid for his tuition at a private school out of his own pocket."

"And?" Leah was intrigued.

"He ran away from the foster home and the school about a dozen times. Turns out, Mousa wasn't an orphan. He had a father and a mother and nine brothers—all of whom made their living by hoodwinking well-meaning foreigners."

"How terrible. Was your father angry?"

"Not really. Perhaps angry with himself for not investigating the situation further. But these things happen. We can't not offer aid just because someone might occasionally take advantage of us."

"I suppose that makes sense. There's the farmhouse." Leah pointed. "It's new. The community pitched in to build it last summer when Ruth and Eli got married."

"But I thought you said that Charley and Miriam lived here."

Leah laughed. "They do. Ruth and Eli live in the bottom part of the house. Charley and Miriam have the top floor. It works out great because Miriam is good with animals and can't make toast without burning it."

"And Ruth, I suppose, cooks like your mother."

"Exactly." He drove slowly down the narrow dirt road that led to the little farmhouse.

"And what about you? Are you a fabulous cook?"

She smiled back. "I'm learning. I have to admit, I'm a better seamstress than a cook."

"I don't cook at all. My mother kept trying to tell me that I might have to cook for myself, but I was always too busy to learn. And I had three sisters. They're notorious for spoiling brothers."

"I wouldn't know about that," she replied. "I only have sisters—six of them."

"More than me. I only have three sisters and two brothers, but they're all special."

"I'm sure they are," Leah said. *They must be, if they're anything like you.* Suddenly, she felt as though she'd known Daniel all her life. What was there about him that made him so easy to talk to? If only he was Amish, she thought.

If only…

Chapter 6

For nearly an hour, Leah sat motionless in her chair, her eyes fixed on the screen as Daniel led his audience through the narrow alleys and bazaars of foreign cities with names that rolled off his tongue as sweet and sour as Aunt Fannie's chow-chow. It was nearly impossible for her to keep from weeping as Daniel's pictures showed the plight of ragged, beggar children, or the ill-fed and overburdened horses and donkeys that fought for space on the crowded streets among the honking flood of dilapidated cars and trucks.

And if the pitiful sights touched Leah's heart and soul, so too did the hopeful scenes of the clinic where Daniel had assisted volunteer doctors and midwives in offering free medical care to the poor. Equally inspiring was the orphanage and school that the Mennonites supported to provide for homeless children, lost souls who otherwise might have turned to crime to survive.

"In Morocco, we are not allowed to preach or offer any public worship services," Daniel explained. "Instead, we try to do what good we can in the Lord's name and attempt to influence people by example."

He paused for a short break when the talk moved from Morocco to Spain. There, life was much freer for missionaries; they were permitted to move around the country, preach the Gospel, offer educational programs and teach in the schools. Leah was fascinated by the old buildings, the parks and gardens, and the slides of farms, scenic mountains and ocean beaches. Daniel said that he'd liked the Spanish people and had been impressed by their loyalty to family and the sense of history and culture that held a place in every part of their lives.

When the lights came on and Daniel thanked everyone for coming, it took a few seconds for Leah to realize that Susanna was chattering away to her. So absolute was her concentration on Daniel's world that Miriam had to take hold of her arm before she broke out of her reverie.

"Did you fall asleep?" Miriam asked, teasingly.

"Lemonade," Susanna repeated. "Pink. Want some?"

Leah met her little sister's excited gaze. "No. You go on with Miriam." As the two followed Charley and the Gleaners to the refreshment table, Leah found herself drawn to the desk where Daniel was shutting down his laptop.

"Daniel?"

He glanced up and his face creased in a big smile. "Leah. I hope I didn't waste your evening."

"No." She shook her head. "It was wonderful. *You* were wonderful."

His green eyes lit up with pleasure. "I'm glad." He shrugged modestly. "I tend to run on. Speaking's not really my strong suit. I like the work… What I mean is, this speaking thing wasn't my idea. But Douglas Wheeler—he's on the mission board—thought that because I'm younger than most of our speakers and not a pastor that I might attract more teenagers to…" He stopped and chuckled. "There I go again. I told you, I talk too much."

"I don't think so," she said, smiling back at him. "I think you're…inspiring."

"It's nice of you to say so." He hesitated, carefully wrapping up an electrical cord. "I wondered…"

"Yes?"

Daniel cleared his throat and grimaced, for just a moment looking more like fifteen than however old he really was. "I don't know if you'd be interested, or if it's allowed, but on Tuesday, Caroline, Leslie and I are helping out at the food bank in Dover. It's only open once a week. My aunt usually volunteers there, but she's having a root canal. Do you think—"

"I'd like to help?" Leah suggested. "I would. Very much."

"That's great. It wouldn't be a problem for you, would it? I mean, your church doesn't usually allow you to do volunteer work for outsiders."

"That's true," she said, never having thought about it that way before. "But that doesn't apply to me because I haven't joined the Amish church yet. I'm allowed to do what I want." Leah chuckled. "Within reason. And I think that helping out at the food bank would be something I'd like to do."

"Great." He laughed. "I said that before, didn't I?"

"It's all right." She suddenly felt shy. "I don't mind."

"I think I like you, Leah Yoder."

She glanced up into his pleasant face and, for a moment, felt giddy, as if the floor had suddenly swayed under her feet. "And I think I like you, Daniel Brown."

"Good." His crooked smile widened. "The girls and I will pick you up at twelve-thirty on Tuesday, if that's okay?" She nodded and he went on. "And wear comfortable shoes. You won't get a chance to sit down until our shift ends at five."

The kitchen clock was striking nine-thirty when Leah, Susanna and Rebecca arrived home to find Mam and Aunt Jezebel waiting up for them. "Oh, you should have come with us!" Leah exclaimed. "It was wonderful! The pictures of Spain and Morocco were beautiful! And Daniel… Daniel is just—"

"Goot!" Susanna said, bouncing from foot to foot. "I saw camels and monkeys. Silly monkeys."

Rebecca nodded. "It was fun. And Miriam and Charley agreed it was educational for the young people. The kids loved it, and even Herman Beachy was on his best behavior."

"Daniel's a wonderful speaker," Leah added. "When he talks about the desert or the noisy marketplace, he makes you feel as though you're right there, smelling the spices and hearing the clamor of the crowded streets."

"It sounds as if they had a good time." Aunt Jezebel's voice was breathy and soft. She hesitated before asking, "There was no preaching the Mennonite faith at the talk, was there?"

"Ne," Rebecca assured her. "Even Bishop Atlee would have approved of tonight's program."

"I'm glad," Mam said with a smile. "It's good for you to see something of the outside."

"But I wouldn't want to live like that—like Daniel and his family," Rebecca said. "In some foreign place where we wouldn't know anyone and everything was strange."

"*Ya,* the Mennonites differ from us," her mother said. "They feel called to spread the word of God, while we Amish believe the Lord has instructed us to live apart from the world."

Susanna wrinkled her nose and tugged on her mother's sleeve. "I want a camel. With a hump. I like camels."

"No camels." Mam sighed. "The feed store doesn't sell camel chow. We'll have to make do with horses and cows."

Aunt Jezebel's eyes twinkled. "*Ya,* Susanna, what would the bishop think if we hitched a camel to our buggy instead of a horse?"

Leah laughed. Aunt Jezzy was always more fun after *Grossmama* went to bed. Her shy aunt had a real sense of humor. The two older women had spent years living under the same roof, and as uncharitable as it might be to judge, Leah felt that *Grossmama* often bullied and was unkind to her younger sister. Aunt Jezebel always seemed happier on the days that *Grossmama* went to the senior center.

"Camels are not *Plain,*" Rebecca said with a giggle.

"Ne," Mam agreed solemnly. "Definitely not *Plain.*" And then they all laughed.

Leah went to the window and pulled aside the curtain. Daniel's Aunt Joyce's van was gone. She hadn't expected to still see him there, but still, the dark yard left her with a sense of longing. "Daniel drove us home," she said.

"Home," Susanna echoed, her word nearly lost in a yawn.

"Bedtime for you, sleepyhead," Mam said. "Time we all turned in, I think."

Leah nodded. Three mornings a week, *Grossmama* was picked up to go to Maple Leaf, the Englisher senior center, where she taught other women how to make beautiful braided rugs. On those days, Leah went to help Anna with the children and housework. Leah was naturally an early riser, so being at Anna's by seven a.m. was not a problem. Usually, she would sit up until at least ten, doing puzzles with her sisters or listening to Rebecca read news from the *Budget*. But tonight, as much as she loved being with her family, Leah wanted to be alone.

She wanted to climb into bed and think about all she'd seen and heard.

She wanted to remember how Daniel's face had seemed to glow with an inner light when he'd told about the work of the Mennonite missionaries in faraway places where impoverished people lived difficult lives and had to struggle to find enough to eat. He wasn't preachy, but when he spoke, she could feel his honesty and dedication to serving God. And maybe, most of all, she wanted to remember how he'd smiled when he said he liked her.

Being part of a tight-knit Amish community, Leah had always been involved in hands-on sharing days, sewing bees and school fund-raising auctions. But none of those efforts seemed as worthwhile or as exciting as what Daniel was doing, and she couldn't help wishing that her church could reach out to help strangers.

As everyone made final preparations for bed, Leah let Jeremiah, Irwin's little terrier, outside to relieve himself. Mam had gotten her share of disapproving looks from her neighbors for permitting a dog to sleep in the house instead of in the barn with Flora, the family's sheepdog, but Mam had stood her ground. Irwin had been a lost and troubled boy, and Jeremiah an abandoned mutt. The two had bonded from the first day that Leah's sister Ruth had carried the starving pup home, and Mam insisted that Jeremiah and Irwin had healed each other. Usually, Jeremiah curled up at the foot of Irwin's bed, but tonight Irwin was spending the night with his Beachy cousins, and it fell to Leah to see to the terrier's needs.

"Don't take all night," Leah called to the little dog. It was very dark, with only a few stars piercing the heavy cloud cover. She thought that it might rain again this evening. In the west, she caught sight of a flash of lightning. "Jeremiah!" Leah called. "Come on!"

The kitchen door squeaked and Leah's mother stepped out on the porch beside her. She didn't have to turn to see who it was, and Mam didn't need to speak to be recognized. There was no mistaking the scent of lavender soap that Mam favored.

"Daniel asked me if I wanted to help at the Mennonite Food Bank in Dover on Tuesday afternoon. Caroline and Leslie Steiner will be there." Leah hesitated. "I told him I would, and he's going to pick me up after lunch."

"I see."

When silence stretched between them, Leah called for the dog again and then said, "He must be chasing a mouse or one of the cats."

"He'll come when he's ready," Mam said. "I wanted a minute alone with you. It seems that my instincts were right." Soft fingertips brushed Leah's chin. "You find Daniel Brown attractive, don't you?"

"Daniel?"

Her mother chuckled. "He is a nice young man." Her

voice grew more serious. "But he's not for you, Leah. He's not one of us."

"I went to see his program," she defended. "And I'm helping to give out food to people who need it. I'm not walking out with him."

"*Ne,* you're not, but you've imagined what it might be like, haven't you?"

Leah didn't answer. She wasn't ready to admit to Mam or even to herself that the attraction she felt for Daniel was different…stronger than for any of the boys with whom she'd grown up. Instead, she called for Jeremiah again. Still no ragged little black-and-white dog with a silly plumed tail. "Where can he have gotten to?"

"Leah."

She sighed. "I know he's Mennonite, Mam, but it doesn't hurt to think what might be, does it?"

Her mother's hand closed around hers. "It is your running around time, and it's only right that you see how others live, but don't look too far. It could make you unhappy when you choose the *Plain* life."

"It's not like I'm smoking cigarettes or making a show of myself with the English boys at Spence's. I'm going to be helping those less fortunate, families in need. Is that so wrong?"

"No, not wrong, but dangerous all the same."

Her shoulders stiffened. "Are you forbidding me to go?"

"*Ne,* child. That's not my place. You're a woman grown."

Again, Leah couldn't answer. Would she have gone anyway if her mother told her not to? She suspected that she might.

Mam's voice took on a thread of steel. "Have you

never wondered about my other family? My mother? My father? My sisters and brothers?"

"Ruth used to ask when we were kids, but you told us that was in the past. We were your family then and now."

Mam squeezed her hand. "I should have been honest when Ruth asked, but it was still too hurtful for me. I was weak, and it was easier not to talk about them. I'm afraid I'm a work in progress. You don't know how many nights I've gone on my knees praying for the strength to be a good mother."

"But you are," Leah said. "No one could have a better one."

"That's sweet of you to say, but—"

"It's how I feel, Mam—how we all feel."

"Thank you for telling me. But now, I need you to listen."

"I am."

Mam nodded. "When I married your father and joined the Amish church, it broke my father's heart. My grandmother closed the door in my face, and my father forbade me to come home. He returned the letters I wrote to my sisters and mother, unopened."

"Oh, Mam." Leah hugged her. "It must have been awful for you. Why didn't you tell us?"

"I never wanted you children to feel that I was sorry for the decision I made. I've never regretted it, not for a moment. But that doesn't mean that I don't miss my old family, that I didn't want to see you in my mother's arms. You look like her, you know. She was fair of face and beautiful in spirit."

Leah felt her cheeks flame. All her life, she'd known that other people considered her pretty, but it wasn't something that the *Plain* folk were supposed to remark on, or that she was supposed to take pride in. Pride was *Hochmut*. Forbidden. It was against the *Ordnung*, the laws that governed every aspect of Amish life.

"Your mother turned her back on you after you married Dat?" Leah looked at Mam. "How could she?"

"She had no choice. In our home, my father's word was final. He was ordained, a leader in our church. By leaving our faith for Jonas's church, my father felt that I had rejected him and shamed him before the members of his community. My mother was raised among the Old Order Mennonite, and it would have been unthinkable for her to go against her husband."

"Did you know…before? That they would disown you if you married Dat?"

"*Ya*. My oldest brother enlisted in the military. His name was Timothy. He was funny and kind, and he always had time to listen to my chatter. He taught me to bait a fishhook and to ride a horse bareback. I adored Tim. I was twelve the last time I saw him."

"I have an uncle who's a soldier?"

Her mother made a small sound that was almost a sob. "Tim came home once, after he graduated from basic training. My father wouldn't let him see my mother—see any of us. Tim hitched a ride with another serviceman back to their duty station. There was an accident on the interstate."

"He was killed?" Leah asked.

Her mother nodded. "Both of them were. They told us that that they found alcohol in the wreck—that the boys had been drinking. My father refused to allow Tim to be buried in our cemetery. He told the soldiers who came to notify us of Tim's passing that he had no son."

"Dat would never do that," Leah protested. Tears

clouded her vision. "No matter what we did, he'd never have denied one of us."

"Ne," her mother said. "I don't believe that he would. But you're of an age when you'll make decisions that will affect the rest of your life. You have to realize that you are Amish, blood and bone. Nothing will ever change that."

"But I'm free to choose, am I not?" She laid her hand on the porch rail and looked into the darkness. "Isn't that part of our faith?"

"It is. Joining the church, making the commitment to live a *Plain* life is a decision we must each make for ourselves. You're past the age most girls have already been baptized, and I wouldn't be honest if I didn't tell you I was concerned that you have doubts."

"Not doubts, not really. I just…" Leah searched for the right words to explain her restlessness to her mother… to tell her in a way that wouldn't involve Daniel. "I want to be sure," she said, and that much was true. She'd felt this way all her life, as though she belonged…but didn't.

"And so you should be. Just remember, if you chose not to be one of us, you give up everything you've ever known."

"Not my family. You wouldn't stop loving me, would you, Mam?"

"*Ne,* child, never. I want you to be happy, but I also want you to be realistic. And I want you to realize that if you chose a husband from outside our faith, many of your larger family—friends, relatives, neighbors would be lost to you."

"I know that…but I don't know why you're saying this to me. I'm not dating anyone, and—"

"Hush, Leah. Don't say what you'll regret. We've always known each other's hearts. You may look like my mother, but you're a lot like me. There's an independence in you that your sisters don't share. You'll follow your heart, no matter where it leads you." She took a deep breath. "I'm just saying that your life will be a lot simpler if you find a nice Amish boy and start walking out with him."

"Do you have anyone in mind?" Leah went to the steps and whistled for Jeremiah. "I've a mind to leave him out all night."

Her mother joined her. "I wouldn't have you think that your grandfather was a bad man. He wasn't. He was a good man. He loved his children, and we loved him. But he was very set in his ways. My mother always said that Dad would have been a martyr if he'd lived in the bad times in Germany."

Leah stepped back and looked into her mother's face. It was dark on the porch, and her features were hidden in shadow. "So you knew the price you'd have to pay, but you chose to follow your heart and marry Dat."

"*Ya,* I did. For me, I think it was the right choice. I could never have had a better husband—a better father for my children." She sighed. "Maybe I took after my Dad…maybe I'm as stubborn as he was."

"But you wouldn't—" Jeremiah began to bark. "What's wrong with him?"

"I think someone's coming," her mother said. "There." She pointed.

Leah stared into the darkness and saw a small beam of light. "Who'd be coming this late? On foot?"

Chapter 7

"We'll see, won't we?" Mam started down the steps.

"Wait," Leah cautioned. "Let me get a flashlight."

"Hello!" Mam called.

"It's me! Johanna." The flashlight beam bobbed and grew brighter. Jeremiah's excited yips nearly drowned out her sister's voice.

"Johanna?" Leah called. "Is someone sick?" She hurried down the steps after her mother. She couldn't imagine why her eldest sister had walked over in the dark this late at night.

"We're all fine," Johanna answered. But something in her voice told Leah that wasn't quite true.

Leah's nephew, red-haired Jonah, ran into her mother's arms and Mam scooped him up. "How's my big boy?" she asked. "Did you walk all the way over here?"

"Ya," Jonah said shyly. "I did. Katy rode."

Leah heard the squeak of wagon wheels and Johanna materialized out of the dark, pulling Jonah's little red wagon. Katy, the baby, sprawled inside, one small booted foot hanging over the wooden railing.

"Not so far," Johanna said. "We took a shortcut through the fields, came down the woods lane and up through your pasture."

It was still a long way for a four-year-old to walk and her sister to pull the baby. "Is she asleep?" She hugged Johanna. "I wish I'd known you wanted to come. I'd have hitched up one of the horses and driven over to fetch you."

"Too bad we don't have one of those cell phones," Johanna said, switching off her flashlight and putting it in the wagon. "But it didn't take me long. Katy's sleeping like a log. It's way past her bedtime."

Leah looked at her, waiting for some explanation.

"Wilmer's not at home, and Jonah and I decided that it would be fun to spend the night with all of you," Johanna said.

"Wilmer took the horse and buggy?" Mam asked. Leah could tell by her mother's tone that she was suspicious, too. This simply wasn't a spur-of-the-moment decision to come visiting, but Johanna would tell them the real reason when she was good and ready.

"*Ya,* he did. I don't expect him home tonight, and we got lonely for company, didn't we, Jonah?" Johanna said with forced joviality. She lifted Katy, still sleeping and clutching her beloved rag doll, out of the wagon and cradled her against one shoulder. "Has everyone else gone to bed?"

"I think so," Mam replied. "But we've always got

room for you. Leah can take Jonah to bed with her, and you can sleep with me."

"I think there's some rhubarb pie left," Leah said. She knew that Johanna was partial to rhubarb.

"That and a glass of buttermilk would hit the spot," her sister murmured.

"Well, don't just stand there," Mam said. "Let's get these little ones into the house and into bed. Thank goodness I've got that crib still set up in the corner of my bedroom."

Johanna and Leah glanced at each other and laughed. Mam had had that crib there as long as either of them could remember. It was always useful for visiting grandchildren or neighbors' babies or for church services when the whole congregation came for the day. The quilts and sheets changed over the years, but they were always kept fresh and clean, and Leah had lost track of the number of babies who had slept in it.

Inside, they found that Rebecca, Susanna and Aunt Jezebel had gone on to bed. Someone had turned off the propane lamp, leaving just the antique kerosene lantern burning on the kitchen table. Mam passed Jonah to Leah. "Give his face and hands a lick and a promise and tuck him in while we put Katy to bed. Then we'll all have some of that pie and buttermilk."

Jonah's eyes were heavy-lidded and it was clear to see that he was on the verge of falling asleep. "Let's just get this hat and jacket off you," Leah said. "Aunt Rebecca's already in bed. Let's surprise her."

"Go with your Aunt Leah like a big boy," Johanna said to the child. "And in the morning, I'll make you something special for breakfast."

Jonas murmured something and Leah carried him

upstairs, first to the bathroom, and then to the bedroom she shared with Rebecca. Her sister had left a lamp burning, and she sat up when Leah entered the room. "Who have you got there?" she asked teasingly. "It can't be our Jonah."

"Ya." He yawned. "It's Jonah."

Rebecca met Leah's gaze, obviously curious, but Leah shrugged. "Johanna brought the children to spend the night with us," she said. "I suppose we'll know why in the morning. Or not."

Rebecca put out her arms, and Leah tucked him in under the quilt beside her sister. The boy's curly hair, exactly the same shade as Rebecca's, mingled with hers on the white pillowcase. "He smells sweet," Leah said. "Like pumpkin pie."

"Do not," Jonah said, but he giggled sleepily.

Leah smiled at him. He was an adorable child, good-natured, and independent, for four. Whenever she saw Jonah, she couldn't help thinking what it would be like to have a little boy or girl just like him someday. "Make sure he says his prayers," she reminded Rebecca. And then she blew out the lamp and made her way back downstairs in the semidarkness.

As she neared the kitchen doorway, Leah heard Johanna say, "I pray for him, Mam. I think his is a troubled soul."

Leah couldn't make out Mam's reply, but it was obvious that her mother was concerned. As she entered the room, Johanna broke off in midsentence and glanced at her. That was when Leah saw the large purple bruise on her sister's left cheekbone.

Leah's chest tightened. "How did you get that bruise

on your face?" she demanded, but she had a sinking feeling that she already knew.

Her sister's marriage to moody Wilmer Detweiler had been a rocky one from the start, and Leah could never understand why Johanna had accepted his proposal. The church taught that members of a congregation were all one family and should love each other like brothers and sisters, but Leah had never taken to Wilmer.

From the first, Johanna and Wilmer had struggled financially, and difficult pregnancies with both children put even more strain on the relationship. On several occasions, there had been discord, followed by disturbing incidents between Johanna and Wilmer, such as Wilmer's public complaints about his wife and his rough-handedness with her. It was a sensitive subject, because marital relationships were considered private, to be kept within the home, and Johanna never complained.

A husband was expected to be the head of the family, to command respect, but physical abuse directed toward a wife—toward anyone—was not permitted by the Amish. A marriage was supposed to be a partnership. Any type of violence went against their teachings.

Shamed by the difficulties between her and her husband, Johanna had tried to hide her injuries. Eventually, Mam had found out and confronted Wilmer. And when he rejected her intervention, Mam had reported Johanna's plight to the elders of the church. Samuel, as deacon, and other members of the congregation had taken him to task, and the family had hoped that the trouble was in the past.

But if Wilmer had struck Johanna again, the old problems had resurfaced, making Leah frightened for her sister's safety. "Was it Wilmer?" Leah asked. "Did he hit you?"

"*Ne,* an accident." Johanna averted her gaze, making Leah certain that her sister was protecting her husband.

Unconsciously, Leah's fingers balled into fists at her sides. This wasn't the fun-loving and confident big sister she'd always counted on. Leah's heart ached for her. "Oh, Johanna," she said. "How could he?"

"I said it was an accident," her sister repeated. "I was getting some jars of peaches out of the cupboard and one fell and..." She looked up through moist lashes. "Just peaches," she finished softly.

"Peaches, my foot!" Leah threw her arms around Johanna and hugged her tightly. "We should call the police. Wilmer should be locked up."

"Ne, ne." Johanna pulled out of Leah's embrace, covered her face with her hands, and began to sob. "No English." She shook her head. "No police. It's not our way."

"She's right," Mam put in. "We do not involve the English in our troubles."

"But we've tried *our* way," Leah argued. "Wilmer promised that it would never happen again. And now it has!"

"Hush." Mam raised a finger to her lips. "This is Johanna's business. Best you not trouble her further tonight. She's here with us, and she's safe—"

"Until morning!" Leah retorted. "And then what? Wilmer will come for her, and she'll go with him like the last time?"

"He will be better tomorrow," Johanna said. "It was his headache again. Katy has been fussy all day, and Wilmer couldn't sleep. He has terrible headaches. I know not to vex him when he's in pain, but I lost my temper when he scolded Jonah for spilling his milk. It was my fault. It's a father's duty to teach his children proper behavior."

"You can't go on making excuses for him," Leah said. She couldn't take her gaze off Johanna's hands. Although her sister had only recently turned twenty-five, her slender hands were red and calloused from doing hard labor and looked as though they belonged to a much older woman. "We'll send word to Samuel and the church elders," Leah insisted. "They'll—"

"Ne." Johanna shook her head even harder. "If you shame Wilmer, it will be worse for me and the children. Pray for him. He's a good man weighed down by ill health and misfortune."

"I don't think he is a good man." Leah's words came out in a rush. "I think he's lazy—and a bully."

"Enough, Leah," Mam said. "Maybe you should go on to bed. Praying for Wilmer would be the best thing you can do for Johanna and for the children right now. God's power to change hearts is greater than ours."

"Mam, we're past the point of prayer. Your daughter and grandchildren are in danger. Why are you not more upset about this?" Leah settled her hands on her hips. "She should leave him and come home for good."

Johanna wiped the tears from her face. "He is my husband, Leah. If I leave the marriage, I break a contract I made before God. We're not English. I cannot break up a family because we have differences."

"Differences?" Leah motioned to the bruise on Johanna's cheek. "What would you do if he struck Katy like that? Would you stand by and watch him do her permanent harm?"

"Wilmer's never laid a hand on Katy in anger," Johanna said. "You should know I would never allow my children to remain in danger. As for me, I can take care of myself. And it's unfair to call him lazy. His trade is a hard one, especially in bad weather."

"I'm sure he is a good carpenter—when he works," Leah said. "How many days was he off this past winter?"

"Construction is slow. It's not Wilmer's fault if—"

"It's his fault if he's home and still abed while you're out feeding the sheep and turkeys. Or hoeing the garden. Lots of Amish men work forty hours outside the home and then come home and tend the farm. Wilmer leaves the house, the bees, the poultry and the livestock to you. Not to mention the quilts you sew or the canned jams and jellies you sell to the English."

"Leah." Her mother's tone grew sharp. "I won't ask you again to leave us. You're not helping your sister. She needs time to think, to decide for herself the right thing to do. You cannot make such decisions for her, and neither can I. You're young. You don't—"

"I may be young, but I know right from wrong," Leah insisted. "I think Wilmer's dangerous, and I couldn't bear it if anything happened to Johanna or either of the children."

"None of us could," her mother said.

Leah sighed and hung her head. "I'm sorry, Mam. I didn't mean to be disrespectful to you."

"I know you didn't," Mam said. "We'll talk in the morning, after Johanna has had time to pray and to consider her options."

"All right." Swallowing the arguments she wanted to make, Leah left the kitchen and started up the wide stairs to her bedroom. But the unspoken words echoed in her mind. *What Wilmer's doing is wrong, and if neither of you will do anything to stop him, I will.*

But there was no time to speak to her mother about Johanna's abusive husband the following morning. Apparently, Mam and Johanna had stayed up late into the night, and Johanna and the baby were still sleeping in when the rest of the family gathered around the table for breakfast. This was *Grossmama*'s senior center day, and she was too excited to have more than a cup of black coffee before the bus arrived to pick her up.

"We have breakfast and lunch there," her grandmother said loudly. "On trays. Fruit and waffles, bacon and eggs. But not real eggs. They taste funny. And *decaffeinated* coffee." *Grossmama* wrinkled her nose in disgust. "What good is that? I make them give me tea." She scowled at Irwin. "Where are my bags?"

"On'na porch," the boy said.

The rug-making supplies that her grandmother was looking for were in two old-fashioned carpet bags, and it was Irwin's job to lug them out to the gate so that the driver could stow them in the back of the bus. "Irwin carried them out for you," Leah soothed. "Just as he always does." She threw Irwin a sympathetic glance. He ducked his head and slurped his milk.

"I don't trust him. Beachys all have sneaky eyes."

"Irwin has the eyes God gave him," Mam said, smiling at Irwin. "And they serve him well, now that he has new glasses."

Grossmama scrunched up her face and picked at the single black hair on her chin. "The bus is late. It's always late."

"It's not time yet," Leah said. "The bus doesn't come until seven-thirty."

Despite her complaints, Leah knew that her grandmother enjoyed the experience because she complained even more when the center was closed for the holidays. Her grandmother was the first Old Amish woman in Kent County to attend a program for older English people. Anna had been instrumental in convincing the church elders that it was in *Grossmama*'s best interest to allow her to attend Maple Leaf.

This was apparently one of her grandmother's good days, because, even though she was grumbling, her fussing made sense. Of course, *Grossmama* was always sharper in the morning. She rarely asked where Dat was before noon. He'd been her only son, and most days—although he'd been dead and buried for three years—*Grossmama* was positive that he was in the barn milking the cows and would be in any moment.

Leah poured coffee for her grandmother and found the black high-top athletic shoes and long black sports socks with the orange basketballs that her grandmother insisted on wearing to the center along with her traditional black dress, cape and bonnet.

"Have a good day," Leah said as she finished tying *Grossmama*'s shoelaces. "I have to go to Anna's now."

"Why isn't Anna here? It's not decent, an unmarried girl out of the house all night. She wasn't here at supper, either."

"Anna's in her husband's home," Leah reminded gently. "She married Samuel, and I'm going to help with the children and the washing."

"She has children already? Didn't take her much time,

did it? As fat as she is, no wonder I didn't know she was in the family way." *Grossmama*'s mouth puckered. "If Hannah had kept a tighter rein on the girl, she wouldn't have had a baby so soon after her wedding."

Leah didn't attempt to explain that Anna and Samuel hadn't had any children yet or that Samuel had been a widower with five children when they'd married, two months ago. She just smiled and hurried for the back door. As she passed Rebecca, she tugged at her sister's apron. "I won't be back until afternoon," she whispered. "Don't let Johanna leave the house."

"I'll do my best," Rebecca promised.

Mam glanced at them and raised an eyebrow.

"Have a good day in school," Leah called.

"I'm taking the buggy today, instead of walking," her mother said. "And I may be late getting home. You girls will have to start supper."

"We will," Leah replied. She wished she had a chance to give Rebecca more than a brief account of what she suspected had happened last night. She hadn't wanted to talk with Jonah in the bedroom. The child probably knew better than any of them what went on in his parents' home, but Leah couldn't add more grief to the child's lot.

Leah grabbed a scarf off the hook by the door and tied it over her hair. She had a *kapp* in her pocket, but the scarf would do for the walk across the field to Anna's. Because the morning would be hard work—house cleaning and washing clothes—she'd donned her patched but serviceable dark green dress and an old apron of Mam's. Leah wished this wasn't one of her Anna days, because she'd worry about Johanna until she got back. Maybe, if she skipped lunch, she might be finished with the day's chores by two, perhaps even earlier.

* * *

The delicious smell of cinnamon bread fresh out of the oven washed over Leah as she opened Anna's back door. "Aunt Leah!" squealed four-year-old Lori Ann as she flung herself at Leah's legs. "You're here!"

"Yes, I'm here." Leah laughed and unwound Lori Ann's arms from her knees.

"M… Mae wet the bed," Lori Ann proclaimed.

"But me sor-ry," her little sister shouted.

Samuel, a big, hearty man with a full dark brown beard and kind eyes, nodded, drained his coffee and bid Leah a good day. Leah knew that Samuel had probably been up since four a.m.—he looked tired and there were worry lines at the corners of his eyes.

"Is Samuel well?" Leah asked once her brother-in-law had gone outside. As she watched her sister kneading bread dough, it occurred to Leah that Anna didn't appear her usual calm and cheerful self, either.

"He didn't get much sleep last night," Anna confided. "Deacon business."

Naomi looked up from her book. "Wilmer was here," she said. "Talking with Dat."

Leah met Anna's gaze. Wilmer had come here? Leah's thoughts raced as she tried to fill in the blanks. As deacon, it was Samuel's duty to see that all the members of the church community followed the rules and lived in harmony. He would have been the first one to chastise Johanna's husband for abusing her. So why had Wilmer come to Samuel? And what had Samuel done about it?

Chapter 8

Anna pursed her lips and gently shook her head, warning Leah that they couldn't talk in front of the children. Turning to Naomi, Anna smiled and raised a flour-dusted finger to her lips. "*Ne,* my love. We don't tell who comes to talk with your father. A deacon's family must remember that church matters are to be kept private." She went to the table and gave her eight-year-old stepdaughter a hug. "Now, if you want to be helpful, I could use your help packing the school lunches."

Naomi sighed, closed her book and rose to obey.

"Me help," little Mae chimed in.

"Ya," Naomi agreed. "You can wash the apples."

It was difficult for Leah to curb her curiosity. She couldn't wait to discuss Johanna's plight with Anna after the older children left for school, but she knew that her sister was right, so she bit back her questions.

Naomi set her library book safely out of reach of her younger siblings and went to gather the black lunch pails that she and her twin brothers, Peter and Rudy, carried to school. As the girl efficiently began to assemble sandwiches, apples and muffins, Leah couldn't help noticing what a difference Anna had made in Naomi in the short time since the wedding. Already the child looked far better than she had before, happier and more attractive. Her shining hair was neatly braided under a starched *kapp*, and her new, rose-colored dress fit her perfectly.

Samuel had done his best for his five children after his wife had died, but the home needed a mother, and loving Anna filled that spot perfectly. It was clear to Leah that—despite the difference in Samuel's and Anna's ages—the new marriage was off to a solid start. That Samuel would have courted Anna in the first place was a surprise to the community, but not to Leah. From the first, she'd seen real affection between the two, and Leah hoped that when she married, if she ever did, she'd find a man as good as Samuel to call husband.

She was about to ask Anna what time she'd gotten to bed, when Rudy, Peter and Samuel came back in and everyone gathered around the table for breakfast. Leah didn't get a chance to speak privately to Anna until the kids left for school and the two younger girls were settled in the sunny pantry with a litter of fluffy kittens to play with and a basket of washcloths and dish towels to fold.

The washroom was just off the kitchen, and with distance between them and the children and the chug-chug-chug of the wringer washer, Leah finally had the opportunity to question Anna about Wilmer's visit. Alone, it wasn't difficult to get the whole story from her sister.

"Wilmer admitted that he lost his temper and hit her," Anna said. "He knew he had done wrong, and he wants help to change. He asked Samuel to pray with him."

"And what did Samuel say?"

"You know my Samuel." Anna sighed and reached for a clean towel. "He is a good deacon—firm on church rules, but fair. It's not the first time he's admonished Wilmer for his bad treatment of Johanna. I know the Bible teaches us to forgive one another, but I worry for Johanna. Always, the same thing. Wilmer is sorry and he wants forgiveness."

"Only God can grant that kind of forgiveness," Leah answered, digging into the basket for a towel to fold. "And not unless we truly repent of what we have done wrong." She grimaced. "I'm afraid she'll go back to him. When he's sorry, he promises her that it won't happen again. And Johanna wants to believe that things will change..."

"Maybe you'd best go home and talk with her some more," Anna suggested. "I'll finish this folding. If you can just get those sheets through the wash, I can manage the rest here today."

"Are you sure?" Leah grabbed a sheet and began to feed it through the washer rollers, careful not to get her fingers too close to the mechanism.

"Johanna is more important than having my parlor floor scrubbed. We can do it together when you come back on Wednesday." Anna slid the heavy basket of clean wet laundry aside and gazed at her sister. "So, what is this I hear about you and the Mennonite missionary? Be careful, Leah. You know how people talk."

"Not you, too?"

"You rode to the Grange with him last night?" Anna

rested her hands on her ample hips. "Lucky for you that he's going back to Africa soon."

"Africa?"

Anna shrugged. "Well, someplace foreign. I heard he was waiting to see where he'd be sent."

Leah didn't ask where Anna had heard that. The Amish didn't have telephones, but that didn't keep them from spreading every morsel of news from one end of the county to the other faster than the English could manage it on their fancy computers. *Amish telegram,* the English called it.

"I went with Daniel and Miriam and Charley and the Gleaners…and Rebecca and Susanna…to see the missionary program. He gave a bunch of us a ride in his aunt's van."

"And?" Anna waited.

"And after the program, Daniel asked me if I'd like to help out at the food bank in Dover tomorrow. Both of his cousins will be there. Caroline and Leslie Steiner. You know them. They buy eggs from us."

"And you are going to this Mennonite place?"

"Yes, I am. To help people in need. I told Mam I was, and she didn't tell me not to."

"Umm." Anna's expression was thoughtful. "Is he handsome, this Mennonite boy?"

"Nice-looking, yes, but…"

"You like him, don't you? You can tell me."

"There isn't anything to tell." Leah retrieved a stray sock that had dropped to the concrete floor and guided that through the washer rollers.

"Ah. That's what I told Samuel. You wouldn't do anything to cause a scandal. And not with a Mennonite."

"And if I did?"

"I would tell you to think over what you do…but I would love you all the same." Anna reached for her bag of wooden clothespins. "Help me hang out these sheets and then go on home. Johanna will listen to you if she'll listen to anyone."

"I think I should," Leah said. "I told Rebecca not to let her take one step out of the house, but Johanna…"

"It's hard to tell Johanna anything," Anna agreed. "But this time, I think we have to try."

Leah climbed the stile and hurried across the pasture. All the way home, she went over and over in her head what argument she would use to convince Johanna to stay at Mam's with the children. But when she met Susanna, who was on her way to the pigpen with a bucket of potato peelings and kitchen scraps, Leah's worse fears were realized.

"Johanna went home," Susanna said.

"Did Wilmer come to get her?"

"Ya." Susanna nodded. "In the buggy."

Leah sucked in a breath. "Rebecca was supposed to keep her here."

"Ya." Susanna's round face crinkled and her eyes grew large. "'Becka is sad."

"It's all right," Leah told her. "I'll go and talk to Johanna."

"Me, too."

"*Ne,* you stay here and help Rebecca and Aunt Jezzy. Tell them I'm going to take Dat's buggy and drive over to Johanna's. I should be home before Mam gets home from school."

"Okay." Susanna's brow furrowed.

"What is it, Susanna-banana?" It was the name that always made her laugh.

"I'm thinking."

"What about?" Leah was anxious to get to Johanna's, but it was important to listen to Susanna. Just because she'd been born with Down syndrome—which made speech and some tasks difficult for her—didn't mean that Susanna was a child. She understood far more than most people realized.

Her little sister's chin firmed in an expression that looked exactly like their mother's. "Ruffie is married."

Leah nodded. "Yes, she is. To Eli."

"And Miriam is married to Charley."

Leah waited.

The tip of Susanna's tongue touched her upper lip. "And…and Anna…"

"Married Samuel," Leah finished.

"Can I marry Samuel, too?"

"No. Samuel is Anna's husband. You'd have to marry someone else."

"Who?" Susanna wrinkled her nose. "Not Irwin. I don't want to marry Irwin."

"Good. I'm glad you don't want to marry Irwin." Leah smiled at her to cover her sudden rush of sorrow. It was impossible to tell this precious sister that she'd never marry, never have a home and children of her own. "Because we can't have any more weddings now," she said, making a joke of it.

"Why not?"

"Because. Mam used up all her celery. You'll have to wait to get married, Susanna. Until you're older." Celery was traditionally served in large quantities at Amish weddings, and the joke was that you could tell who had a courting daughter by how many rows of celery a couple grew in their garden.

"Old as you?"

"Older than that," Leah said. "Twenty-five, at least. How old are you now?"

"Eighteen."

"Right. So that's years and years to be Mam's helper before you're old enough. Now, you go on and feed the pigs and then tell Rebecca where I went."

"To Johanna's house." Susanna picked up the bucket.

"That's right."

"Okay. Tell her to plant celery." Susanna giggled. "Maybe you want to get married. Next week!"

Leah drove Blackie and the courting buggy to Johanna and Wilmer's small farm at a fast trot. She didn't take pleasure in driving, as her sister Miriam did, but she was at ease around horses. She wasn't afraid to take them out on the road, and she was undaunted by cars and trucks. Once, when she'd been driving home with Anna and Rebecca from Spence's Auction, she'd heard the wail of fire engines coming toward them. She'd jumped out of the buggy, put her apron over the horse's eyes and led horse and carriage off onto the grass until the noisy vehicles had safely passed.

She hoped that once she reached Johanna's, she'd get a chance to be alone with her, but she doubted that she would. That was all right. She wasn't afraid of Wilmer. Church member or not, she'd tell him what she thought of him. For once, she wished that she had studied and taken her baptism when Anna did. Baptized women were treated as full adults, regardless of their age, and her word would have more sway in the community if she had joined the church. Surely, none of that would matter to Johanna. If they had a chance to talk this out, she'd be able to convince her sister that the only sensible course to take was to gather up Katy and Jonah and come home to Mam's to live.

Leah was still going over in her mind what argument she would use when she guided Blackie into Johanna's rutted dirt driveway. The small farmhouse had seen better days. The roof leaked and Leah suspected that the walls weren't insulated. Sometimes, in the winter, the children had to wear their coats while playing inside, and Katy got a lot of colds. Still, the rent was what they could afford, and the farm had a lot of outbuildings that Johanna was able to use for her poultry and sheep.

As she tied Blackie to the hitching rail, her sister stepped out on the porch. "Leah." Johanna's face was strained, but Leah couldn't see any new bruises. "Why are you here?"

"You know why." Leah started toward her.

Johanna came down the wobbly wooden steps and embraced her. "I know you mean well," she said, "but I have to work this out for myself."

"I'm afraid for you," Leah answered.

"Pray for me—pray for us."

"I have, and I still wish you'd come home with the children. Home to stay, at least for a few months."

Johanna shook her head. "I can't, Leah. Wilmer is my husband. He needs me—now, more than ever. He's not well."

"You won't be either, if you stay with him."

"We'll be all right. Really. Wilmer's been to talk to Samuel, and he plans to make a full confession in front of the church elders. He's sorry, and he's praying that nothing like that will ever happen again."

"And if it does?"

"I'll face that if I have to." She forced a smile. "But I don't want you and Mam to worry about me. Wilmer's sister, Emily, is coming to stay with us for a while. I like her. She's easy to get along with, and there won't be any trouble in the house while Emily is here."

"You're sure?" Leah stepped back and folded her arms. "I wish…"

"If wishes were horses…" Johanna said. It was an old saying of Dat's. *If wishes were horses, beggars would ride.*

They laughed together, and for an instant, Leah saw a flash of her old fun-loving and strong sister. "I love you," Leah said. She glanced toward the house.

"And I love you. But I know better than to let you and Wilmer under the same roof together until this whole thing blows over."

"What he did was wrong, Johanna. Don't make light of it."

"I'm not. Believe me, I'm not. But I have to accept that he can change—that God can show us a better way to live, in peace and harmony, for the sake of our children."

"I hope you're right," Leah said. She hugged Johanna again and then went back to where Blackie stood, patiently waiting.

"I see you're driving Dat's courting buggy," Johanna said. "Not planning on going riding with that Mennonite boy, are you?"

"Nooo." Leah chuckled and shook her head. "Mam had to tell you about Daniel, didn't she?"

"I'm your big sister. Just because I don't live in the house doesn't mean I can't know what's going on."

"And try to boss me around as you did when we were kids," Leah teased.

Johanna smiled. "Exactly. Sometimes, I wish we were still children. Everything seemed so easy then." Leah unsnapped Blackie's bridle and rolled the length of rope around the hitching rail. "Tell Mam I'll be fine. I'm sorry I worried all of you. With God's help, I can handle this."

As she drove out onto the blacktop road again, Leah wished that she could feel as confident as Johanna that she and her husband would be able to work out the problems in their marriage. She wished that she had Johanna's faith. It wasn't that she doubted that God could work miracles, but she'd always believed that God wanted her to take an active role in finding solutions.

Now, her thoughts wandered from Johanna's problems to her own. She had always believed that she would eventually find a good Amish boy, marry him and lead the same life as her mother and older sisters. It was what was expected of her—what every faithful young woman was supposed to do. And yet… She had always felt constrained by the rules, rules that Johanna, Ruth, Miriam and Anna accepted without question. Now she wondered if what she'd been struggling with hadn't been her own willful disobedience, but something else. Could it be that God's plan for her was different than that of her sisters? And if it was, would she have the courage to heed His will and follow a new road into the unknown?

The consequences of such a departure from all she'd ever known—from everyone she'd ever loved—were frightening. Once, before she was too young to go to school, Mam and Dat had taken them to the ocean for a day of picnicking, fishing and playing on the beach. She and her sisters had been playing tag with the waves, running down the wet sand and letting the cold salt water wash over their feet and legs. But she had grown bold, dashing farther and farther into the surf, until suddenly the force of the water swept her off her feet.

She'd been tumbled over and over in the waves. She was terrified, as salt water burned her eyes and filled her nose and throat. She'd been certain that she was dying, but then, just as abruptly, her father's hand had closed around her waist. Dat had pulled her, choking and coughing out of the ocean, and the light was so bright that it nearly blinded her.

When she could see again—when she could make out her beloved father's face—she realized that she wasn't where she'd thought she was. She didn't see Mam or her sisters or the rock jetty. The undertow had carried her down the beach to a new spot, and her father had rescued her there. She'd always remembered that feeling and that exhilaration of being alive and safe…but in a new place.

Could that be what was happening to her now? Could meeting Daniel and stepping into his world be a repeat of her childhood experience of dashing into the waves? And if the undertow caught her again, would she be saved or lost? And if she survived, would she surface in a new and unknown life?

Blackie snorted and tossed his head, jerking Leah back to the present. Just ahead of her, on the side of the road, was a gray van. And getting out of the vehicle was a familiar figure, with soft brown hair.

Daniel…her Daniel.

Chapter 9

Daniel slapped his palm on the van's steering wheel and groaned. How could he have forgotten the last thing his aunt had said to him before he left for the grocery store in her minivan? "Don't forget to put gas in the tank. Otherwise, you'll be walking home."

He *had* forgotten, and he *would* be walking. He'd tried to reach the house on his cell, but no one answered. He tried Leslie, but got her voice mail. *How could he have been so absentminded? Again!* He couldn't help but laugh.

He'd been so proud of himself for remembering to use Aunt Joyce's detergent coupons, getting everything on the list, including the twenty cans of tuna and the dozen boxes of raisins that he'd purchased with his own money. He hadn't wanted to show up at the food bank without his own donation.

Caroline would tease him unmercifully for forgetting to put gas in the van and getting stranded, and he had to admit that he deserved it. The truth was, he'd been thinking about Leah Yoder. He'd hardly been able to think of much else since the night they'd searched for Joey Beachy. He'd mentioned it to his aunt at breakfast this morning, and she'd rolled her eyes.

"What's wrong with Leah?" he'd asked, stung by the expression on her face.

"Nothing. Everything." Aunt Joyce had patted his shoulder as she slid his plate of eggs and grits in front of him. "She's a lovely girl…but…"

"She's Amish," Uncle Allan had finished.

Daniel had tried to make a joke of it. "Didn't you just say that Mom was hinting for you to introduce me to some nice girls while I was here?"

Aunt Joyce took her seat across from him and gave him an *I'm saying this for your own good* look. "She did. But what she meant was that I should introduce you to some nice *Mennonite* girls. Girls like Kelsie Rhinehart or Janelle Warner. Girls from our church."

"The Amish are a closed society," his uncle said as he buttered a slice of rye toast. "Leah Yoder's people have no interest in spreading the Gospel or in serving God by contributing to society. That's *our* way, Daniel. Leah's a beautiful girl, someone that I'd be proud to have as a daughter, but she's not a wise choice for you to show an interest in."

"What your uncle's trying to say," his aunt interjected, "is that we know these people. Fewer than two percent of the young women ever leave the church. Leah might date you, but if you have any other hopes, you're going to be sadly disappointed. None of Hannah Yoder's girls will ever leave the fold."

His uncle had folded his newspaper and set it aside. "And you're not just any Mennonite young man," he said. "You've had a calling to serve, and you're about to leave on another mission, probably to some place thousands of miles from home. You need to find a young woman who shares your faith and commitment."

"Someone like Kelsie," his aunt added. "I know she's interested. Her mother hopes you'll accept their invitation to dinner before you leave."

"You know how much we think of you," Uncle Allan said. "...And how proud we are of you. We just don't want to see you get hurt."

Daniel had tried to reassure them that he wasn't going to do anything stupid or anything to embarrass them, but he couldn't deny that he was interested in Leah... more than interested—fascinated. Yet, in all honesty, he wasn't ready to tell anyone how deeply he felt for Leah, especially since they were still practically strangers.

What his uncle had said was true. Every lesson Daniel had ever learned in his church and family had encouraged service to those less fortunate. Not every Mennonite felt called to serve as a missionary, but most who were active in the church helped to provide a safety net for those in need. They acted as volunteers in homeless shelters and youth programs, provided support for abused women and teen mothers. The Amish, while good, God-fearing people, kept to themselves. The sensible thing would be to find someone like Kelsie Rhinehart, someone who shared the same beliefs and sense of purpose.

But, Daniel thought as he got out of the van and

locked the door, rational thinking had gone out the window when Leah walked into his life in that wet and windy dark pasture. Kelsie Rhinehart was a pleasant young woman, with a nice smile, but she wasn't Leah.

He'd only met Leah three times. It was ridiculous that he could be so attracted to her after knowing her for such a short time—laughable, really. Only he wasn't laughing. All he could think of was Leah...how she talked...the way she smiled...the sparkle in her eyes. He'd never met a girl like her—a girl who made him feel as though she lit up the room when she walked into it. And he'd never expected an Amish girl to be so outspoken or so easy to talk to. She was a puzzle, one he found fascinating.

He wanted to date Leah, but more than that, he wanted her to be his wife. It was insane. He'd never even had a steady girlfriend. He had lots of friends who were female, and he'd participated in coed youth outings, Sunday School picnics and organized sports. In Spain, he'd met lots of pretty girls and worked with them on festivals and charity affairs. He'd gone to movies and museums with a circle of friends from his high school, but he never felt comfortable asking a girl out.

He was probably getting way ahead of himself, anyway—he didn't even know if Leah liked him. She'd agreed to help out at the food bank, but that was probably because she had a kind heart. If she knew that he wanted to ask her out, she'd probably refuse to ever speak to him again. And her family would certainly shut the door to their home in his face.

Daniel grimaced. What was he thinking? There was absolutely no way that he has a chance with a girl like Leah Yoder, especially one as beautiful as she was. No, his hopes would come to nothing. He would end up as alone as he'd ever been in the girlfriend department, and Leah would be the wife of a farmer like Samuel Mast—one of her own kind.

He walked a few yards from the van, and then turned back to make certain he'd locked the door. He hadn't seen any cars come by since he'd run out of gas and coasted off the road, but with all those groceries in the back, he didn't want to take chances. He took out his cell and tried his aunt's home again, but no one answered. As he retraced his steps, he couldn't help wondering how he'd gotten to this age without ever becoming seriously involved with a girl, any girl.

He supposed that part of it was that he'd always looked younger than he was. At eighteen, he could have passed for a middle school student, and he'd been nearly twenty before he'd shot up another four inches and begun to shave. The girls he talked to at lunch and between classes all treated him like a younger brother and wanted to tell him their problems with their boyfriends.

In college, he'd been so engrossed in his nursing studies and the multiple part-time jobs that he'd worked to support himself—that there hadn't been time for dating. And even though he was lonely, at times, the girls in the too-tight clothing with flirtatious personalities didn't seem like a good fit for him, and the more studious ones, who did interest him, he'd been too shy to approach.

Daniel considered himself a normal guy, but he'd never been able to understand the games that a lot of young men and women played or the way they flirted with each other. He wasn't interested in parties, where the main attraction seemed to be alcohol, and he didn't want to hang out in bars, hoping to meet some girl who'd go home with him. As geeky as it sounded, even to himself, he'd wanted to save some important parts of life for the one woman he was certain God intended for him.

For Daniel, marriage was a sacred pact between one man and one woman. He'd always felt that the greatest gifts he could bring to that union was a pure heart, a sense of responsibility and a strong faith. He'd thought that when the right girl came along, the one God intended for him, he'd know it. He just hadn't expected that girl to appear in an Amish *kapp* with a good flashlight and a better sense of direction than he'd ever possess.

Daniel glanced down the road. He hoped that the nearest gas station would have a sympathetic attendant willing to lend him a gas can and perhaps offer a ride back to the van. He had money. He even had a credit card that his church had secured for him so that he wouldn't travel on this speaking tour without an emergency backup. But he hadn't used church money for gasoline or tolls, at least not so far. He'd saved most of the small salary he'd collected while working at the clinic in Spain, and he'd been using that for his day-to-day needs.

The rattle of wheels on the blacktop behind him and the clack-clack-clack of a horse's hooves pulled Daniel out of his reflection. He stopped walking and turned to see an open buggy approaching. There was one person inside, a woman in a dark green dress and a white head covering. For an instant, he thought it might be…

But then he laughed and waved at the driver. What was he thinking? Just because he had Leah Yoder on his brain didn't mean that she could materialize out of thin air just when he needed a ride.

The woman waved back, and as she came closer, excitement rose in Daniel's chest. It couldn't be…but the driver was young and pretty, and she was…

"Daniel? Did your aunt's van break down?"

Daniel stared. "Leah?"

She laughed. "*Ne,* it's Bishop Atlee." She reined up the horse. "Of course it's me." She paused. "Well, are you getting in, or are you going to keep walking?"

"You're here." He still couldn't believe it. It was Leah. *His* Leah. "What are you doing here—on this road?"

The horse tossed its head and pawed at the road with one iron-shod hoof. "Hurry up," Leah urged. "Get in before he starts acting up."

"In the buggy?"

She laughed again. "Did you fall and hit your head, Daniel Brown? Of course, in the buggy. Are you on your way home? I'm afraid I don't have any tools in the back for fixing car engines." Her eyes sparkled with mischief. "And if I did, I wouldn't know the first thing about repairing one."

"Yes, all right." He moved cautiously up to the buggy. "How do I…"

She chuckled. "Just climb in."

The horse shifted from side to side and switched his tail as Daniel scrambled up onto the seat beside Leah. He'd no sooner gotten his balance than she clicked to the animal and the buggy started forward with a jolt. Daniel grabbed for the front panel. "I've never ridden in one of these before," he admitted.

"I can see that." She flicked the long leather lines and the black horse began to trot. A truck came down the road toward them, and Leah tightened her grip on the reins but didn't slow the horse.

"I ran out of gas," Daniel explained. "I was walking to a gas station."

"Does it happen a lot?"

"Does what happen?" He tried not to stare at her, but she was so pretty with her red hair and the modest dark green dress.

"Running out of gas," she said. "Do you do it a lot?"

"More than I should." He laughed with her. "You've probably guessed. I'm a little absentminded. I get so engrossed in what I'm doing or what I'm thinking about that I forget to do stuff. I lay down my keys and can't remember where I put them. I misplace my textbooks or—"

"Forget it's time to go to work?" she suggested.

"No." He grinned at her. "My work is the only place I don't forget things. I'm on time, and I know what I'm doing." His voice grew earnest. "I'm a good nurse, Leah. I might not pay attention to what time I'm supposed to leave at the end of the day and work a double shift, but—"

"Then you have nothing to be ashamed of," Leah put in. "I probably wouldn't think to put gas in an automobile, either."

"No, you wouldn't forget." He grimaced. "You don't forget to feed this horse, and you wouldn't forget what a van needs to run. I don't see you as a distracted person. You have purpose."

"You think so? I wonder." She made a soft clicking noise to the horse and guided it off the road as a large brown delivery truck passed them. "Mam says that everyone is born with strengths and weaknesses. We have to do our best with what God gave us. It seems to me that you do just fine." She chuckled. "For an Englisher."

"I'm not an Englisher," he protested. "I'm Mennonite."

She shrugged. "Same as. You aren't *Plain*. You've lived in foreign cities and flown in airplanes."

"Guilty." He smiled at her, thinking that talking to Leah was the most natural thing he'd ever done. "If you could take me to a gas station, that would be great," he said. "I can probably get a ride back to the van from—"

"I'll just take you back to the van," she interrupted. "Unless you're afraid people will laugh at you, riding in an Amish buggy."

"No, that doesn't bother me. I like being with you."

She nodded. "Me, too, Daniel."

"I like the way you say my name."

She chuckled. "So it's settled. I'll bring you back to your van. Do you think it will start?"

"Oh, sure. It's a reliable vehicle. It wasn't completely empty. It started sputtering, and I knew instantly what I'd done wrong. I turned the key off and steered it onto the grass."

"Smart."

Daniel laughed. "Trying to fix what I'd already messed up. I would have had my truck, but my uncle borrowed it this morning to bring home some lumber. We're going to repair the back porch." He shrugged. "He's the carpenter. I'm the run-and-fetch guy."

"Someone has to run and fetch, with any job."

He glanced down at her slender hands, so small and yet strong enough to control the big horse. "I've never driven a horse and carriage," he said.

"Would you like to learn?"

"You mean now?"

Her eyes twinkled with amusement. "Well, there is a horse available right now."

He hesitated, feeling totally out of his element,

but wanting to try. "I warn you, I'm not familiar with horses."

She smiled at him, and he felt as though the oxygen had suddenly disappeared from the air. *She's the one,* he thought. *Bonnet or no bonnet. If I mess this up, I'll regret it for the rest of my life.* "You look so pretty today," he managed. "So confident, holding those reins."

"I don't look so good, I think." She smoothed down her skirt. "It's my day to help out my sister, Anna. We were doing the wash. I think I got more water on me than on the clothes." She passed the reins to him and a thrill ran up his arms as her hands brushed against him. "Hold them like this," she instructed. "Firm, but not too tight. A horse's mouth is sensitive."

"His mouth?"

"The lines lead to the bridle, and the bridle has a bit that fits into his mouth. Without the bridle, it would be hard to control such a large animal."

"He's big, all right." Daniel tried not to show how nervous he was.

"Big, but not as smart as a pig or a dog. Horses frighten easily. You have to let them know that you're the boss."

"Even when I don't *feel* like I'm the boss?"

"Exactly." She nodded in approval. "Good. You have good hands, Daniel, gentle hands. Not clumsy."

The horse continued to move along the blacktop, almost as if it didn't know he was holding the reins instead of Leah. Daniel's mouth was dry, but he was having a good time. He tried to think of something sensible to say, so that Leah wouldn't think he was a total dork. "Anna's married to Samuel, isn't she?" was the best he could come up with.

Leah nodded. "They're newlyweds. Samuel was a widower with five children. Anna is a good housekeeper, and she'll make a good mother, but it takes a while to get into a routine. I go over a few days every week to do what I can."

"That's good of you. You get along well with your sister, then?" Another vehicle came up behind them and honked the horn. The horse raised its head and made a little jump to the left. Daniel tensed up and tightened his hands on the reins.

"Easy, boy," Leah said to the horse. She laid a hand over his and he felt the same jolt of excitement. "Don't wrap the line around your fist," she said. "That could be dangerous. You're doing fine. Keep the lines gripped so."

He did as she instructed. "Like this?"

"Yes, very good. A few more lessons and you'll be fit to go." She settled back onto the bench seat as the driver raced around the buggy and continued on down the road. "Everyone gets along with Anna," she said, answering his question. "…Even my *Grossmama*." Leah wrinkled her nose. "My grandmother. You met her. She is a strong…" She searched for a word.

"Personality?"

They laughed together. "*Grossmama* doesn't like my mother so much, but she likes Anna. They get along fine. Anna and Samuel have asked her to come and live with them, so it will make life easier for Mam, too. But that won't happen 'til later, Anna and Samuel being newlyweds and all. They need their time alone together." She felt her cheeks grow warm, with the embarrassment of such talk, but Daniel didn't seem to notice.

"Where were you going now? Am I taking you out of your way?" he asked. "I'm sorry if—"

"No." Leah shook her head. "Just on my way home. My sister Johanna..." She hesitated and then went on in a softer voice. "Her husband is not well, not sick but... troubled. I worry about Johanna and her children."

"You were on your way to her house?" Daniel straightened his spine. Driving the horse was easier than he'd thought, at least with Leah beside him. She was a good teacher.

"On my way back home from Johanna's." She turned her face away, seemingly staring at the horse's rump. For a long moment, she didn't speak, and then she sighed. "I shouldn't say anything, especially to an outsider, but I feel like you're not the kind of man to judge." She hesitated. "Wilmer, that's Johanna's husband, he does things to her."

Daniel took his gaze off the road ahead and glanced at Leah. "What kind of things?"

"He gets angry and shouts at her. A lot. And he hit her. She had a bruise on her cheek." Leah touched her cheekbone. "Here. An ugly bruise."

"No man should ever hit a woman. Ever."

"I agree. I wanted Johanna to bring the children home and stay with us. But it's not easy. We...the Amish don't believe in breaking up families. A marriage is for life."

"With us, too," Daniel agreed. "But not if there's abuse. That's against the law."

Leah reached over his hands, gripped the reins and pulled back. The horse stopped short. "I shouldn't have said anything to you. My sister...my family would be angry with me. It's private, what happens in our homes."

"But hitting a woman—hitting anyone is wrong."

"Yes, it is."

"Your mother must..." He broke off, not sure what

her mother thought about such behavior. "I mean, surely, she…"

"My mother is worried, but she says that Johanna must make her own decision, that we can't make it for her. And Johanna is still trying to mend things between her and Wilmer."

"And you're afraid your sister is in danger."

"Exactly."

"And you say there are children?"

"A four-year-old boy and a baby girl. Johanna says he won't harm the children. I think Wilmer is too hard on Jonah. He favors their daughter. He has since she was born. Wilmer says he's sorry for what he did to Johanna, and I know we should forgive, but—"

"If it were my sister, I don't know if I could forgive a man for striking her."

Moisture glistened on Leah's lashes. "You understand how I feel."

He nodded. "Maybe you should report this to the police."

"No, I can't. Not yet. My sister would never forgive me. We try to fix things inside our church…in our community. But Johanna will be safe now, at least for a while. Wilmer's sister is coming to stay with them. He wouldn't lose his temper in front of her." Leah released the leather lines and clicked to the animal. "Walk on, Blackie." She rested her hand on his forearm. "Promise me that you won't tell anyone."

The horse obeyed her command and the buggy moved forward. "Not if you don't want me to," Daniel said.

"Please," she pleaded. "It was wrong of me to talk about my sister's marriage, but I had to talk to someone…someone outside the family."

"I won't break your confidence."

"Oh, no!" Leah pulled her hand from his.

Daniel glanced up to see another horse and buggy, a larger, covered, black carriage coming toward them. "What's wrong?" he asked.

Leah grimaced. "That's my Aunt Martha."

"Is that a problem?"

"I'm afraid so, Daniel. My Aunt Martha is always a problem."

Chapter 10

Leah's heart sank as she smiled and waved. Of all the people she knew, it would have to be Martha and Dorcas who saw her with Daniel. "I wonder where they're going," she said, trying to keep her voice light.

Dorcas stared but waved back, while Aunt Martha only gave a grudging nod as the buggies passed each other.

"Will you be in trouble because of me?" Daniel asked.

Leah hesitated. *How could she make him understand Aunt Martha without being uncharitable?* "It's not your fault," she said. "Don't worry about it. You've done nothing wrong. What would be wrong would be for me to leave a friend walking, instead of picking him up."

"So…are we friends?"

Her heart skipped a beat. "Yes, Daniel, I think we are. Since the woods and the dark…" She glanced at him and smiled. "And the rain." She nodded. "Yes, I'm sure of it—friends."

"It was a miserable night for a walk in the woods—but we found Joey."

"Yes, we did. We found him together." Daniel grinned at her, and Leah found herself drawn into the depths of his warm green eyes.

"You found Joey. I just tagged along."

"Is that what you think?" She shook her head. "No, *we* did it. If it wasn't for you, I wouldn't have been so brave. I don't like the dark. My sisters always tease me about being afraid to go out to the barn at night. It's why I always have a flashlight." She reached under the seat and showed him the one she kept in this buggy. "And I wouldn't have been able to save that baby goat."

"You don't know that."

"You're too hard on yourself, Daniel."

"Maybe, sometimes." He swallowed and his gaze became serious. "You're different than most girls, Leah. Easy to talk to. I feel like I've known you forever."

She smiled. "Me too, with you, I mean."

"Okay, one friend to another—why is my being in this buggy with you a problem?"

"It's my aunt. She's..." There was nothing to do but be honest with Daniel. "My aunt is something of a *retschbeddi*."

He chuckled. "A tattletale?"

She covered her face with her hands. "You know more *Deutsch* than you let on."

"A little, but my accent is awful."

"It's what I think about my English. In the home we speak German a lot...and with other Amish. My mother wanted us to use good English out in the world."

"I like your mother," he murmured.

"I've been blessed to have her…and my father. Both good people."

"And your Aunt Martha? Is she your mother's sister?"

Leah shook her head. "My Dat was her only brother. She was older. He said she tried to always boss him when they were growing up. My *Grossmama*—you met her at our house—she is their mother. Aunt Martha takes after her, I think. My aunt watches what my sisters and I do, and she tells whoever will listen."

He chuckled. "She's judgmental?"

"Exactly." Leah sighed. "My sister Miriam thinks Aunt Martha has a grudge against my mother. It's true Aunt Martha never cared much for Mam, but I don't believe she intends harm. Beneath her stern outside is a tender heart. I have to think Aunt Martha means well and is trying to guide us to live a *Plain* life."

"So, in her eyes, us riding together is wrong."

Leah nodded. "She definitely won't approve, especially since we're riding in this buggy, and you're driving." She flashed him a mischievous smile. "Aunt Martha will make a lot more of it than it is."

"Why *this* buggy?"

"Because it isn't closed. Anyone can see us—see what we're doing. It's called a courting buggy. If you were Amish, and I was with you, people would think we were *walking out* together."

"By *walking out,* you mean dating?"

"Dating, yes, but a little more serious than that. If we were coming home from a young people's frolic—a singing or a picnic—that would be one thing. But we're together in the middle of the day, not part of a group, so other Amish would see us as getting serious about one another."

"And they wouldn't if we were together in a closed buggy?"

"If I'd been driving Mam's closed buggy, I would have picked you up, but I would have worried some. I might even have offered to find you help or go for the gas, but not asked you to ride with me."

"I'm not sure I understand the logic."

She chuckled again. "It's logical to me, but I'm Amish. I wouldn't expect you to understand."

"Pretend I was Amish. Would I be suitable to ride with you—in your Aunt Martha's eyes?" The buggy bumped over a rough spot in the road. "Do you want to take the reins? Am I driving all right?"

"You're doing fine."

He glanced at the front left wheel. "That looks a little wobbly. The whole carriage seems small and light. Are you sure it's safe to drive on this road?"

"It's a solid buggy," she assured him. "My Dat brought it with him from his home in Pennsylvania. He courted my mother in this buggy, and he always kept it in great shape."

They reached the intersection of a busier road. "I'll take over now," she said. "Blackie gets a little skittish when the big trucks pass." He handed over the reins and Leah guided the animal onto the blacktop and then onto the right shoulder. A car whizzed by them without slowing down. The horse flinched but kept trotting.

"If you were Amish, hmm." Leah took a moment to consider his question. "First," she said, "it might depend if you were from our church or one equally conservative. We're very strict, compared to some communities. You see?" She pointed to the waistband on her dress. "No buttons. Our women use straight pins. In some churches, men are allowed to use buttons, but they must be small and not fancy. It's because back in the old countries, in Germany and Switzerland, before we came to America, soldiers wore shiny buttons on their uniforms. We were driven from our homes, tortured and sometimes burned at the stake by soldiers because of our religion."

He nodded. "I know the history of the persecutions. It was the same with the Mennonites. You know that the Amish, your Amish, were once members of the Mennonite church?"

"Of course. Jacob Amman broke away from the Swiss Mennonites because he felt that they weren't strict enough. But we Amish still share many of the same customs with your church, such as foot washing after communion and believing in adult-only baptisms."

"Okay." Daniel ran a hand through his short hair. "Say that I am from your Amish church or one just as conservative. Then what would I have to do to satisfy your Aunt Martha?"

Leah turned her attention to a tractor-trailer coming down the road toward them. "Easy, boy," she cooed to Blackie. "Steady." And then to Daniel, she said, "It might depend on how well prepared you were to provide for a family. Are you a serious boy or one who has paid attention to lots of girls? Do you have a good trade? If you're a farmer, do you own land or have hope of inheriting some?"

"So, if I'm poor, I don't have a chance with you?"

"It depends. Do you own a good horse and buggy? Are you willing to work hard to learn new skills? How respectable is your family? Would your bishop or church elders speak for your character?"

"Sounds like your aunt is hard to please."

"She would be right to take all those things into consideration. Marriage is more than just between a man and a woman," Leah said. "It's of great importance to the family and the community. It's not a decision to take lightly."

"I agree," Daniel said. "But what if I didn't own land and didn't have a bishop to recommend me, but we really liked each other. Would you let me ride with you, then?"

Her pulse quickened. "I might," she answered softly. "I *am* riding with you. Tomorrow? The food bank? Will you and Caroline pick me up at the house?"

"Yes, about twelve-thirty, if that's all right."

For the next quarter of an hour, Leah steered the conversation to safer topics: what her duties would be as a volunteer and how many clients they could expect to serve. As they approached a quieter side street, she guided the horse left past several new houses with well-kept front yards. "There's a small convenience store at the next corner. They sell gas, and I'm sure they'll let you borrow a gas can."

"I'm glad you came along when you did and took pity on me," Daniel teased. "It would have been a long walk."

She laughed, then smiled shyly. "I want to thank you for listening...about Johanna."

"I know you're worried about her. I would be too. I wish I could do something to help."

"You have," she said sincerely. "Sometimes just talking to someone makes you feel better... But you won't say anything to anyone else, right?"

"Absolutely not, not unless you want me to. You can count on me, Leah."

A few minutes later, they reached the store with its two gas pumps outside. Daniel bought her a bottle of iced tea, and while she was waiting, a pickup pulled into the lot with Roland Byler sitting in the truck bed. By the time Daniel got his gas, Leah had invited Roland to ride home with them.

Leah quickly made the introductions. "Roland is Charley's brother. His usual ride was sick today and his boss drove out from the job site to pick him up. It will be a tight squeeze, but we can all fit, and it will save Roland's boss from driving him home."

Having Roland in the buggy kept her and Daniel from continuing their discussions about Johanna and Aunt Martha. Luckily, the two men seemed to hit it off, and by the time they got back to Daniel's van, the three of them were all laughing and joking as if they'd been long time friends.

"Thanks for the ride," Daniel said, once he got the big van's engine running. "See you tomorrow."

"Twelve-thirty," Leah replied.

As they drove away, she asked Roland how his wife was doing. A few weeks earlier, Pauline had suffered a miscarriage of twins. Due to juvenile diabetes, her health was unstable, and the pregnancy had been very stressful on her body. The community had rallied around the young family, helping out by bringing meals and taking care of two-year-old Jared so that Pauline could regain her strength. The medical bills were high, and Roland had taken a construction job for a few weeks to take up some of the slack.

"Better, by the grace of God," Roland answered as

she passed the reins to him so that he could drive. "So many praying for her had to help. But she mourns the two she lost."

"That's natural," Leah said. "There can be nothing worse than the loss of a child for a mother."

"I hate to see Pauline grieving. But if I'd lost her, I don't know how I would have stood it. We've had so many close calls over the last few years. Having Jared is our miracle."

"A fine little boy he is, too. A blessing to you both."

Roland flicked the reins and Blackie crossed the intersection at a trot. "We were afraid he might be born with Pauline's sugar, but he wasn't. Not yet, at least. She worries over him day and night. Too much, I think." He sighed deeply. "It's good of the neighbors to watch him for her, and we appreciate it, but she's so afraid something will happen to him when he's away from her that I wonder if it's worth it."

Leah wasn't sure what to say. Miriam had mentioned the same thing to Mam, and she wasn't the only one. Other women in the congregation, including Aunt Martha, had noticed how obsessed Pauline had become with her son's health since she'd lost the babies. However, Leah didn't feel it was her place to add weight to Roland's burden.

But he didn't seem to notice that she hadn't spoken and continued on. "Don't get me wrong, Leah. I understand how much Pauline must be hurting, but Jared's not sick. He's strong, and it's not good for him to be shut up in the house with her so much. She doesn't trust me to take him in the buggy to church services or even to the barn anymore, for fear the cow will kick him or he'll climb the hayloft ladder and fall."

"We'll keep praying for her—for all three of you," Leah said. "And if there's anything we can do to help, just ask. Anything."

"Your family's been good to us—all of you. I can't thank you enough."

A van full of Amish men, driven by an English woman, passed. The men waved, and Leah and Roland waved back. "People will be saying we're courting, us being in your Dat's courting buggy."

It was good to see him smiling. Everyone in Seven Poplars liked Roland, and his name had been mentioned as a possible candidate for preacher the next time there was an opening. But, according to Charley, Pauline's illness had been hard on Roland. Usually a jolly and good-natured person, he'd become much more serious and quiet.

"Ya," she teased. "Maybe they'll say you're turning to one of those religions where you can have two wives at one time."

"Lord forbid! One wife is all I can manage. God gave me a good one, and I'll not tempt fate by looking elsewhere, not for love nor money." They came to Roland and Pauline's lane and he brought Blackie to a stop. "This is fine," he said. "I can walk up the drive." He swung down and got his tools out of the back. "But I'm curious. Is there something going on between you and that Mennonite, Daniel?"

"He's a friend. I found him with his van broke down. Was I to just drive by and leave him?"

Roland raised a brow suspiciously. "There's bound to be talk, and not about me. You be careful, Leah. A good reputation is the finest thing a woman can own. You wouldn't want to give people reason to think you'd stray from the path. Especially since your mother was born Mennonite."

"I'll keep that in mind, Roland," she answered, trying to keep from showing how the question peeved her. "After all, you know I'm at the running-around time." She lifted her brows. "No telling what I'll get up to."

"Amen to that." He grinned. "So long as you come to the church, be baptized and put on the black. We all think too much of you and your family to have it any other way."

"It's a matter of choice," she reminded him.

"It's a matter of your soul." He slung his tools over his back, turned, and strode up the lane. "Thanks for the ride," he called. "I appreciate it."

The next afternoon, Leah joined Daniel and Caroline at the food bank. Leslie was supposed to help as well, but she'd lost a filling and had to go to the dentist. That left the three of them to unload food donations, keep the boxes filled and wait on clients. Not only were they on their feet from the moment they'd walked into the building, but they barely had time to catch their breath.

Leah was busy dealing with all sorts of people, including several women who spoke only Spanish, an elderly man in a wheelchair with a hearing problem and a young mother with three small, shrieking children.

At first Leah filled cardboard boxes with rice, beans, canned fruit, powdered milk, pasta, jars of spaghetti sauce and an assortment of canned vegetables, while Daniel carried perishable goods in from a refrigerated truck and moved cases of food to the assembly tables. But soon Caroline had a line of waiting and sometimes impatient customers. Leah came to the front to assist her, and when the crowd thinned out to just a steady stream, Caroline traded jobs with her. Leah had rarely spoken to so many Englishers in one day, and she'd rarely had to deal with so many questions and different situations.

The problem for her wasn't that she was overwhelmed by the task; rather it was that she had such a good time meeting new challenges. Most of the strangers she met were surprised to be waited on by an Amish woman, and the majority of them had questions about her clothing and her faith. She answered as simply and as clearly as possible while managing to retain her good humor. Many of the clients were facing hard times financially, and it was so rewarding to be able to help, if only in a small way.

Truly, Leah thought, she was getting more from volunteering than those who'd come to accept the donations. Ever since she could remember, her mother had kept in mind those in the community who were less fortunate. Leah and her sisters had helped prepare meals, can food to share with the elderly and the sick, and welcomed guests to their table at mealtime. But in her home, charity had always been offered within the Amish circle.

Mam had warned her that being among the English might tempt her to question her faith, but Leah was learning that it might not be in the way her mother thought it would be. Simply by taking part in assisting strangers who were having a difficult time feeding their children made Leah wonder why her church didn't extend a hand to outsiders. She'd always been taught that her people were God's chosen ones, that if they lived according to His word as revealed in the Bible and followed the rules of the *Ordnung*, they were living a good and proper life. But was it possible that God wanted something more from her? And had he meant for Daniel to cross her path and throw open a window to a larger world?

Leah was pondering that question when she realized that Daniel was speaking to her. She blinked, looked around and saw that Caroline was locking the front door and lowering the blinds.

"Leah? Did you hear me?"

"Yes...no." She chuckled. "Sorry, I was caught up in my own thoughts. Gathering hay in the mist, Mam would call it." She looked at Caroline. "Is it quitting time?"

"Past time," Caroline said. "We stayed open an extra twenty minutes. There's another shift coming later. The food bank is open three hours this evening, for people who work a day shift and can't get here in the afternoon, but we're done."

"I never expected so many to come," Leah said. She looked up into Daniel's expectant face. "Sorry, I didn't hear a word you said to me."

"He wants to know if you'll come to our house, this evening," Caroline said, removing her apron and hanging it on a hook. "We're filling shoeboxes for Daniel's orphanage."

"Not *my* orphanage," he said, "but one I volunteered at when we lived in Marrakesh, in Morocco. It was a haven for homeless boys who live on the street. Caroline and Leslie organized a drive to collect toothbrushes, toothpaste, pencils, toys and other small items that boys might like. Some of them have never had anything new that belonged to them personally—at least nothing that they didn't steal."

"Some of our friends are coming over," Caroline said. "Teenagers and young adults. Afterwards, Mom always has a movie party for us in the basement. Popcorn and DVDs."

"Movies?" Leah asked. "What kind of movies?" She loved movies and she'd been to them several times with Mennonite friends when she was in Ohio. But she didn't want to see anything with violence or foul language. It simply wasn't something she thought she would enjoy.

"Usually Disney," Caroline assured her. "Nothing that would upset our pastor or my friends' parents. Mom would love for you to come. She told us to be sure to invite you."

Leah hesitated. A movie and popcorn sounded good, but what would Mam think? "Could I bring Susanna?" she asked suddenly. "She would love to see a movie."

"Of course," Caroline said. "Bring all your sisters if you like."

"All right," Leah said, nodding. "Thank you. I will come." She smiled at Daniel. "And thank you for asking me."

"I'm glad you're coming," he said as his cousin walked away, "but that wasn't what I asked you."

Her eyes widened.

He took a deep breath and stepped closer. "I wanted to know…" He swallowed. "I wanted to know if you would go out with me."

Leah didn't know what to say. "You mean…like a date?"

He nodded. "Yes, a date. More than one. I want to get to know you, Leah. I'm asking if you'll walk out with me."

Chapter 11

"Can I think about it?"

That was the answer she'd given Daniel when he'd asked her if she'd date him. And she *had* been thinking about it. For hours and hours. She kept going over and over in her mind whether it was the right thing to do and what it might mean if she said *yes*. She'd prayed for God to tell her what she should do, but so far, He hadn't answered. Either that…or she hadn't listened hard enough.

Leah knew what she *wanted* to do. She wanted to accept, to go out with Daniel, to get to know him and his family. But was that rebellion against the rules that she felt were too strict? Did she want to be with Daniel because she was attracted to him, or was she attracted to the bigger world that Daniel represented? Was it Daniel's stories of the colorful Moroccan *souk*, the marketplace with snake charmers, acrobats and camels, that fascinated her? Or was it Daniel himself? How could she know what her heart was telling her and what was earthly temptation?

And if she did date Daniel and they liked each other, how would she explain that to her mother? She'd only known Daniel since Saturday. Surely, going against everything she'd ever believed for someone she'd just met was foolhardy, not worthy of one of Hannah Yoder's daughters.

Leah continued to wrestle with her conscience as she and Susanna helped fill the colorfully decorated boxes in the Steiners' basement. As she'd suspected, Susanna was thrilled at the idea of a movie and popcorn party. Everyone had been kind and welcoming to her sister, and Daniel had given her the special job of putting six pencils in every box.

"After pencils, I'm going to do cow…cow…cowalators!" Susanna said excitedly. "Daniel said I could."

"Calculators," Leah corrected softly.

Daniel smiled and winked at her, and she smiled back at him. After he and Caroline and Leslie had picked them up at the house, they'd made a quick stop at the dollar store. Daniel had purchased several dozen solar calculators, bags of marbles, index cards and other personal items for the boxes. Leah didn't need to buy anything to contribute. Mam had produced bags of erasers, packs of sticky notes, rulers and small pencil sharpeners shaped like basketballs to add to the donations, which Daniel said would be perfect.

"I still don't know how your mother could pull all these things out of a hat on such short notice," Leslie said. She and another friend, Gail, were rolling T-shirts and securing them with thick rubber bands.

"Not out of her bonnet," Susanna corrected proudly. "Out of her school chest."

Leah smiled. "Mam has a teacher's savings card for the big office supply store in Dover. In the fall, they have wonderful specials for back-to-school items, and she always comes home with baskets full of stuff for our kids."

Daniel laughed and shook his head. "I can just picture your mother driving up to the store in her buggy and loading her cart."

"We watch our budget like anyone else," Leah explained. "And if there's a bargain for good stuff, we're going to take advantage of it, just like everyone else. Amish are allowed in Staples, you know."

"Owwll." Daniel clutched his heart. "Stung again." Everyone laughed and he laughed with them. "Every time I open my mouth, I say something stupid."

"You're not stupid," Susanna said, pausing in her careful counting of pencils. "Nobody is stupid. Just sometimes slow."

"But slow is good," Daniel's Aunt Joyce said as she approached the table with a pitcher of lemonade and homemade ginger cookies. "If you go slow, you don't miss anything good in life." She smiled as she looked at the rows of boxes. "This is wonderful. I didn't know how you'd manage to get all these donations in, but somebody here is organized."

"Leah!" Daniel, Leslie and Gail all said in unison.

"She thought of rolling the T-shirts instead of folding them, and they fit perfectly around the rulers," Caroline explained. "And when the box is full, we stuff the small stuff in the corners and tape it shut."

"I know the children will appreciate all your work," Joyce said.

"They will," Daniel agreed. "Some of the kids have never had a new T-shirt or school supplies that weren't worn or broken. But they don't whine about what they don't have. Most are grateful to have a safe place to sleep and enough food to eat." He exhaled softly. "I wish you could see these boys and look into their eyes. Even the little ones seem far older than their years. Anything we can do to help them is greatly appreciated."

Leah wished she could have been there with Daniel to see the orphanage and meet the children who needed so much. Again, she was thankful to be of some assistance, however small. She was glad Mam had agreed to allow them to come this evening, even if *Grossmama* had put up a fuss. Of course, Mam wouldn't have forbidden her to go, but she could have kept her from bringing Susanna if she'd truly believed the evening was inappropriate. "Leah?"

Daniel was standing at her side. "I'm on popcorn detail. It seems *someone*—" He gave Caroline an amused look and everyone laughed. "Someone we all know and love has decimated the popcorn supply and I've been designated to run out and buy more. Would you ride with me while the rest finish taping up the boxes?"

Leah glanced at Susanna.

"She'll be fine," Daniel's aunt said. "She can help me pick out a movie. What do you think, Susanna?" she asked. "*Swiss Family Robinson, Old Yeller,* or *The Yearling?*"

"All of them!" Susanna cried.

Leah nodded. "I'll go with you, Daniel." She followed him up the narrow basement steps, through the kitchen and outside to where his truck was parked. He opened the door for her and she climbed in.

"So," he asked as he got behind the wheel. "Is tonight a date?"

"No." She smiled at him. "This is not a date. We're helping the homeless children. It's a service frolic."

"And working in the food bank today—was that a date?"

She shook her head. "Definitely not."

"Hmm." He turned the key and put the truck into gear. "You're not going to make this easy for me, are you?"

She didn't answer.

"But would you go out with me…on a *date* date?"

"I told you, I'll think about it." She straightened her *kapp.* She'd thought that she and Susanna might feel out of place here tonight in their Amish dress, but Caroline's friends all wore prayer caps, some small and lacy, yet all had head coverings. Their clothing wasn't *Plain*, but it wasn't fancy, either. Caroline's skirt and blouse were homemade, simple and modest, nearly identical to those of her mother and sister except in color. Daniel and the two other young men who'd come to help wore blue jeans and white button-up shirts.

If Daniel had some misconceptions about the Amish, she had her own about the Mennonites. Far from ungodly people, Daniel's relatives and friends seemed to put God first in their work and play. The Mennonite young people seemed open about their faith and willing to share God's word with others. It wasn't what she'd expected.

"I like you a lot, Leah," Daniel said, tugging her back into the moment. He eased the truck out onto the country road. "I think you like me, too."

"I do," she admitted in a small voice. "But I'm afraid."

"I'd never do anything to hurt you." He reached over and took her hand. "You have to believe that, Leah."

She let her hand lie in his for just a few seconds before withdrawing it. "That's the problem. If we walk out together…if we find out that we aren't a good match, then that would almost be better. But what if we found that we liked each other even more?" She sighed. How could she explain how she felt to Daniel? "We've only just met. This is all too fast for me."

He slowed the truck, put on his signal and pulled over along the side of the road. "I know it's happening quickly," he said. "But every good change I've made in my life has been a spur-of-the-moment decision. I think I knew that you were the one that very first time we met." He took a deep breath. "I've prayed over this, Leah, and I think God brought us together. I may not have much time in Delaware before I get my new assignment. I don't want to waste a single moment."

"I've prayed over it, too," she said. Her heart was racing, and she could still feel a warm tingling in the palm of her hand from where he'd touched her. "But God hasn't answered. I don't know what He wants me to do."

"All the more reason we should date, so that we can make a rational decision."

"Dating you would mean going against my family, my community."

He met her eyes. "My aunt and uncle aren't too happy about it, either, probably for the same reasons."

"If we…if we got serious, it would mean…"

"We'd marry," he finished for her. "I think that's what I want. I think I love you."

She turned to look at him, a little shocked by his forwardness, but at the same time…fascinated by how sure he was of himself. "How can you love me? How can I love you? We don't know each other." Now she was a little flustered. "You're Mennonite and I'm Amish," she blurted out.

He chuckled. "I think that's pretty evident, but what's more important than the church we worship in is a commitment to God and to each other. Don't you see—we share the same values, Leah. I want you to be my wife and the mother of my children."

"Wow." She sank back against the door. "I tell you that this is all too fast—your wanting to date me and your talking about children. You're the one who's not making this easy, Daniel."

"You know I'm right."

"What I know is that, if we did…if we even considered marriage…" *I'd have to give up my church,* she thought, *give up being Amish. I'd have to become Mennonite.* That was the *Plain* way. Usually, a woman joined the man's church, went to live among his people, as her own mother had done. Leah didn't know if she was brave enough…or strong enough to consider such a thing.

"Do you want to walk away without even giving us a chance? What if you live to regret it? What if one day you wish that you could go back and say, 'Yes, Daniel, we should date.'" He paused. "Don't you think this is the best way to know for certain?"

She didn't answer. Was he right? Did she want him to be right? "When God speaks to you, what does He sound like?"

It was dark in the cab of the truck, but she could feel Daniel's intense gaze. "I don't hear Him speak the way I hear you. It's more of a feeling, inside." He touched his chest. "And after I follow that path, it feels good. It happened when I decided to go to the Univerity of Ohio, instead of the college my parents wanted me to attend. And it happened when I gave up the computer science major to study nursing."

"But if computer science wasn't right for you, then how can you say that God directed you to make the decision to go to that college? God couldn't tell us to do something wrong."

"The college was the right place for me. I just needed some time to figure out what I was supposed to be doing there. Maybe I needed to see more of the world, to try something that didn't fit so I would eventually find my true calling and serve where I was needed most." He turned his face away. "Does that sound too pompous, Leah? Am I too full of myself?"

It sounds like the most honest thing anyone has ever said to me, she thought. "*No.* I'm honored that you'd share it with me."

"So you admit that I'm not completely crazy?" He looked back at her. "So will you go out with me?"

"I said I'd think about it." She shivered, but she wasn't cold. Suddenly, it was hard to breathe. "I don't think I'm ready to take that step yet."

"So, there's no sense in my inviting you to help out at the school bazaar in Felton on Saturday? Since I'm not gainfully employed at the moment, Uncle Allan is working double-time finding volunteer jobs for me." He hesitated. "Caroline and Leslie won't be there. It would be just you and me and half the congregation of Oak Forest Mennonite Church."

"You want me to go with you Saturday and work at the bazaar?"

"Not as colorful as a Moroccan *souk*, but fun, all the

same. I was going to ask you, yes. And I do want you to come with me."

"I don't think that selling crafts and jellies in a room full of people qualifies as a date."

"So you'll go?" he pressed.

"Maybe."

"No maybe, Leah. Be bold. Say yes. You're not a wishy-washy woman. It's what I admired about you from the moment I first laid eyes on you."

She hesitated, then spoke quickly before she chickened out. "All right. I'll come—but..."

"But?"

She held up her finger in warning. "It's not a date. I haven't decided about that yet, and I won't let you push me into anything."

He beamed at her. "I'll pick you up at eight Saturday morning. Is that too early?"

"No, but you don't have to come to the house. I'll walk over to the school where Mam teaches, Seven Poplars. It's closer to your aunt's. We can meet there."

"You're not going to tell your mother that you're going with me?" he asked.

"It's not our way. Not until...unless we were walking out. Until then, what I do and where I go—within reason—is up to me."

"So, we still aren't *dating* per se, but you will go out with me on Saturday?"

She nodded. "To help at the school bazaar."

He laughed. "It's a deal, Leah Yoder." He pulled back onto the road. "Now, we'd better get that popcorn and get back to Aunt Joyce's before we miss half the movie."

Daniel switched on the radio and turned the dial to

a contemporary Christian station. "Do you mind?" he asked. "I really like this song."

"No, it's nice," she said. She wasn't familiar with the singer, but the words were those of a popular hymn and they filled her heart with joy. It was all she could do to keep from tapping her foot to the music.

Among her people, no instrument was allowed except a harmonica, but Leah secretly loved to hear guitar and organ music. She liked the rhythm of some of the country music that Miriam enjoyed, and she appreciated the wholesome songs, but too often the lyrics told stories of drinking or violence or cheating husbands. This music made her feel good inside.

Leah sneaked a peek at Daniel. He was singing along and smiling. The music made him feel good, too.

Daniel glanced at her and caught her looking at him. "I think you're special," he said.

She looked away, feeling bold and shy at the same time. "You too."

Leah arrived at the schoolhouse early Saturday morning, scared, excited, and anxious, all at the same time. All week, she kept replaying in her mind the conversation she and Daniel had had in the cab of his truck on the way to buy popcorn. She kept thinking of how much she loved being with him in the warm darkness, listening to the sweet notes and enthusiastic voices of the artists on the radio…wondering how praising the Lord and giving thanks in a modern tune could possibly be wrong.

Today, she hadn't brought Susanna, and she hadn't asked Mam's permission to go with Daniel. She hadn't even said where she was going, only that she might not be home in time for supper and not to worry.

Rebecca had thrown her a suspicious look, but if Mam had been curious, she hadn't asked. She'd merely slipped her $10 and advised her to wear her bonnet over her *kapp*, because it looked like rain.

Tomorrow was church Sunday, and it would be held at Aunt Martha's home. Mam and her sisters were all preparing food to share at the communal meal after services. Since no cooking could be done on a church Sunday, sandwiches, salads, meat dishes and desserts all had to be made today. Even Johanna would be joining them to help, and Miriam, Ruth and Rebecca would go over to Aunt Martha's to help wash windows and do a final cleaning after the young men moved all the furniture out of the downstairs and brought in the church benches.

Leah had seen Johanna again on Thursday, and she felt a lot better about her sister's situation. Wilmer's sister had been afraid to travel alone with a driver, so Wilmer had gone out to escort her back to Delaware, leaving Johanna and the children at home. Leah had spent Thursday night and most of Friday at her house, and had been relieved to find that Johanna seemed much more like her old self.

"I'm sure that things will be better for us," her sister had said. "With God's help, Wilmer will get better."

"I hope so," Leah had answered. She loved Johanna and the children fiercely, and she wanted things to turn out right for her marriage and her family, but she still wasn't ready to trust Wilmer. He'd promised to change before and had always slipped back to his old, sullen ways.

Without Johanna's husband watching them, Johanna's house had seemed as warm as ever. It was a simple home, but Johanna's quilts and spotless housekeeping made the old house, with its leaky roof and splintered wood floors, seem larger and more welcoming. Her sister was a hard worker, and her curtains were always bleached white and her floors scrubbed and waxed. Leah knew that Johanna struggled to pay her bills and put away a small savings for doctor bills and the occasional medicine the children needed, but she never complained. Strong and vibrant—those were Leah's most powerful memories of her eldest sister, and she had been that way on this visit.

Leah had almost told Johanna about what Daniel had said to her, about thinking she was *the one* and wanting to date her. If any one of her sisters would understand her attraction to Daniel, she thought it might be Johanna. But, in the end, she'd kept her secret. What need was there to discuss Daniel with Johanna if they were simply friends? There would be plenty of time later, if anything came of the relationship.

A truck horn honked and a smiling Daniel pulled into the schoolyard. He jumped out of the cab and came around to open the door for her, looking handsome in a green button-up shirt and brown corduroy trousers. He certainly wouldn't have passed for Amish, but Leah approved. He looked exactly like Daniel, which was right for him…right for the Mennonite boy who had her keeping secrets from her sisters and lying awake at night wondering *what if.*

Chapter 12

Leah had been afraid that riding with Daniel to the school bazaar would be awkward and that there might be uncomfortable silences between them. She wasn't a person who needed constant chatter, but this was all so new between her and Daniel. She didn't know if he would feel as though they had to maintain a conversation.

But Leah had always believed that there were other ways to communicate, besides verbally. And sometimes, just being with a person you cared about was what mattered. Some of the best times she had had with her sisters or mother were when they worked side by side in the house or garden or rode in the buggy with only the squeak of the wheels and the clip-clop of the horse's hooves to keep them company. There was a warm satisfaction that came from being so at ease with someone that you could simply enjoy being together without feeling compelled to speak. And to her surprise and delight, sitting beside Daniel as the truck rolled down the country roads was like that.

The day, with all its possibilities, stretched out before her like a table of fresh-baked pies. She was excited at the prospect of meeting new people, of seeing and hearing new things…of doing something different than she'd ever done before. Volunteering for workdays, school auctions, picnics and helping at frolics was familiar. She had taken part in those since she was a small child. But those experiences had always been for another Amish person or family, for someone who shared her faith.

At the food bank and then, later, when they'd packed the boxes for the children's home, she'd felt, somehow, as if this was doing something more. The members of her church were her family. It was natural and right to help your family, but it thrilled her to think that something she could do, in some small way, would help strangers. It made her feel as though she was part of a much bigger family. And with that excitement came shivers of apprehension. What if this was the temptation that the world offered to lure young people away from God's path?

"I'd feel better if I'd picked you up at your house," Daniel said, breaking through her reverie. "It almost seems dishonest, this way…as if we were ashamed of being together, sneaking around."

She smiled at him and shook her head. Daniel was such a good man to worry about her so. "No. It's an Amish thing." She chuckled. "Young people are allowed some freedom. Parents look the other way and pretend not to see what's right in front of them. It isn't really deception because if they told everything, and waited for their parents' permission, how do they learn to make the right choices?"

His green eyes narrowed as he tried to follow her reasoning. "So your mother knows where you are?"

"No, but it's all right with her that she doesn't know."

He exhaled slowly. "I'm still confused, but if you say so, I'll believe you. I'm new to this."

"Driving girls to school bazaars?" she teased. She sat up tall on the seat and looked around. It was a beautiful day, sunny and warm, and she was certain she was going to have fun. "It's new for me, too, being driven in a pickup by a Mennonite boy…alone."

She'd ridden in motor vehicles, of course. She didn't live in an egg basket under a porch. Many times, it was safer and more convenient for Old Order Amish to travel by van. She'd visited relatives in Pennsylvania with her mother since she was eight, and she'd made several trips back and forth to *Grossmama*'s home in Ohio with a hired driver.

"It's nice, though, riding with you," he murmured quietly.

She smiled at him as a small tremor of excitement slid down the nape of her neck. She liked Daniel Brown, and the longer she knew him, the more she liked him. He was such a good man…such a gentle man. For her, he was trouble, and if she had the sense God gave a goose, she would ask him to stop the truck. She'd get out and walk home to her sisters and mother. Spending just one more hour with Daniel was a threat to everything she knew and believed and expected out of life. Instead, she smiled again, settled back against the cushioned seat and asked, "Did you drive cars in Marrakesh?"

He laughed. "Hardly. There don't seem to be many

rules of the road in Morocco. I drove in Barcelona, but not in Marrakesh."

Leah looked out at the fields and farmland on either side of the blacktop and tried to imagine the foreign land of Morocco. "What were the people like?"

"Most are warm and friendly," Daniel replied. "Really good people. With an interesting culture. I loved the food there, especially the yogurt and the olives. And the flat bread. There's one called *khobz bishemar* that has onions and chili peppers in it. It's wonderful."

"My mother makes the best bread and biscuits," Leah said, "but I've never tasted any bread with peppers in it." She wondered what Susanna would say if Mam sprinkled her baking powder biscuits with black pepper or chili powder.

She could just picture Susanna wrinkling up her nose and making a face. She wouldn't complain. She'd just slip the food under the table to Jeremiah. Irwin's little terrier was like Irwin. He would eat anything and everything. Neither one ever got fat, and it was a family joke that if you cooked half a cow, Irwin could eat most of it by himself and Jeremiah would finish the rest.

"You'd love the bread. I promise," Daniel went on with enthusiasm. "My mother learned to make it, and we used to have it every Sunday with roasted chicken and vegetables. I can't make the bread, but I make a mean bread pudding with dates and raisins."

"You cook?" She glanced at him in surprise. Mam had always joked that Dat couldn't boil water, and that he'd starve to death without his mother, sisters or wife to cook for him. She didn't know any Amish men who had much skill in the kitchen. Anna said Samuel's children told her that their father always burned the oatmeal and they didn't know it wasn't supposed to be black and crunchy.

"Just eggs and French toast mostly, and sweet muffins and pudding. Stuff I like. Not pie, though. I love pie, especially raisin pie, but I can't make a pie crust fit to eat."

"Pie crust is hard," she agreed. "Anna and Mam make the best. Aunt Jezzy makes hers with a little vinegar, and that's good. Mine are okay." She smiled up at him. "Not bad, but nothing like Anna's."

"Would you make me a raisin pie, if I asked nicely?"

"I might."

On the right side of the road, two boys ran across an open meadow, followed by two puppies. To her left, an English farmer was plowing with a large green tractor. Seagulls swooped down to snatch up bugs and earthworms, and Leah could smell the rich, freshly turned earth. She thought it must be the sweetest scent on earth.

High overhead, she saw a plane headed toward Dover Air Force Base, and she wondered where on earth the people inside had traveled from. Lots of planes passed over her family farm, but most were so high that you never heard a sound. "I know you must have flown in a plane across the Atlantic Ocean to come home from Spain," Leah said. "I've always wondered what it would be like, up in the clouds with the birds."

"A little scary if you hit a rough patch, but most of the time, it's good. It's a long trip from Europe—seven hours, give or take, and sometimes longer, once you are waiting to land. When I came back this time, I flew into Cincinnati. That's not a bad airport."

"I can't imagine all the places you've been, all the things you've seen," she said. "Our life in Seven Poplars...it must seem very small to you."

"No." He shook his head. "Not at all. I think… I think that it must be wonderful to feel that God has directed you to live at a slower pace. Money or education can't buy the peace and sense of purpose I see among your people. It must be very satisfying and…" He seemed to search for the right words. "Full of grace."

"But not right for you."

He was quiet for a second, as if he was seriously considering her words. She liked that about Daniel.

"No. I'm not a farmer. I don't feel this pull of the land that I see in others."

"But you find that sense of grace in what you do? In doing God's work in the missions?"

"I try," he admitted. Then he smiled. "Yes, I do. I don't know what tomorrow or the next day will bring, but I believe that if I listen, I'll hear what's right for me. I'll try to do it." He shrugged. "It's all we can do, isn't it? Follow our hearts and try to do our best?"

"Yes," she said. "Try to do our best every day." *And maybe,* she thought, *it was all right to not know what tomorrow would bring...as long as you kept listening for His voice in your heart.*

By ten o'clock, the room that served as both cafeteria and gym to the school was overflowing with students, volunteers and customers. Daniel and Leah had been assigned to the refreshment stand and kitchen, and Leah quickly became the short-order cook when Daniel's methods resulted in a lot of high flames and smoke. Still, they worked well together and quickly figured out a system to serve up hot dogs, hamburgers, scrapple sandwiches, Dutch fried bread, cheesy fries and lemonade without getting in each other's way.

Tables offering used books, toys and baby clothes lined the walls. There were baked goods, plants and crafts for sale as well as a display of local honey and beeswax candles. Jams and jellies vied for space amid jars of homemade spaghetti sauce and a table of birdhouses and feeders. Despite the chaos, the atmosphere in the spacious room was light and airy, with everyone clearly having a good time. Laughing children darted from table to table, and slipped quietly in and out of the adjacent room where a group of high school girls were showing cartoons depicting Bible stories.

Outside, on the playground, there were games, pony rides and a petting zoo. Leah had seen the animals amid the preparations when she and Daniel had arrived. At that point, she wished that she'd brought Susanna with her. Her little sister would have loved it. Susanna had a special fascination with chicks, ducks and other farm animals and the fair atmosphere would have delighted her. But today, selfishly, Leah hadn't wanted to bring her sister. She'd wanted to spend the day with Daniel. She promised herself that she'd do something special with Susanna next week to make it up to her, but today was hers alone.

Later, when the lunchtime rush had passed, two of the teachers took Daniel and her places and Leah went to help sell fresh herbs while Daniel taught a class in CPR. The potted mint and basil and chives went quickly, and soon Leah was down to several flats of cilantro and a planter of rosemary and oregano. Then Daniel's uncle bought those for his wife, and Leah was left to sweep the empty area. Someone had questions about making a quilt, and she was soon involved in a lively discussion with two young, married Mennonite women, one with a small baby. Leah ended up rocking the baby to sleep while one of the teachers showed the mother a new stitch. By the time Daniel came to fetch her, Leah felt that she had made three new friends.

"I was wondering," Daniel said as they walked back to the truck together. "Would you like to go to the beach with me?"

"To the beach?" The bright sunshine had given way to clouds, and soon it would be getting dark. The breeze from the east was cool, and the warmth of the spring day had fled.

"The boardwalk, actually. In Rehoboth. Not that much will be open, but I love the ocean. We could just walk and look at the water and maybe find a place to get a slice of pizza. If you like pizza, that is?"

She laughed. "I love the ocean, and I love pizza. I keep telling Mam we should buy one of those pizza stones. Rebecca and I buy pizza for lunch whenever we go to Spence's and we make our own at home. I'd like to go with you, Daniel…very much, but…"

"But?"

"Remember, this isn't a date—not a real one."

"Well, it could just be two friends looking at the ocean and sharing pizza," he teased.

"Exactly."

And that's what they did. The wind off the water was cool, so Daniel found a jacket of his behind the seat and he lent it to her to throw over her shoulders. They bought a pepperoni pizza with black olives and extra cheese, which Leah insisted on chipping in for, and an extra-large cup of root beer. They found a bench on the boardwalk, and sat and talked until the sun went down, without ever running out of things to say.

They talked about everything, about Ohio and Daniel's cousins and the fun Leah had had at the State Fair with them last summer, about Spanish food, and the best vegetables to put on pizza and how Noah had managed to stow enough grain and hay on the ark to feed all the animals during the Great Flood. Daniel told her about his family and how his father had taught him to juggle rubber balls when he was eight, and Leah told him about sometimes fasting with her family on Thanksgiving Day.

And, finally, when it was growing really dark, neither could put off that it was time to head back to Kent County and home before Leah's mother began to worry about her. "When can I see you again?" Daniel asked as they walked back to where his truck was parked. "Tomorrow?"

"Not tomorrow. Tomorrow is church at Aunt Martha and Uncle Reuben's."

"Maybe I could come," he suggested.

She shook her head. "Amish only. Singing and prayers and preaching. Five or six hours, maybe more, but definitely no outsiders."

"Is that what I am? An outsider?" He walked beside her, tall and slim and just a little awkward in the fading light. "Because I don't want to be. Not with you."

Not sure what to say, she went on about church. "It's not bad, even though it sounds like a tedious day." She thought for a moment. "It's wonderful, actually. I love church, even when Uncle Reuben forgets pieces of his sermon and hunts for his notes. The singing is like nothing else—we sing in old German. It makes me feel so…so much a part of something special. I love to look around the house and see my friends and neighbors and relatives, babies sleeping, little children playing with their rag dolls, everyone together, wrapped in God's loving arms." She sighed. "It makes me feel so safe."

"I understand exactly what you mean. That's how I feel whenever my family gets together, after Bible School or a holiday dinner." He paused and then said softly. "I miss them, Mom and Dad, and my brothers and sisters. Growing up in another country, I think you get really close to your family. Most of them are up in Canada now. I hope I'll get to see them before I go to my next assignment."

"You couldn't have gone there with them?"

"I suppose I could have, if I'd asked. But they didn't need a nurse, and there are other places where the people have no available medical care. It only seems fair that I go where I can do the most good."

She nodded. She didn't want to think about him going away and never seeing him again, but she'd known all along that Daniel was only here for a short time. There was no way they could continue their friendship after he left Delaware, not really. "And after the worship service, we have a communal meal," she continued. "The host is supposed to feed everyone, but most families bring food to share."

"It sounds like a good time," he agreed.

"It is. I always feel so clean afterwards, as though I left all my troubles on the floor by my bench."

"I'm sorry I can't come, then," he said.

"Me, too."

"You would be welcome at a Mennonite church service."

She nodded, actually saddened by the idea that she couldn't invite him to church. "It just isn't our way, Daniel. We are a people apart."

"I wish you weren't," he said. "Or I wish there were some way we could bring both our faiths together, so that everyone would understand how much alike we really are."

"There *is* something you would be welcome at," she said. "On Wednesday evening, the Gleaners are going to repair a chicken house and fence in the poultry yard for a family. Anyone can go. Rebecca and Miriam and Susanna and I are going to whitewash the chicken house and help with refreshments. Samuel's going to lend his team, and Charley's going to drive us in a straw wagon. If you'd like to come, we can always use an extra pair of hands."

"A hay ride and a chicken fence." Daniel laughed. "Sounds like fun."

"Then it's settled." They were walking on the sidewalk now, almost to the truck. "Mam is hosting the Gleaners for a haystack supper at five. Come and eat with us. There will be so many people here, no one will notice one extra Mennonite missionary."

"I've never eaten a haystack before, but you can count on me to try anything."

She laughed. "You'll like it, I promise. It has onions, but no chilies, and definitely no figs."

"And I suppose this isn't a date you're inviting me on, even though it is a hayride?"

"*Ne,* Daniel," she teased. "Not a date, and not even a hayride. Straw is a lot less prickly when it gets down the back of your neck."

He opened his arms wide. "In that case, how can I refuse?"

Chapter 13

Leah shivered with anticipation as she saw Daniel turn his truck into the school driveway and get out. The swings, where she usually waited for him, were half-hidden by the trees and the corner of the schoolhouse. She could see him, but he couldn't see her, and it gave her a secret thrill to watch him walk toward her through the tall grass.

It was mid-May, and the Seven Poplars Amish School had closed for the summer. In the past few weeks, since the children no longer came every day, the weeds had begun to take over the playground and creep up the side of the neat white building. She'd have to remember to mention to Mam that the grass needed cutting, if she could think of some way to bring it up without admitting that she'd been meeting Daniel here. The school had a three-rail fence around it. Maybe Irwin could lead one or two of the heifers over so that they could crop the grass.

"Leah?" Daniel called. "Are you here?"

"I'm here, Daniel," she answered. Just saying his name made her happy. Daniel made her happy. Despite the unsuitability of their friendship, she didn't want to think about not seeing him…about what it had been like before she'd known Daniel. She didn't want to think about him going away.

Leah smiled and waved. She was seated on one of the swings, and now she gave herself a small push with her feet. She wanted to leap off the swing and run into his arms. She wanted to hug him tightly, but, of course, she wouldn't. As long as they weren't doing anything to be ashamed of, as long as her behavior was properly *Plain*, she didn't have to feel guilty for seeing him secretly. Did she?

Daniel stopped directly in front of her. "We need to talk," he said.

She looked up at him and her stomach clenched. Something was wrong. Gooseflesh rose on the back of her neck. "What is it?" she asked.

He reached out and caught hold of the ropes. The swing stopped and she half rose and then sat down hard on the seat. The schoolyard was suddenly still. In the distance, she could hear peepers and the cooing of a mourning dove. It was a sad sound, and she felt a sudden wash of apprehension. Was this the moment when everything changed between them? Moisture clouded her vision.

"What's wrong?"

"It's been a couple of weeks. It's time to have this out, Leah," he said. Daniel's tone was firm. "We've been avoiding it too long."

She blinked away the tears. *No,* she thought. *I don't want to lose him.*

His voice grew husky. "We can't keep doing this, Leah," he said, taking the swing next to her. "You know we can't. It's not honest."

She twisted so that she could look into his eyes. "What's not honest? Us seeing each other? Being friends?"

"We're more than friends. We both know that." He took a deep breath. "I need to talk to your mother, to tell her that we're serious. It's time, Leah."

He was right. She knew he was right, but she still wasn't ready. She gripped the ropes harder. The swing wasn't moving, but she felt as if the ground was far away and she might fall off, and keep on falling. "I never meant to be dishonest," she said. The tight prickling sensation behind her eyes grew stronger and she was afraid that she was going to burst into tears and shame herself.

For the past few weeks, they'd been seeing each other several times a week. She'd kept up the pretense, insisting that they weren't dating, and maybe they hadn't been, at first. But they were now. By Amish standards, Mennonite standards and probably even English standards. And she couldn't bear for it to end.

"Say it," he said quietly. "We're dating."

She took a breath, but she didn't have enough air. She felt dizzy. The ground was still so far beneath her feet, and the warm May twilight was taking on a damp chill fast.

"You have to admit it, Leah. To me and to yourself."

She nodded. "Yes," she agreed. "We're dating."

"All right." Some of the lines smoothed around his eyes and he gave her the hint of a smile. "So, if we're dating...if we're *walking out together,* then it's time we told someone. I want to make my intentions clear to your mother and to my aunt and uncle."

She nibbled at her bottom lip.

"You know I'm right," he said.

"It's not easy...what you're asking me to do," she murmured.

"But we can't go on like this." He reached across the distance between them and took her hand in his. "I've tried to reason this out. I've tried to be logical, but all I can think of is how much I care about you and how inappropriate this is."

"Because of who I am?" she asked. "Because we... we come from different faiths?"

"Because we're not being honest with our families." He paused and went on, his words tumbling over one another in his haste. "I've prayed over it, Leah. I'm certain that God wants us to be together, that He wants us to marry. But we have to do this right. We can't hurt the people who love us most just because we're a little scared."

"You want to tell everyone how you feel about me, but you haven't asked me how I feel about you," she said. "You have to ask me."

"Okay. I'm asking you."

She shook her head. "That's the problem, Daniel. I'm not sure of how I feel."

"But you care for me?"

"Of course, I do. You know I do. But..." *Why was she such a coward?*

He nodded. "If you're still unsure, I can understand that. It's all happened so fast. But... I have to know...is there a possibility? Do you think I'm a man you *could* love? A man who could make you happy?"

"I think so," she said softly.

"Do you?" He squeezed her hand. "I'm certain of how I feel. I love you and I want you to be my wife."

"I've prayed, too," she answered, holding onto his hand with all her might. "But God's not answering me. I can't hear Him. It can't be just you who's sure. It has to be me, too. I have to be certain this is right…right for both of us."

Daniel nodded. "I agree. Pushing you into something you don't want is the last thing I'd ever do. But you must have some idea of how you feel…inside."

"I do," she said. "I think I'm in love with you, but…"

"But?"

She smiled at him through her tears. "It's hard, because I've never been in love before. It's hard to know if it's real or just…wishing."

"Do you trust me, Leah?"

She nodded. "Yes." Of that, she was certain. She trusted Daniel Brown with all her heart, utterly…completely.

"Does being with me make you feel happy or unhappy?"

"Happy. But for us to…to marry, it would mean…"

He stood and gathered her in his arms. She leaned against him, soaking up his strength and warmth. *This is right,* she thought. *This must be love I feel.* And just being near him gave her the courage to say what had to be said.

"If we were to marry, one of us would have to change our faith," she said.

"I'd become Amish for you," Daniel said. "I would if I could. If I were free, I'd give up nursing and learn to plow fields and grow wheat, if that would make you happy. But I'm not free, Leah. I've already given my promise."

"To whom?" she asked.

"To God. I know it sounds…sounds prideful, that God spoke to me. But I believe He has. I believe that God's called me to serve Him. I can't refuse Him. Can you understand that? As much as I love you, I can't turn my back on the promise I made to God."

"Of course, you can't," she said. "I wouldn't want you to. But that's why I have to be absolutely certain. If I marry you, I'll be like Ruth, in the Bible. I'll go with you, wherever you go, and I'll worship as you worship. Your people will be my people, and my children raised in your church. If I say *yes*, Daniel, it will be with a fully willing heart, not halfway."

He stepped back and raised her chin so that he could stare into her eyes. "You are the most wonderful woman in the whole world," he whispered, "the only woman I'd ever ask to be my wife. And no matter what your answer is, I'll love you for the rest of my life, and only you."

And as he said those words, Leah felt a loosening in her chest and a sudden rush of joy. There was no voice in her head, no jolt of electricity, just a sense of release and warm happiness that made her certain. "Yes," she said. "You're right, Daniel. It's time my mother knew of our decision. Only…only, I need to speak to her first. I've been acting like a child. I haven't been fair to her, and I'm going to tell Mam."

"Tell her what?" he urged.

She smiled at him with all her heart. "Tell her that a very good young man has done me the honor of asking me to be his wife."

A wide, silly grin split his face. "Get in the truck, Leah. We're going right now to find her."

"Oh, no," she said, suddenly giggly with relief. "Not tonight. Tomorrow. I have to have time to break this to her gently. Otherwise, she might take your head off with her wooden spoon."

"She can't hit me," he protested, still grinning. "You're peace-loving people."

"Mam may be peace-loving," Leah said, "but when it comes to protecting her family, she can be pretty scary."

Leah slipped into the kitchen just as the rest of the family was sitting down to supper. Aunt Jezzy looked up and smiled. "Here's our girl, Hannah," she said.

Susanna waved. "*Grossmama* isn't here tonight," she said. "Samuel came to get her."

Rebecca carried a pitcher of iced tea to the table as Leah washed her hands, dried them on a towel and slid into her place at the table. Irwin caught her attention and rolled his eyes. Leah ignored him and addressed her mother. "The ham smells delicious, Mam."

"Anna sent cinnamon buns with Samuel when he came for *Grossmama*," Susanna said. "And strawberry pie."

Leah remembered that her grandmother was spending the night at Anna's tonight. They were in the process of moving *Grossmama*'s belongings to Anna and Samuel's, and Anna had felt that it might make it easier for *Grossmama* if they made the change gradually. They'd been inviting her to supper several times a week, and having the senior bus drop her off there on the days she went to the center.

Irwin cleared his throat, and Leah looked around,

realizing that everyone had bowed their heads in preparation for silent grace. Speaking to Mam about Daniel would have to wait. As much as she might want to get it over with, Leah knew that mealtime was family time, and not the place to announce that she wanted to turn Mennonite, marry Daniel Brown and go off to be a missionary.

Leah had no doubt that her mother loved her, and that she'd support her decision in the end, but it was all the fussing in between that had her worried. And just thinking about the explosion to come made her sister Anna's featherlight cinnamon rolls go down like lead.

Supper was usually earlier, but tonight Mam had outdone herself and they were eating late. There was fresh asparagus, coleslaw, turnips whipped with potatoes, cold fried chicken, chow-chow, pickled beets, deviled eggs, and steamed cabbage with caraway seeds to go with the smoked ham. Irwin ate enough for two grown men, but Leah could only swallow a few bites.

What would she do if her mother refused to speak to Daniel or if she cried? Mam never cried, at least almost never, but when she did, it was a disaster. Even her mother's temper was better than tears. And it would be worse if she called in Ruth and Miriam to back her up. How could Leah possibly explain her decision to all of them at once? And she could expect no help from Rebecca. Leah wished she'd asked Daniel to give her a week, rather than a day, to explain things to her mother.

Without *Grossmama* at the supper table, Aunt Jezebel was jovial and bursting with stories about Dat's childhood. She was in the middle of a particularly funny one involving a visiting bishop and Dat's pet billy goat when Jeremiah flew out from under the table and began to bark furiously.

"I think someone's here," Mam said.

"I'll see who it is," Leah offered, going to the screen door.

"Mam!"

The voice was Johanna's, and as Leah rushed out onto the porch, she could see at once that her sister had been crying. "Johanna, what's wrong?"

Johanna stood there, shaking from head to foot and clutching little Jonah by the hand. Jonah was white-faced and looked scared to death. He was bareheaded, his red hair sweaty and sticking out in tufts, his bare feet dusty.

"Wilmer," Johanna said, on the verge of breaking down. She shook her head. "I've never seen him this bad."

Their mother swung the kitchen door wide. "Come in, child," she said, gathering Jonah up in her arms. "Susanna, take this tired little boy. Wash him up and give him some strawberry pie."

Jonah began to sob and reach out to Johanna, but Mam cradled him against her breast. "Shhh, shhh, it's all right. Go with Aunt Susanna like a big boy. Your mam's right here."

"Where's Katy?" Leah demanded. Johanna didn't stir out of her house without the baby...without either of her two children. "Is she—"

Johanna threw a meaningful glance at her small son, and Leah nodded. "Susanna," she said with false cheerfulness. "See if you can find out who's under that dirty face."

"It's Jonah," Susanna said.

Mam smiled at her and passed the boy into her arms.

Murmuring to him, Susanna carried him out of the kitchen. "Irwin," Mam said sternly. "Best you go out to the barn and check on that milk cow. I think her calf may be coming before morning."

"It's too early for that calf," Irwin said, clearly bewildered by whatever was going on. "It won't be for another two weeks or so."

"You heard Hannah," Aunt Jezzy said. "Best you go and keep an eye on her."

"But my supper…"

"Take your pie and milk with you," Mam said. "You and Jeremiah stay with the cow until I send someone for you."

As soon as Irwin was out of the house, Leah drew Johanna to a chair and the rest of them gathered around her. Anger flared in Leah's chest as she saw the puffy eye and the bruises on her sister's arms, injuries that had obviously been made by a man's hard hands.

"Now, tell us what's happened," she urged her sister.

"Wilmer got mad. It was over nothing, but he got madder and madder. Jonah started crying, and Wilmer…" A single tear rolled down Johanna's sweat-streaked cheek. "He…he grabbed me and shook me. Then he picked up Jonah and threw him at me. He told us to get out." She choked back a sob. "He wouldn't let me take Katy. He said Katy was his and I couldn't have her!" Another tear rolled down her cheek.

Without a word, Aunt Jezebel brought ice wrapped in a washcloth and pressed it against Johanna's black eye.

"What about Wilmer's sister?" Mam asked. "How could she stand by while this happened? Wasn't she there?"

Johanna nodded. "She's there. She has Katy. I think

she was scared too. He doesn't usually get like that around his own people. I didn't want to leave Katy, but I was afraid of what he might do. He was so angry… and I didn't do anything. It was about nothing at all…a crack in his coffee cup that's been there for weeks. Jonah had nothing to do with the cup. Wilmer just got so mad, so fast."

Leah put her arm around Johanna's shoulders. "It's him," she said. "Wilmer. Of course it's not Jonah's fault."

"Wilmer wouldn't believe me. He said Jonah broke his mug…that I spoiled him…that he had to spend his life working for a willful brat. He was so angry that it scared me." She looked at their mother with tear-filled eyes. "I want my baby, Mam. I had to get Jonah here, where it's safe, but I'm going back for my Katy."

"Ne." Mam stiffened. "You will stay here with your sisters and Aunt Jezebel. I'm going to fetch Samuel. He'll get the baby. Wilmer might not let you have Katy, but he won't stand against Samuel."

"I'll come with you," Leah offered, trying to hide her own apprehension. "I'll hitch up the buggy." She didn't want to think of small Katy in that house with her angry father. How frightened she must be without Johanna and Jonah. Wilmer's sister was kind enough, but she was a meek and soft-spoken woman, not strong enough to stand up to him when he was in one of his moods.

Mam shook her head. "I'll cut across the field," she said. "It's faster. We can take Samuel's horse and buggy. You stay here with Johanna. Your sister needs you."

"I can't just sit here and wait," Johanna protested. She pushed the washcloth away.

"You can and you will," their mother insisted. "Wilmer is not well. You, of all people, know that. He could be dangerous. We will take no chances with you and your children. Samuel will know how to manage Wilmer."

"Did I do wrong to leave her?" Johanna asked tearfully. "I didn't know what to do, but I thought—"

"You did right," Leah said, trying to remain calm. "Exactly right. We have you and Jonah safe, and now Mam and Samuel will go and get your Katy."

Chapter 14

It was two days before things calmed down enough at home for Leah to approach her mother concerning Daniel. Mam was picking strawberries in the new berry bed at the far corner of the garden. It was a brilliant morning, with a blue, blue sky, sunshine and enough of a breeze to send the blades of the big windmill spinning. As she walked across the lawn toward her mother, Leah could smell the sweet scent of honeysuckle from the hedgerow, where a mockingbird warbled a joyous song.

How can I think of leaving all this behind? she wondered. Would she ever find the peace and happiness she'd known here in this quiet corner of Kent County? Was she making the biggest mistake of her life?

She thought back to her meeting with Daniel at the schoolhouse the morning after Johanna had come home with the black eye and only one of her children. As Mam had assured them, Samuel had taken care of Wilmer, or at least he'd solved the immediate problem of getting little Katy back. According to Mam, Wilmer had been almost ashamed of himself when the two of them had arrived at Johanna's home. Wilmer denied roughly grabbing Johanna, but he'd handed over a sleeping Katy without a fuss.

As Leah explained to Daniel, Samuel had taken Johanna's plight to the bishop and to the church elders, and everyone agreed that she was better off at Mam's until Wilmer could work through his crisis. As much as Daniel wanted to be open about their *walking out together,* he understood that Johanna's troubles were much more pressing. But Leah had promised to talk to her mother as soon as possible, and this morning seemed like the best time.

"Leah! Leah!" Susanna waved to her from the clothesline where she was hanging out towels and children's clothes to dry in the sunshine. "See our scarecrow!" she shouted.

"It's lovely!" Leah called back.

Susanna and Irwin had made a new scarecrow to keep the blackbirds out of the strawberry patch. They'd taken old clothes, good for nothing but scrub cloths, stuffed them with straw, and plopped a ragged bonnet on top. Then Susanna had added sparkly streamers of aluminum foil and strung can lids to the broomstick that served as arms. It was a good scarecrow, and Leah didn't know who was more pleased, Susanna or Irwin. It was Dat who'd taught his girls how to make scarecrows, and back in Pennsylvania, when he was a boy, Dat had made such funny ones that he'd been able to sell them to the English for their gardens.

Leah reached the edge of the strawberry patch and started picking near the scarecrow, in the next row over from her mother. The berries were fat and ripe, bursting with juice, and it was all Leah could do not to eat more than she put in her split-oak basket. What she had to tell her mother was daunting, and she concentrated on filling her container as she gathered her nerve.

For the past two days, Mam's face had shown the worry she felt over Johanna's disastrous marriage, but this morning, here in the garden with the birds singing and the sun shining, she looked years younger. And thinking of the possibility of her own marriage to Daniel, Leah wondered if Mam would ever take a new husband.

Thinking of her mother marrying someone was a little disturbing. However, it was expected. Few Old Amish widows in their forties remained widows for long, but it would take a lot of getting used to. With her daughters leaving to set up homes of their own, Mam and Susanna would soon need help running the farm. But she had her own way of doing things, and a new husband might bring as many problems as solutions.

Leah retrieved a particularly large cluster of strawberries and tried to think of the best way to approach her mother. Once she'd told Mam, there would be no going back, and maybe that was part of her reluctance. She did love Daniel. She was certain she did, but what she wasn't sure of was her ability to leave home—to leave her family and her entire way of life to go off and be with someone else. The farm, her mother and sisters, even Irwin, would always be a part of her. What kind of a wife and partner would she be for Daniel? Was she doing the right thing for both of them? Doubts haunted the shadowy corners of her mind.

"You have something to say to me, daughter?" Mam asked, startling Leah so badly that she dropped a strawberry and it rolled into the center of the open space between the rows. "You've been following me around all morning with that guilty expression on your face."

"Me?"

"Ya," Mam said. "You, Leah. You may be a woman grown, but in some ways you'll never change. Remember when you poured the big crock of honey in Aunt Martha's church bonnet?"

"I was four and I thought it would make her sweet," Leah protested. So long as she lived, her sisters or Aunt Martha would never let her live it down.

"You may as well come clean. What have you done now?"

Leah glanced away, then back at her mother. "This is more serious than a child's prank, Mam. It's Daniel. Daniel Brown. We're...we're seeing each other."

Mam set down her strawberry basket and straightened her back. "More than that, I'd say. And isn't this a little late to be telling me?"

Leah felt the sting of her mother's disapproval in her gaze. "You knew?"

"I knew. It isn't like you, Leah, to sneak around. But a Mennonite boy? Have you thought what this would mean? Not just for you, but for our whole family? How your sisters will feel if anything comes of it?"

Leah looked at the ground, suddenly ashamed. "I didn't mean to hurt you," she said. "I just didn't know that I'd feel this way about Daniel."

"Is it serious? Has he asked to court you?"

Leah nodded. "He has...and I've said I would...let him, I mean."

Her mother closed her eyes for a second and hugged herself, rubbing her arms with her fingertips. "I always wondered what I'd say if one of my girls came to me and said that," she said. "I wondered, but I never had the answer. I still don't."

Leah raised her chin and looked her mother eye to eye. They were the same height. "I think I love him, Mam."

"Love of a man is one thing, daughter. Living a lifetime with him is another. Daniel Brown is Mennonite. I know you've considered what that would mean."

"A hundred times. Every waking minute."

"And you think you could give up your faith for him?"

"Why shouldn't she follow her heart, Mam?" Johanna walked from the grape arbor toward them. She didn't seem shocked; her sister must have been standing only a few yards away, listening to their conversation.

"This is between Leah and me," Mam chided. "You shouldn't interfere."

"Why not? She's my sister, isn't she? I owe her the wisdom of my experience, too." Johanna turned to look into Leah's face. "Do what's right for you. If you don't, you may live to regret it."

"Johanna," Mam said. "Don't—"

"Don't what?" Johanna cried emotionally. "Don't say what we all know is the truth?"

"You're upset," Mam soothed. "Things are bad now between you and your husband, but—"

"I was a fool," Johanna said. "I turned down the man I loved over a foolish misunderstanding. And now, I'll never be happy again." She took hold of Leah's arm, tears filling her eyes. "Don't make the same mistake. Daniel's a good man. So what if he's a Mennonite? Don't they worship the same God? If you love him, marry him, Leah. Because the one thing you don't want is to be tied into a marriage with the wrong man."

Mam fussed, but in the end, she softened enough to invite Daniel to dinner that night. The meal was awkward, with long periods of silence and black looks from Rebecca and Ruth, but as the days passed, the family seemed to tolerate having Daniel among them. Leah continued to attend church with Mam and her sisters on alternate Sundays, but she also began to take part in Mennonite worship services, such as a weekly Bible school for adults. Daniel's aunt and uncle were polite, if not enthusiastic, about the two of them keeping company.

"It will take time for them to accept us," Daniel said soothingly. "All of them."

Leah had her doubts. Her grandmother and Aunt Martha took no pains to hide their disapproval of the match, and Bishop Atlee became a regular visitor to the Yoder farm. Through it all, she and Daniel continued to volunteer for the food bank and to help with Amish work frolics, but generally, the Amish community—other than Leah's immediate family and Samuel—ignored Daniel.

It wasn't easy to be at odds with people she'd known and loved all her life, but the longer she and Daniel knew each other, the more Leah felt that he was right for her. Of her sisters, only Johanna—who remained at Mam's with her children—seemed totally supportive of the romance.

"How long will you have together before you have to make a final decision?" Johanna asked, one afternoon when they were making strawberry jam. Susanna had taken Jonah and Katy outside to play, and Mam and

Rebecca had gone next door to Ruth's to help her and Miriam can asparagus.

"There's no way to know," Leah answered. "He expects to get word soon, though, and then he could be sent anywhere. It will probably be back to Spain or maybe even Mexico. Daniel speaks Spanish, and that would make working in a medical clinic easier for him and for his patients."

Johanna used pot holders to transfer the hot jars of jam from the counter to a butcher-block table near the window to cool. So far, they had finished thirty-two pints, and the rows of ball jars shone like jewels in the afternoon sun.

"So, if you do marry him, you'll have to go away for a long time?"

"It could be as long as a year." Leah smiled at her sister. "I can't imagine what it would be like—living in a foreign country and learning to cook and eat the different foods. But wherever we are, there will be a Mennonite community. It may be small, but we'll be able to have our own worship services and celebrate holidays as if we were home."

"So you have decided to marry him?" Johanna arched an auburn brow. "You're certain?"

"Almost. Yes, I think I am." She didn't want to admit to Johanna that she was still hoping to hear God's answer to her prayers loud in her ears. She thought she knew what God's plan was for her—Daniel certainly was sure of it. But, so far, she hadn't received any personal messages. Maybe it was prideful, but she was still waiting and listening. "Almost," she repeated. "I know I love Daniel. It's not Daniel, it's me I still have doubts about."

"You wonder if you have the courage to take a leap

of faith," Johanna said, speaking aloud the words Leah had been thinking.

"Yes," she admitted.

"Have you prayed about it? Asked for the Lord's guidance?"

Leah nodded. "But..." She sighed. "I don't think God has heard me."

Johanna wiped her hands on her apron, went to the table, and began to write the date on the labels for the jars of jam. "He always hears us," she said. "Sometimes, I think we don't listen when He speaks to us."

Leah approached the table and leaned on the back of a chair. Her sister's writing was bold and clear as she used the permanent marker to fill in one pretty label after another. Leah and Rebecca had picked out the labels from a catalog, and they showed a basket overflowing with fruit. They made the ordinary canning jars look special and attracted customers at Spence's.

"Why did you speak up to Mam for me?" Leah asked. "When I talked to you before...about Daniel, I thought you were warning me to stay away from him."

Johanna's blue eyes sparkled with moisture. "It was my duty as a big sister and a member of the church. If you had listened to me and decided not to see Daniel again, then your love for him wouldn't have been more than a flirtation. But if you're willing to go against all of us, he must be right for you."

"Is that what I'm doing, Johanna? Going against my family?"

"Ne." Johanna smiled and shook her head. "Not me, and in the end, not Mam, either. Remember, she was born Mennonite. They must be good people if she was one of them. But I'll expect to get letters from you every

week with foreign stamps on them, letters that tell me everything you do and everything wonderful you see."

"Thank you." Leah hugged her. "You don't know how much it means to me—to have you on my side."

"We're all on your side," Johanna said. "It just depends on where you're standing." She rose. "Now, let's get this jam put away and start on the birthday cakes for Aunt Jezzy. I think we'll need four, at least."

Leah nodded. "At least. Daniel and Irwin can eat a whole one between them. What kind are we making?"

"With all these strawberries?" Johanna shrugged. "Strawberry shortcake. What else?" Leah laughed and went to get the big sheet cake pans from the pantry.

The following day, Anna and Samuel, *Grossmama*, and the children, Aunt Martha, Uncle Reuben, and Dorcas, Roman and Fannie and their little ones, as well as Ruth and Miriam, Eli and Charley were all coming to share a birthday supper on the lawn. Samuel had put a pig on to roast over hot coals at six in the morning, and Anna was preparing baked beans and coleslaw. Charley and Eli were in charge of setting up tables and benches outside. Miriam was making a huge fruit salad, and Ruth had promised enough potato salad to feed the whole church.

Leah, Rebecca, Susanna and Johanna would cook the rest of the food this afternoon. Leah couldn't wait to have Daniel enjoy a meal with her extended family. She was even looking forward to his meeting Aunt Martha. She was Aunt Jezebel's niece, and could hardly be left out of the birthday party. Besides, maybe once Aunt Martha got to know him, she wouldn't be so critical of their courting. It wasn't likely, Leah thought, but you never knew. Mam kept saying that under her crusty exterior,

Aunt Martha had a good heart. If that was true, her shell must be pretty tough.

As it happened, Aunt Martha didn't come.

"Mam slipped in the wash water and pulled her back," Dorcas explained. "She said to tell your mother and Aunt Jezzy that she's sorry, but she thought it would be best if she just went to bed with a hot water bottle."

"Ya," Uncle Reuben chimed on. "But she said be sure and bring her a plate. You know how she likes roast pork."

"And she wants a big slice of birthday cake," Dorcas finished. "Or two if you have extra. Her appetite isn't quite what it used to be and she fancies a little cake now and then."

Leah glanced at Johanna, and her sister rolled her eyes. It was all Leah could do not to giggle. Aunt Martha always said she wasn't hungry, but Mam said Aunt Martha could eat more than Anna and Samuel put together, and she always wanted a plate of leftovers to take home. Not that anyone minded. Mam always had enough food to feed the county, and today was no exception.

Eli put Daniel to work helping with the tables, while Leah and her sisters carried out platters of food. Samuel brought his roast pig in his daughters' pony cart and drove it right around to the grassy backyard. The pork smelled wonderful, almost as good as the bushel of yeast rolls that Fannie had baked that afternoon.

There was a bustle as Mam supervised the food, and Charley and Irwin carried out two armchairs for either end of the tables. One was for *Grossmama*, and the other for Aunt Jezebel. Leah's aunt was as giggly as a girl. She kept saying that she couldn't believe all this fuss was for her or that she was sixty years old today.

"I remember when I was ten," she said excitedly. "My uncle took me fishing to a lake and we went in a boat. I caught the biggest fish and my mother cooked it for my supper."

Eventually, everyone was seated, grace was finished, and the eating, laughing and talking began. Daniel sat directly across from Leah, between Eli and Charley, and it was hard for Leah to take a bite with him watching her. *He fits in,* she thought. *He may be different, but he fits in.* Here, for the first time, she could feel her family and friends slowly lowering the fences.

Halfway through the meal, Rebecca stood up and read a poem she had written about Aunt Jezebel. Aunt Jezzy's face turned beet-red and she covered her face with her hands, but it was easy to see that she was pleased. Leah smiled at Mam, so glad that her mother had thought to honor Dat's aunt's special day. Not everyone understood Aunt Jezebel or knew how deeply she felt things. Some even said she was touched. It was true that she had her odd ways and that she'd never married. But Leah loved her.

"I'm thirsty," *Grossmama* said loudly from the far end of the table. "Is there more lemonade? My glass is empty."

Rebecca leaned close to Leah's ear and whispered, "She probably isn't thirsty. She probably doesn't like all the attention Aunt Jezzy is getting."

"I'll get some more from the house," Johanna offered. She rose and put little Katy into Mam's lap. "I'll just be a minute."

Roman began a story and Samuel had funny comments to make. Soon, everyone was laughing.

"Where's that Johanna with my lemonade?" *Grossmama* demanded.

"I'll go see what's keeping her," Leah offered.

"Probably spilled the whole pitcher," her grandmother grumbled. "Bring me water if there's no more lemonade. Better yet, buttermilk. You must have buttermilk. It's good for my stomach."

Daniel got to his feet. "I'll come with you," he said. "In case you need to carry anything."

"No, stay here and finish your supper," Leah said. If they went off together it would *look* as if they'd planned this—as if it was a scheme to be alone together. As long as Daniel was at the table, even Samuel couldn't think they were doing anything wrong.

Instead of going in through the back, Leah walked around the house. Out front, she saw a buggy standing in the middle of the yard—Wilmer's buggy. The horse was white with sweat, foam bubbled from his nostrils and his head hung down. Worse, the animal's knees were scraped and bloody. Someone had driven him hard, so hard that he'd fallen on the gravel and injured himself.

Fear sent goose bumps rising across the tops of her arms. She quickened her pace toward the house, and as she neared the porch, she could hear Wilmer's angry voice.

"You didn't invite me!" he shouted. "A family gathering and you forget your husband!" Something heavy crashed to the floor. "You're coming home with me! Where you belong!"

Leah ran up onto the porch and flung open the kitchen door. Wilmer rushed after Johanna, but she ducked around the table. He made a dash to grab her, but Leah seized the nearest object she could find—a broom—and thrust it between Wilmer's ankles. He tripped and fell, giving Johanna and Leah time to run out onto the porch.

Wilmer came after them, roaring like a bull. His face was white, his eyes bulging. Leah caught the stink of alcohol radiating off his dirty clothing. Johanna's husband looked like a tramp. One suspender hung loose, and his shoes were untied. His hands and arms were streaked with mud.

"Go home!" Johanna cried. "You're drunk, and I'm not going anywhere with you."

He dove at her. She leaped off the porch and Leah darted between them. "Leave her alone," she shouted. Wilmer brushed her away with one swing of his arm.

From somewhere, the dogs had come. Jeremiah circled Wilmer, barking furiously, while the Shetland sheepdog crouched, growling. The dogs had never been hostile to Wilmer before. Leah sensed that they knew he wasn't himself.

"Go home!" Johanna repeated. "You're sick. I'm staying here with my children until you get help."

Wilmer raised a meaty fist and advanced on her.

"Run, Johanna!" Leah shouted. She ducked behind Wilmer, grabbed the rope that hung from the big iron bell and rang it as hard as she could.

Wilmer beat Johanna to the gate, and he trapped her in the corner of the picket fence. She hitched up her skirt, put a foot on the cross-rung and attempted to climb over the fence, but he caught her bonnet string and yanked her head back. Her bonnet slipped off, and she dodged around him, running for the open gate. She dashed through just ahead of Wilmer.

Still shouting, he pounded after her, but, suddenly, Daniel appeared. He stepped in front of Wilmer and Johanna's husband stopped short. "Get out of my way!" he threatened. "This is no business of yours, Mennonite!"

"Put your hand down," Daniel said quietly. "This is no way to treat your wife."

Wilmer put it down, all right. He smashed his fist into Daniel's jaw. Daniel fell back onto the ground, but he scrambled up and put himself between a weeping Johanna and Wilmer again. "You don't want to do this," Daniel said, rubbing his chin. "Violence solves nothing. Better to talk this—"

Wilmer swung at him again. Leah screamed, but Daniel weaved out of Wilmer's reach. "You need help," Daniel said calmly. "I'm a nurse. I can help you get the medical attention you need."

Behind Leah, people were gathering: Mam, Roman, her sisters and their husbands. Eli and Charley rushed forward and seized Wilmer. He cursed in German and tried to shake them off, but they were too strong for him. After a minute or two, Wilmer sagged to his knees, weeping. "She's my wife," he wailed. "It's her duty. She has to come home. Tell her, Samuel. Tell Johanna she has to come home."

Samuel strode forward and knelt in the dirt in front of Wilmer. He put his broad hands on Wilmer's shoulders. "Shh, shh, brother," he said, before glancing at Roman. "Bring your buggy. Not his buggy, yours. His horse is in no shape to be driven. We'll take him to Bishop Atlee."

Johanna threw herself into Mam's arms. Her shoulders were shaking, but she wasn't crying.

"It's all right," Mam said. "You're safe. The children are safe."

Everyone stared in silence as Eli and Charley and Samuel ushered a blubbering Wilmer into Roman's buggy. "Did you see his horse?" Miriam said. "It's a disgrace. He must have tried to run him on the blacktop." She and Rebecca were already unhitching the trembling animal from its traces.

"Poor Boomer," Johanna crooned. "I need to—"

"Go with Mam," Ruth said. "Miriam and Susanna will look after the horse."

Leah moved away from her family to where Daniel stood, still rubbing his jaw. "You were wonderful," she said. "If you hadn't come, I don't know what would have happened."

"I wouldn't have hit him," Daniel said. "I don't believe in physical violence, but he wouldn't have hurt you or your sister again. I promise you that."

She looked up into his determined green eyes and felt a surge of what could only be admiration. "But you got hurt," she said. "Your poor jaw."

He shrugged. "Nothing serious. I've gotten lots worse playing soccer."

Chapter 15

"Wilmer's problems are too serious for your church elders to deal with," Daniel said, later that evening, as he prepared to leave the Yoder farm. Leah had walked to the pickup with him, and they were standing close in the twilight. "He needs professional help. He's suffering from depression; from what you've said, it sounds like he's been suffering from it for some time. And your sister should file charges against him. I don't understand why Samuel advises against it."

"He's her husband, and he didn't hit her. Not this time," Leah answered. "You prevented that from happening. The bishop won't allow it to happen again. And Johanna and the children are staying here with Mam indefinitely, so Wilmer won't have another opportunity to hurt her."

Daniel gritted his teeth, trying not to allow his impatience to show. How could he make Leah understand how grave the situation was? Domestic violence cut across all races, incomes and religious groups. "Sometimes calling the authorities is the kindest thing to do," he said as he rested his hand on the driver's door of the truck.

"But it would be against our *Ordnung*."

"Still, it might force Wilmer into the kind of treatment he needs." Daniel wondered if he'd done the right thing by not calling the police himself. But he was an outsider, and if he interfered, Hannah might forbid Leah to see him again. His acceptance into this community was tenuous at best, and he didn't want to make things more difficult for Leah.

On the overseas missions, Daniel had watched his father tread the difficult path between doing what was right to prevent injustice and not interfering with the cultural practices of the host country. Daniel had believed he understood. Now he had an inkling of just how difficult his father's task had been. Daniel had always loved and admired him, as a teacher, a missionary and as a father. He only hoped he could do as well.

"What you did was very brave," Leah said.

Daniel shook his head. "I'm a man. Younger than Wilmer, and probably stronger. It's you who showed courage. You put yourself in danger to protect your sister."

She shrugged. "I had to. I couldn't let him hurt her."

Even now, hours after the incident, Daniel was still shaken by how close Leah had come to being harmed. The feeling of protectiveness that had swept over him, when he'd seen Wilmer shove her, had barely faded. Daniel wanted to draw her into the circle of his arms and hold her safe. Suddenly, keeping her from harm seemed like the most important thing in the world.

"Leah..." He broke off, unable to express his feelings.

She was gazing off into the distance. "This is such a difficult situation. I think Wilmer loves Johanna, no matter how he behaves."

"Maybe he does, but he shouldn't be anywhere near her."

"I agree, and so does my family. That includes Samuel. He's our deacon, and his opinion is important in a situation like this."

"What will happen if Wilmer refuses treatment? Will the bishop ignore it?"

"I don't think so. Bishop Atlee, our preachers and Samuel are good men, and they care about Johanna, as well as Wilmer. If he doesn't change, it's possible they could shun him."

"They still do that?"

She nodded. "They can. We don't look at it as punishment, but as an act of love—a last attempt to turn someone we care about from a terrible mistake. If Wilmer was shunned, no one would eat with him, talk to him or permit him in their homes."

"And your sister? Would she shun him as well?"

"She would. It would hurt her terribly, but Johanna's faith is strong. She wouldn't go against the bishop's ruling. And neither would Mam, at least not for Wilmer," Leah said.

"Let me make sure I understand this shunning." He met her gaze. "Your mother wouldn't turn against you if we married, would she?"

"Oh, no, Daniel. I haven't been baptized yet. It's my right to choose. It's only those who are full members of the church who can be shunned. At least in our community."

"If your bishop shunned Wilmer, would that include Johanna?"

"No. She and the children haven't done anything wrong. And if Wilmer was shunned, there's always a chance that he could redeem himself and then he could become one of us again."

"Good. That makes me feel a little better. I never like to see families separated, but it's better than what happened here today." He opened the vehicle door. "Can I see you tomorrow?"

She was so close that he could smell the shampoo in her hair and the scent of sunshine in her crisp Lincoln green dress and apron. She was so beautiful, his Leah. And for just a moment, uncertainty filled him. How could he think that a girl like her would leave her family and church for him? How could he be so arrogant to believe that he could be worthy of her?

"Tomorrow?" he repeated.

"I think I need to stay close, in case Mam or Johanna needs me," she said. "But you could come back after supper. We could walk down by the creek. It's pretty there, under the willow trees."

"If you need me before that, don't hesitate to call. You have my cell number." He knew that there was no phone at the farm, but he also knew the Yoders had phones available to them. "I'll come if you need me. Don't worry about the time. Day or night."

She laid her small hand over his, and a surge of warmth flowed up his arm. "I will call if I need you," Leah promised, "but we'll be fine. Bishop Atlee and the elders will take care of Wilmer." She removed her hand

and smiled at him. "Your poor chin will be black and blue tomorrow and then you'll have to explain to your family what happened at our picnic dinner."

Daniel knew that he should start up his truck and go back to his aunt's house, but he didn't want to leave Leah. Not yet. "Would it be all right… Could we take that walk tonight?"

"I'd like that," she said, smiling up at him. "Stay here, while I tell Mam. I'm sure it will be okay."

Daniel got out of the pickup and leaned against it, waiting as Leah went back to the house. He wished he could talk to his dad, explain Johanna's situation and get his opinion, but it was too late to call. His parents rose early and were probably already in bed. Besides, talking to his father would mean also talking with his mother, and the last phone conversation he'd shared with her had centered on Leah.

His mother agreed with his aunt and uncle that marrying someone of the Amish faith would put a strain on the marriage from the start. "I'm sure she's a wonderful girl," his mother had said. "But it's so hard, as a young woman, to be in a strange country where you don't speak the language. You remember that your father and I married quickly so that he could accept a position in a mission overseas. I underestimated how difficult it would be. You don't know how many times I broke down and cried, how many times I wanted to leave our assignment and come home."

"You were younger than Leah, Mom. She'll be twenty-one in a few days."

"I was, but twenty-one is still young to go so far from home and family. I was nineteen, stranded in an isolated village in Panama, alone when your dad had to travel. I felt so out of place that I doubted my own dedication to God's work. Nothing against your Leah, but you have to think of her happiness. You may be asking too much of her. If you marry in haste and the marriage fails, you could ruin her life as well as your own."

"Leah hasn't agreed to marry me yet, Mom," he'd answered. "And I've wrestled with every argument you can make against us marrying, but I can't get past the belief that we're meant to be together—that this is God's plan for us."

"Make certain you aren't confusing your own desire with that of the Lord's," she said, quietly. "Remember that we love you, and we'll support any decision you make—even if it's to marry a girl you haven't known more than a month."

His mother hadn't convinced him that Leah was wrong for him, but he knew that he hadn't convinced his mother that she was right for him, either. She would continue to worry and to give her advice, as she always had. His mom and Hannah Yoder would both be surprised to know they had that in common. Both mothers would rather see him and Leah part than marry.

Leah came toward him in the soft darkness. Daniel took his cell phone out of his pants pocket, turned off the power and tossed it on the front seat of the truck.

"I didn't bring a flashlight," she said, "but I could go back and get it—"

"No need," he said. "The moon is bright enough for us to find our way."

"Yes," she agreed. "It is, isn't it?" She caught his hand and led the way around the barn. Lantern light spilled through a small window. "Miriam's with Wilmer's horse," Leah said. "We think Wilmer drove him too hard and he fell on the road. His knees are a mess."

"I hate to see any animal mistreated."

"It just shows how sick Wilmer must be. He's not even able to care for his animals. Johanna brought the baby turkeys here the day after she came. We have them in the little shed off the utility room. You have to have a heat lamp if the temperature drops too low."

"Even in May?" He savored the feel of Leah's fingers clasped around his. *If we marry,* he thought, *I can hold her hand whenever I want.* A surge of joy rose in his chest. If Leah would only accept his offer of marriage, they'd share so much. He'd never know loneliness again.

"It can get cool on May nights," she said.

As they walked past the enclosed corral behind the barn, Daniel saw the white shapes of sheep. "I didn't know you had sheep," he said.

"Johanna's. She bought the original breeding pair with her quilt money. Wilmer never liked them, and she knew he wouldn't take care of them, so Uncle Reuben, Charley and Eli brought them here, too. A neighbor has been milking the cow for her."

"A shame she lives so far away."

"Yes, too far for Irwin to go back and forth to care for the animals twice a day. Last year, they rented a house at the end of our lane, the green farmhouse on the right. That was nice, to have her so close to all of us. But Wilmer's never satisfied. He's always looking for a better deal. They've moved four times since they were married."

"That's not a lot of moves," he said with a chuckle. "I can't tell you how many homes I've lived in."

"I've never moved. I was born in this house."

"My older brother and sister were born in Panama. I was born in Ohio. Matt in Oregon, and one of my younger sisters in Spain, the other one in South Dakota."

She glanced at him. "You lived in South Dakota?"

"I've lived a lot of places."

He'd thought that they would be talking about Johanna and her problems with Wilmer, but they didn't. Instead, they found themselves pouring out their hearts to each other. He told her about a Sunday school play he'd been in when he was four.

He'd been assigned the role of a shepherd who'd followed the star to Bethlehem and found the baby in the manger. He'd wanted to be Joseph, but that was a speaking part, reserved for an older boy. His brother was one of the three kings and wore a shiny crown. Somehow, when the time came for the shepherds and kings to make their grand entrance, Daniel found himself wearing the tinfoil crown on top of his washcloth headdress. The audience had howled with laughter, sending him wailing off stage, which pretty much ended his acting career.

Leah laughed heartily and quickly followed with an incident in her own childhood that had caused her much embarrassment in her later years. Soon they were so engaged in each other's stories that they were finishing each other's sentences and so much at ease that it seemed the most natural thing in the world was to find a mossy spot near a peach tree, sit down, lean back and stare up at the stars.

There were no airplanes overhead, and the sky was exceptionally clear. The stars shone so brightly that they seemed like glistening diamonds against a velvet blue-black heaven. Somehow, Leah's head was nestled against

Daniel's shoulder and his arm was draped around her shoulders. It felt so good…so right.

"There's something I want to tell you," she said softly.

"You can tell me anything."

"Today, when Wilmer hit you and knocked you down, I was afraid for you, but more than that…" He heard her inhale deeply. "You were the strong one, Daniel. It's what I thought. That you were kind and strong and good. He hurt you, but you didn't get angry. You saw his pain and you just wanted to help him."

He didn't know what to say. It made him feel good that she thought he wasn't afraid, that he'd held to his nonviolent principles. But he hadn't had time to decide what to do. It was like that when he was treating someone with a medical emergency. He simply did what he had to and agonized over it later.

"I heard Him when you did that," Leah said. "Just as you told me that you hear Him. The Lord. Not with words in my ears, but in my heart. A feeling that it is right between us, that you have always been intended for me. And…" She hesitated and went on shyly. "And I realized then that I want you to court me, Daniel. I don't care what other people think—not even my family. I want to *walk out* with you, not to hide anymore, but to have everyone see us together. If you still want me?"

"I do," he said, tightening his arm around her. "I want it more than anything."

"Other than keeping your promise," she reminded him. "To God."

"Yes," he said. "But it seems to me that we can keep that promise together."

"I think so." She rose to her feet and took a few steps away from him. "We should get back," she said.

He got up and crossed the distance between them. She stood there, her heart-shaped face beautiful in the moonlight. As she took his hand, he couldn't help himself. He lowered his head and brushed her lips with his. For just an instant, she returned his kiss, and her lips were warm and soft and sweet.

"Oh, Daniel." She backed away from him. "That was nice."

"Yes," he said. "Better than nice."

"I think that means it's official," she said. "But you're supposed to ask me again."

"Ask you?" His stomach turned over. And his heart hammered in his chest.

She laughed, a joyous sound in the hushed darkness of the peach orchard. "To marry you, Daniel. You're supposed to ask me again."

"Will you do me the honor of becoming my wife, Leah Yoder?"

Laughing, she turned and darted away, her bonnet strings streaming behind her. "I'm thinking about it," she flung back over her shoulder.

He raced after her. For a few minutes, he was certain he'd catch her, but Leah was faster on her feet than he'd expected. And as he reached his pickup, she clattered up the back steps to the kitchen door. "Tomorrow," she called.

"I love you!" he shouted, not caring who heard. "I love you!"

With another peal of laughter, she flung open the door and went inside. Upstairs, a window opened and Susanna stuck her head out. She was giggling. "I love you, too!" Susanna shouted.

Red-faced and sweating but so happy that he was

about to burst out of his skin, Daniel climbed into his truck. He turned around in the yard, stopped long enough to stare at the dark windows on the second floor, and finally drove away, whistling.

His aunt met him at the back door of her house. "Daniel! We've been trying to reach you. You've had a call from Pastor Bennett, from the committee. He wants you to contact him right away."

"He called *tonight?*" Daniel looked at his wrist to check the time before remembering that he'd forgotten to put his watch on that morning. It was probably still lying on top of the dresser in his bedroom along with his wallet. "Is it too late to return his call?"

"No. John was adamant. He wants you to call him, no matter the time." She hugged him. "They've found a place for you! Wait until you hear where it is."

"He told you? Where is it? Do they want me to go back to Spain?" Usually, volunteers had several months to tie up their affairs in the States before going overseas. Unless the new post was in the United States. There'd been talk about an Indian reservation in New Mexico that might need help in their tribal clinic. Would his next assignment be in the Southwest? "Did Pastor Bennett say when I had to report to the mission? Will I be working in an established clinic?"

His aunt laughed and hugged him again. "I'm not telling. All I can say is that your uncle is very pleased. So am I, Daniel. We'll miss you terribly, but this will be such an adventure for you—a real chance to make a difference."

Uncle Allan was sitting at the kitchen table. "All

things come to he who waits." He handed Daniel the wall phone. "Go ahead. Call Pastor Bennett."

Daniel was too nervous to sit. He found the number, punched the buttons and held his breath as he heard the faint ring on the other end of the line. The pastor answered on the third ring. As pleasantries were exchanged, Daniel walked outside, onto the porch, to have a little privacy.

"We've had a bit of a scramble here," Pastor Bennett said in his deep, husky voice. "If you feel called to accept this responsibility, you're going to make a lot of people happy. Another family was scheduled to take the post. The wife was a nurse-practitioner, but one of their children was just diagnosed with juvenile diabetes, and they had to refuse the assignment since this is such a remote location."

"I'm sorry to hear that," Daniel said.

"As we all are. But you should know that two committee members submitted your name, Daniel. You're young, but we feel you're the right one to head up this mission."

"Head it up?" Daniel was certain he'd heard wrong. "I'm sorry, Pastor Bennett. Would you repeat that?"

"You heard me correctly, son. We're badly in need of an experienced RN with leadership qualities."

"I'm honored, but..." Suddenly he felt as if he couldn't get enough air in his lungs. He couldn't get his head around what John Bennett had said. "I'm not ordained. I can't be in charge of the mission."

"Not necessary. We have three other families going. For one young couple, this will be their first mission. The other two families are old hands at this. We have several teachers, a farmer, a carpenter and an excellent pastor with twenty years of mission experience. We spoke with him, and he agreed that you would be a wonderful addition. And you should know that the committee voted unanimously to have you take charge."

"I'm speechless. I never expected..."

"You'll be setting up your own clinic. There isn't a medical facility for a hundred miles, and the population desperately needs your skills."

"My own clinic?"

"We have the funds for a small but fully supplied station. The post used to be a cattle ranch, but the jungle has reclaimed much of the pastureland. We've purchased some land on a navigable river to set up a school, a store and a self-sustaining farm. We also have a private donation to build a lovely church."

"Jungle? Did you say jungle? Pastor, where is this post?"

"Oh." Pastor Bennett laughed. "I thought your uncle and aunt would have told you. It's in the Amazon, Daniel. Brazil. Extremely remote. Your only electricity will be generator enabled, and the only practical way in or out is by boat or a float plane."

"But they speak Portuguese," Daniel reminded him. "I'm fluent in Spanish, not Portuguese."

"Not that important. Most of your patients will speak only one of a myriad of tribal dialects so interpreters who also speak Portuguese will be available. With a solid background in Spanish and your skill with languages, you'll soon make the switch to Portuguese. There is a locally trained woman with basic nursing skills who will act as your assistant. It's my understanding that she speaks both Portuguese and English."

Daniel tried to organize his thoughts. The Amazon?

The area had always fascinated him. When he was a boy, he'd read every book he could find on the subject. "Would this be a two-year post?"

"Afraid not. The position is longer than usual because of the unique nature of this project. Starting from scratch, as it were. Your assignment will be for seven years."

Daniel felt light-headed. "Seven years?"

"Yes, but there're always opportunities to come back to the States on leave during that time."

Seven years? How could he ask Leah to leave her home and family for seven years? Daniel dropped into the porch swing.

"So what do you say? Do you feel up to this?"

Daniel was about to say *no*, that this had to be some mistake, that he wasn't qualified to take on such a challenge. But as he opened his mouth to refuse the post, he found himself thinking of the possibilities that stretched out in front of him. "I'd like to have a few days to consider…to pray for guidance," he said. "And there's… there's a young woman. I've asked her to be my wife. We just became engaged tonight, and she…" He trailed off.

"Good, good. Excellent. The only real issue is that the committee is hesitant to send a single man to head this project, especially one as young as yourself. But your engagement is the best news you could have given me. Tell your young woman that you're going to have to marry at once."

"And if I said yes…if she agreed, how long before we would leave?"

"We'd want you on location in thirty days, Daniel, so I'll need your answer within the week. A bit of a stretch, on both counts, I know, but we have faith you'll think this over and realize that when the Lord calls, sometimes we have to run to catch up with Him."

Chapter 16

"The Amazon jungle? For seven years?" Leah stared at Daniel in disbelief as she tried to grasp what he was saying. "How is that possible?" A cold sensation coiled in the pit of her stomach and for a second, she felt light-headed.

Daniel had come back to the farm the following day, as he'd said he would, and she'd taken him down to the willows by the pond where they could be alone. When he'd gotten out of the truck, she'd sensed that something was wrong. His normally ruddy cheeks were pale, and his expression strained. She'd been afraid that he was coming down with something, or that he'd changed his mind about courting her, but she'd never expected to hear this.

"I didn't accept," Daniel said quickly. "I have a week to make my decision. Saying *yes* would mean that we'd have to marry within the next few weeks. The board can help with getting you a passport, but I have to go to Ohio to meet with the rest of mission group." He took her hand and squeezed it. "I'm as shocked as you are," he told her. "This isn't what I expected at all."

Leah swallowed, trying to dissolve the thickness in her throat. Daniel had waited so long for this assignment. She'd thought they might be getting a call to go to Spain or even back to Morocco, but the Amazon? Weren't there jaguars there? Giant snakes and alligators? She'd pictured herself in a city apartment or living in a tiny house on a busy street, but never in a jungle. "Seven years is a long time." She felt as if she might start weeping. Could she possibly leave her family for seven years?

"There are vacations," Daniel said. "There will be money for us to fly home, and we can always have visitors. We'll have our own home."

Leah's thoughts scattered in a hundred directions. "Could I have a garden?"

"A garden, a cow, whatever you like."

"But what would I do? Besides taking care of our house? I'm not a nurse. What help would I be in a jungle mission?" Leah turned her head away from him and stared at the pond. A mallard duck and her yellow and brown babies paddled by on the far side, the ducklings little more than balls of fluff. Home…all she'd ever known. How could Daniel ask her to leave this peaceful world to go to live in Brazil?

"There would be more work than hands to do it," he said in a burst of excitement. "The native population is sorely lacking medical attention. The infant mortality rate is high, nutrition is poor, the poverty overwhelming. Education is key in a place like this. We won't just be treating them medically, but we'll be helping them to help themselves. We can do so much to help them, to offer them a better way…to bring them to an understanding of God's love."

She looked at Daniel, still unable to speak.

"If you say you won't go, I'll turn them down," Daniel said.

"You have to let me think." She covered her face with her hands. "This is such a shock." So many questions surfaced in her mind and she groped for something sensible to say. "I took high school classes by mail. I got my diploma, and I wanted to teach in one of our Amish schools, but no position ever opened up. The elders won't allow college, but there was so much more that I wanted to learn. Do you think that would be possible? That I could continue studying by mail?"

"Not only by mail, but by computer. I'll need to be in contact with the nearest hospital, so we'll have satellite Internet. And the Internet would allow us to keep up with our families. Your mother and sisters could go to my aunt's house and use her computer. You could see them and talk to them, and they could see you."

Leah plucked a cloverleaf from the grass and tossed it on to the surface of the water. The breeze whirled it away. Like me, she thought, never to return. "So far away…" she murmured.

"I could refuse the post. I'm serious. I will if you say so. It won't be the only one offered."

Leah raised her head and looked into his eyes. "But how long before you're asked to be the leader again? These are special circumstances, Daniel."

"I don't have to be in charge. All I want to do is help

people who are sick or injured. Being the leader of a mission is a heavy responsibility. It takes a rare person."

"If they chose you, they must think you are the best one for the job," Leah said.

"Maybe… I don't know." He pressed the heel of his hand to his forehead and then lowered it. "I only know that I don't want to go if it means losing you. I love you, Leah."

"And I love you," she said, gazing earnestly into his face. "But if it weren't for me, would you take this post?"

"I won't answer that…it isn't fair. You come first. You'll always come first in my life."

She shook her head. "No, be honest with me, Daniel. We've always said that God comes first, haven't we?"

"Yes, but… Maybe this is something *I* want. Maybe it's a test, not what God has planned for me, but a test to see—"

"No," she said firmly. "Either I'll marry you right away and we'll go to the Amazon together, or I won't marry you." She felt moisture well up in her eyes and spill over. "I have to decide. If I really love you, then where we go and what we do doesn't matter. I'd go with you with a willing heart."

"This is too much for me to ask of you. Too much too soon."

"With God and love on our side, nothing is too much," she answered. "I don't doubt *you*. It's *me*. It's been me all along. I'm not certain I'm strong enough to be the wife you deserve. I need time to think…to decide." She reached out and squeezed his hand. "Go home. When you're near me, I can't think of anything but you. Come back tomorrow afternoon, and I'll give you my answer then."

"Is it changing your faith to mine?" He rose and offered his hand to help her up. "Is that what troubles you?"

She shook her head, getting to her feet. "No, I think I could do that. It feels right. Maybe I was always meant to return to the church my mother was born in. Maybe that's my heritage, from all the Mennonites who came before her."

"If it's not that, then what—"

"Please, Daniel." She faced him. "If you really love me, you'll let me think this through." She took a deep breath. "Whatever I decide, I'll stick by. You have my word on that."

He went home as she asked…reluctantly, but he went.

After he was gone, Leah didn't return to the house. Instead she wandered through the meadow and into the peach orchard. She remembered the previous night so well… She could still feel the warmth of Daniel's lips on hers and the way it had made her feel. She hadn't felt wicked or daring, and she hadn't been ashamed of letting him kiss her. He was the first boy she'd ever kissed, and it had been worth waiting for. There was something about him so sweet and tender…so strong. How could it be wrong for them to be together as man and wife?

But doubt still tugged at her. She was certain Daniel would be a good husband and father, if the Lord saw fit to bless them with children. But was she worthy of him? Could she remain strong when the weeks, months and years stretched between her and her beloved family…when she'd broken the bond with her Amish faith? Or would she become weak and needy of his time and attention? Would she compromise Daniel's calling to serve as leader and medical caregiver for people who needed him so much?

She wanted to talk to Johanna…ask her opinion. Johanna knew her as well as Mam or any of her other sisters, and Johanna would be honest. If her sister thought she was too weak or might falter, she wouldn't hesitate to say so. And if Johanna believed that Leah had the strength, she would see past all the obstacles and urge her sister to follow her heart.

Leah started back for the house, walking fast, taking long strides. She'd find Johanna and pull her aside where she could spill out her heart. Leah knew what she wanted, but she needed to hear Johanna say it. But when she reached the farmyard, she stopped short and stared.

Bishop Atlee's buggy was there, and so was Samuel's. A red-faced Irwin stood stock-still by the windmill with a bucket of chicken feed in each hand and tears running down his face. As Leah tried to think what could be wrong, she saw Eli running up the lane.

Something was terribly wrong. Someone was dead.

"Mam!" Leah cried as she broke into a run.

Susanna sat on the back step, her face in her hands, weeping.

"What's happened?" Leah cried as a terrible feeling of dread washed over her. "Is it Mam?" Not her mother or one of her sisters! Not Johanna's baby or little Jonah! Not Charley, with his laughing ways and easy manner of taking charge! "Aunt Jezzy?"

Susanna raised her head. She was sobbing so hard that she could barely speak. "Johanna," she managed. "Johanna's…" She began gasping and hiccupping.

Leah dashed past her and flung open the kitchen door. "Johanna!"

But there was Johanna sitting stone-faced and dry-eyed at the table with both children in her arms, and there was Mam standing behind her, her complexion pale with shock. Leah searched the room with her gaze, counting off those who were dearest to her: Anna, Ruth, Miriam, Rebecca. *Grossmama* sat in the rocker, face pinched, mouth tight. Charley stood behind Miriam, his hand on her shoulder. Anna wasn't crying, so it couldn't be one of Samuel's children who'd come to misfortune.

"What is it?" Leah asked. Familiar faces turned toward her.

Anna caught her hand and drew her aside. "Wilmer," she whispered. She shook her head. "God rest his soul."

Leah didn't understand. "What did he do? He didn't try to hurt Johanna or the children, did he?"

Anna's eyes were kind as she tugged Leah back out onto the porch. "My Samuel found him. Wilmer was staying with the bishop until his brother could come from Ohio to take him back there, but last night, he climbed out a window. They looked for him everywhere at the Atlees'. They thought it better not to say anything until they found him. But Samuel, he had a hunch. He went back to the farm and searched. He found him in the corncrib. He had taken his own life, probably last night." Anna eyes brimmed with compassion. "So awful for Johanna and the children."

"Poor Johanna," Leah choked out. "How is she?"

"You know our Johanna. Strong. She hasn't cried, not one tear, but I know she weeps here." Anna touched the spot over her heart.

"I am so sorry."

"Ya," Anna murmured. "We all are. He was very troubled, Wilmer. Maybe so sick that God will not hold him responsible for what he's done." She squeezed Leah's hand. "We will pray for him."

"And for Johanna and the children."

"*Ya,* for Bishop Atlee as well. He is such a good man, and now he will feel responsible that he tried to help Wilmer and couldn't."

Just what Daniel said, Leah thought. *We should have listened to Daniel and called the police. If we had, Wilmer might still be alive.*

"And your Samuel," she said to her sister. "Poor Samuel."

Anna bit her lower lip and nodded. "Better it was him than Johanna or one of the children." Then she opened her arms, and Leah went into her embrace and they cried tears of regret together.

Leah walked across the field and crossed the road to the chair shop. A *Closed* sign hung in the window; normally, the business would have been open until six on a weekday, but Roman had closed early. She'd passed him and Fannie on their way to Mam's, so no one was at home there but the children, and they would be in the house or the barnyard. At the shop, she retrieved the key from a nail under the porch and let herself inside the salesroom.

She had to talk to Daniel; Wilmer's death changed everything. She couldn't wait for Daniel to come tomorrow for her answer. She had to see him face-to-face, as soon as possible. She went behind the counter where a black phone hung on the wall. Hands damp with moisture, Leah punched in the number for Daniel's cell phone, and when he answered, she asked him to come.

"What's is it, Leah? Have you been crying?" Daniel asked.

"Just come to the chair shop. Come now," she said before hanging up the phone.

Too agitated to sit, she folded her arms and paced up and down the large room. Daniel would understand what she had to do. It would break both of their hearts, but there was no other way. Leaving her family now, when they needed her most—when Johanna needed her most—was impossible. Daniel would understand. And maybe it would be easier this way. Now, she didn't have to make a decision. The decision had been made for her.

The church would come together to support Johanna and her children in her time of grief. Neighbors would arrange for any work that had to be done at her farm, there would be food to feed all those who would come to offer condolences, and later attend the funeral. Considering the manner of Wilmer's passing, there was no way to keep the authorities from getting involved, but when they were finished, and Wilmer's body had been prepared for burial, he would be laid out in Mam's parlor.

Johanna would sew white trousers and a shirt for Wilmer to be buried in, and the men would place him in a simple pine coffin. Johanna and the family would sit up all night, keeping vigil and praying. The house would be full of visitors until the third day, when the preachers would offer a final service for the deceased and a procession of buggies would file slowly to the *Graabhof*—the Amish cemetery.

The church and the Amish community would unite to help Johanna, but it would be her family that she would need most. Ruth and Miriam and Anna lived nearby, but they had husbands and responsibilities of their own. Leah was the eldest daughter still at home. Supporting Johanna would fall on her shoulders, and it would be impossible to let down those who counted on her. She could no more go off to the jungles of Brazil with Daniel than she could fly off a roof.

The sound of truck tires on gravel tore Leah from her thoughts, and she went out on the porch and down the steps. Daniel got out of the truck and hurried toward her. Each step she took felt as if her shoes were made of concrete, but she forced herself to be brave. She could not be selfish and think of her own happiness. She had to think of Johanna.

"Daniel..." A lump rose in her throat. She would not cry. If she cried, she might not get through what she had to say.

"Leah, I'm so sorry. I just heard about your sister's husband. My uncle's a volunteer on the fire department and he called my aunt as I was going out the door."

He put out his arms, but she stepped away and shook her head.

"I can't marry you, Daniel. I'm sorry, but I can't."

"You're upset," he argued. "We don't need to talk about this now."

"Follow your dream," she said. "Find someone who will be the wife and helpmate you need. But it can't be me."

"I'll tell them *no*. I'll stay here, Leah—here in Kent County. Maybe, in time—"

She shook her head again. "I can't leave my family. Not now, not ever. I was wrong to let you think I could."

"But, Leah—"

"I need you to go, Daniel." Dry-eyed but weeping inside, she turned and walked back into the chair shop, locked the door behind her and pulled down the blind.

He followed her to the door and banged and called

her name, but she didn't answer. It would be better this way, she told herself, better for her family and better for Daniel. In time, he'd understand that she was right. And the quicker she freed him to go, the kinder it would be for both of them.

"Just let me talk to you," he begged.

It pained her to hear him crying, but she didn't answer. And finally, after nearly an hour, she heard his footsteps on the steps and the crunch of gravel. The truck door shut, the engine roared to life and Daniel drove out of her life.

Chapter 17

Back home, the house was teeming with people. Mam, Susanna and Johanna sat in the parlor while friends and neighbors offered condolences and promised to offer prayers for Wilmer. Lydia and Fannie were there, as well as Wilmer's sister and Aunt Martha. For once, Aunt Martha had nothing critical to say. She'd hugged Johanna, offered to help in any way she could and took baby Katy to Rebecca and Dorcas in the backyard.

Leah asked Mam what she should do first. In moments, she and Ruth were laying white material out on the floor in the upstairs hall. Ruth went up to the attic and came down with an old suitcase. In it was a pattern that Mam had used to make their father's funeral clothes, and they used that to pin and cut the garments that Johanna would need to sew for Wilmer.

Leah tried not to think about Daniel, about what she'd

said to him, about how she'd hurt him. She hoped he wouldn't hate her, and she wished there had been some other way to send him away. She felt empty inside, as cold and black as a fireplace when the last coals have gone out and the winter wind blew down the chimney. She told herself that she'd done the right thing, the only thing. Only a selfish woman would have put her own happiness ahead of her sister's need. This was where she belonged…where God wanted her.

She was busy through supper and afterwards. It wasn't until after Katy and Jonah had been tucked into bed with Mam, and an exhausted Johanna had retired to her room, that Leah had time to think. Anna, Ruth and Miriam had gone home, promising to come back first thing in the morning. Samuel had taken the last load of *Grossmama*'s things to his house. The neighbors had left, and only Rebecca, Irwin and Aunt Jezebel remained at the kitchen table talking and eating slices of a pie that Anna had baked.

But Leah didn't want to join them. She didn't want to talk to anyone, and she didn't want pie. She didn't care if she ever ate again. She wanted to be alone, but she could think of no place in the house that didn't have someone sleeping there. Even the parlor was taken. Wilmer's sister refused to stay at his house, and Mam had gotten Miriam and Irwin to make up a borrowed air mattress in the parlor for her. Leah thought of going outside, maybe to sit on the porch and look at the stars, but that would mean going through the kitchen, and Rebecca would want to know why she was going outside at ten o'clock at night. And worse, she might ask why Daniel hadn't come to offer his condolences.

Instead, Leah found matches in a hall closet, lit a kerosene lantern and carried it up two flights of stairs to the attic. The third story had once been used as bedrooms; now it was just storage. And like the rest of the house, Mam believed in keeping it free of dust and cobwebs. When she was small, Leah had loved to come up here with her sisters to play games on rainy days. The rooms on either end of the attic had exposed brick chimneys. No fireplaces or stoves, but the heat from the downstairs warmed the bricks and made the space cozy, even on a damp and windy day. The room on the west end held furniture not needed downstairs, and it was to this retreat that Leah fled and finally let the tears fall.

She wasn't sure how long she'd been there when she heard footsteps on the bare wood floors. For just an instant, *Grossmama*'s ghost stories surfaced in her mind and gooseflesh rose on the back of her neck. But then, her own good sense took over, and she called out, "Who's there?" A shadowy figure appeared and Leah's breath caught in her throat. "Who—"

"Child, child, whatever are you doing up here all by yourself?"

"Aunt Jezzy?"

"I wondered who'd found my secret spot. Why, Leah, sweet, you've been crying." Aunt Jezebel sat down beside her on the day bed mattress. "Weeping for poor lost Wilmer or your sister?"

Leah tried to answer, but found herself sobbing uncontrollably. Aunt Jezzy put her arms around her and pulled her against her soft bosom. "There, there, child. It will be all right. It will. God's in his heaven, and Wilmer's in a better place. As bad as things look right now, Johanna will be happy again someday. I promise you that."

"Ne...ne." Another round of sobbing followed. "It's..."

it's me I cry for," Leah wailed. "Oh, Aunt Jezzy, I sent Daniel away. He wanted to marry me…and now I'll never see him again."

"Shh, shh." Her great aunt patted Leah's back. "Sent him away? But I thought you loved him."

"I did… I do, but now…" The words tumbled out, one after another, and by the time Leah had finished explaining why she'd had to do what she'd done, her storm of tears had passed.

The older woman fumbled in her apron pocket and produced a clean, white handkerchief. "Blow," she ordered, handing Leah the handkerchief. Leah did as she was told. "We all thought you were going to marry him and turn Mennonite," Aunt Jezzy said. "Even Hannah thought so."

"I was," Leah said faintly. "But after what's happened… Johanna needs me. Mam needs me. It would be wrong to go and leave them in the midst of all this trouble."

"Wrong, is it?"

"And selfish to want to go," Leah said.

Her great aunt shook her head. "Child, I don't believe that. You don't have a selfish bone in your body. I saw how you looked after Levina when she broke her hip. She's not an easy person, and she has a sharp tongue, but you persevered. She's my sister and your grandmother, but there are times, I can tell you, I've wished her at the far end of the country from me. So, don't tell me you're selfish. *Ne,* I won't accept that."

Leah sniffed. "I'm sure staying home… I'm sure it's what God would want me to do."

Aunt Jezebel arched one graying eyebrow. "Certain, are you?"

"I think so." Leah nodded. "Yes, I'm certain of it."

"Well, I think you're wrong." She used the corner of her apron to wipe a tear off Leah's cheek. "Listen to me, child. I wasn't always a withered old woman that some people call touched in the head. I had a beau, a poor boy without a horse or a buggy or an acre to his name, but I loved him. My mother and father were set against him, and so I refused his offer of marriage and sent him away."

"And you were sorry afterwards?"

"Sorry every day of my life," Aunt Jezzy said. "He married someone else, had children, worked hard, made a good life. She was happy, his wife. It could have been me if I'd had the courage to follow my heart instead of listening to other folks."

"It's why you never married."

"Never found anyone else who held a candle to him. Didn't want second best. Maybe I'm a one-man woman, a foolish one, but faithful. You see, Leah, I think God sent Benjamin to me, hard though the road might have been, and I turned my back on him." She pursed her lips. "Why do I think you're making the same mistake?"

"But Johanna needs me."

"Johanna would want you to be happy, Leah. She would want you to find a good man, to marry him and to live the best life you can. You're not indispensible. Johanna has a circle of family here to help her. Have you thought that you might be using Johanna's sorrow as an excuse to keep you from taking a leap of faith?"

They slept there, the two of them, on that daybed in the attic…or rather Aunt Jezzy slept. Leah lay awake, dry eyed, praying and thinking. And when the first rays of dawn spread coral feathers of light across the sky in the east, she crept down the stairs and out to the barn.

She was harnessing Blackie to Dat's buggy when Miriam came into the stable to start the morning milking. "Coming in late or going out early?" her sister asked.

"I'm going to Daniel," Leah said. Her voice was husky from lack of sleep, but she wasn't a bit tired. "I made a mistake. I turned down his offer of marriage, but I've changed my mind. I'm going to marry him if he'll still have me."

Miriam frowned. "I was afraid of that."

"Don't be angry with me. It feels right," Leah said. "Daniel feels right to me. I think this is what was always meant to happen…for one of us to go back to the faith Mam left for Dat."

Miriam nodded. "I'll take the rails down. It hasn't rained in days. You'll make better time if you cut across the pasture, let yourself out of the woods' gate and follow the logging trail to the road beyond Samuel's."

"Tell Mam and the others where I've gone."

"I will." She stepped close and touched Leah's cheek. "It wouldn't be my choice, but maybe it is the right one for you. Daniel's a good man."

"I think Dat would have liked him."

Miriam chuckled and began to check the straps on the gelding's harness. "I think Dat would have run him off this farm with a pitchfork. Go with God, little sister. And mind Blackie. He's full of ginger this morning."

Miriam was right about Blackie. By the time they reached the hard road, the horse was eager to go. He started off at a smooth trot, his shod hooves flying over the pavement. But Leah didn't care. This was one time that she wanted Blackie to go as fast as he could. She had to get to Daniel and tell him how foolish she'd been.

But when she pulled into the driveway of Joyce and Allan's house, the first thing Leah saw was the empty spot where Daniel always parked his truck. *He's gone,* she thought. *I'm too late. I've really lost him.* She didn't cry; there were no tears left. She was turning Blackie around in the yard when Daniel's aunt came out the back door and saw her.

"Leah? What are you doing here?"

Leah stared at her, numbly. How could she explain what she'd done? How wrong she'd been? "I was looking for Daniel," she called raggedly.

"You just missed him. He has a flight out of Baltimore." Joyce approached the buggy. "He loves you, Leah. I'm so sorry about your sister, and sorry that the two of you couldn't..." She broke off, obviously choked up with emotion. "I know I wasn't as welcoming as I should have been. It's just that we think of Daniel as our own son, and we didn't want to see him hurt."

"I understand," Leah said, turning the reins in her hands. "My mother was against it, too. She was afraid that we...that it wouldn't..."

"I was wrong," Joyce said. "When we saw how Daniel was last night, Allan and I realized that we should have been more supportive. We want you to know that you're always welcome in our home and at our worship services."

"Thank you," Leah said, looking out into the barnyard. "He's really gone?"

"Yes." Joyce nodded. "I'd offer to call him for you, to see if I could get him to turn around and come back, but he left his cell phone in the bathroom. You know how he is. That boy would leave his head if it wasn't attached."

Leah nodded. "I know how he is." *How he was,* she thought. Aunt Jezebel was right. She had been so busy trying to guess what God wanted her to do that she hadn't been listening to His answer. He'd sent her a wonderful man to be her husband, and she'd sent him away because she was too scared to put her trust in Him. She lowered her head and then looked up again. "I'm sorry to bother you. I guess I'll just go home."

"No bother at all. Tell your sister how sorry we are. Some of us from the church will be bringing over food next week. I'm sure you're well stocked now. And we'd like to come by and pay our respects, if that's all right."

"Yes," Leah said. "Johanna would like that, I'm sure." She waved to Joyce and turned Blackie's head down the drive. Her great aunt's words echoed in her head. *"Sorry every day of my life..."* Moisture clouded her vision and she blinked away hot salt tears. "Oh, Daniel, I'm so sorry," she whispered. "So sorry."

Suddenly, Blackie came to an abrupt halt, planted all four feet and reared in the traces. At the same instant, the pickup truck that had turned into the drive screeched to a stop, tires sliding in the gravel, and Daniel flung himself out of the driver's door.

"Leah!"

"Daniel!"

She pulled hard on the reins, and when the buggy stopped rocking, she jumped down and ran to catch hold of Blackie's bridle. Daniel rushed toward her, and together they settled the horse. Somehow in the excitement, Daniel's aunt and uncle had come out of the house.

"Let me hold that horse," Allan said.

"Thank you," Leah and Daniel said at the same time.

Daniel caught hold of Leah's arm and pulled her around to the back of the house and into the relative seclusion of the grape arbor. "You're here," he said. "I thought… You told me… But you're here."

She was breathless, giddy. Her knees felt weak. "You left," she managed. "You left for the airport."

"I forgot my ticket."

Leah began to laugh. "And your cell phone."

"My phone, too?" He pulled her into his arms. "Tell me that I'm not dreaming. That you're really here? That you've changed your mind?"

"You're not dreaming," she murmured. "I'm here, and I changed my mind."

"Why? Why would you ever want to be with such a dunce who can't even get to the airport with all his belongings?"

"Hush," she said, slipping her arms around his neck and raising on her tiptoes to kiss him. "Because I love you and want to marry you."

"Really?"

"Daniel Brown, will you quit talking and kiss me?"

And when he finally did kiss her, there was no need for them to say anything else at all.

Epilogue

Amazon Rain Forest—Eighteen Months Later...

"Wake up, wife." Daniel kissed the tip of Leah's nose.

She stirred, snuggled down deeper into her bed and pulled the pillow over her head. Daniel sat on the mattress beside her and bounced.

"Mmm," Leah murmured. "Just a little longer."

Daniel laughed. "Open your eyes, darling. I have a surprise for you."

Groaning, she pulled the pillow aside and peeked up at him. Daniel waved a thick brown envelope in front of her nose.

"Mail? Really?" She flung the pillow back and sat up, reaching for the packet. "For me?"

Still chuckling, he waved the envelope just out of her reach. "A boat arrived this morning with supplies, books, your new sewing machine and what looks like six months of the *Budget,* all addressed to Mrs. Daniel Brown, Bethesda Mission. I suppose that must be you."

Leah flung aside the sheet. "Give me my letters, please." Excitement thrummed through her, sending ribbons of joy to the tips of her toes.

"Breakfast first," Daniel said. "Midwife's orders. Caridade came by with a ripe pineapple, a bowl of figs and mangos, and a pitcher of fresh-squeezed orange juice. Nothing too good for *little teacher in the family way.*"

Leah wiggled out from under the sheet, pushed aside the mosquito netting and slid to the floor. Daniel handed her a white organdy duster to cover her modest white cotton nightgown and shook out each of her soft leather huaraches to make certain no spiders were hiding there before slipping them onto her feet.

"How's the tummy?"

Leah took a deep breath and smiled at him. "Good." She quickly pinned up her braids, took her small, lacy Mennonite prayer *kapp* off the nightstand, and fastened it on the back of her head. "Really good. I think I'm hungry." She was only three months along, and had had morning sickness for weeks, but it seemed to be passing.

He laughed. "It's about time. I made you breakfast—fig and Brazil nut muffins and a soft-boiled egg."

"Mmm, sounds delicious, but I'd rather have my letters first, then eat."

Daniel shook his head and chuckled. "Oh, no. First the egg—"

"One bite?" she bargained as she followed him through the tiny thatched-roofed cottage. Out on the covered porch, Daniel had set the breakfast table for two, complete with fresh-cut pink orchids floating in a hand-thrown pottery bowl and a basket of fruit.

As she sat down, she looked around her, marveling at the beauty of the Amazon rain forest and the slow-moving river that bordered the clearing. "This must be what the Garden of Eden looked like," she said as she drank in the wonder of the soaring capirone, capok and leafy cercropia trees that sheltered her jungle home.

"You say that every morning," he teased as he took his chair.

"It's true, isn't it?" As she watched, a scarlet macaw took flight from a lower branch of a Brazil nut tree, his colorful feathers a slash of brilliance against the green backdrop of the jungle. "You've brought me to paradise."

"Not every wife would think that." He chuckled as he poured her a brimming glass of orange juice. "No running water, electricity only a few hours a day, no grocery stores or shopping malls."

"But bananas and lemons grow in our backyard." She held out her hand. "My letters from home?"

"Actually, you might want to wait on the letters." He looked over his shoulder again. "There's another surprise. Why don't you have some egg while we wait?"

"Another surprise?" She gazed into his handsome face. *I couldn't have found a more devoted husband, not if I'd searched the world over,* she thought. And the chasm she'd thought she was crossing—from the Amish faith to the Mennonite faith, had turned out to be only a series of slow, easy steps. Now, to her joy, they were expecting a child who she hoped might inherit Daniel's beautiful green eyes and his loving spirit. "How can I eat when you tell me you have another surprise?"

"You need to eat for the baby."

Leah started to argue, then bowed her head and closed her eyes for grace. Daniel Brown could be a stubborn man, she'd learned; sometimes it was just easier to play along with him.

"Thanks be to the Lord for all His blessings," Daniel said. "And for you, who left so much behind for me."

She opened her eyes and smiled at him. "I do miss my family," she said, "but there's so much to do here. My preschool and Sunday School classes, and the sewing circle with the women."

She remembered that Daniel had said the new sewing machine had come on the boat. That would make her sewing group's fledgling enterprise so much easier. Many of the young women who had come to live near the mission were single mothers or widows without education and no means to support their children. Leah had proposed that they start a business making a high-quality line of baby clothing that could be sold at Mennonite-owned stores and bazaars in the United States. They'd begun the project only eight months ago, and already they were showing a profit, with a potential for selling as many garments as the women could produce.

"When the baby's old enough to travel, we'll go home on leave," Daniel assured her. "Three months. And you'll get to show off Rachel to your mother and sisters."

"Or David," she teased. "I think this is going to be a boy."

"Boy or girl, I'll be happy with, either." He slid a muffin, sliced banana and a small bowl with the soft-boiled egg onto her plate.

"You spoil me, Daniel."

"You deserve to be spoiled," he answered.

Leah nibbled at the egg. Surprisingly, she found it

delicious and devoured every bite of the egg, the banana and half a muffin before taking a swallow of orange juice. "Now, what's the other surprise," she asked.

Mischief sparkled in Daniel's eyes.

"Is it a monkey?" Leah clasped her hands. "You've found me a baby squirrel monkey?" One of the women who attended her sewing circle had a pet squirrel monkey with a pretty little white face and a brown cap of fur that Leah had found adorable. Orphan monkeys were sometimes brought to the mission, and Daniel had been promising that the next time one appeared, she could have it.

"No," he said. "Better than a monkey."

"Not a sloth." She wrinkled her nose. "I don't want a sloth." Daniel had argued that a sloth would be a lot less trouble than a monkey with the baby coming.

"You'll like this, I promise. Close your eyes." He rose, stepped behind her, and covered her eyes with his hands.

"Hurry," Leah said impatiently. Then she heard footsteps on the porch.

"Surprise," Daniel said, as he dropped his hands.

Leah stared, not certain she could believe her eyes. Standing there on her porch were Miriam and Charley. "Miriam!" she cried, leaping out of her chair. "Charley! Am I dreaming?"

And then they were all laughing and hugging each other, and Leah was crying for joy. "How?" she demanded. "How did you get here?"

"It was Susanna's idea," Miriam said between hugs. "She said she missed you and we should come to see if you were all right. Everyone in Seven Poplars agreed it was time someone looked in on you two, so everyone contributed a little to pay for the plane tickets. Even Aunt Martha." She chuckled.

"Even Aunt Martha?" Tears filled Leah's eyes. She knew her pregnancy was making her emotional, but she was truly touched that Aunt Martha, who had little money, would contribute to Charley and Miriam's trip. "Does that mean she's forgiven me for marrying Daniel, leaving the church and moving to South America?"

"No one at home is angry with you, silly goose." Miriam hugged her sister again. "You're serving God here, just in a different way than we do."

"How long can you stay?" Leah demanded, squeezing Miriam's hands in hers. "A long time, I hope."

"Through Christmas." Miriam grinned. "Almost three weeks. So you won't be alone for Christmas."

"I couldn't ask for a better Christmas gift." Leah looked at Daniel. "Did you know they were coming?"

He nodded. "Just for a few weeks. I thought that since you'd been feeling under the weather, this would cheer you up."

Miriam looked back to Leah, her face falling. "You're not sick, are you?"

"Nothing that another six or seven months won't cure," Daniel teased.

Blushing, Leah turned and pressed her face into her husband's chest and his strong arms drew her in to a warm embrace. "You shouldn't say that," she whispered. "Not in front of Charley."

"Why not?" Charley asked. "We're all family, aren't we?"

"Ya," Miriam said, clasping Charley's hand. "We're all family. Even if some of us do wear smaller *kapps*."

* * * * *

HIDE IN PLAIN SIGHT

Marta Perry

This story is dedicated to my gifted editor,
Krista Stroever. And, as always, to Brian.

For everything there is a season, and a time to every purpose under heaven: a time to be born and a time to die; a time to plant and a time to uproot; a time to kill and a time to heal.

—*Ecclesiastes* 3:1–3

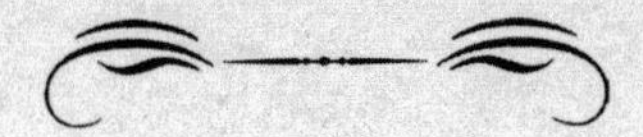

Chapter 1

She had to get to the hospital. Andrea Hampton's fingers tightened on the steering wheel as that call from the Pennsylvania State Police replayed in her mind in an endless loop. Her sister had been struck by a hit-and-run driver while walking along a dark country road—like this one. They didn't know how badly she was injured. Repeated calls to the hospital had netted her only a bland voice saying that Rachel Hampton was undergoing treatment.

Please. Please. She wasn't even sure she believed any longer, but the prayer seemed to come automatically. *Please, if You're there, if You're listening, keep Rachel safe.*

Darkness pressed against the windows, unrelieved except for the reflection of her headlights on the dark macadam and the blur of white pasture fence posts. Amish country, and, once you were off the main routes, there were no lights at night except for the occasional faded yellow of oil lamps from a distant farmhouse.

If she let herself picture Rachel's slight figure, turning, seeing a car barreling toward her… A cold hand closed around her heart.

After all those years she had protected her two younger sisters, Rachel and Caroline were independent now. That was only right. Still, some irrational part of her mind seemed to be saying: *You should have been here.*

A black-and-yellow sign announced a crossroads, and she tapped the brakes lightly as she approached a curve. She glanced at the dashboard clock. Nearly midnight.

She looked up, and a cry tore from her throat. A dark shape ahead of her on the road, an orange reflective triangle gleaming on the back of it… Her mind recognizing an Amish buggy, she slammed on the brakes, wrenching the wheel with all her strength. *Please, please, don't let me hit it—*

The car skidded, fishtailing, and she fought for control. Too late—the rear wheels left the road and plunged down into a ditch, tipping crazily, headlight beams spearing toward the heavens. The air bag deployed, slamming into her. For an instant she couldn't breathe, couldn't think.

As her head began to clear she fought the muffling fabric of the air bag, the seat belt harness digging into her flesh. Panic seared along her nerves, and she struggled to contain it. She wasn't a child, she wasn't trapped—

A door slammed. Voices, running feet, and someone yanked at the passenger door.

"Are you hurt? Can you talk?"

"Yes." She managed to get her face free of the entangling folds. "I think I'm all right, but I can't reach the seat belt."

"Hold on. We'll get you out." A murmured consultation—more than one person, then. The scrape of metal on metal, and the door shrieked in protest as it was lifted.

"The buggy." Her voice came out in a hoarse whisper. "I didn't hit it, did I?"

"No," came a curt male voice, and then a flashlight's beam struck her face, making her blink. "You didn't."

Hands fumbled for the seat belt, tugging. The belt tightened across her chest, she couldn't breathe—and then it released and air flowed into her protesting lungs.

"Take a moment before we try to move you." He was just a dark shadow behind the light. In control. "Be sure nothing's broken."

She wanted to shout at him to pull her free, to get her out of the trap her car had become, but he made sense. She wiggled fingers, toes, ran her hands along her body as much as she could.

"Just tender. Please, get me out." She would not let panic show in her voice, even though the sense of confinement in a small, dark space scraped her nerves raw with the claustrophobia she always hoped she'd overcome. "Please."

Hands gripped her arms, and she clung instinctively to the soft cotton of the man's shirt. Muscles bunched under the fabric. He pulled, she wiggled, pushing her body upward, and in a moment she was free, leaning against the tip-tilted car.

"Easy." Strong hands supported her.

"Are you sure she is all right, Calvin Burke?" This

voice sounded young, a little frightened. "Should we take her to the hospital?"

"The hospital." She grasped the words. "I'm all right, but I have to get to the hospital. My sister is there. I have to go there."

She was repeating herself, she thought, her mind still a little fuzzy. She couldn't seem to help it. She focused on the three people who stood around her. An Amish couple, their young faces white and strained in the glow of the flashlight.

And the man, the one with the gruff, impatient voice and the strong, gentle hands. He held the light, so she couldn't see him well—just an impression of height, breadth, the pale cloth of his shirt.

"Your sister." His voice had sharpened. "Would you be Rachel Hampton's sister?"

"Yes." She grabbed his hand. "You know her? Do you know how she is? I keep calling, but they won't tell me anything."

"I know her. Was on my way, in fact, to see if your grandmother needed any help."

"Grams is all right, isn't she?" Her fear edged up a notch.

"Just upset over Rachel." He turned toward the young couple. "I'll take her to the hospital. You two better get along home."

"*Ja,* we will," the boy said. "We pray that your sister will be well." They both nodded and then moved quickly toward the waiting buggy, their clothing melting into the darkness.

Her Good Samaritan gestured toward the pickup truck that sat behind her car. "Anything you don't want to leave here, we can take now."

She shoved her hand through the disheveled layers of her hair, trying to think. "Overnight bag. My briefcase and computer. They're in the trunk." Concern jagged through her. "If the computer is damaged…" The project she was working on was backed up, of course, but it would still be a hassle if she couldn't work while she was here.

"I don't hear any ominous clanking noises." He pulled the cases from the trunk, whose lid gaped open. "Let's get going."

She bent over the car to retrieve her handbag and cell phone, a wave of dizziness hitting her at the movement. Gritting her teeth, she followed him to the truck.

He yanked open the passenger side door and shoved the bags onto the floor. Obviously she was meant to rest her feet on them. There was no place else to put them if she didn't want them rattling around in the back.

She climbed gingerly into the passenger seat. The dome light gave her a brief look at her rescuer as he slid behind the wheel. Thirtyish, she'd guess, with a shock of sun-streaked brown hair, longer than was fashionable, and a lean face. His shoulders were broad under the faded plaid shirt he wore, and when he gave her an impatient glance, she had the sense that he carried a chip on them.

He slammed the door, the dome light going out, and once again he was little more than an angular shape.

"I take it you know my grandmother." Small surprise, that. Katherine Unger's roots went deep in Lancaster County, back to the German immigrants who'd swarmed to Penn's Woods in the 1700s.

He nodded, and then seemed to feel something more was called for. "Cal Burke. And you're Rachel's older sister, Andrea. I've heard about you." His clipped tone suggested he hadn't been particularly impressed by whatever that was.

Still, she couldn't imagine that her sister had said anything bad about her. She and Rachel had always been close, even if they hadn't seen each other often enough in the past few years, especially since their mother's death. Even if she completely disapproved of this latest scheme Rachel and Grams had hatched.

She glanced at him. As her eyes adjusted to the dim light, she was able to see a little more, noticing his worn jeans, scuffed leather boots and a stubble of beard. She'd thought, in that first hazy glimpse as he pulled her out of the car, that he might be Amish—something about the hair, the pale shirt and dark pants. But obviously he wasn't.

"I should try the hospital again." She flipped the cell phone open.

Please. The unaccustomed prayer formed in her mind again. *Please let Rachel be all right.*

"I doubt they'll tell you any more than they already have." He frowned at the road ahead. "Have you tried your grandmother's number?"

"She never remembers to turn her cell phone on." She punched in the number anyway, only to be sent straight to voice mail. "Grams, if you get this before I see you, call me on my cell." Her throat tightened. "I hope Rachel is all right."

"Ironic," he said as she clicked off. "You have an accident while rushing to your sister's bedside. Ever occur to you that these roads aren't meant for racing?"

She stiffened at the criticism. "I was not racing. And if you were behind me, you must have seen me brake as

I approached the curve. If I hadn't…" She stopped, not wanting to imagine that.

His hands moved restlessly on the wheel, as if he wanted to push the rattletrap truck along faster but knew he couldn't. "We're coming up on Route 30. We'll make better time there."

He didn't sound conciliatory, but at least he hadn't pushed his criticism of her driving. Somehow she still wanted to defend herself.

"I'm well aware that I have to watch for buggies on this road. I just didn't expect to see anyone out this late."

And she was distracted with fear for Rachel, but she wouldn't say that to him. It would sound like a plea for sympathy.

"It's spring," he said, as if that was an explanation. "*Rumspringa,* to those kids. That means—"

"I know what *rumspringa* means," she snapped. "The time when Amish teenagers get to experience freedom and figure out what kind of life they want. You don't need to give me the Pennsylvania Dutch tour. I lived in my grandparents' house until I was ten."

"Well, I guess that makes you an expert, then."

No doubt about it, the man was annoying, but she hadn't exactly been all sweetness and light in the past half hour, either. And he was taking her to the hospital.

"Sorry. I didn't mean to snap. I guess I'm a little shaken."

He glanced at her. "Maybe you should have them check you out at the hospital. You had a rough landing."

She shook her head. "I'll probably be black-and-blue tomorrow, but that's it." She touched her neck gingerly. Either the air bag or the seat belt had left what felt like brush burns there. The bruises on her confidence from the fear she'd felt wouldn't show, but they might take longer to go away.

Apparently taking her word for it, he merged onto Route 30. The lights and activity were reassuring, and in a few minutes they pulled up at the emergency entrance to the hospital.

"Thank you." She slid out, reaching for her things. "I really appreciate this."

He spoke when she would have pulled her bag out. "I'm going in, too. May as well leave your things here until you know what you're doing."

She hesitated, and then she shrugged and let go of the case. "Fine. Thank you," she added.

He came around the truck and set off toward the entrance, his long strides making her hurry to keep up. Inside, the bright lights had her blinking. Burke caught her arm and navigated her past the check-in desk and on into the emergency room, not stopping until he reached the nurses' station.

"Evening, Ruth. This is Rachel Hampton's sister. Tell her how Rachel is without the hospital jargon, all right?"

She half expected the woman—middle-aged, gray-haired and looking as if her feet hurt—to call security. Instead she gave him a slightly flirtatious smile.

"Calvin Burke, just because you've been in here three or four times to get stitched up, don't think you own the place." She consulted a clipboard, lips pursing.

Andrea stole a look at him. It wasn't her taste, but she supposed some women went for the rugged, disreputable-looking type.

Ruth Schmidt, according to her name badge—another good old Pennsylvania Dutch name, like Unger—picked up the telephone and had a cryptic, low-voiced conversation with someone. She hung up and gave Andrea a professional smile.

"Your sister has come through surgery fine, and she's been taken to a private room."

"What were her injuries?" She hated digging for information, as if her sister's condition were a matter of national security. "Where is my grandmother? Isn't she here?"

The woman stiffened. "I really don't know anything further about the patient's condition. I understand Mrs. Unger was persuaded to go home, as there was nothing she could do here. I'd suggest you do the same, and—"

"No." She cut the woman off. "I'm not going anywhere until I've seen my sister. And if you don't know anything about her injuries, I'll talk to someone who does."

She prepared for an argument. It didn't matter what they said to her, she wasn't leaving until she'd seen Rachel, if she had to stay here all night.

Maybe the woman recognized that. She pointed to a bank of elevators. "Third floor. Room 301. But she'll be asleep—"

She didn't wait to hear any more. She made it to the elevator in seconds and pressed the button, the fear that had driven her since she left Philadelphia a sharp blade against her heart. Rachel would be all right. Grams wouldn't have gone home unless she was convinced of that. Still, she had to see for herself.

A quick ride in the elevator, a short walk across the hall, and she was in the room. Rachel lay motionless in the high, white hospital bed. Both legs were in casts, and hospital paraphernalia surrounded her.

Light brown hair spread out over a white pillow,

dark lashes forming crescents against her cheek. Rachel looked about sixteen, instead of nearly thirty. Her little sister, whom she loved, fought with, bossed, protected. Her throat choked, and the tears she'd been holding back spilled over.

Cal picked up a five-month-old newsmagazine and slumped into a molded plastic chair. The dragons guarding the third floor wouldn't have let him in, obviously, so he'd just wait until the sister came back down again. Maybe tonight wasn't the time, but he had a few things he'd like to say to Andrea.

He frowned, uninterested, at the magazine, seeing instead the face of the woman who'd just gone upstairs. On the surface, she'd been much like he'd expected from the things her sister and grandmother had said and from the photo on Katherine's mantel.

Glossy, urban, well dressed in a rising young executive way, with silky blond hair falling to her collarbones in one of those sleek, tapered cuts that every television newswoman wore now. Eyes like green glass, sharp enough to cut a man if he weren't careful.

Well, he was a very careful man, and he knew enough not to be impressed by Ms. Andrea Hampton.

Not that her sister or grandmother had ever badmouthed her, but the picture had formed clearly enough in his mind from the things they said, and from her absence. Her elderly grandmother and her sister were struggling to get their bed-and-breakfast off the ground, and Ms. Successful Young Executive couldn't be bothered to leave her high-powered life long enough to help them.

Not his business, he supposed, but despite his intent

to live in isolation, he'd grown fond of Katherine and her granddaughter in the time he'd been renting the barn on the Unger estate. He'd thought, when his wanderings brought him to Lancaster County, that he just wanted to be alone with his anger and his guilt. But Katherine, with her understated kindness, and Rachel, with her sweet nature, had worked their way into his heart. He felt a responsibility toward them, combined with irritation that the oldest granddaughter wasn't doing more to help.

Still, he'd been unjust to accuse her of careless driving. She'd been going the speed limit, no more, and he had seen the flash of her brake lights just before she'd rounded the curve.

Her taillights had disappeared from view, and then he'd heard the shriek of brakes, the crunch of metal, and his heart had nearly stopped. He'd rounded the curve, fearing he'd see a buggy smashed into smithereens, its passengers tossed onto the road like rag dolls.

Thank the good Lord it hadn't come to that. It had been the car, half on its side in the ditch, which had been the casualty.

Come to think of it, somebody might want to have a talk with young Jonah's father. The boy had said he'd just pulled out onto the main road from the Mueller farm. He had to have done that without paying much attention—the approaching glow of the car's lights should have been visible if he'd looked. All his attention had probably been on the pretty girl next to him.

He didn't think he'd mention that to Andrea Hampton. She might get the bright idea of suing. But he'd drop a word in Abram Yoder's ear. Not wanting to get the boy into trouble—just wanting to keep him alive.

Giving up the magazine as a lost cause, he tossed

it aside and stared into space until he saw the elevator doors swish open again. Andrea came through, shoulders sagging a bit. She straightened when she saw him.

"You didn't need to wait for me."

He rose, going to her. "Yes, I did. I have your things in my truck, remember?"

Her face was pale in the fluorescent lights, mouth drooping, and those green eyes looked pink around the edges. He touched her arm.

"You want me to get you some coffee?"

She shook her head, and he had the feeling she didn't focus on his face when she looked at him. His nerves tightened.

"What is it? Rachel's going to be all right, isn't she?"

"They say so." Her voice was almost a whisper, and then she shook her head, clearing her throat. "I'm sure they're right, but it was a shock to see her that way. Both of her legs are broken." A shiver went through her, generating a wave of sympathy that startled him. "And she has a concussion. The doctor I spoke with wouldn't even guess how long it would be until she's back to normal."

"I'm sorry to hear that." His voice roughened. Rachel didn't deserve this. No one did. He could only hope they caught the poor excuse for a human being who'd left her lying by the side of the road. If he were still an attorney, he'd take pleasure in prosecuting a case like that.

Andrea walked steadily toward the exit. Outside, she took a deep breath, pulling the tailored jacket close around her as if for warmth, even though the May night didn't have much of a bite to it.

"I'll just get my things and then you can be on your way." She managed a polite smile in his direction.

"How do you plan to get to your grandmother's? I

called to have your car towed to the Churchville Garage, but I don't imagine it'll be drivable very soon."

She shoved her hair back in what seemed to be a habitual gesture. It fell silkily into place again. "Thank you. I didn't think about the car. But I'm sure I can get a taxi."

"Not so easy at this hour. I'll drive you." He yanked the door open.

"I don't want to take you out of your way. You've done enough for me already, Mr. Burke." Her tone was cool. Dismissing.

He smiled. "Cal. And you won't be taking me out of my way. Didn't you know? I'm your grandmother's tenant."

He rather enjoyed the surprised look on her face. Petty of him, but if she kept in better contact with her grandmother, she'd know about him. Still, he suspected that if he were as good a Christian as he hoped to be, he'd cut her a bit more slack.

"I see. Well, fine then." She climbed into the truck, the skirt she wore giving him a glimpse of slim leg.

He wasn't interested in any woman right now, least of all a woman like Andrea Hampton, but that didn't mean he was dead. He could still appreciate beautiful, and that's what Andrea was, with that pale oval face, soft mouth and strong jawline. Come to think of it, she'd gotten the stubborn chin from her grandmother, who was as feisty a seventy-some-year-old as he'd met in a long time.

She didn't speak as he drove out of the hospital lot. He didn't mind. God had been teaching him patience in the past year or so, something he'd never thought of before as a virtue. He suspected she'd find it necessary to break the silence sooner than he would.

Sure enough, they'd barely hit the highway when she stirred. "You said you were my grandmother's tenant. Does that mean you're living in the house?" Her hands moved restlessly. "Or inn, I guess I should say, given Grams's and Rachel's project."

She didn't approve, then. He could hear it in her voice.

"I rent the barn from your grandmother. The newer one, behind the house. I've been there for six months now, and in the area for nearly a year."

Healing. Atoning for his mistakes and trying to get right with God, but that was something he didn't say to anyone.

"The barn?" Her voice rose in question. "What do you want with the barn? Do you mean you live there?"

He shrugged. "I fixed up the tack room for a small apartment. Comfortable enough for one. I run my business in the rest of it."

"What business?" She sounded suspicious.

He was tempted to make something up, but he guessed she'd had enough shocks tonight. "I design and make wood furniture, using Amish techniques. If you pick up any wood shavings on your clothes, that's why."

"I see." The tone reserved judgment. "Grams never mentioned it to me."

"Well, you haven't been around much, have you?"

He caught the flash of anger in her face, even keeping his eyes on the road.

"I speak with my grandmother and my sister every week, and they came to stay with me at Easter, not that it's any of your concern."

They were coming into the village now, and he slowed. There wasn't much traffic in Churchville, or even many lights on, at this hour. The antiques shops and quilt stores that catered to tourists were long since closed.

He pulled into the drive of the gracious, Federal-style Unger mansion, its Pennsylvania sandstone glowing a soft gold in the light from the twin lampposts he'd erected for Katherine. He stopped at the door.

He wouldn't be seeing much of Andrea, he'd guess. She'd scurry back to her busy career as soon as she was convinced her sister would recover, the anxiety she'd felt tonight fading under the frenzied rush of activity that passed for a life.

"Thank you." She snapped off the words as she opened the door, grabbing her bags, obviously still annoyed at his presumption.

"No problem."

She slammed the door, and he pulled away, leaving her standing under the hand-carved sign that now hung next to the entrance to the Unger mansion. The Three Sisters Inn.

Chapter 2

Andrea had barely reached the recessed front door when it was flung open, light spilling out onto the flagstones. In an instant she was in Grams's arms, and the tears she didn't want to shed flowed. They stood half in and half out of the house, and she was ten again, weeping over the mess her parents were making of their lives, holding on to Grams and thinking that here was one rock she could always cling to.

Grams drew her inside, blotting her tears with an unsteady hand, while her own trickled down her cheeks. "I'm so glad you're here, Dree. So glad."

The childhood nickname, given when two-years-younger Rachel couldn't say her name, increased the sensation that she'd stepped into the past. She stood in the center hall that had seemed enormous to her once, with its high ceiling and wide plank floor. Barney,

Grams's sheltie, danced around them, welcoming her with little yips.

She bent to pet the dog, knowing Barney wouldn't stop until she did. "I went to the hospital to see Rachel. They told me you'd already gone home. I should have called you…."

Grams shook her head, stopping her. "It's fine. Cal phoned me while you were with Rachel."

"He didn't say." Her tone was dry. Nice of him, but he might have mentioned he'd talked to Grams.

"He told me about the accident." Grams's arm, still strong and wiry despite her age, encircled Andrea's waist. Piercing blue eyes, bone structure that kept her beautiful despite her wrinkles, a pair of dangling aqua earrings that matched the blouse she wore—Grams looked great for any age, let alone nearly seventy-five. "Two accidents in one night is two too many."

That was a typical Grams comment, the tartness of her tone hiding the fear she must have felt.

"Well, fortunately the only damage was to the car." She'd better change the subject, before Grams started to dwell on might-have-beens. She looked through the archway to the right, seeing paint cloths draped over everything in the front parlor. "I see you're in the midst of redecorating."

Grams's blue eyes darkened with worry. "The opening is Memorial Day weekend, and now Rachel is laid up. I don't know…" She stopped and shook her head. "Well, we'll get through it somehow. Right now, let's get you settled, so that both of us can catch a few hours sleep. Tomorrow will be here before you know it."

"Where are you putting me?" She glanced up the

graceful open staircase that led from the main hall to the second floor. "Is that all guest rooms now?"

Grams nodded. "The west side of the house is the inn. The east side is still ours." She opened the door on the left of the hall. "Come along in. We have the back stairway and the rooms on this side, so that'll give us our privacy. You'll be surprised at how well this is working out."

She doubted it, but she was too tired to pursue the subject now. Or to think straight, for that matter. And Grams must be exhausted, physically and emotionally. Still, she couldn't help one question.

"What was she doing out there? Rachel, I mean. Why was she walking along Crossings Road alone after dark?"

"She was taking Barney for a run." Grams's voice choked a little. "She's been doing that for me since she got here, especially now that things have been so upset. Usually there's not much traffic."

That made sense. Rachel could cut onto Crossings Road, perpendicular to the main route, without going into the village.

She trailed her grandmother through the large room that had been her grandfather's library, now apparently being converted into an office/living room, and up the small, enclosed stairway. This was the oldest part of the house, built in 1725. The ceilings were lower here, accounting for lots of odd little jogs in how the two parts of the Unger mansion fit together.

Grams held on to the railing, as if she needed some help getting up the stairs, but her back was as straight as ever. The dog, who always slept on the rug beside her bed, padded along.

Her mind flickered back to Grams's comment. "What do you mean, things have been upset? Has something gone wrong with your plans?"

She could have told them, had told them, that they were getting in over their heads with this idea of turning the place into an inn. Neither of them knew anything about running a bed-and-breakfast, and Grams was too old for this kind of stress.

"Just—just the usual things. Nothing for you to worry about."

That sounded evasive. She'd push, but they were both too tired.

Her grandmother opened a door at the top of the stairs. "Here we are. I thought you'd want your old room."

The ceiling sloped, and the rosebud wallpaper hadn't changed in twenty years. Even her old rag doll, left behind when her mother had stormed out of the house with them, still sat in the rocking chair, and her white Bible lay on the bedside table. This had been her room until she was ten, until the cataclysm that split the family and sent them flying off in all directions, like water droplets from a tornado. She tossed her bags onto the white iron bed and felt like crying once more.

"Thanks, Grams." Her voice was choked.

"It's all right." Grams gave her another quick hug. "Let's just have a quick prayer." She clasped Andrea's hands, and Andrea tried not to think about how long it had been since she'd prayed before tonight.

"Hold our Rachel in Your hands, Father." Grams's voice was husky. "We know You love her even more than we do. Please, touch her with Your healing hand. Amen."

"Amen," Andrea whispered. She was sure there were

questions she should ask, but her mind didn't seem to be working clearly.

"Night, Grams. Try and sleep."

"Good night, Dree. I'm so glad you're here." Grams left the door ajar, her footsteps muffled on the hall carpet as she went to the room across the hall.

Andrea looked at her things piled on the bed, and it seemed a gargantuan effort to move them. She undressed slowly, settling in.

She took her shirt off and winced at the movement, turning to the wavy old mirror to see what damage she'd done. Bruises on her chest and shoulder were dark and ugly where the seat belt had cut in, and she had brush burns from the air bag. She was lucky that was the worst of it, but she shook a little at the reminder.

After pulling a sleep shirt over her head, she cleaned off the bed and turned back the covers. She'd see about her car in the morning. Call the office, explain that she wouldn't be in for a few days. Her boss wouldn't like that, not with the Waterburn project nearing completion. Well, she couldn't make any decisions until she saw how Rachel was.

Frustration edged along her nerves as she crossed to the window to pull down the shade, not wanting to wake with the sun. This crazy scheme to turn the mansion into a bed-and-breakfast had been Rachel's idea, no doubt. She hadn't really settled to anything since culinary school, always moving from job to job.

Grams should have talked some sense into her, instead of going along with the idea. At this time in her life, Grams deserved a quiet, peaceful retirement. And Rachel should be finding a job that had some security to it.

Andrea didn't like risky gambles. Maybe that was what made her such a good financial manager. Financial security came first, and then other things could line up behind it. If she'd learned anything from those chaotic years when her mother had dragged them around the country, constantly looking for something to make her happy, it was that.

She stood for a moment, peering out. From this window she looked over the roof of the sunroom, added on to the back of the house overlooking the gardens when Grams had come to the Unger mansion as a bride. There was the pond, a little gleam of light striking the water, and the gazebo. Other shadowy shapes were various outbuildings. Behind them loomed the massive bulk of the old barn that had predated even the house. Off to the right, toward the neighboring farm, was the "new" barn, dating back to the 1920s.

It was dark now, with Cal presumably asleep in the tack room apartment. Well, he was another thing to worry about tomorrow. She lowered the shade with a decisive snap and went to crawl into bed.

Her eyes closed. She was tired, so tired. She'd sleep, and deal with all of it in the morning.

Something creaked overhead—once, then again. She stiffened, imagining a stealthy footstep in the connecting attics that stretched over the wings of the house. She strained to listen, clutching the sheet against her, but the sound wasn't repeated.

Old houses make noises, she reminded herself. Particularly her grandmother's, if her childhood memories were any indicator. She was overreacting. That faint, scratching sound was probably a mouse, safely distant from her. Tired muscles relaxed into the soft bed, and exhaustion swept over her.

She plummeted into sleep, as if she had dived into a deep, deep pool.

Andrea stepped out onto the patio from the breakfast room, Barney nosing out behind her and then running off toward the pond, intent on his own pursuits. A positive call from the hospital had lifted a weight from her shoulders and she felt able to deal with other things. She paused to look around and take a deep breath of country air.

Not such pleasant country air, she quickly discovered. Eli Zook must be spreading manure on his acreage, which met the Unger property on two sides. How were the city tourists Rachel expected to have as guests going to like that? Maybe they'd be pleased at the smell of a genuine Amish farm.

They'd have to admire the view from the breakfast room. The flagstone patio had stood the years well, and now it was brightened by pots overflowing with pansies and ageratum. The wide flower bed dazzled with peonies and daylilies. She had knelt there next to Grams, learning to tell a weed from a flower.

Moving a little stiffly, thanks to her bruises, she stepped over the low patio wall and followed the flagstone path that led back through the farther reaches of the garden, weaving around the pond and past the gazebo with its white Victorian gingerbread. When she glanced back at the house, morning sunlight turned the sandstone to mellow gold, making the whole building glow.

Rounding the small potting shed, she came face-to-face with the new barn. An apt expression, because she'd always thought the barn had more character than a lot of people. Lofty, white, a traditional bank barn with entries on two levels, it had the stone foundation and hip roof that characterized Pennsylvania Dutch barns. More properly Pennsylvania Swiss or German, her grandfather had always said, but the name stuck.

It hadn't seen much use since her grandfather had stopped farming and leased the fields to the Zook family, but the stone foundation showed no sign of deterioration, and the wooden planks looked as if they had a fresh coat of white paint.

A small sign on the upper level door was the only indication that Cal Burke did business here. And how much business could he do, really? The only way into his shop was via the rutted lane that ran along a hedge of overgrown lilacs that bordered the house. She glanced toward the road. Yes, there was a tiny sign there, too, one that could hardly be read from a passing car. The man needed a few lessons in marketing.

She walked up the bank to the door and tapped lightly. Stepping inside, she inhaled the scent of wood shavings and hay. Music poured from a CD player that sat on a wooden bench. Cal apparently liked Mozart to work by. He bent over a pie safe, totally absorbed as he fitted a pierced tin insert to a door.

He obviously hadn't heard her, so she glanced around, wanting to see any changes before she spoke to him. There weren't many. In the center threshing floor he'd installed a workbench and tools, and the rest of the space was taken up with pieces of furniture in various stages of construction. The mows and lofts on either side already held hay and straw, probably stored there by Eli Zook.

She took a step forward, impressed in spite of herself

by his work. They were simple oak pieces, for the most part, done in the classic style of Pennsylvania Dutch furniture. There was a three-drawer chest with graceful carving incised on the drawer fronts, a chest stenciled with typical tulips and hearts, a rocking chair with a curved back.

Cal did have a gift for this work, and he was certainly focused. Sun-bleached hair swung forward in his eyes, and he pushed it back with a sweep of one hand, all of his movements smooth and unhurried. He wore faded jeans and a blue plaid shirt, also faded, the sleeves rolled up to the elbows. A shaft of sunlight, beaming down from the open loft door, seemed to put him in a spotlight, picking out gold in his brown hair and glinting off tanned forearms.

She moved slightly just as the music stopped. The sole of her loafer rustled stray wood shavings, and he looked up. The pierced tin clattered to the floor, the sound loud in the sudden stillness.

"I'm sorry. I didn't mean to disturb you."

"It's all right." He straightened, leaning against the pie safe, and watched her approach.

She hadn't noticed his eyes last night. The light had been too dim, for the most part, and she'd been too upset. Now she saw that they were a light, warm brown, flecked with gold like his hair.

He waited until she stopped, a few feet from him, before he spoke again. "Any news from the hospital?"

"We called first thing. Rachel had a good night, and she's awake and asking for us." She couldn't stop the smile that blossomed on the words.

"Thank God." He smiled in return, strong lips curving, lines crinkling around his eyes, his whole face lighting. For an instant she couldn't look away, and something seemed to shimmer between them, as light and insubstantial as the dust motes in the shaft of sunshine.

She turned to look at the furniture, feeling a need to evade his glance for a moment. She wouldn't want him to think he had any effect on her.

"So this is your work." She touched a drop leaf table. "Cherry, isn't it?"

He nodded, moving next to her and stroking the wood as if it were a living thing. "I've been working mostly in oak and pine, but Emma Zook wanted a cherry table, and Eli had some good lengths of cherry that I could use."

"It's beautiful. Emma will be delighted, although if I remember Amish customs correctly, she won't say so."

A faint smile flickered in his eyes. "'For use, not for pretty,' she'll say. Anything else might sound like pride."

"That's Emma, all right." Nostalgia swept through her. Emma Zook had helped Grams in the house for years, and her sturdy figure, always clad in a long dress and apron, was present in Andrea's earliest memories.

As children, they'd played with the Zook youngsters, so used to them that they never saw the Amish clothing or dialect as odd. She'd caught up a bit with Emma over breakfast. As she'd expected, all the children except Levi were married and parents by now. Levi—well, Levi would always be a child, no matter how old he was.

"The Amish have the right idea," Cal said. "No reason why something can't be both useful and beautiful."

She traced the scalloped edge of the drop leaf. "This certainly qualifies."

"Two compliments in as many minutes." He drew back in mock surprise.

"I believe in giving credit where credit is due. You

make lovely furniture. I just can't help but wonder why you're doing it in my grandmother's barn."

Where did you come from, and why are you here? That's what she was really asking. How could this man have made such inroads into her family when she hadn't even known about him?

He shrugged. "I came to this area to learn Amish furniture techniques. When I needed a place to set up shop, she had an empty barn. We came to an agreement."

She'd like to ask what that agreement was, but he could answer that it wasn't her business. Which it wasn't, but anything that affected her grandmother and sister mattered to her, whether she'd been back recently or not.

"You're not from around here," she tried.

"No. I'm not."

Most people liked talking about themselves. Cal Burke seemed to be the exception.

"You're a little hard to find. How do you market your work?"

He shrugged again. "There are plenty of machine-made copies out there, but if people are asking around for good, handmade furniture done in the old Amish style, they'll find me or one of the others who do it."

"That's no way to do business." His marketing strategy, if that's what it was, exasperated her so much that she couldn't stop the words. "You have something people want, so make it easy to find you. You could probably double or triple your business if you did a little advertising."

"I don't want to double my business. There are only so many pieces I can make by hand in a month, and they sell okay. What am I going to do with more customers than I can satisfy?"

She blinked, looking at him. As far as she could tell, he was serious. "If you hired a few people to help you—"

"Then it wouldn't be my furniture people were buying."

"But you could make more money—"

He shook his head with an impatient movement that made the hair flop in his eyes again. "I make enough to get by, and I enjoy my work. Your corporate approach wouldn't work for me."

She stiffened. "If you mean I'm practical, I don't consider that an insult. Although I suspect you meant it that way."

"Just recognizing a difference in how we see things, that's all." His voice was mild, but his eyes had turned frosty. "If you came out here to tell me how to run my business, I thank you for your interest."

"No." She bit off the word. The world needed practical people like her. They kept the dreamers afloat. But she didn't suppose it would do any good to tell him so. "My grandmother wants you to know that we'll be going to the hospital shortly. She asks if you'll keep an eye out for the painters and let them in." Somehow it seemed important that he know the favor was for Grams, not her.

"I'd be glad to."

"I thought she could call you, but she said you never answer your phone."

"Really bugs you, doesn't it?" His expression suggested internal laughter. "I don't like to jump when the phone rings. If anybody wants me, they leave a message."

She bit back another comment about his business methods. Or lack of them. Why should she care if the man frittered away his prospects for want of a few sensible steps?

"I see." She kept her tone perfectly polite. "Thank you for taking care of the painters. My grandmother will appreciate it."

She turned and walked away quickly, suspecting that if she looked back, she'd find an amused smile on his face.

"But I can't. I really can't." Andrea looked from her grandmother to her sister. Both faces were turned toward hers, both expectant, waiting for an answer she couldn't possibly give. "I'm extremely busy at work right now."

"Surely your employer will give you the time off." Grams was serenely confident. "Your family needs you."

Rachel didn't say anything. She just leaned back against the raised head of the hospital bed, her face almost as white as the pillow.

She'd tell herself they were ganging up on her, but that wasn't true. They were depending on her, just as Rachel and her baby sister, Caroline, had depended on her during those years when Mom had relocated the family from place to place, nursing her grudge against Grams and Grandfather and depriving her children of the only stable home they'd ever known.

Andrea was the oldest. She was the responsible one. She'd take care of it.

The trouble was, she was responsible to her job, as well, and there couldn't possibly be a worse time for her to take off. Gordon Walker would not understand his right-hand woman requesting a leave to help her family. He hadn't even taken time away from work when his wife was in labor with their twins.

Of course, he and his wife were now divorced, and he saw his daughters once a month if he was lucky.

She tried again. "I'm in the middle of a very important project, and I'm on a deadline. I couldn't take time off now. It wouldn't be fair to the company."

It wasn't fair to her, either. Maybe that thought was unworthy, but she couldn't help it. The promotion her boss had been dangling in front of her for the past year would be hers when this project was completed. Her position with the company, her stable, secure life, would be assured.

"Can't someone else take over for you?" Grams's brow furrowed. "We've already accepted reservations for our opening weekend. All the rooms are booked. We can't turn those people away now."

Grams's sense of hospitality was obviously offended at the thought, even though these would be paying guests. Andrea could see it in her eyes. An Unger didn't let people down.

I'm a Hampton, too. She thought bleakly of her father. *They're pretty good at letting people down.*

Rachel tried to push herself up on the bed a little, wincing, and Andrea hurried to help her.

"Take it easy. I don't think you should try to do that on your own. Those casts must weigh a ton."

"If they don't, they feel like it." Rachel moved her head restlessly on the pillow.

Looking into Rachel's eyes was like looking in a mirror. Green eyes, cat's eyes. All three Hampton girls had them, even though otherwise they didn't look at all alike.

She was the cool, conservative blonde. That was how people saw her, and she didn't find anything wrong with that. It fit with who she wanted to be.

Rachel, two years younger, was the warm one, with her heart-shaped face and her sunny-brown hair. She had the gift of making friends and collecting strays everywhere she went. Sweet, generous, she was the family peacemaker, always the buffer.

And they'd needed a buffer, she and Caroline. Her youngest sister had been born an exotic orchid in a family of daisies. She certainly looked the part. In her, the green eyes sparkled and shot fire. Her hair, a rich, deep red, had been worn in a mass of curls to below her shoulders the last time Andrea had seen her. Currently, as far as she knew, Caroline was making pottery in Taos. Or maybe it was turquoise jewelry in Santa Fe. Andrea couldn't keep up.

"I could come home in a wheelchair. We could get some extra help and I could supervise." But the tears that shone in Rachel's eyes belied the brave words, and she thumped one hand against the side rail of the bed, making the IV clatter.

"Honey, don't." Andrea caught the restless hand, her heart twisting. "It'll be all right."

But how would it be all right? How could she be true to herself and yet not let them down?

Rachel clung to her, much as she had when Mom had taken them away from Grams and Grandfather so many years ago. "You mean you'll do it?"

"We'll find some way of handling the situation. I promise."

Rachel gave a little sigh, relaxing a bit, though worry still puckered her brows.

"Good," Grams said. "I knew we could count on you."

She'd told her boss she couldn't be back until Monday, though she'd continue working while she was here. She was only a phone call or an e-mail away, after all. By then, she'd somehow convince Grams and Rachel that with Rachel laid up for who knows how long, starting a bed-and-breakfast didn't make sense.

A glance at Rachel's face assured her that now was not the time to mention that. Rachel was far too fragile.

She'd discuss it with Grams later. Giving up the inn was the best thing for everyone, especially Rachel. Once she was healed, she could get another restaurant job in a minute with her skills, and if she needed help to get through until then, Andrea or Grams would certainly provide that.

Right now she had to do something to wipe that strained expression from Rachel's eyes. "Did you hear about my adventure getting here last night? Rescued from a ditch by your handsome tenant. Hope you don't mind my using your car while mine's in the body shop."

"Grams told me Cal brought you to the hospital. He is a hunk, isn't he?" Some of the tension eased out of the pale face. "So, you interested, big sis?"

"I wouldn't want to tread on your territory." She smiled. "We made a deal a long time ago, remember? No boyfriend poaching."

"Sad to say, Cal doesn't see me as anything but little-sister material." She wrinkled her nose. "I have to admit, when I first met him, I thought there might be something, but the chemistry just isn't there."

Andrea didn't bother to analyze why she was relieved. "I understand he's been around for about a year?" She made it a question for both of them.

"Just about," Grams agreed. "He stayed over at the Zimmerman farm for a while, I think, when he first came to the area."

"You never mentioned renting the barn to him when we talked." Grams and Rachel had come into the city for dinner just a month ago, but in all their talk about the inn, they hadn't brought up their resident tenant.

"Didn't we? I thought you knew about him."

The vagueness of it got under her skin. "Where did he come from? What did he do before? What does Uncle Nick think of him?" Her grandfather's business partner had a solid, no-nonsense attitude that Grams lacked.

"I don't know. Does it matter?" Grams frowned a little, as if Andrea had said something impolite. "And it's not James Bendick's business."

Rachel moved slightly. "He's a nice guy. That's all we need to know."

It wasn't all *she* needed to know. Perhaps the truth was that Grams hadn't mentioned him because she'd known exactly the questions Andrea would ask and didn't want to answer them. Grams did things her own way, and she'd never appreciated unsolicited advice.

"I believe I'll get some coffee." Grams stood, picking up her handbag.

"I'll get it for you, Grams," she offered.

Her grandmother shook her head. "You stay here and talk to Rachel. I want to stretch my legs a bit."

Andrea watched her leave, her heart clutching a little. Grams wouldn't admit it, but she was slowing down. Grams had always been so strong, so unchanging, that age had sat lightly upon her. It had seemed she would never let it get the better of her. But that had been an illusion.

A weight settled on Andrea's shoulders. She had to make the right decisions now. Rachel, Grams—she was responsible for both of them.

"Are you okay, Dree?"

She shook off the apprehension before she turned to look at her sister. "Sure. Just worried about you. Did the police talk to you about the accident?"

Rachel nodded. "The township chief was in before you got here. It doesn't sound as if they have much evidence. He wanted to know if I remembered anything."

"Do you?"

Rachel moved restlessly. "I don't remember anything that happened after about noon yesterday."

Chapter 3

Cal let himself in the side door of the Unger mansion, toolbox in hand. He'd told Katherine that he'd fix the loose post on the main staircase, but that wasn't his only reason for being there.

He'd been mulling it over, praying about it, most of the day. Prayer was still new enough to him that he wondered sometimes whether he ought to be asking for guidance about simple everyday things. Still, it was comforting to feel that Someone cared.

And this wasn't a selfish thing. He wanted a sense of whether he should speak to Andrea about her grandmother. Seemed to him the answer was yes, although that might just be his need to do something.

Two years ago, he'd have found it laughable to think he'd be so concerned about an elderly woman who wasn't even a relative, but he hadn't been much of a human being, either, back then. Now—well, he cared about Katherine Unger.

Katherine was kind, proud and too stubborn to ask for help even when she needed it. She'd be appalled, probably, if she realized how much he'd learned about her concerns just by listening. If she knew he intended to talk to Andrea, she'd be outraged.

But someone had to. Emma Zook could, but she might be too much in awe of Katherine to do it. So he would. He reached the stairs and pulled out a hammer. He'd been watching for an opportunity to speak to Andrea alone since she'd returned from the hospital, but she'd been holed up in the second-floor family quarters. Maybe a little noise would draw her out.

Sure enough, it didn't take more than a few hearty blows with the hammer before Andrea appeared at the top of the stairs, looking annoyed. She marched down to him.

"What are you doing?" She'd exchanged the pants and jacket she'd been wearing this morning for a pair of dark jeans and a green top that matched her eyes. "I'm trying to do some work upstairs."

"Sorry. You brought work with you?"

"Of course. I couldn't just walk out in the middle of the week."

Even when rushing to her sister's side, she hadn't left the job that seemed so important to her. She reminded him of himself, the way he used to be. That probably went a long way toward explaining why she annoyed him so much. He wasn't too fond of that guy.

He rested his elbow on the banister. "Wouldn't your boss give you a break under the circumstances?"

For a moment she hesitated, and he could almost read

her thoughts. She had the kind of superior who wouldn't, as a matter of fact, and she didn't want to admit it.

"I didn't ask," she said finally. "I have responsibilities, and I meet them." She frowned. "What are you doing here, anyway?"

"Katherine asked me to take care of this loose place in the banister." He wiggled the carved wood gently, mindful of its delicate reeding. "I had time to get to it this afternoon."

"I didn't realize you work for my grandmother."

"I don't. I'm just being neighborly." He still hadn't figured out the best approach. "Look, I know this is none of my business—"

"But it's not going to stop you," she finished for him. "All right. You won't be content until you have your say, so get it over with." She planted one hand on the railing, standing up a step so that their faces were level.

"You don't beat around the bush, do you?"

"I try not to." A slight frown appeared between her brows. "Does that bother you?"

"On the contrary, it makes it easier." If she wanted it straight from the hip, she'd get it. "Your grandmother and sister have been running themselves ragged, trying to get the inn ready. They needed help even before Rachel was hurt, but now it's worse. With Rachel in the hospital, your grandmother shouldn't be in the house alone. Did she tell you she's spotted a prowler out in the grounds recently?"

She sent him a startled glance, hand tightening on the railing. "No. Did she call the police?"

"By the time they got here, the person was long gone." He shrugged. "They didn't take it too seriously, figuring it was just someone curious about the inn. Still, there have been some minor incidents of vandalism in the area lately and a few break-ins. I've been trying to keep an eye on things. But she shouldn't be staying here at night by herself."

"You're right about that." She sounded faintly bewildered that she was agreeing with him. "As for the rest, I'm not sure how best to help her."

He was surprised that she was taking it so well, but perhaps she'd been giving some thought to the problem. She just hadn't come to the right conclusion yet.

"Move in, take over for Rachel, get the inn up and running," he said promptly. "Your grandmother can't do it by herself."

"My job—"

"—can get along without you for a while."

"You don't know that." If her glare had been a blow, it would have knocked him over. "I'd be risking a lot to stay here now."

"I get it. I had bosses like that once." He had a feeling he'd *been* that kind of a boss.

"Then you should understand. Maybe I can hire someone to help out."

He shook his head. "I'm not saying more workers wouldn't make things go faster, but what's needed is someone to oversee the whole project. Your grandmother isn't up to that anymore."

"You think I don't know that?" She fired up instantly. "She shouldn't be attempting something so ambitious at her age. She ought to just relax and enjoy life."

"How is she supposed to do that? What's she going to live on, air?" He clamped his mouth shut. He'd gone too far, even though his intentions were good.

"What are you implying?" She grabbed his arm to

keep him from stepping away. "My grandmother doesn't need to worry about money."

Was she putting on a front?

"Maybe you ought to have a serious conversation with your grandmother."

Her grip tightened. "Tell me what you meant. What do you know, or think you know?"

Fine, then. "I know I offered to lend her the money for the renovations, but she took out a loan on the house instead. I know Emma works for free half the time. I know the signs of financial trouble. If someone doesn't step in, namely you, your grandmother could lose this place that means the world to her."

He yanked his arm free and grabbed the toolbox. "I'll come back later and fix this."

Andrea was actually shaking. She watched Cal's broad back as he retreated down the hall. She should talk to Grams—no, she should find out first from someone she trusted if there was any truth to Cal's allegations. Emma. Emma knew everything that went on here.

But even as she thought it, there was a tap on the front door, followed by a quick, "Anyone here?"

"Uncle Nick." She hurried to the door, to be swept into a hug. Soft whiskers and a scent of peppermint—that was Uncle Nick.

He held her at arm's length. "Well, if you're not a sight for sore eyes, Andrea. You're looking beautiful, as always."

"And you're the biggest flatterer in town, as always. You haven't aged a bit."

She made the expected response automatically, but it was true. Maybe the beard and hair were a little whiter, his figure in the neat blue suit just a bit stouter, but his cheeks were still rosy and firm as apples. He had an aura of permanence and stability that was very welcome.

"Ah, don't tell me that. I know better." He shook his head. "This is a sad business about Rachel."

She linked her arm with his. "She's going to make a complete recovery—the doctors have promised. Come into the library. We have to talk."

He lifted bushy white eyebrows. "Where's your grandmother?"

"Taking a nap, thank goodness. She needs one, after yesterday's upsets."

He nodded, glancing around the room and taking in the computer setup and file cabinets. "It's sad to see this fine old room turned into an office. What your grandfather would have said, I don't know."

There didn't seem to be an answer to that. She gestured him to a chair, sitting down opposite him.

He was surveying her with shrewd, kind blue eyes. "You're worried, aren't you? Tell Uncle Nick about it."

She had to smile. He wasn't really their uncle, nor was his name Nick. Caroline had called him that when she was three because to her eyes, James Bendick, Grandfather's junior partner, looked like St. Nicholas.

"That's what you always said. And you solved our problems with chocolate and peppermints."

"It's a good solution."

"Not for this problem." The worry, dissipated for a moment in the pleasure of seeing him, weighed on her again. "Tell me the truth, Uncle Nick. Is Grams in financial trouble?"

"Who told you that? Not your grandmother." His voice had sharpened.

"No. Cal Burke told me. He seems to think she could lose the house."

"I'd call that an exaggeration." He frowned. "And I'm not sure what business it is of his, in any event."

"Never mind him. Tell me what's going on. I thought Grandfather left her well-off. I've never questioned that."

"Your grandmother never questioned it, either. Sad to say, maybe she should have."

"But the properties, his investments..." She couldn't believe it. "Explain it to me."

Uncle Nick's lips puckered. "I'm not sure I should. Your grandmother—"

"Grams is depending on me." Normally she'd appreciate his discretion, but not now. "I have to know what's wrong in order to help her."

He hesitated, looking distressed. Finally he nodded. "Your grandfather decided, a few years before his death, to sell most of his properties. He didn't want to take care of them."

"I thought he enjoyed that." One of her earliest memories was of riding along with Grandpa when he went out the first day of every month to collect the rents from his tenants. That had been her first taste of business, and she'd wanted to be just like him.

Uncle Nick shrugged. "People change. He wanted to invest the money himself." His gaze dropped. "He wasn't very good. If only he'd held on to the property until the real estate market went up, your grandmother would be sitting pretty."

"As it is..." She could hardly take it in. Still, she'd certainly known how determined Grandpa was to do as he chose. Something chilled inside her. She, of all people, knew just how stubborn he could be.

"She has this place left, but not enough to maintain it." His voice was brisk, as if he didn't want to dwell on what had been. "I'm not sure how you feel about this idea of theirs to turn the place into an inn."

"I think it's a bad move," she said promptly. "Rachel is a great cook, but she doesn't know anything about running an inn. And Grams doesn't need the stress at her age."

Nick beamed at her as if they were the only two sensible people left on earth. "The practical course is for your grandmother to sell. She could pay off the home equity loan she took for the renovations and have enough to live very comfortably for the rest of her life."

"I wish she agreed."

He nodded. "She has her own stubborn streak, that's for sure. I was worried about her living here alone since your grandfather died, but she'd never listen to me. It was a little better after Rachel moved back, but even so…"

"Cal Burke is out at the barn." With the phone he never answered. What good did that do?

"Burke." He repeated the name. "I suppose he's better than nothing, but what do we know about him?"

Not much. She shared his concern.

"And there have been a rash of thefts. People breaking in to isolated farmhouses. You know what this area is like—folks have lived here for generations, never giving a thought that Great-aunt Eva's dough box might be worth a small fortune to a crooked dealer."

She almost wished she hadn't asked, but it was better to face the facts, no matter how unpleasant.

"What are we going to do?" It was good to feel that she had an ally. "Rachel and Grams want me to stay and open the inn. They don't seem to understand that I have a position I can't walk away from."

He patted her hand. "If you make it clear you can't, they'd have to face facts."

"I've tried. Without success."

"You'll have to keep trying." He rose. "Give my best to your grandmother, and tell Rachel that I'll see her later." He gave her a quick hug. "I know you'll do the right thing. You always do."

"Can I carry that for you, Andrea?"

Andrea stopped reluctantly. She'd noticed Cal down the block when she'd left Snyder's General Store to walk back to the house, but she hadn't been eager to talk to him. Just because he was right about her grandmother's finances didn't mean she had to like it.

He caught up with her, and she handed over the shopping bag, taking in the dress shirt and neat gray slacks he wore. She blinked, exaggerating her surprise.

"You didn't know I'd clean up this well, did you?" He smiled, apparently ready to forgive and forget.

"Have a hot date?"

"No, just out for supper at the Dutch Inn. It's chicken and dumpling night. What about you?"

She gestured toward the bag he now carried. "Grams needed a few things from the store, and I didn't want to drive to New Holland to the supermarket."

"So you went to Snyder's, where you get a hot serving of gossip with every bag of groceries."

She couldn't stop a smile. "Some things never change."

"Did you get the latest popular opinion on who I am and why I'm here?"

She was surprised that he spoke so easily about it. "Opinion is divided. You're either a famous author hiding from a deranged fan or a bank robber sitting on his loot until it cools off. That one came from Etta Snyder's ten-year-old son. Her teenage daughter considers you a tragic figure recovering from a terrible loss."

She felt a sudden qualm. What if any of them proved true?

But he didn't seem affected. "I'll let you guess which it is." They walked past the Village Soda Shop and Longstreet's Antiques, their steps matching. "Did you get the whole scoop from Bendick? I saw him come in."

She stiffened. Her family troubles weren't his affair. Didn't he understand that?

His eyebrows lifted. "Okay. Right. I'm interfering."

She fought with herself for a moment. Interfering. Aggravating. But he already knew, so who was she kidding by refusing to answer him?

"Uncle Nick confirmed what you said." She bit off the words, resenting the fact that he'd known what she should have.

"Sorry. I wish I'd been wrong." His voice had just the right degree of sympathy.

Some of her resentment ebbed away. This wasn't his fault. "I can't grasp it. When I was small, I thought my grandfather was the wisest, kindest man in the world."

Her opinion about the kindness had changed when Grandfather let them go without a word, writing them out of his life except for the college funds he'd provided. Surely he could have mended the quarrel with Mom if he'd really cared about them. But even so, she'd never doubted his business acumen.

"You can still have good memories of him." His tone warmed.

She could only nod, her throat choking up. She would like to remember Grandfather as she'd once seen him, without thinking about how he'd let her and her sisters down. Or how he'd apparently failed Grams.

"Why didn't my grandmother tell me? I would have helped."

She could feel his gaze on her face. "Maybe it doesn't matter why. Now that you know, you'll do the right thing."

He sounded like an echo of Uncle Nick, except that they didn't agree about what that right thing was.

"Uncle Nick told me he's been worried about Grams. He said there have been problems with antiques thieves. That prowler you mentioned—" She came to a stop, frowning at him.

He stopped, too, leaning an elbow on top of the stone wall that surrounded the church across the street from Grams's house. "Could be connected, I suppose."

"Nick said they hit isolated farmhouses. Grams's place is right on the edge of the village."

"It's also big, concealed by plenty of trees and outbuildings, and for the most part has had only one elderly woman in residence. There aren't any houses to the east, and in the back, the farms are too far away for troublemakers to be spotted." His frown deepened as he looked across the road toward the house.

She shivered a little at the thought. He was right—the mansion was isolated in spite of the fact that it fronted on the main road. Crossings Road, where Rachel had been injured, snaked along one side, leading toward distant farms and making it easy for someone to approach from the back. "Surely no one would try to break in to the house."

"They wouldn't have to. The outbuildings are crammed to the roof with stuff. Furniture, mostly. And that's not including the attics of the house itself. No one knows what's there."

"You mean there's no inventory?"

His lips twisted in a wry smile. "I'm sure you'd have a tidy inventory, with the approximate value listed for every item."

"Of course I would." Her voice was tart. He didn't need to act as if efficiency were a sin. "For insurance purposes, if nothing else."

"That's how your mind works, but not your grandmother's."

"I suppose not." Her grandmother was an odd mixture—clever about people, but naive about business, which had been her husband's prerogative. "You're trying to give me nightmares, aren't you?"

He gave a rueful smile and shoved away from the wall. "Sorry about that." He touched her hand in a brief gesture of sympathy. Warmth shimmered across her skin and was gone. "I figured I shouldn't be the only one."

Andrea was still wrestling with the difficulties when she went up to her room that evening, hoping to concentrate on some work. A half-dozen times she'd nearly confronted Grams about the financial situation, but each time a look at her grandmother stopped her. Grams looked so tired. So old.

She'd never thought of her grandmother as needing someone to take care of her. Now she'd have to, even though she suspected Grams wouldn't take kindly to any suggestion that she couldn't manage her own affairs.

Well, she'd let the topic ride until tomorrow, at least. Maybe by then she'd have come up with some tactful way of approaching the subject and Grams would, she hoped, have had a decent night's sleep.

She opened her laptop. In an instant she was completely engrossed in work.

Finally the numbers began to blur on the screen. She got up, stretching, and walked to the window. Full dark had settled in, and her attention had been so focused on the computer screen that she hadn't even noticed. Maybe she'd been trying to shut out the human problems that she found so much more difficult to deal with than figures.

Her eyes gradually grew accustomed to the darkness. She could make out the pond now, the forsythia bushes along it, and the pale line that was the flagstone path.

She stiffened. There—by the toolshed. That wasn't a bush—it was a person. She froze, watching the faint gleam of a shielded light cross the door of the shed.

He was breaking in. She whirled, racing out of the room and across the hall to burst in on her grandmother, who sat up in bed with a Bible on her lap. Barney jumped up, ears pricking.

"Andrea, what—"

"There's someone prowling around by the toolshed. Call the police and alert Cal. I'm going to turn the outside lights on."

She could hear Grams protesting as she bolted down the stairs, the dog at her heels.

Chapter 4

Andrea reached the back door and slapped the switch that controlled the outside lights. They sprang up instantly, bathing the area with soft illumination. The yellow glow was probably intentional on Rachel's part. It fit well with the style of the two-and-a-half-century-old building, but at the moment, Andrea would rather have harsh fluorescents that lit up every shadowy corner.

She peered through the glass pane in the door, shivering a little. The dog, pressing against her leg, trembled, too, probably eager to get outside and chase whatever lay in the shadows.

The flowers were mere shapes that moved restlessly in the breeze, as if they sensed something wrong. She strained to see beyond the patio. There was the pale outline of the pond, and beyond it nothing but angular shadows.

She heard a step at the top of the stairs behind her.

"I tried Cal, but there was no answer. Perhaps it's him you saw outside."

If so, she was going to feel like an idiot for overreacting. "Does he usually look around the grounds at night?" He'd mentioned looking for the prowler, and after their conversation, that seemed likely. The tension eased.

"Sometimes. But I called the police anyway. Now, don't start worrying about it." Grams seemed to be reading her mind. "I'd rather be safe than sorry."

But she couldn't help the chagrin she felt. City-dweller, jumping to conclusions at the slightest thing.

Well, if so, Cal was the one who'd spooked her, with his talk of prowlers and thieves. He and Uncle Nick had done the job between them.

A heavy flashlight hung on the hook next to the back door, just where Grandfather had always kept one. Clutching the collar of the excited dog, she opened the door, then reached up and took the flashlight.

"Andrea, don't go out," Grams said. "I'm sure it's fine, but wait for the police. Or Cal. He'll come to the house when he sees all the lights on."

Obviously Grams wasn't worried. A little embarrassing, to have her elderly grandmother reassuring her.

"I'll just step outside and flash the light around. See if I can spot Cal. Or anyone."

The dog surged forward, tail waving, apparently welcoming this change in his usual routine. Did the waving tail indicate he sensed a friend?

She edged down the two steps to the patio, lifting the flashlight to probe the shadows beyond the pond. Even as she did, the wail of sirens pierced the night.

She must have relaxed her grip at the sound, because

Barney pulled free and darted off toward the lane, letting out an excited bark. Turning, she caught a glimpse of what might be a dark figure. Her heart jolted. She swung the light toward it, but the beam didn't reach far enough to show her anything suspicious.

The dog barked again, a high, excited yip.

If it had been an intruder, he'd be thoroughly scared away by the dog, the lights and the sirens. The lane led to the road—if he went that way, he might run straight into the arms of the police, although he'd hardly be so foolish.

She swung the light back toward the shed where she'd first glimpsed the figure. Everything was still. Reassured by the wail of the police car as it turned in the drive, she crossed the patio, flashing the light around. Nothing seemed to be disturbed.

Cal had said the outbuildings were stuffed to the rafters with furniture. She focused the flashlight on the toolshed. Nothing moved now. The shed was a dark rectangle, with a darker rectangle for the door.

She frowned, trying to pick out details in the shaft of light. Memory provided her with an image of the door as she'd seen it earlier, and tension trailed along her nerves. There had been a padlock on the door. If it was open, someone had been breaking in.

She glanced toward the house. Grams stood in the lighted doorway, peering out.

"Grams, I'm going to check the toolshed. Please don't come out."

"Be careful." Grams sounded a little shaky.

"I will. But if anyone was here, he's long gone by now." She called the words back over her shoulder, moving toward the shed. If something had been stolen on her second night here, she was going to feel responsible.

A mental list began to take shape. Get better outdoor lighting, whether it enhanced the ambience or not. Ask the police to make a regular swing by the property. New locks on any building that held something of value. If what Cal had said was right, that could be any of the half-dozen or more outbuildings.

Every building should be properly inventoried. If it hadn't been done when her grandfather died, it should be done as soon as possible.

Grams and Rachel hadn't thought of that—their minds didn't work that way, as Cal had pointed out. Hers did. He hadn't intended a compliment, but she considered her organizational skills an asset. If her mother had been a bit more meticulous, maybe they wouldn't have spent so much time evading the bill collectors.

She shook that thought off, because remembering those days gave her a queasy feeling in her stomach and an inclination to check her bank balance, just to be sure she was all right.

Hardly surprising. Other children's bogeymen had been monsters and snakes. Hers had been collection agencies.

"Barney! Come, Barney." Her grandmother's voice fluted over the dark garden.

She glanced back the way she'd come to see the dog's pale coat as he bounded toward Grams. Apparently Barney hadn't been in time to take a piece out of their intruder.

Ahead of her, the entrance to the toolshed yawned open, sending a faint shiver of fear across her skin. She hadn't been imagining things. Someone had been here.

A few steps took her to the shed door. With a vague thought of fingerprints, she didn't touch it. She'd shine the light inside, that's all. There was no way of knowing if anything was missing, but at least she could see if it looked disturbed. And get an idea of what she had to deal with.

She leaned forward, light piercing the darkness, giving her a jumbled view of wooden pieces—straight chairs, tables, shelves, even an old icebox, jammed on top of each other…

A quick impression of movement, a dark figure. She couldn't react, couldn't even scream as a hand shot out, shoving her into the toolshed.

She barreled into the edge of a table, cracking her head on something above it. Stars showered through the darkness. She stumbled, hitting the floor just as the door banged shut.

For an instant dizziness engulfed her, followed by a wave of sheer, uncontrollable panic. She was shut in, she was alone in the dark—

She bolted to her feet, grabbed at the door, fumbling for a handle, a latch. "Let me out!"

Shout, don't cry, don't let yourself cry or the panic will take over.

"Help! Help me!"

The door jerked open, and she hurtled out. She caught back a sob, her hands closing on the soft fabric of a shirt and solid muscle. She knew him by instinct before she could see him.

"Cal—there was someone here. Did you see him?"

He pulled her clear of the door and slammed it shut. "Are you okay?"

"Yes." They'd had this exchange before, hadn't they? "I'm fine. Did you see him?"

"I saw him." He sounded grim. "Not enough to describe him, unfortunately. You?"

She shook her head. "Just a blur of movement when he pushed me into the shed. I'm sorry."

He grunted, a frustrated sound. "I was following him. If you hadn't sounded the alarm, I might have caught him."

Cal shook his head in response to Katherine's repeated offer of another cup of chamomile tea. "No, thanks, I've had plenty." One cup of the pale brew was surely enough to satisfy the demands of politeness.

"I think that's everything we need." The young township cop sat awkwardly at the kitchen table, looking half-afraid to touch the delicate Haviland cup and saucer that sat in front of him.

"Do you think you'll catch the thief?" Katherine was as much at ease in her kitchen, wearing a fuzzy red bathrobe, as if she sat in the parlor.

"That might be too much to expect, Grams." Andrea spoke before the cop could come up with an answer. "None of us actually saw the man, and he didn't take anything, as far as we know."

While the cop's attitude toward Katherine was one of respect bordering on awe, the glance he turned on Andrea was simply admiration.

Cal understood. Even casual and disheveled, wearing jeans and a loose blue shirt, Andrea was cool and elegant.

And frosty, when she looked at him. Apparently his comment about her interfering with his pursuit of the intruder still rankled.

"I'd best be on my way, ma'am." The cop rose, settling his uniform cap over a thatch of straw-colored hair as he headed for the back door. "We'll do the best we can to keep an eye on the place."

"Thank you, Officer." Katherine was graciousness itself. "We appreciate that."

Once the door closed behind him, Cal shook his head. "That won't be often enough. The township cops have too much territory to cover and too few men. What you need out there is better lighting."

"That's just what I was thinking." Once again Andrea looked faintly surprised to find herself agreeing with him. "I'll call about it in the morning."

"I don't think that's necessary. If we leave on the lights we have, that should suffice." Katherine set a cup and saucer in the sink, the china chattering against itself, betraying her emotion.

"I can install them," he said, knowing she was probably worrying about the cost, "if Andrea gets the fixtures."

Andrea nodded. "Of course." Her gaze crossed his, and he knew they were thinking the same thing. "It'll be my contribution to the renovations."

"I don't want you to spend your money on this." Katherine's eyes darkened with distress. "After all, you didn't think the inn was a good idea."

She probably still didn't, but she managed a smile. "I have to take part. The sign does say The Three Sisters Inn, after all." She put her arm around her grandmother's waist and urged her toward the stairs. "You go up to bed, Grams. I'll just talk to Cal about the lights, and then I'll see him out."

"Thank you, dear." Katherine patted her cheek, and then came over to touch him lightly on the shoulder.

"And you, Cal. I don't know what we'd have done without you tonight."

"No problem," he said easily. "Have a good night's sleep."

She nodded. "Come, Barney." The dog padded obediently after her. "That's my good, brave dog," she crooned, starting up the stairs. "You were so clever to chase the bad man away."

He waited until he heard her door close to shake his head. "I've never been overly impressed with Barney's intelligence, and tonight confirmed that. He ran to me, recognizing a friend, instead of chasing the prowler."

Andrea frowned. "Even if he's not the brightest dog in the world, you'd think he'd go after a stranger."

That thought had occurred to him, too, but he didn't see anything to be gained by pursuing it now. If this was the same person who'd broken into several farmhouses, he could be someone local, even someone who'd been to the house before.

She sat down across from him, apparently willing to forget her annoyance in the need to talk with someone. "Do you think he was planning to steal something tonight, or just checking things out for a future visit?"

"I'm not sure." He balanced the silver teaspoon on his finger. Silver, good china, antiques—there was plenty here to tempt a thief. "He may have wanted to see where the best stuff was. I would expect him to come with a truck of some sort if he planned to haul away any antiques. Pennsylvania German pieces tend to be pretty hefty, to say the least."

"I suppose you're right. He did break the lock, though."

"Meaning he wouldn't have done that unless he

planned to take something? I'm not sure you're right. He couldn't know what was there unless he got in to have a look around."

"I guess." She ran her hands through the silky strands of blond hair in a gesture of frustration. "I don't even know what's in the shed. How could they get away without a proper inventory when my grandfather died?" She sounded slightly outraged, as if lack of the right paperwork was a moral failing.

"Maybe that's a good job for you." It would keep her busy, anyway.

"I can't imagine how long that would take. More time than I have, at any rate. But I'll call a locksmith and have decent locks put on all those buildings."

A slight feeling of sympathy surprised him. Andrea was trying to do the right thing for her grandmother, even if she didn't agree with her decisions.

"I can put new locks on. We'll get them when we go for the light fixtures tomorrow."

"We?" Her eyebrows lifted.

"We. Unless you're well-informed as to the best type of light fixtures and locks to use."

Her eyes narrowed, and he could almost see her trying to pigeonhole him. "I thought you were a carpenter, not a handyman."

"I know a little about a lot of useful things."

"In that case, I'm surprised you didn't offer to do the lights and the locks before," she said tartly. "Since you were so quick to warn me about the danger."

"I did. Numerous times." He rose, carrying his cup and saucer to the sink. "Katherine always turned me down. She held tightly to the illusion that this place was still safe. After tonight, I don't think that's an issue, sadly. She'll let us do it."

"You really don't need to help." Andrea's chair scraped as she shoved it in, the only sound in the room other than the ticktock of the ornate Black Forest mantel clock. "I'm sure my grandmother appreciates your offer, but I can hire someone. I'll pay—"

He swung around, annoyed that she thought this was about money. "I said I'd do it."

"It's my responsibility." That stubborn jaw was very much in evidence. "Why should you be involved?"

"Because I live here, too. Because your grandmother and your sister have both been kind to me."

Because they can accept me as I am, without needing a dossier on my past.

Her hands moved, palms up, in a gesture of surrender. "All right, then. If you feel that way about it, I guess we'd better head out to the hardware store tomorrow."

"Fine." He strode toward the door and pulled it open. "Be sure you lock this behind me."

"You don't need to remind me of that." The ghost of a smile touched her lips as she came to the door and reached for the dead bolt. "I'm a city-dweller, remember? Locking up is second nature to me."

She stood close in the dim light, with the half-opened door between them like a wedge. Her face looked softer in the shadows, more vulnerable.

The way it had looked when she'd catapulted out of the shed practically into his arms. He'd felt her heart racing in the instant she'd pressed against him. She'd been panic-stricken, although she was hardly likely to admit that to him.

"Katherine could use a few street smarts. But I can't

see her changing at this time of her life, so we'll have to take care of it for her."

She nodded, but he thought there was still a question in her eyes. About him. She wasn't like Katherine and Rachel in that regard. She didn't accept anyone at face value.

No, if Andrea stuck around for long, she'd be trying to find out more about him. She'd have to know, just so she could fit him into her neat classification system. And if she did, it would only raise more questions in her mind. Why would a rising young attorney in a prestigious firm throw it all over after winning the case of his career? She'd want to know the answer.

She wouldn't. No one here knew but him. His conscience would never let him forget the mistake he'd made in his rush to get ahead, or the child his stupidity had returned to an abusive father. It had cost his career to right that wrong, and he didn't figure he was finished paying yet. But that wasn't Andrea's business.

"Good night." His fingers brushed hers lightly as he grasped the door to pull it shut behind him. "Pleasant dreams."

"So basically it was much ado about nothing." Andrea gave Rachel her most reassuring smile the next morning. "Really. Stop looking so worried."

Of course Rachel couldn't help it, tethered as she was to a wheelchair by the two heavy casts. The chair was parked by the window, but she didn't look as if she'd been enjoying the view of the hospital's helipad.

"I knew we should have taken more security measures, especially after thieves broke into the Bauman farmhouse and vandals knocked over some of the gravestones in the church cemetery." She brushed a soft brown curl behind her ear with a quick gesture, brow crinkled. "But Grams still thinks this place is as safe as it was fifty years ago, and anyway, she said—" She stopped abruptly, guilt plainly written on her face.

"Relax, Rachel. I talked to Uncle Nick. I know about Grams's finances."

Rachel blinked. "He told you?"

"Yes. What I want to know is, why didn't you tell me?" She forced the hurt out of her voice.

Discomfort made her sister move restlessly in the wheelchair. "You know Grams. She's proud. The only reason I found out was because I happened to be visiting when she hit a low point."

"So you came up with the idea of starting the bed-and-breakfast to help her." How disapproving did she sound? Apparently some, because Rachel's gaze slid away from hers.

"It seems like a good use for the house. Nobody needs a huge place like that just to live in."

"Exactly." She sat down in the vinyl padded chair that was all the room offered for a visitor, turning it to face Rachel. "So wouldn't Grams be better off to sell? The place is way too big for her, and I don't think she should have the worry of starting a business at this time of life."

"You don't understand." Rachel straightened, eyes flashing. "Grams loves that place. Unger House has been her home for fifty years. How can you act as if it would be easy for her to give it up?"

That was as much anger as she'd seen from Rachel since Caroline stole her boyfriend in tenth grade. She leaned forward, resting her hand on her sister's.

"I know it wouldn't be easy, but doesn't that point

come to everyone? When people get older, they usually have to move into a place that's more manageable. I'm sure Grams understands that."

Rachel's expression was unusually stubborn. "She's not ready for that. Besides, she always assumed there'd be family to take over Unger House one day. Us."

That was like a blow to the stomach. "She—why would she think that? It's been years since we left."

"Not that long, as Grams sees it." Rachel tilted her head, surveying Andrea with an expression that suggested she just didn't get it. "You're the one who had the most time here. I'd think you'd have lots of good memories."

"Good memories?" Something hardened in her. "What I remember is being dragged out of the house with half our belongings, Caro screaming, Grams crying, and Grandfather standing there like a statue. As if he didn't care."

"Oh, honey." Rachel patted her hand as if she was the one who needed comfort. "I know how bad that was, but can't you think about all the good times, instead? We were happy here once."

She jerked her feelings back under control, shoving the images from that day behind a closed door. In her ordinary life, she never let them out. Here, she'd been tripping over them every other minute, it seemed.

"You've always been the peacemaker, Rachel, trying to make everyone else feel good." Lucky Rachel had the gift of being able to separate out the bad stuff and remember only the happy times. She didn't, it seemed.

"There were lots of good things," Rachel insisted. "Remember the time the power went off in the big snowstorm, and Eli and Levi Zook brought the horse and sleigh and took us for a ride over the fields to their place? Having the power go off wasn't a problem for them, since they don't depend on it anyway."

"I remember." She couldn't help a smile. "Caroline tried to teach Eli and Emma's kids how to do the hokey-pokey. I don't think they appreciated it."

"The point is that if Grams wants to stay at Unger House, I'm ready to help her do it. The bed-and-breakfast seemed like the logical answer." She rubbed the wrinkle that formed between her brows. "My getting hurt wasn't part of the plan, but I still think if they'd let me go home, we could work it out. Emma's a good cook, and if I'm there to supervise—"

"Absolutely not." That was one thing she was sure of in this situation. "I've talked to the doctors. You need rest, healing and therapy, in that order. No coming home until they give the okay."

Rachel looked at her steadily. "If I do that, how is Grams going to get the inn ready to open? She can't do it herself. Just making all the decisions, let alone the work—"

"She won't be doing it by herself." She'd reached the point she'd probably known all along she would. This wasn't her dream, but she couldn't let her family down. "I'll stay and do my best to get the inn off the ground."

She could only hope that she wouldn't have to sacrifice her job in order to do it.

Chapter 5

Andrea hurried through the center hallway toward the rear of the house, pausing in the small room that had been first a summer kitchen, then later a playroom for her and her sisters. They'd loved the huge fireplace, big enough to roast a whole side of beef. They'd pretended they were Cinderella, sweeping the hearth. Come to think of it, Caroline had always gotten to play Cinderella. She'd been the wicked stepmother.

That was how Rachel had made her feel at her suggestion of selling Unger House—like the wicked stepmother. That stung, with its implication that Rachel cared more, understood more, than she did. She still thought selling was the logical solution, but she was smart enough to know when a plan, logical or not, didn't stand a chance of success.

So she was heading to the hardware store with Cal,

putting off the two things she was least eager to do today. Confronting her grandmother about the financial situation, for one. And then telling her boss she needed a leave of absence. Knowing him, she'd be lucky if he didn't simply give her a choice—her family or her job.

Something winced inside her at that. She deserved that promotion. She'd worked hard for it, sacrificing everything else in her drive to succeed. It wasn't fair that she might lose it now.

She pushed through the swinging door to the kitchen. "Emma, do you need anything—"

She stopped, nerves jumping. Emma was not in sight, but a man stood with his back to her—tall, broad, black pants and a black jacket, his hand in a drawer of the hutch that held the everyday china.

"What are you doing?" The edge to her voice was put there by fear, but she wouldn't give in to the feeling. Wouldn't let herself think about the dark figure that had shoved her into the toolshed. It was broad daylight now, and she wasn't afraid.

The man froze, then turned slowly toward her. It was like watching a mountain move. His face became visible, and something jolted inside her. The face was oddly unformed, as if a sculptor had started working on it and then walked away, uninterested in finishing. Blue eyes, rounded cheeks like a child's…

Emma hurried in from the pantry, her white apron fluttering, eyes worried behind wire-rimmed glasses. "What are you doing, Levi? You remember Andrea, don't you?"

"I remember him." Andrea tried to soften her embarrassment with a smile. Of course. She should have recognized him at once. Emma's oldest son was two years older than she was chronologically. Mentally, he was still the child he'd been long ago. "How are you, Levi?"

"Say good day," Emma prompted, but he just shook his head, taking a step back until he bumped the hutch.

"That's all right," Andrea said, trying to smooth over the uncomfortable moment. "Maybe later Levi will want to talk to me."

Levi's round blue eyes filled with tears. With an incoherent sound, he turned and ran from the kitchen, the screen door slamming behind him.

She could kick herself. "I'm so sorry." She turned to Emma. "I didn't mean to upset him that way."

"He will be fine." Emma didn't seem upset. "He just needs time to get used to new people."

"Doesn't he remember me?" Her own childhood memories were flooding back faster and faster, no matter how much she tried to block them out.

Emma shook her head. "He knows you, for sure. He just doesn't understand about how people change. I'll tell him a couple of times about how you're Andrea all grown-up. He'll be fine."

Certainly Emma didn't seem worried about the incident. Her oval face, innocent of makeup, was as serene as always. Whatever grief she'd endured over Levi's condition had long ago been accepted as God's will, the way she'd accept a lightning strike that hit the barn or a bumper crop of tomatoes to take to market as God's will.

Andrea went to press her cheek against Emma's, affection surging within her. Maybe she'd be a better person if she had a little of that kind of acceptance.

"Well, you tell Levi I was happy to see him, anyway." She dismissed that flare of apprehension that had gripped her when she'd seen him at the hutch. "Rachel was just reminding me of the big snowstorm, when we came to your house in the sleigh. Levi helped his father drive the horses, I remember."

"Ach, I will tell him." Emma beamed at the reminiscence, rubbing her hands on the full skirt of her plain, wine-colored dress. "He will remember that, he will."

They'd all played together then—Amish and English—it hadn't mattered to the children. Emma's oldest daughter, Sarah, had been her exact age. She'd longed go to school with Sarah in the simple white schoolhouse down the road, instead of getting on the yellow school bus for the trip to the consolidated elementary.

"How is Sarah? Married, I know from my grandmother."

"Married with six young ones of her own, and training to be a midwife, besides." Emma's pride was manifest, though she'd never admit it.

"Please greet her for me, too." They'd all grown and gone their separate ways. Only Levi had remained, a child still, but in a man's body. "I'm going to the hardware store with Cal to get some new lights and locks. I wondered if you needed anything."

Emma's plump face paled. "Locks? Why? Has something happened?"

She'd assumed Grams would have mentioned it, but possibly they hadn't had a chance to talk before Grams set off for the hospital.

"We had a prowler last night." She didn't want to alarm Emma, but surely it was better that she know. "He tried to get into the old toolshed."

"Did you—did you get a look at this person?" Emma's hands twisted together under her apron.

She shook her head, sorry now that she'd mentioned

it. She didn't want to distress Emma. Probably she, like Grams, still thought of this area as perfectly safe.

"He ran away when he heard the dog and the sirens." Maybe it was just as well not to mention her closer encounter with the man. "We're going to put up brighter lighting in the grounds. Hopefully that will keep any troublemakers away."

"Ja." Emma pulled open the door under the sink, peering inside. "*Ja,* maybe it will. I can't think of anything that I need from the store."

Andrea hesitated a moment, studying the tense lines of Emma's shoulders under the dark dress, the averted face. The thought of a prowler had upset her more than expected, but Andrea didn't know what to do to ease her mind.

"Don't worry about it, please, Emma. I'm sure the lights will solve the problem. And if you're concerned about walking back and forth to the farm, I'd be happy to drive you."

"No, no." Emma whisked that offer away with a sweeping gesture. "I am fine. No one will bother me."

There didn't seem to be anything else to say, but Andrea frowned as she walked to the door. They couldn't afford to have Emma upset. Grams needed her more than she ever had.

They both did, if they were really going to open the inn on time, and though she could hardly believe it of herself, it seemed she was committed to this crazy venture.

From his perch on the stone wall that wound along the patio, Cal watched the black-clad figure vanish from sight around the barn. He and Levi had reached the point that Levi would sometimes speak to him, but today he'd rushed past without a word. Something had upset him, obviously.

Cal latched his hands around his knee. Andrea had said she'd meet him, and he'd guess she was the type to be on time. So he'd come a bit early, not wanting to give her a reason to say he'd kept her waiting.

Sure enough, she hurried out the back door, checking her watch as she did. She looked up, saw him and came toward him at a more deliberate pace.

"Sorry. Have you been waiting?"

"Only for a couple of minutes." He got up leisurely. "I saw Levi come running out."

"I suppose you think I frightened him."

He held both hands up in a gesture of surrender. "Peace. That wasn't aimed at you. I know how shy he is. It's taken months to get him to the point of nodding at me."

A faint flush touched her cheeks. "I guess that did sound pretty defensive, didn't it? I was startled that Levi didn't seem to remember me."

He fell into step beside her as they walked toward the stone garage that had started life as a stable. "I take it you knew him when you were children."

What had she been like as a child? Flax hair in braids, he supposed, probably bossing the others around because she was the oldest.

She nodded, those green eyes seeming fixed on something far away. "They were our neighbors. Emma's daughter Sarah was my closest friend." She shook her head. "It seems odd now, when I think of it. As if it happened in a different world."

That, he thought, was the most unguarded thing she'd

said to him yet. "I suppose it was, in a way. Childhood, I mean."

"The differences didn't seem so great to a child. We drove my grandfather crazy by talking in the low German dialect the Zook children used at home."

"He didn't like that?" He gestured her toward the truck. When she hesitated, he opened the passenger door for her. "We may as well take this. Rachel's compact doesn't have much trunk room."

She nodded, climbing in. When he slid behind the wheel, she went on as if the interruption hadn't happened.

"I'm not really sure why he objected. His family was what the Amish call 'fancy' German, just as they call themselves the 'plain folk.'" She shrugged. "He didn't insist—maybe he knew that would just make us more determined. Or maybe he saw that Emma's family was good for us." Some faint shadow crossed her face at that.

"Sounds as if you and your sisters had a good childhood here," he said lightly. "I was an urban kid, myself. Never saw a real cow until I was twelve."

"Good?" Again that shadow. "Yes, I guess. Until it ended."

He glanced toward her. "Ended sounds rather final."

She blinked, and he could almost see her realizing that she'd said more to him than she'd intended. She shrugged, seeming to try for a casual movement.

"Everyone outgrows being a kid. Can we get what we need at Clymer's Hardware, or do we have to go farther?"

Obviously the subject was closed. Maybe only the encounter with Levi had opened her that much. Something had happened to put a period to that innocent time, maybe the same thing that had kept her away from here for so long. Whatever it was, she wasn't going to tell him.

So be it. He wouldn't pry, any more than he wanted someone prying into his life. "Clymer's. I know your grandmother likes to use local businesses if she can."

"Fine."

He pulled into the lot next to the frame building with old-fashioned gilt lettering on the glass windows. He loved going into the village hardware store. It was nice to be in a place where people knew your name, as the song said.

Clymer's was as much a center for male gossip as the grocery store was for female gossip, in the way of small towns. Here they'd be talking about who needed new fencing and how the alfalfa was coming along.

Andrea slid out quickly, and he followed her to the door. She stepped inside, pausing as if getting her bearings.

"Lighting fixtures are in the back." He nodded toward the aisle.

Detouring around kegs of nails and the coil of rope that hung handy to be measured off, they headed back to where sample fixtures hung, gleaming palely in the daylight. Ted Clymer looked up from the counter where he was working a crossword puzzle and raised a hand in greeting. Ted seemed to figure if his customers needed any help, they'd ask for it. Otherwise, he left them alone.

Andrea came to a halt in the midst of racks of light fixtures. She turned toward him. "I'm not too proud to admit when I'm out of my depth. What do you think we need?"

Since he'd already decided, he was relieved that they weren't going to argue about it. He chose two brands and set the boxes in front of her. "Either one of these would do the job."

"Which do you recommend?"

He put his hand on the more expensive brand. "This will cost more to begin with, but it's higher rated. Still, the other one will serve."

She shook her head decisively. "I don't want to worry that they'll have to be replaced in a couple of years. How many do you think we need to cover the area?"

"I'd say six would do it." He glanced at the racks. "Ted doesn't have that many out, but he probably has more in the back."

She picked up the box. "I'll ask him to get them while you're picking out the locks." Her smile flickered. "You don't need to ask my opinion. Just get what you think will work best."

So apparently Andrea trusted him in that, at least, and she wasn't grudging the money spent on something her grandmother needed. He watched her walk toward the counter. Even in khaki pants and a fitted denim jacket, she had just enough of an urban flair to let you know she didn't belong here.

Too bad. Because Katherine would like having her around, not because it mattered to him.

It took a few minutes to find locks that satisfied him. Nothing would keep out a really determined thief, but these would discourage anyone who was looking for a lock that could be popped quickly and quietly.

He headed back to the counter, his hands full, but checked when he saw the person who stood next to Andrea, talking away as if they were old friends. Margaret Allen. He'd be willing to bet that no legitimate errand had brought her into the hardware store. It was far more likely that she'd spotted them from across the street and decided to check up on the competition.

He approached and dropped the locks on the counter, their clatter interrupting the conversation. "That's it for us, Ted. Ring us up."

He turned, forcing a smile. "Hello, Margaret. How's business?"

She returned the smile with one that had syrup oozing off it. Margaret looked, he always thought, like a well-fed, self-satisfied cat, and never so much as when she was asserting her position as the owner of the finest inn in the county. Just how far would she go to maintain that status? The question had begun pricking at the back of his mind lately.

"How nice to see you, Cal. I was just telling Andrea how wonderful it is of her to come and help her grandmother at such a sad time. Poor Rachel. I'm afraid all their visions of starting a bed-and-breakfast will be lost. Still, I always say that every cloud has a silver lining, and I'm sure in the end, this disappointment will be for the best. Don't you agree, Andrea?"

Andrea looked a little dazed at the flood of saccharine. "Yes, I mean—"

"We have to go." He handed Andrea the credit card Ted had been patiently holding out. "Lots to do. Nice seeing you, Margaret." He scooped up boxes, handing the bag containing the locks to Andrea, and nudged her toward the door.

She shot him an annoyed look. "I'm glad to have met you, Ms. Allen. I'll tell my sister you asked about her."

They reached the pickup, and he started loading fixtures quickly, not having any desire to hang around for another interrogation from Margaret.

Andrea dropped the bag with the locks into the pickup bed. "You didn't have to be rude to that poor woman. She was just expressing her concern."

"Right." He shook his head. "That was Margaret Allen." He pointed to the Georgian mansion across the street with its twin weeping willows overhanging the wrought iron fence. "That Margaret Allen, owner of The Willows bed-and-breakfast."

"She said she was a friend of my grandmother's." Andrea climbed in, frowning at him as he got behind the wheel. "Maybe she did gush a bit, but I'm sure she meant well."

"A bit?" He lifted an eyebrow. "You looked as if you were drowning in it."

Her lips twitched. "Just because she runs another B and B, that doesn't make her the enemy."

"In her mind, it does. Believe me. She takes pride in having the only inn in Churchville, and she doesn't like to share the limelight, or the tourist dollars, with anyone." He pulled out onto Main Street for the short drive home.

"Surely there's enough tourist trade to go around."

He shrugged. "Ask Rachel, if you don't believe me. She's the one who's had to deal with her. The other B and B operators in the county have been supportive, by and large, but Margaret created one problem after another."

"What could she do? Surely you don't think she was our prowler."

That was a thought that hadn't occurred to him, and he filed it for future consideration. "I don't see her wandering around in the dark, no, but she has played dirty. Complaints to the township zoning board, complaints to the tourist bureau, complaints to the bed-and-breakfast owners association. All couched in such sickeningly sweet language you'd think she was doing them a favor by putting up roadblocks."

"Maybe she was." It was said so softly he almost missed it.

"Is that what you'll tell your grandmother when you bail and leave them on their own?" The edge in his voice startled him. He hadn't meant to say that.

He felt Andrea's gaze on him and half expected an explosion. He didn't get it.

"Think what you like." Her tone dismissed him, as if he were no more important in the scheme of things than the barn cat. "But as a matter of fact, I'm not leaving. I'm staying until I can be sure that my grandmother and sister are all right."

It silenced him for a moment. "What about your job?"

Her fingers clenched in her lap. "I don't know. Talking to my boss is a pleasure I haven't had yet."

"I'm sorry. I hope he understands."

"So do I." Her fingers tightened until her knuckles were white.

"It means that much to you?"

"Yes. It does." She clipped off the words, as if he didn't have the right to know why.

She was willing to sacrifice something that was important to her for the sake of someone else. The few people who knew the truth about him might say he'd done the same, but he'd done it as much for himself as for anyone else, because he'd known he couldn't live with himself if he hadn't.

It had brought him unexpected benefits in the long run—helped him to know what he wanted from life, brought him to faith. Still, he couldn't assume that would be the result for Andrea's sacrifice.

"I hope it works out for you, Andrea. Really."

He glanced across the confines of the front seat at her. There was something startled, a little wary, in her eyes. As if she wasn't sure whether she believed him. Or maybe as if it mattered what he thought.

Chapter 6

Andrea sat in the room she still thought of as her grandfather's library that afternoon, frowning over the rather sketchy records Rachel seemed to be keeping on the inn's start-up. Sketchy didn't cover it. Surely Rachel had better records than this. If not, they were in more trouble than she'd imagined.

She flipped through the file folder, her frustration growing. Hadn't Rachel been saving receipts, at least? Grams might know if she had records elsewhere. Maybe, like Grandfather, she preferred to do it all by hand, although he had been far more organized than this.

Grandfather's tall green ledgers had been a fixture of their childhood. Presumably the insurance and real estate business he'd shared with Uncle Nick had long since been computerized, but she'd always associate her grandfather with those meticulously handwritten ledgers. She glanced at the shelf where they'd once stood in a neat row, but it was now occupied by a welter of tourist brochures and bed-and-breakfast books. Rachel must have moved them.

The front door closed, and Barney gave the excited yelp that meant the center of his existence had returned. The scrabble of his nails on the plank floor was followed by the crooning voice Grams reserved for him. Andrea had to smile. She couldn't imagine her dignified grandmother talking baby talk to any other creature but Barney.

"Andrea?" Her grandmother came in, followed by the excited dog. "Good, you're here. I'd like to speak with you."

The determined set to Grams's jaw told her that any questions about Rachel's record-keeping would have to wait. Grams clearly had an agenda of her own.

Andrea swung the leather swivel chair around so that she faced the wingback tapestry chair that was Grams's favorite. The desk chair had been Grandfather's. It was too big for Andrea, and she felt slightly uncomfortable in it, as if she sat in the boss's chair without permission.

"How's Rachel? Did you tell her I'll come to see her this evening?"

Grams sat down, her expression lightening a little. "I thought she seemed a bit stronger today. She didn't look quite so pale. Nick had been in with a lovely arrangement of roses, and Pastor Hartman came just as I was leaving."

"That's good." Good that Rachel seemed better, and good that she was having other company. Perhaps that would keep Grams from feeling guilty if she couldn't be there every minute.

"Yes." Grams fondled the dog's ears for a moment, frowning a little. "I understand from Rachel that you know about my financial situation. That James Bendick told you."

That must really rankle, or Grams would be using the nickname that she'd adopted along with the children. "Please don't blame Uncle Nick, Grams. I'd already guessed some of it, and I made him tell me what was going on."

That didn't seem to have the desired effect. Grams still looked severe. "Nevertheless, he doesn't have the right to discuss my affairs without my permission. I'll have to speak to him about it."

The threat to be spoken to by Grams had been such a part of her childhood that it almost made her smile. *Andrea Katherine, do I have to speak to you?* The words echoed from the past.

Grams was taking this too seriously for smiling, however, and they had to discuss the situation, whether Grams wanted to confide in her or not.

"Uncle Nick probably thought I'd heard it already, from you. Which I should have. Why on earth didn't you tell me about the financial problems? You must know I'd help any way I can."

Grams turned her face away, and for a moment Andrea thought she wasn't going to answer. Then she realized that her grandmother was looking at the portrait of Grandfather that hung over the mantelpiece on the other side of the room.

"I didn't want you to think ill of your grandfather. Or any more than you already do."

The words were spoken so softly that it took a moment for them to register. And when they did, Andrea felt a flush rise on her cheeks. "I don't know what you mean."

Grams looked at her then, her blue eyes chiding. "Yes, you do, Andrea. You've never forgiven him for the quarrel with your mother."

It was like being slapped. She'd never dreamed that Grams guessed her feelings. Obviously she hadn't been as good at hiding them as she'd thought. She took a breath, trying to compose herself. She couldn't let whatever lingering resentment she had affect what she did now.

"It was a long time ago, Grams. What's important is what's going on now."

Her grandmother shook her head slowly, delicate silver earrings echoing the movement. "The past is always important, Andrea. Your grandfather was a good man. He gave me a comfortable life, and I won't hear a word against him just because he made a few wrong business decisions."

It must have been more than a few, some practical part of her mind commented, but she shooed away the thought. She had to help Grams, but she'd hoped to steer clear of Grandfather's mistakes, knowing that would hurt her.

"He loved you very much, Grams."

For the first time since her return, Andrea stared directly at the portrait. Her grandfather's image stared back—blue eyes as piercing as she remembered, the planes of his face still strong even when the painting was done, to commemorate Grandfather's retirement from the state legislature at sixty-five. He looked like a man you could count on.

But he also looked stubborn. In the case of his daughter, the stiff-necked stubbornness had won out over any other consideration, including his grandchildren.

"He loved you, too, dear. I know you find that hard to believe, but he did."

"He let her take us away." The voice of her childhood popped out before she could censor it.

Grams reached out to grasp her hand. "He couldn't stop her. She was your mother." She shook her head. "I know you think he could have mended things with her, but you must be old enough now to see how it was. He was proud, and your mother—well, she was willful. They could never stop the quarrel long enough to admit they loved each other."

Willful, reckless, lavish with both affection and temper—yes, she knew what her mother had been like. How had two such solid citizens as her grandparents have produced Lily Unger Hampton? That had to be one of the mysteries of genetics.

"I'm sorry, Grams." To her horror, she felt tears well in her eyes. "I know it hurt you, too." But her grandmother would never know just how bad it had been for her precious grandchildren, at least not if Andrea could help it.

"He grieved when you were taken away." Grams's voice was soft. "You have to believe that, my dear."

Not as much as we did. You were the grown-ups, you and Grandfather, and our mother and father. Why didn't you take better care of us? She wouldn't say that, but she couldn't help feeling it.

Shaking her head, Grams got up. She dipped her hand into a Blue Willow Wedgwood bowl that sat on top of the desk, retrieving the small key. She handed it to Andrea.

"It fits the bottom drawer on the right." She nodded

to the massive mahogany desk that had been Grandfather's. "I want you to look inside."

Something in her wanted to rebel, but she couldn't ignore the command in her grandmother's eyes. She bent and unlocked the drawer, pulling it open. Inside were long rectangular boxes, three of them—the sort of archival boxes that preserved documents. The top box had a name, written in black ink in Grandpa's precise lettering. *Andrea.*

She lifted that one, setting it on the desk blotter to remove the lid. Her throat tightened. A picture, drawn by a child's hand, showed two figures—a white-haired man in a navy suit, a child with yellow braids. Before she could dwell on it, she flipped through the rest of the contents.

Report cards, more drawings, dating back to the earliest attempts that were no more than ovals on sticks for figures. Always two of them—grandfather and granddaughter. A handmade valentine, with a lopsided heart pasted onto a white doily, signed with a red crayon. *To Grandfather from your helper.*

She remembered making that one, sitting at the kitchen table, asking Emma to aid with the spelling. Emma, always more adept in German than English, had called Grams in to advise.

Tears stung her eyes, and she fought to keep them from falling. Grams meant well. She was trying to prove that Grandfather had loved her. But if he'd loved her enough to save all these things, why hadn't he loved her enough to do whatever it took to stay a part of her life?

A hot tear splashed on the valentine, and she blotted it away. Yes, Grams meant well. But looking at these reminders didn't make the situation better. Seeing them just made it worse.

* * *

Cal rounded the shed on his way to the kitchen. His stride checked abruptly.

Andrea sat on the low stone wall where he'd sat earlier, but she didn't seem to be waiting for anyone. Her cell phone was pressed to her ear, and judging by the expression on her face, the conversation wasn't going well.

He detoured to the walk that circled around, taking him toward the door at a safe distance from her. She'd probably come out to the garden to ensure her privacy, and he wouldn't intrude. But he couldn't prevent a certain amount of curiosity. Was it her boss who put that expression on her face?

Or was it a boyfriend, unhappy at her prolonged absence from the city? That thought generated a surprisingly quick denial. No one had mentioned a boyfriend in Andrea's life, but then again, why would they, to him?

He went on into the kitchen, where he consulted Emma about the exact finish on the piece he was making for her, enjoying prolonging the conversation with a smattering of the low German he'd been attempting to learn. It must still be plenty fractured, judging by her laughter.

That had been one of the things that had surprised him about the Amish when he'd come here. He'd expected, from outward appearances, a dour people, living an uncomfortable life as if it were a duty.

Instead he'd found people who laughed readily and who took as much enjoyment in plowing all day in the sun as they did from sitting on the porch on a summer's evening. Work was not something that was separate from play—all things held their own intrinsic satisfaction, because they were done in obedience to God's will.

It was a lesson he'd been trying to learn, but he suspected that even the trying was self-defeating. He couldn't will himself into finding peace and joy in the everyday things of life. That only happened when he forgot the effort and simply lost himself in what he was doing.

When he went out the back door again, Andrea still sat on the wall. Afternoon sunlight, filtering through the leaves of the giant oak that shaded the patio, turned her silky blond hair to gold. The cell phone lay next to her.

"Hi." He nodded toward the phone. "I didn't want to interrupt you."

"An interruption might have improved the conversation." She grimaced. "No, I take that back. It would just have prolonged it."

"Your boss?" That instinctive sympathy came again.

"He did *not* take the news well. Not even when I assured him I'd keep working on the project from here."

"Did you point out that telecommuting is fast becoming the norm in some businesses?"

"He doesn't think telecommuting will do the trick at this point." She shrugged. "I can't really argue with that. He's probably right."

He propped one foot on the wall and leaned an elbow on his knee. "I assume he finally accepted the inevitable."

"Well, he's not firing me outright, so I suppose that's a good sign. But I suspect my promotion has just moved off into the distant future." Her eyes clouded at that. "I'll do everything I can from here, and my assistant will do what she can, but he'll still be inconvenienced."

"A little inconvenience never hurt anyone. Maybe he'll learn to appreciate you more." He'd like to remove the dismay from her face, but that wasn't within his power.

"Somehow I doubt that."

He sat down next to her. No use pretending he didn't care about her troubles. He couldn't help doing so. "This promotion—it means a lot to you."

A fine line formed between her brows. "It means… security."

Whatever he'd expected her to say—recognition, success, the corner office—it hadn't been that. "Security? That sounds like something I'd expect from a fifty-year-old who's thinking about retirement."

She stiffened. "Security is generally considered a good thing, believe it or not. You don't have to be fifty to think about it. In fact, if you wait until you're fifty, you've put it off too long."

"You're young, smart and, I suspect, talented at what you do." He smiled. "And those are good things, too. They'd be appreciated in plenty of places. Your grandmother says—"

"My grandmother doesn't know anything about business. But you do, don't you?" She swung the full impact of those green eyes on him.

"What makes you say that?" He backtracked, wondering where he'd made a mistake. "I'm just a craftsman."

"You do a pretty good imitation of the country hick from time to time, but that's not who you are, is it?"

He shrugged, almost enjoying parrying with her. She'd never hit on the truth, so what difference did it make?

"I told you I grew up in the city. Any little vestiges of urban sophistication should wear away, in time."

"I'm not talking about growing up in the city." She

brushed that away with a wave of her hand. "I'm talking about the corporate mind-set. You understand it too well to be a bystander."

He rose, the enjoyment leaving. He didn't like the turn the conversation was taking. "Hey, I was just trying to be sympathetic."

She studied him for a long moment, her brow furrowed with uncertainty. And he suspected she didn't like being uncertain about anything.

"If that's true, I appreciate it," she said finally. "But I still don't believe you're just a simple craftsman."

His tension eased. She wasn't going to make an issue of it, and even if she did—well, he hadn't committed any crime. At least, not any that the law would call him to book for. Whatever guilt he still carried was between him and God.

"And you're not just a simple financial expert, are you? You're also a granddaughter, a sister, and now an innkeeper."

"Don't remind me." She rubbed at the line between her brows, as if she could rub it away. "I know you won't appreciate how this pains me, but my sister's idea of keeping track of start-up costs consists of throwing receipts in a file."

"She uses a file? I thought my cigar box was pretty sophisticated."

That got a smile, and the line vanished. "You're not going to make me believe that, you know."

"Maybe not." He sobered. "But I hope you'll believe that if anything happens that worries you, you can call me. Any time. I promise I'll answer my phone."

She looked startled. "You mean—but surely with the new lights and the locks, no one would try to break in."

"Sounds a little melodramatic with the sun shining, but I'm still not comfortable about the situation." An ambitious thief might want to see what he could get before the inn opened, filling the place with visitors. And an ambitious rival might think one more incident would be enough to scuttle the inn plans for good. "Just—call me."

Her gaze seemed to weigh him, determining whether and how much to trust him. Finally she nodded.

"All right. If I see or hear anything that concerns me, I'll call you. I promise."

She'd made a promise she didn't expect she'd have to keep, Andrea thought as she drove home from the hospital that evening. She appreciated Cal's concern, but surely the measures they'd taken would discourage any prospective thief.

Now all she had to worry about was hanging on to her future at work, ensuring Rachel's healing, and getting the inn off and running. Those concerns had actually begun to seem manageable.

The layer of dark clouds that massed on the horizon didn't dampen her optimistic mood. Rachel had looked almost normal tonight, joking about the casts and finally rid of the headache that had dogged her since the accident. Andrea hadn't realized how worried she was about her sister until the weight had lifted with the assurance that Rachel was her buoyant self again.

They had spent nearly two hours going over all of Rachel's plans for the inn, and in spite of her sister's undoubted lack of financial expertise, they probably had a reasonable chance of success. They had a beautiful, historic building in an unmatched setting, and Grams was a natural hostess. With Emma's housekeeping ability and Rachel's inspired cooking, they should be in good shape.

The cooking was the immediate problem, but surely they could find a way around that until Rachel was well. If Andrea could just get them set up on a sound financial system, the whole thing could work. She might still have doubts about the wisdom of Grams taking on such a project at her age, but at least she was no longer convinced they were headed for disaster.

She pulled up to the garage, giving an approving nod to the lights Cal had installed. It would take a brazen thief to attempt to break in now, even though darkness took over beyond the buildings with only the pale yellow glow from a distant farmhouse to break it.

She parked and walked quickly to the side door that led directly into the family quarters. From upstairs, Barney gave an experimental woof and then quieted, apparently recognizing her step. Grams must have already gone to bed.

Andrea made the rounds of the ground floor, checking the doors that Grams had already no doubt checked. Everything was locked up and secure. She hurried through the library, not looking toward the portrait. Thinking about her grandfather was not conducive to a good night's sleep.

Upstairs, she opened the door to Grams's bedroom. Her grandmother was already asleep, her Bible open on her lap. Barney looked up, tail slapping the floor. Andrea removed the Bible, open to the twenty-third Psalm. Had that comforted Grams enough to send her to sleep? Faint longing moved through her. She wanted…

She wasn't sure what. Faith, like Grams had? Like Cal apparently had? But faith wasn't to be manufactured just because she felt responsibility weighing on her. She turned off the bedside lamp, tiptoed out and shut the door.

A cool breeze wafted into the hall from the open window. She glanced at it, deciding to leave it open, and went on into her bedroom.

The new lights cast reflections on her ceiling. Comforting reflections. They could all sleep well tonight, including Cal. She wouldn't be calling him.

Andrea jolted awake. Shoving the sheet aside, she reached for the bedside lamp, heart pounding. Then the noise came again, and she subsided, relaxing. Thunder, that was all. The threatening storm had arrived. Even as she thought that, rain slashed against the house.

Jumping out of bed, she hurried to the windows, but no sprinkles dampened the wide sills. The rain wasn't coming in this direction, but it might well be raining in the hall window.

She hurried out into the hallway. The sheer white curtains on the window billowed inward, and she rushed to pull down the sash, bare toes curling into a slight dampness on the floor beneath her feet. She could imagine Grams's reaction if she woke to soaked curtains.

There were no lights on this side of the house. Darkness pressed against the panes, mitigated only by reflections of the dim night-light Grams always left on in the hall. She stood there for a moment, looking into the dark, until it was split by a vivid flash of lightning.

She jerked back, gasping. In the brief instant of light—had that been a figure, standing just by the shelter of the lilac hedge?

She pressed her hand against her chest, feeling the

thud of her heart. Imagination, that was all. She was spooking herself, seeing menace where there was nothing… But there had been something that night by the toolshed. Was their prowler making another visit?

Lightning snapped again, closer now, one sharp crack illuminating the grounds below as sharply as a spotlight. Showing her the dark figure of a man.

She drew back, clutching the curtain instinctively in front of her, as if he could see her standing there in the flimsy cotton nightshirt. She slid to the side of the window. Stared out, focusing her eyes on the spot, trying to still the rasp of her breath. If the lightning flashed again, she'd be ready.

A volley of lightning, thunder following it so fast that the storm must be right over the house. It showed her, as if in a series of jagged still pictures, the figure turning, the brim of a hat, tilting up toward the window where she stood, frozen. The face was a pale blur, but the clothing—even in dark outline, the clothing looked Amish.

Impossible. But she had to believe the evidence of her own eyes, didn't she? Even as she watched, the figure moved, raising one arm as if he shook his fist at her.

She stumbled backward, heart thudding, breath catching, and then bolted for the bedroom and her cell phone. The doors were locked, he couldn't get in, call Cal, call the police….

Cal answered on the first ring, sounding as if he fought his way awake. "Yes, what?"

"There's someone, a man, out on the east side of the house."

"Andrea?" His voice sharpened. "Are you sure?"

"The lightning makes it as bright as day. He's there, watching the house. We didn't put lights—"

They hadn't thought they needed to where there were no outbuildings to be broken into. Maybe the intruder's goal wasn't the outbuildings. Maybe it was the house itself.

"I'll be right there. Don't go out, you hear me?"

"I won't. I'll go down to the side door and meet you there." She glanced across the hall. "My grandmother's exhausted. I don't want to wake her again unless I have to."

"Right. Don't call the police until I see what's up. And don't open the door." He clicked off without a goodbye.

It wasn't until she stood there shivering in the dark that she realized that at least one part of her relief at hearing his voice on the phone was the conviction that it couldn't be Cal out there in the dark, playing tricks.

Quickly she pulled sweatpants and a sweatshirt on, stuffing her feet into slippers. She hadn't realized she'd been considering that possibility, even subconsciously. But what, as Uncle Nick had said, did they really know about Cal?

Well, she knew now that he wasn't their prowler. And she knew that comfort had flooded through her at the sound of his voice.

Maybe it was better not to dwell on that. She grabbed a flashlight and went softly down the stairs. Should she have called the police? Maybe, but if she did, Grams would waken, would be subjected to that upset yet again.

Wait, as Cal had said. See what he found.

She huddled against the side door, gripping the flashlight, wishing for even the dubious comfort of Barney at this point. If Cal didn't appear soon, she'd have to do something.

A dripping face appeared outside the glass, and her

heart threatened to leap from her chest before she recognized Cal. She unlocked the door, trying to ignore the shaking of her fingers, and pulled him in out of the rain.

She switched on the hall light. Like her, Cal wore sweatpants and sweatshirt, but his were wet through.

"I'm sorry. You're soaked." Well, that wasn't very coherent. "Should I call the police?"

"No use." He shook his head, water spraying from his drenched hair. "He's not there now."

"If he ever was?" She knew her quick anger was just reaction to strain. "I saw him. He was there."

"Relax, I believe you. The lilac bushes were broken, the grass tamped down, as if he'd stood there for some time." His fingers closed over hers. They were wet and cold, but somehow they warmed her. "Tell me what you saw."

"A man. I can't say how tall he was—I was looking down from the upstairs window." She kept her voice low, not wanting to stir up the dog. "I didn't make out the face, but Cal—he was wearing Amish clothing."

He frowned. "Are you sure?"

"I know it doesn't make any sense, but I'm sure. Dark pants and jacket, white shirt, the hat—if it wasn't an Amishman, it was someone doing a good imitation."

"I'd almost rather believe that." His voice was troubled. "The Amish aren't exactly noted for producing prowlers. You never met a more law-abiding bunch."

She shivered. "That's not all. It—he—the figure seemed to be looking up at the window where I was standing. He raised his arm, as if he were shaking his fist at me. And if you tell me I was dreaming—"

"I don't doubt you." Without seeming to know he was doing it, Cal pulled her closer. "But we've got to think this through before we do anything. Can you imagine the repercussions if something like this hit the newspapers?"

"I hadn't thought of that, but I see what you mean." Like it or not, and they didn't, the Amish were newsworthy. A story like that could get out of control in hours. She glanced up the stairs. "I don't want Grams upset, and that would devastate her."

"Well, whoever he was, he's gone now." Cal brushed damp hair back from his brow. "Are you okay if we hold off making a decision until we can talk this over in the morning?"

She was insensibly comforted by the way he said *we.* Whatever came, she wasn't alone in this. "Yes, all right. After all, he didn't really do anything except lurk. The house is locked up securely."

"Good." He squeezed her hand. "I'll take another look around before I go back to the barn. We'll talk in the morning. Meantime, try to get some sleep, or your grandmother will want to know why your eyes are so heavy." He turned to go back out into the rain.

"Wait. Do you want an umbrella?"

"Why?" Cal paused on the threshold, his smile flashing. "I can't get any wetter than I already am. Good night. Lock the door."

"No chance I'll forget that."

He vanished almost at once into the darkness beyond the reach of the light. She locked the door, realizing that she was smiling.

Amazing. If anyone had told her fifteen minutes ago that she'd find anything to smile about tonight, she'd have said they were crazy.

Chapter 7

Cal frowned at the mug of coffee in his hand and then set it out of the way on the barn floor. He needed something to get his brain moving after the previous night's alarms, but caffeine wasn't doing the job.

He picked up a sanding block and knelt next to a reproduction of an old-fashioned dry sink, running the fine sandpaper along its grain. This was better than coffee for what ailed him.

What he really needed was to talk with Andrea, but he'd known better than to go to the inn first thing this morning. Katherine would be up and Emma already busy in the kitchen, making it impossible to have a private conversation. He'd have to wait until after their breakfast was over, at least.

He ran his hand along the curved edge of the dry sink's top. Smooth as silk—that was what he wanted.

Taking shortcuts at this stage would show up eventually in the finished product, ruining the piece for him.

Even the work didn't chase away his troubled thoughts, unfortunately. He couldn't stop chewing on the implications of what Andrea had seen. Or thought she'd seen.

A few days earlier, he might have been tempted to believe she was making up her tale of a prowler, just to convince her grandmother to sell. Now, he knew her better. Andrea wouldn't do that.

No, he didn't doubt that she'd seen someone, but was it beyond belief that the man, whoever he was, wasn't Amish? She'd seen a figure in dark clothes, but peering out into the storm from an upstairs window, she couldn't have seen all that much. Maybe her imagination had taken the prowler's dark clothing and filled in the rest.

Somehow he didn't relish the idea of bringing that up with her.

"Cal?"

He straightened at the sound of Andrea's voice, dismayed at the flood of pleasure he felt at the sight of her. She stood for a moment in a stripe of sunlight at the barn door.

"Come in. How are you? Nothing else happened, did it?"

She came toward him, the sneakers she wore making little sound on the wide planks of the barn floor. In jeans and a loose denim shirt worn over a white tee, she almost looked as if she belonged here.

"It was quiet enough," she said. "I didn't sleep much, though. I woke at every creak, and believe me, a house that old creaks a lot."

"How about some coffee?" He gestured toward the

pot that sat on a rough shelf against the wall. "It won't be as good as Emma's, but at least it's hot."

"None for me, thanks. Grams insisted on giving me three cups of herbal tea this morning, because I looked tired. I don't have room for coffee."

"She didn't ask any difficult questions, I hope." If she'd told her grandmother about what had happened…

Andrea shook her head. "No. And I didn't mention anything about last night." She ran her hand along the top of the dry sink, much as he had done, a wing of silky hair falling across her cheek as she looked down. "But I can't just ignore what happened."

"I know." He frowned, wondering if it were wise, or even possible, to keep her from voicing her suspicions. "Do you want to go to the police?"

"Depends upon what moment you ask me." Her smile flickered. "I spent my wakeful night going over and over it and changing my mind every thirty seconds or so."

He bent, picked up a couple of sanding blocks, and tossed one to her.

She caught it automatically. "What's this for?"

"Try it." He knelt, running his block along the side of the piece. "It's very soothing."

"Just what I need—to be soothed while intruders trample through Grams's yard and try to break in." But she sat down on the floor in front of the dry sink and began sanding lightly.

"Trample?" He raised an eyebrow.

"You know what I mean." She sanded for a moment longer, frowning. "He was there. He was watching the house."

"I know." He silenced the urge to tell her what he thought she should do. It was her decision, not his.

"You're right. This is soothing. How did you learn to do this? The furniture, I mean, not just sanding."

"My dad's father." His voice softened, as it always did at the thought of his grandfather. Whatever he knew about being a good man, as well as a good carpenter, came from him. "He figured everyone should know how to do something useful, just in case."

"He sounds like a wise man."

She glanced up at him, smiling. For an instant their faces were close—so close he could see the flecks of gold in those green eyes, mirroring the gold of her hair. So close he could feel the movement of her breath across his cheek.

Her eyes widened, and he heard the catch of her breath. He put the sanding block down with a hand that wasn't entirely steady and sat back, away from her. That was—well, unexpected. Not surprising that he found her attractive, but shocking in the strength of that pull toward her. And disturbing that she felt it, too.

Andrea looked down at the sandpaper in her hand. She cleared her throat. "Well, I have to make a decision about calling the police."

So they were going to ignore what had just happened. Maybe that was best.

"If you tell the police the person you saw was Amish—"

"I know. It will cause problems, problems for the community, problems for Grams. I don't want that. But I have to do something. I can't help wondering..." She looked at him again, eyes guarded. "What if it was Levi?"

"Levi." He had to adjust his perspective. "That didn't

occur to me. Do you have some reason for thinking that?"

She shook her head. "Only that I've seen him around the house. At one time, I'd have said I knew him, but not any longer. Does he ever come over here at night?"

"I've never seen him." Everything in him wanted to reject the idea. "Look, you know he's like a child—a gentle child. If it were Levi last night, he certainly didn't intend any harm. From what I've seen, his parents keep close tabs on him, so it's hard to believe he could have been wandering around after dark."

"Somebody was." She moved restlessly. "You mentioned there'd been some vandalism in the area. Could it have something to do with that?"

"I don't know. The incidents have been pretty harmless, as far as I've heard. Mailboxes knocked down. Somebody threw a bucket of purple paint at an Amish house. The police seem to think it's caused by teenagers looking for a little excitement. Nothing here was damaged, but maybe they're branching out into intimidation." He'd rather imagine it was random mischief, not deliberate malice toward the inn.

She nodded, frowning. "What do you think we should do?"

We. The simple pronoun stopped him for a moment. Andrea considered him an ally. She didn't want to make this decision alone, and she didn't want to worry her elderly grandmother, or Rachel, stuck in a wheelchair. So she'd turned to him.

All the resolutions he'd made about living a detached life here were on the line. Panic flickered. He couldn't make himself responsible for them.

But he'd put himself in this position. He'd interfered,

and he couldn't back away and say it was none of his concern just because his emotions were getting involved.

"It seems to me that the police are already doing about all they can do, under the circumstances. The fact that you saw a prowler again probably wouldn't change anything."

He was being drawn in. He was starting to think like a lawyer again. He didn't want to, but he couldn't help it.

"I suppose not, but doing nothing doesn't resolve the situation."

"Look, why don't you give it a day or two? Let me talk to some of my Amish friends, sound them out about it. See if there's any animosity toward the inn among the Amish community." Doing so might harm the delicate balance of his relationship with them, but the alternative was worse.

She studied him for a moment, as if weighing his sincerity. "All right." She got to her feet too quickly for him to reach out a helping hand. "If you'll do that, I'll talk to Uncle Nick. He may have some ideas, and I'm sure he'd keep anything I tell him in confidence. He wouldn't want to upset Grams."

Obviously Andrea wasn't one to leave everything in someone else's hands, but maybe she was right. Bendick did seem to have his finger in a lot of pies in the township.

"What about Levi? Do you want me to talk to Emma?"

"No. I'll see if I can bring it up without upsetting her." She shook her head. "I'm not looking forward to it."

"Better to talk to her than let the suspicion affect your attitude toward him."

"True enough. If I didn't say it before, thank you, Cal.

For last night, and for being willing to help. I appreciate it. And Grams would, if she knew."

"Any time."

He meant it, but he had to be careful. Andrea had broken through barriers he'd thought were completely secure, and trying to deny the attraction he felt was pointless.

But that attraction couldn't go anywhere. The life Andrea prized was the kind of life that had nearly destroyed his soul.

The gold lettering on the plate glass window jolted the cool facade Andrea had meant to maintain for this visit. Unger and Bendick, Real Estate and Insurance. She hadn't imagined that Grandfather's name would still be on the business.

It was a name that stood for something in this quiet country village. Uncle Nick probably hadn't been eager to give that up, and she couldn't blame him.

Grams had assured her that Uncle Nick would be in the office on a Saturday morning. Fortunately she hadn't asked why Andrea wanted to see him.

A bell tinkled when she opened the door. Clever of Uncle Nick to retain the old-fashioned flavor, even when he was dealing with visiting urbanites looking for a little piece of country to call their own. Or maybe especially then.

The woman behind the mission oak desk looked up inquiringly, and in an instant Andrea went from being the appreciative observer to being that ten-year-old trailing her grandfather around town. There was Betty Albertson, her grandfather's faithful secretary, peering at her over the half-glasses she wore at her desk.

Those half-glasses had fascinated Andrea. Betty wore them so far down her pointed nose that they seemed in constant danger of sliding right off, like a sled down Miller's Hill.

"Betty, how nice to see you. It's been a long time." Conventional words, giving her the moment she needed to remind herself that she was no longer ten, no longer interested in the stash of chocolate bars in Betty's top right desk drawer.

Sharp gray eyes now matched gray hair, pulled smoothly back into the same sort of French twist Betty had worn when her hair had been a mousy brown. For a moment she thought the secretary didn't recognize her, but then she smiled.

"Andrea Hampton. Land, it has been a while. You look as if life agrees with you."

Did she? With everything she valued turned upside down in the past few days, it hardly seemed likely.

"I see you're still running Unger and Bendick single-handedly."

The joke had always been that Betty knew more about the business than both partners combined. She'd been so fiercely loyal to Grandfather that it occasionally seemed she resented even the distraction of his family.

Betty's smile tightened. "Mr. Bendick offered to hire more help, but I prefer to handle things on my own."

She'd given offense, even though it hadn't been intended. "I'm sure no one could do it better. My grandfather often said you were worth more than a dozen assistants."

"Did he?" A faint flush warmed Betty's thin cheeks. "That was kind of him. He was always so thoughtful."

Betty had her own memories of Grandfather. "Is

Uncle Nick—Mr. Bendick—in? I'd like to see him for a moment."

Betty's gaze flicked toward the closed office door that bore his name, again in faded gold. "This isn't a good time. We get swamped on Saturdays. Why don't I ask him to stop by the house later?"

Andrea glanced around, half amused, half annoyed. "It doesn't look that busy right now. Surely he can spare me a few minutes."

Betty's lips pressed together, nostrils flaring, but then she mustered an unconvincing smile. "He's on the phone. If you want to wait, I'll try to slip you in when he finishes."

Plainly Betty had transferred the devotion she'd once had for Fredrick Unger to his junior partner. "I'll wait." She crossed the faded Oriental carpet to the row of wooden chairs against the far wall and sat.

Betty blinked, perhaps wondering if she'd gone too far. "Well, that's fine. I didn't mean anything, I'm sure."

"I won't take long, I promise."

She couldn't get into an argument with the woman, just because she was hyperprotective of her employer. If anything, she ought to feel sorry for Betty, leading such a narrow life. She probably didn't get out of Churchville from one year to the next. Andrea vaguely remembered an elderly mother that Betty looked after.

The schoolhouse clock on the wall above the desk ticked audibly. As a child, sitting on this same chair, legs swinging, she'd been mesmerized by the jerky movement of the hands. Photos surrounded the clock, recording events from the early days of Churchville. Grandfather at the ground breaking for the school, at the dedication of the bank, at some long-ago Fourth of July celebration.

The door to the inner office opened. Uncle Nick blinked and then hurried toward her, hands outstretched.

"Andrea, this is a surprise. Betty, why didn't you tell me Andrea was waiting?"

Betty slid the half-glasses down to look over them. "You were on the phone. And now you have an appointment to show the Barker place."

"I certainly have a few minutes to talk with Andrea."

"You know how interested those people are. You don't want to be late."

"Why not? They've kept me waiting at every appointment." He took Andrea's arm, winking at her once his back was turned to Betty. "We have time for a little chat."

He led her into his office and closed the door, then gave her a quick hug. "I'm sorry about that. The woman thinks I can't do a thing unless she reminds me."

"I don't want to mess up a sale."

He shook his head. "Pair of uptight yuppies who think they want a country place but don't like anything that's in their price range." He beamed at her. "I'm glad you stopped in for a visit before you head back to the city."

"As a matter of fact, I'm not going back for a while."

"Now, Andrea, don't tell me you let them talk you into doing something rash. Your job—"

"My job will wait. Right now my family needs me."

His dismayed expression was almost comical. "My dear, I'm sorry. Is your boss all right with your taking time off?"

She shrugged. "He's not happy, but I'm afraid it can't be helped." Her mind flickered to Cal, saying that maybe he'd learn to appreciate her more. "I have to stay, at least until the inn is up and running."

The elderly swivel chair creaked when he sank down in it. His eyes were troubled, and he ran his hand along his jaw.

"I wish we could find some other way of dealing with this."

"I appreciate your concern, Uncle Nick, but it's all right. Really." She took a breath. How to word this without alarming him or sending him running to Grams? "That's actually not what I came to talk to you about."

He blinked. "Is something wrong? Something else, I mean?"

"Not exactly. Well, you know about the prowler. We haven't had any damage, but it made me wonder if there's anyone who might have a grudge against the family."

"Against Katherine?" He sat upright, outrage in his voice. "Your grandmother is universally respected. You know that."

It was said with such vehemence that she couldn't doubt it was true of him. "Has there been anything—someone who thought Grandfather had treated him unfairly, or some dispute about property lines?"

He was already shaking his head. "Nothing at all. I'm sure the prowler was simply an isolated incident. Those security lights you put up should do the trick."

So he knew about the lights already. She'd forgotten how quickly the township grapevine worked.

"What about turning the house into a bed-and-breakfast? Have there been any ill feelings about that?"

"Mostly from Margaret Allen, maybe a few other old-timers who hate change, don't want to see any more tourists brought in." He shook his head. "They're fighting a losing battle on that one. But I'd say they're not the type to prowl around in the dark, especially Margaret."

He had a point. "She's more likely to bury a person under a pile of platitudes."

"That's our Margaret." He chuckled, then sobered again. "But I'm concerned about you. Your grandmother, dear woman that she is, doesn't understand the sacrifice she's asking you to make. Maybe I could hire someone to help out—"

"Thanks, Uncle Nick." She was touched by his kindness. "I appreciate that, but no."

"Really, my dear." He rose, coming back around the desk. "I want to help. It's the least I can do—"

The door opened and Betty marched in, holding out a briefcase. "Mr. Bendick, you must leave or you'll keep those people waiting." She sounded scandalized at the thought.

"Yes, yes, I'm going." He snatched the case and sent Andrea an apologetic look. "Think about what I said. I'll talk to you later."

She nodded. "I will. Thank you, Uncle Nick."

He hurried out, letting the front door slam behind him.

"He worries about your grandmother," Betty said, her voice almost accusing.

Several annoyed retorts occurred to her, but she suppressed them. "There's no need. I'm there with her, and Cal Burke has been very helpful."

"Well, he would be, wouldn't he?"

Andrea blinked. "What do you mean?"

"It's none of my business, of course." Betty patted the smooth twist of gray hair. "But I'm the one who typed the lease, so I can't help knowing, can I?"

She resisted the impulse to shake the woman. "Knowing what?"

"Why, about his lease on the barn. Mr. Bendick warned your grandmother, but she wouldn't listen."

She took a step toward Betty. "What?" she snapped.

"She's renting that barn to him at a ridiculously low price. Almost nothing. It worried Mr. Bendick something awful. Cal Burke is bound to help out. He doesn't want your grandmother to sell, because then he'd lose the nice deal he talked her into."

The lease clutched in one hand, Andrea charged toward the barn, anger fueling her rush. When she found Cal, he wasn't going to know what hit him. She held on to the anger, knowing at some level that if she let it slip, even more hurtful feelings would surface.

Betrayal. She'd already experienced enough betrayal in her life.

She hurried up the slope and shoved the heavy door aside. Her rush carried her several feet into the barn before she realized she was alone.

She stood for a moment, looking at the scattered pieces of furniture as if Cal might be hiding behind one of them. Nothing split the silence except her own labored breathing.

Instinct sent her outside again, where she looked around, frowning. The inn grounds and the surrounding farmland dozed in the Saturday-afternoon sunshine.

And already the anger was seeping away, leaving space for pain and regret. How could she have been so foolish as to trust the man? She knew better than to let herself be taken in by a plausible stranger, the way Grams undoubtedly had.

Maybe he was in the apartment he'd created for himself in the tack room. She followed the path around the corner of the barn. She'd find him and make him admit that he was taking advantage of her grandmother. If there was an explanation for this…

But there couldn't be. She stifled that notion. There could be no logical reason for Cal to have talked Grams into renting him the barn at what anyone would consider a token amount. No wonder Uncle Nick had been upset.

Upset didn't begin to cover it for her.

She rounded the corner and stopped. She'd been prepared to find the story-and-a-half tack room annex changed, but she hadn't expected this.

The rough-hewn door had been replaced by a paneled one with nine-pane beveled glass. A bow window curved out at the front of the building, with a flagstone path leading to the entry.

Irritation prickled along her skin. He'd probably talked Grams into paying for all this, creating a cozy nest for himself at someone else's expense.

Her feet flew over the stones, and she gave a peremptory rap on the door.

The door swung open before she had a chance to raise her hand for another knock.

Cal stood there, smiling. Welcoming.

"Good, you're here. How did you make out with Bendick?"

For a moment she could only stare at him. They'd become partners. She'd agreed to investigate with him.

Before she'd known he was a cheat.

She stalked inside. The old tack room had certainly been transformed. Wooden built-ins lined the walls on either side of a fieldstone fireplace. The wide plank floors were dotted with colorful Navajo rugs that contrasted with the solid Pennsylvania Dutch furniture. The open space was living room, dining room, and kitchen combined, with an eating bar separating the kitchen section. An open stairway led up to a loft that must be the bedroom.

Cal closed the door. "Do you like it?"

Anger danced along her nerves. "Yes. Did my grandmother pay for this?"

He blinked. Then his face tightened, brown eyes turning cold. "Maybe you should ask your grandmother that."

"I'm asking you." Small wonder Grams hadn't confided in her about this dubious rental. She'd have known how Andrea would react. If Grams planned to run the inn on these lines, she'd be bankrupt in a month.

Cal looked at her steadily. "You'd better tell me what this is about, Andrea. I'm not good at guessing games."

He leaned against the bar between kitchen and living room, elbows propped on it. The pose might have looked casual, if not for the muscle that twitched in his jaw, belying his outward calm.

"This." She thrust the lease at him, appalled to see that her hand was shaking. "How did you talk my grandmother into this? She might be naive about business, but surely she realized how ridiculous the rent is. And for both your home and your business—you really got a great deal, didn't you?"

He made no move to take the paper, but his hands curled into fists. "Did you talk to your grandmother?"

"I'm talking to you. The person who's cheating her." *The person who lied to me and made me let my guard down. The person I thought I could trust.*

Cal thrust himself away from the counter, taking a step toward her. "You don't believe that." He stopped, shaking his head. "My mistake. I guess you do."

"I was the one who made the mistake. I trusted you." She would not let her voice break. "How could you do this to an old woman?"

His face might have been carved from a block of wood. "That lease is between your grandmother and me. You don't come into it at all."

"My grandmother asked me to help her with her business."

He raised an eyebrow. "As far as I know, Katherine didn't sign a power of attorney, turning her affairs over to you. If she wants to talk to you about my rental, she will. Are you worried that she's squandering away your inheritance?"

Fury boiled over, threatening to scald anyone in its path. "I'm trying to protect my grandmother from people who would take advantage of her."

Like you, Cal. It wouldn't have been hard to get her to trust you. I did, and I'm a much tougher case than Grams. Something twisted and hurt under the anger.

"I see." Nothing changed in his expression, but he seemed suddenly more distant. "I can't help you, Andrea. The details of my lease are between me and Katherine."

"Anyone who knows the rent you're paying would know you're cheating her."

"That's for Katherine to decide. You're not the owner. And even if you were, you can't throw me out." He nodded toward the paper in her hand. "I have a lease, remember?"

She stared at him, baffled and furious. Then she turned and slammed her way out.

Chapter 8

"I don't know what you thought you were doing." The glare Grams directed at Andrea left no doubt about what Grams considered her actions. Interfering.

"I'm trying to help you. That's all." Andrea sat up a bit straighter. Being called onto the library carpet made her feel about eight.

"Going to my tenant behind my back is not helpful, Andrea Katherine."

When Grams resorted to using both names, the situation was serious. "I'm sorry, but I'm worried about you. If you'd let me know how bad the financial situation is—"

"You'd have told me I should sell the place." Grams finished the thought for her. Her face tightened, and she suddenly looked her age. "That's why I didn't tell you. I didn't want to argue about it."

That was more or less what Rachel had said, but how could Andrea keep silent when the people she loved best in the world seemed bent on the wrong course?

"Are you so sure selling wouldn't have been for the best?" She kept her tone soft.

Grams shook her head. "You're more like your grandfather than you want to admit. That's what he would have said, too, even though this place has been in his family for close to two hundred years."

Grams was right about one thing. She didn't care to be told she was like her grandfather.

If saving Unger House meant enough to Grams that she'd go against what she believed Grandfather would have wanted, then no argument of Andrea's would sway her.

"I've already agreed that I'll do all I can to help you. But if you want to involve me in the business, I have to understand what's going on. When Betty told me—"

"Betty!" Grams's nostrils flared. "What right does she have to talk about my concerns, I'd like to know."

"I'm sure she was just reflecting Uncle Nick's feelings." She shouldn't have mentioned Betty. Relations had always been strained between Grandfather's wife and his secretary.

"Nick is a good friend." Grams's face softened. "He worries too much, but he means well."

"I mean well, too, even if you think I'm going about it the wrong way."

"I know that." Grams's voice gentled a little. Maybe the storm was over, even if the problem wasn't resolved. "Rachel and I appreciate the fact that you're willing to stay here and help us."

"I want to get you on a good business basis, so that

you have a chance to succeed. As far as the rental is concerned..." She couldn't let it go without trying once more to show Grams that Cal was taking advantage of her. "The barn is yours to do as you like with, but I have to tell you that the rent you're charging is extremely low by current standards."

Grams was already shaking her head. "You don't understand."

"How can I, when you won't tell me about it?"

For a moment the situation hung in the balance. If her grandmother continued to treat her like a child who had to be protected from the facts, this would never work.

Finally Grams nodded. "I suppose you ought to know." She glanced toward the portrait over the fireplace. "When Cal approached me about renting the barn, I couldn't imagine how he'd live there. But he was willing to do all the work on the apartment himself. If you've seen it, you'll have to admit he's done a fine job, and he insisted on paying for everything that went into the renovation."

She'd misjudged him in that respect, at least. To her surprise, Andrea was relieved.

"He's certainly increased the value of the building," she admitted. "But even so, to lock yourself into a contract with that low a rent could be a problem." Cal's turning the lease against her still rankled.

"We agreed that as his business picked up, the rent would increase." Grams flushed, as if she found the discussion of money distasteful. "He insists on paying me more every month, more than he should. I don't want to feel as if I'm accepting charity."

No, Grams wouldn't like that feeling. She had always been the giver, not the recipient.

Andrea took a deep breath. "I'm sorry, Grams. I shouldn't have gone to Cal without talking to you about it first."

"No. You shouldn't have." Grams gave her the look that suggested Andrea's manners weren't up to what was expected of an Unger. "Now I think we'll both see Cal and apologize."

"Both…"

Words failed her. Grams proposed to lead her by the hand and make sure she apologized properly, the way she had when Andrea had left the farm gate open and the Zook cows had gotten out.

"Grams, I can handle this myself. It's my mistake."

Her grandmother stood, every inch the lady. "It was my error, as well, in not telling you. We'll both go."

Apologizing to Cal alone would have been embarrassing. Doing it with Grams looking on was humiliating. It didn't help to know that she deserved it.

If she kept herself busy enough, maybe she could forget that awkward scene with Cal. At least that's what Andrea had been telling herself since Grams left to spend the evening with Rachel at the hospital. Unfortunately, it didn't seem to be working.

She shoved away from the desk in the library, blinking as she tried to focus her eyes on something other than the computer screen. It was getting dark, and she hadn't bothered to turn on any lights.

She stretched, rubbing at the tension in the back of her neck. She'd started entering data for the inn into the desktop hours ago. As far as she could tell, neither Grams nor Rachel had touched the computer since they'd bought it, supposedly for the business, and that increased her worries over their chances for success. Running a B and B wasn't just about being a good cook or a good host. It was a business. She hadn't been kidding when she'd told Cal about Rachel's idea of a filing system.

And that brought her right back to Cal again. He'd been gracious when she'd apologized. Pleasant, even.

She frowned at Barney, who'd taken up residence on the hearth rug, seeming to transfer his allegiance to her when Grams wasn't around. "I'd be just as happy if he hadn't been so nice about it. You understand, don't you?"

Barney thumped his tail against the rug. The only thing he understood was that someone was talking to him. He rose, stretching very much as she had, and padded over to her. She patted the silky head that pressed against her leg.

"I'm being ridiculous, I suppose."

He didn't comment.

It had been a difficult situation, made worse by Grams accepting part of the responsibility for the misunderstanding. She'd actually admitted that she should have told Andrea the whole story.

That had hit her right in the heart. She didn't want her grandmother to feel any less in charge than she'd always been.

I don't know how to balance all this. The discovery that she was actually taking her problems to God startled her, but it felt right. Maybe Grams's quiet faith was having an impact on her. *Usually I think I can handle anything, but I can't. I need guidance. I have to know what I should do—about Grams, about the inn, even about Cal. Please guide me. Amen.*

Maybe it wasn't the most perfect of prayers, but the

admission that she couldn't see her way somehow made her feel a bit better.

And as for Cal having such an inside glimpse of their family dynamics—well, maybe she'd be lucky enough not to be alone with him for the next few days. Or ever.

Barney whined, his head coming up, and he let out a soft woof.

"What is it, boy? Do you hear Grams coming?" She peered out the side window, but there was no sign of a car turning into the drive.

The sheltie whined again, then paced to the door and nosed at it.

"You want to go out? I guess it has been a while." She opened the library door and then followed the dog through to the back hallway.

"Okay, out you go." The lights Cal had installed showed her the garden, the outbuildings, the barn, and beyond them, the dark, silent woods and pasture. All was quiet.

Barney bounded out, the screen door banging behind him. He'd be a few minutes at least, needing to investigate every shadow before coming back inside.

She leaned against the doorjamb, tiredness sinking in. Tomorrow was Sunday, and that meant church with Grams in the morning and an afternoon visit to Rachel. Probably she ought to try and find the rest of the receipts Rachel thought she had saved, just in case any of them required an explanation.

In typical Rachel fashion, the receipts had, her sister thought, been tucked away in one of Grandfather's ledgers, which she vaguely remembered putting on the top shelf of the closet which stored kitchen and dining room linens.

Of course. What a logical place to keep receipts they would need to produce come tax time, to say nothing of Grandfather's ledgers. Rachel hadn't inherited any of his organizational genes, that was clear. Obviously Andrea would either have to do the business taxes for them or hire someone locally who'd keep after them all year long.

She opened the closet, frowning at the creaking that came from the hinges. Sometimes it seemed everything in the house had its own sound, all of them together creating a symphony of creaks, cracks, whines and pops. Hopefully none of their guests would be the nervous sort.

The deep closet had shelves against its back wall, accessible only after she'd moved several metal pails, a corn broom and two mops. What the closet didn't have was a light, but the fixture in the hallway sent enough illumination to show her that there appeared to be a book of some sort on the top shelf, stuck between two roasting pans big enough to cook the largest turkey she could imagine. She'd need something to stand on in order to reach the shelf.

She propped the closet door open with one of the mops and retrieved a chair from the kitchen, glancing out the screen as she passed. No sign of Barney yet. She could only hope he hadn't found a rabbit to chase or worse, a skunk. She doubted they had enough tomato juice in the house to cope with that.

The very fact that she knew the remedy for a dog's encounter with a skunk gave her pause. That certainly wasn't part of her normal urban life. Since she'd been back in this house, all sorts of things were resurfacing from her early years.

Grasping the chair with both hands, she carried it into

the closet and climbed onto it. She reached up to find that her fingertips fell inches short of the top shelf. That was what came of having twelve-foot ceilings. How on earth had her sister gotten the book up there to begin with? And why did she think that a logical place to put it?

She could go in search of a stepladder, but maybe if she put her foot on one of the lower shelves, she could boost herself up enough to reach the book.

She wedged her toe between two stacks of table linens that someone, probably Emma, had stored carefully in plastic bags. Bracing her left hand against the wall, she stretched upward, groping with her right. Her fingertips brushed the soft leather cover of the ledger. Memory took her back to Grandfather's desk, sitting on a high stool next to him, watching as he entered figures in a neat row.

This is the proper way to do it, Drea. If I keep the records myself, then I know they're accurate.

She blinked, willing away the childhood memory, and stretched until her hand closed on the edge of the book. Victory in her grasp, she started to pull it down. The palm that was braced against the wall slipped, the chair wobbled, then tipped. In an instant she was falling, tangled helplessly in chair legs and sliding linens, landing with a thud that would probably leave a bruise on her hip.

A board creaked out in the hallway, separate from the clatter of her fall. Before she could look the door slammed shut, leaving her in total darkness.

Her breath caught, and she pressed her lips together. *Don't panic. It's all right. All you have to do is get up and open the door. If you could cope with being trapped in the car and shoved into the toolshed, you can cope with this.*

She untangled herself, willing her heart to stop pounding, and fumbled with sweat-slicked hands for a knob. And realized there was none on the inside of the door.

Be calm. You're all right. Grams will be home soon.

But another voice was drowning out the calm, reasonable adult. It came welling up from someplace deep inside her, erupting with all the violence of a child's terror.

"Let me out!" She pounded on the door, unable to hold back the fear she didn't understand. "Let me out! Someone help me! Help!"

The child inside was crying, hot, helpless tears. *Someone help me. Father, please, help me.*

Cal rounded the corner of the toolshed, his sneakers making little sound on the damp grass. He could see the garage now, illuminated by one of the lights he'd installed, with the door still standing open. Katherine and Andrea must have gone to the hospital to see Rachel.

He frowned absently, coming to a halt and gazing around, probing the shadows, searching for anything that was not as it should be. It would be best if he got back to his own place before they returned. He and Andrea had already butted heads too many times today.

He wasn't sure whether it had been worse to bear her accusations or to listen to her apology. At least when she'd been throwing her fury toward him, he'd had the shield of his righteous anger.

It was only afterward that he began to wonder just how righteous that feeling had been. The hard lessons of the past had driven him to God, but he suspected he still had a lot to learn about living the way God expected.

Andrea had at least been furious with him on behalf of someone else. His feelings had been motivated entirely by something much more personal. He'd thought they'd been on the road to becoming friends. Now it was clear they'd never be that, and disappointment had fueled his anger. Maybe he hadn't expressed it, but he'd felt it, and that was just as bad.

He'd turned to head back to the barn when he saw Barney dash across the garden toward the inn door. Odd. Katherine wouldn't leave the dog outside when the place was empty. How had he gotten out of a locked house?

"Barney!" He took a few steps along the path toward the patio. "What are you doing out here?"

He expected the dog to turn and run to him with his usual exuberant greeting. Instead Barney pawed at the door, ignoring his voice.

The back of his neck prickled. Something wasn't right here. Apprehension pushed him into a trot that covered the rest of the way to the house in seconds.

Even so, by the time he reached Barney, the dog was howling, pawing at the door frantically. Cal grabbed for the collar even as he realized that the noise he heard was more than just the dog.

Somewhere in the house, someone cried for help.

He yanked open the unlocked door, scrambling into the back hall and stumbling over the eager dog. "Barney—"

He shoved the animal out of his way. Barney skidded, claws scrabbling on the bare floor, and then launched his body at the narrow, paneled door of the hall closet.

Dog and door collided with a thud that echoed the

pounding from inside. Cal's pulse thudded so loudly in his ears that it took a second to isolate the voice.

Andrea—but an Andrea who was a far cry from the brisk, efficient woman he knew. She sounded terrified. If someone had hurt her…

"It's okay," he shouted. Anything to dispel that panicky note in her voice. "Andrea, it's okay. I'm here. I'll get you out."

"Hurry." Her voice sounded muffled, as if she'd clamped her hand over her mouth.

He grabbed the small knob that released the catch, turned it, and Andrea tumbled into his arms. She grasped him, her fingers digging into his shoulders, her breath coming in harsh gasps.

He'd sensed her claustrophobia when she'd been closed in the toolshed for seconds. Now—now she was in the grip of a full-blown attack, as terrified as if she'd been faced with death instead of closed-in darkness.

"It's okay." He put his arm around her, feeling the tremors that coursed through her body. "Come with me." He piloted her toward the library, switching on lights as they went, sensing that nothing could be too bright for her at the moment. "You're safe now. Tell me what happened. Did someone hurt you?"

Her hand went up to her mouth as if to hold back sobs. She took one ragged breath and then another, seeming to gain a bit more control with each step they took away from the closet. Barney danced around them, trying to push his way between their legs, making little throaty sounds that sounded sympathetic.

"I'm all right." Andrea probably had to force the words out, and he felt the tension that still gripped her body.

"You're fine," he soothed. He switched on the lamp

next to the sofa and eased her to a sitting position. She still gripped his hand tightly, so he sat down next to her.

Barney, balked of his clear intent to take that space, had to be content with putting his head in Andrea's lap.

Cal smoothed his fingers over hers. "Did someone push you? Attack you?" He thought of the dark figure she'd seen out in the rain, and his alarm ratcheted upward. He should search the house, but he couldn't leave her in this state.

"No, nothing like that." She wiped away tears with her fingers. "At least—" She hesitated. "I don't think anyone was there. Probably the door just slammed shut when I lost my balance."

The slight shading of doubt in her voice had all his senses on alert. "Did you see someone? Hear someone?"

"I didn't see anyone."

Andrea straightened, putting up one hand to rub the back of her neck, as if tension had taken up residence there. Her usually precise blond hair tumbled about a face that was paler than usual, and her jeans and white shirt were smudged with dust. None of that was typical of Andrea, but it was somehow endearing.

Focus, he reminded himself. "You didn't see anyone. Did you hear something then?"

She shrugged, attempting a smile that was a mere twitch of her facial muscles. "You know how old houses are. This place makes all sorts of sounds even when it's empty."

"And it makes noises when someone is there. Someone who shouldn't be." His tone was grim. The back door had been standing open. Who knew how many other entrances had been just as accessible?

"I heard a creak that I thought came from the hallway,

just before the door swung shut, but that doesn't mean anything. All the floors slant, and the door might swing shut on its own." She sounded as if she were trying to convince herself. "Besides, what could anyone gain by shutting me in a closet?"

Just saying the words put a tremor in her voice. The wave of protectiveness that swept over him startled him with its strength. He had no business feeling that way about Andrea.

He cleared his throat. "Maybe he wanted to keep you from seeing him. Or maybe—" Another, more disquieting thought hit him. "You're claustrophobic, aren't you? How many people know about that?"

"What do you mean?" Her fingers tightened, digging into his hand, and her voice rose. "Are you saying someone would do that deliberately to upset me?"

"Or to scare you off." He put his other hand over hers in a gesture of comfort and then frowned, groping for a rational thought that seemed to be lost in a sense of awareness of her.

"That's—that's ridiculous." But she didn't sound convinced.

"Look, Andrea, I'm beginning to think there's more going on here than we realize. First Rachel's accident, and then this business with the prowler—either the Hampton women are prey to a lot of bad luck all at once, or someone is willing to go to extremes to keep the inn from opening."

"Rachel." Her eyes darkened with fear as she zeroed in on the possibility of a threat to her sister. "But that was an accident. The police haven't found any evidence of anything else."

"I'm not trying to scare you." He raised a hand to

brush a strand of silky hair back from her face. His fingers lingered against the smooth skin of her cheek without his mind forming the intent.

"I'm not afraid." She attempted a smile that trembled on her lips. "In spite of the evidence to the contrary. But Grams, and Rachel—"

"I know. I don't like it, either." He wanted to wipe the worry from her face, but he wouldn't lie to her, pretending everything was all right when it so obviously wasn't. "Maybe I'm wrong. Maybe it's all a coincidence. But I don't like you being alone." Vulnerable, he wanted to add, but suspected she wouldn't appreciate it.

"I'm not alone. You're here. I appreciate—" She looked into his eyes and seemed to lose track of the rest of that sentence.

He understood. His rational thought processes had gone on vacation. All he could think was that she was very close, that her skin warmed to his touch, that he wanted to protect her, comfort her...

He closed the inches that separated them and found her lips. For an instant she held back, and then she leaned into the kiss, hands tightening on his arms, eyes closing. He drew her nearer, trying to deny the emotion that flooded through him, wiping out all his barricades in a rush of feeling.

"Andrea." He murmured her name against her lips, not trusting himself to say more. This shouldn't be happening, but it was. He'd probably regret it later, but now all he wanted was to hold her.

He'd told himself they couldn't be friends. Maybe they couldn't, but maybe they could be much more.

Chapter 9

Andrea wrapped her fingers around the coffee mug, absorbing its heat. The warmth generated by Cal's kiss had dissipated when he'd drawn back, looking as confused by what had happened as she was.

Maybe they'd both sensed the need to change the tempo a bit at that point. Cal had gone to search the house, leaving the dog with her. Barney had padded at her heels while she fixed coffee and carried a tray back to the library, apparently mindful of his duty to guard her. The journal, Rachel's receipts tucked inside, lay next to the computer, the innocent cause of her problems.

She stroked the sheltie's head. In spite of Cal's doubts about Barney's intelligence, the dog had seemed to know she was in trouble.

"Good boy," she told him. "If it hadn't been for you…" Well, she didn't want to think about that.

"If it hadn't been for Barney, you'd still have been all right." Cal came into the room as he spoke. "Your grandmother would have come home and found you soon, even if I hadn't heard the dog."

She knew he was trying to make her feel better, but she didn't want to think about what she'd have been like if she'd been closed in the closet all this time. Cal didn't understand the panic. No one did who hadn't experienced it.

"Did you find anything wrong anywhere?"

"No actual sign of an intruder, but there are far too many ways into a house this size." He frowned, looking as if he'd like to go around putting bars on the windows. "And I'm not saying that closet door couldn't have swung shut on its own, or even from the vibration when you fell, but it still seems pretty stable."

"Is that supposed to make me sleep well tonight?"

She watched as he took a mug, poured coffee and settled on the couch opposite her. She liked the neat economy of his movements.

"I'd put safety over a good night's sleep anytime." He looked toward the windows. "Your grandmother should be back soon, shouldn't she?"

She glanced at the grandfather clock in the corner and nodded. "I don't want her upset about this. It was just an accident. You agree?"

"Let's say I'm about eighty percent convinced of that. You're sure it wasn't a person you heard before you fell?"

He leaned toward her, propping his elbows on his well-worn jeans. As usual, he wore a flannel shirt, this time over a white tee, the sleeves folded back. Also as usual, his brown hair had fallen forward into his eyes.

"It was a creak. That's all. I told you—this house has

a language all its own. Surely if someone had been there, I'd have heard him running away."

An image popped into her mind—the large, dark figure she'd seen outlined by the lightning. Her fingers tightened on the mug. If he'd been in the house, he would have made more noise than a gentle creak.

"Well, maybe. Unless he was smart enough to slip away the minute he heard you fall."

"You searched the house. You didn't find any signs someone had gotten in," she pointed out.

Lines crinkled around his eyes. "Does that mean you trust me?"

"Yes." The word came out so quickly that the sureness of it startled her. Maybe tomorrow she'd be back to being suspicious of him, but at the moment she was just glad he was here.

"Well…good." He seemed a little taken aback by her quick response. "Have you given any more thought to what I asked you? Does anyone else around here, other than family, know about your claustrophobia?"

She shook her head, wanting to reject the possibility. "I don't know. I suppose someone could. The Zook family probably knew." Levi popped into her mind, and she pushed him out again. He wouldn't remember something like that. "It was a lot worse when I was a child. I don't even remember what triggered it the first time, so I must have been pretty young."

"It didn't start when you left here, then."

She blinked, surprised at his linking the two things. "No. Why would you think that?"

The light from the Tiffany lamp on the end table brought out gold flecks in his eyes. "It's just that I've gathered it was a pretty traumatic time for all of you."

"Has my grandmother talked about our leaving?" She asked the question carefully, not sure she wanted to hear the answer.

"Only in a general way, saying how much it grieved her when you left."

"It wasn't our choice." Her voice was tart with remembered pain. "The adults in our lives didn't give Rachel and Caro and me any say in what happened."

"They don't, do they? My folks split up when I was twelve, and I always had the feeling that what happened to me was an afterthought. Did your parents—"

She nodded, her throat tight. "Our dad left. Not that he'd been around all that much to begin with." She frowned, trying to look at the past as an adult, not as the child she'd been. "He kept losing jobs, and Mom—well, she couldn't cope. That was why we moved in here, I suppose. Our grandparents were the stable element in our lives."

"And then you lost them, too." Setting his mug aside, he reached across the space between them to take her hands, warming her more than the coffee had.

"My mother quarreled with Grandfather." She shook her head. "I'm not sure what it was all about—maybe about Daddy leaving. It all happened around the same time. I just remember a lot of shouting. And then Mom telling us we were going away, hustling us out of the house before we even had time to pack everything."

"Where did you go?"

She shrugged. "Where *didn't* we go is more like it. Mom never seemed able to settle in one place at a time. We moved constantly, usually one step ahead of the bill collectors."

Her hands were trembling. Silly to be so affected after all this time, but he grasped them tightly in his.

"I'm sorry," he said softly. "I shouldn't have brought it up."

"It's all right. We all grew up okay, in spite of it. And there was a trust fund from my grandparents to see us through college."

"Still, it can't have been easy, having your whole world change so quickly. Is your father a part of your life now?"

"No." Maybe it was odd that his absence didn't bother her more, but he'd never exactly been a hands-on father. "We haven't heard anything from him from that day to this."

"And your mother?"

"She died a couple of years ago. Driving under the influence, apparently. In Las Vegas." She pressed her lips together for a moment. "We hadn't seen much of her since we'd all been out on our own."

He moved his fingers over her hand, offering comfort. "Sounds as if your parents let the three of you down pretty badly."

She shook her head, the words seeming to press against her lips, demanding to be released. "It was Grandfather who let me down. Let us down, I mean. We counted on him. He could have stopped her. But he just stood and watched us leave and never said a word."

All the pain of that betrayal, held at bay over the years she'd been away, came sweeping back, threatening to drown her. That was why she so seldom came here, she knew it now. She didn't want to remember, and the memories were everywhere here.

"You really think your grandfather could have prevented what happened? Unless he was able to have her declared an unfit mother..."

She jerked her hands away. "I don't want to talk about it anymore." He didn't understand. Grandfather—he could do anything, couldn't he? Or was that a ten-year-old's view of the world?

Cal recaptured her hands. "I'm sorry," he said again. He brought her fingers to his lips so that she felt his breath with the words. "I wish I could make it better."

"Thank you." She whispered the words, shaken by the longing she felt to let him comfort her, to close the space between them and be in his arms again...

The sound of car wheels on gravel had her sitting up straight. She drew her hands from his, hoping he couldn't guess what her thoughts had been. She didn't know whether she was glad or sorry that Grams was home, ending this.

"Remember, not a word to Grams. About any of this."

He nodded. Then, too quickly for her to anticipate it, he leaned forward and touched her lips with his.

The organ was still playing behind them when Andrea and her grandmother stepped out into the May sunshine after worship. Andrea tucked her hand unobtrusively into Grams's arm as they went down the two shallow steps to the churchyard. She'd seen the sparkle of tears in Grams's eyes more than once during the service.

Actually, the minister's prayers for Rachel's recovery had made her own eyes damp. She'd expected to feel guilty, if anything, at going back to church after letting regular attendance slip out of her life over the past few years. Instead she'd felt welcomed, and not just by the congregation. The awareness of God's presence, growing in her heart since she'd returned, had intensified to the point that her heart seemed to swell. Grams had looked at her with a question in her eyes once or twice, as if she sensed what was happening.

"I see everyone still gathers out here after the service," she said as they reached the walk and moved away from the steps to allow others to come down. She wasn't ready yet to talk about this renewed sense of God in her life.

People clustered into small groups as they cleared the stairs, exchanging greetings, catching up on the news. A long folding table had been set up to one side, bearing pitchers of iced tea and lemonade. Several children had already started a game of tag among the tilted old gravestones. A few late tulips bloomed, bright red against gray markers.

Grams patted her hand. "Some things don't change. Once you and your sisters did that in your Sunday best."

"I remember. We didn't have any silly superstitions about cemeteries after playing here every Sunday."

The small church, built of the same stone as the inn, was almost completely surrounded by its graveyard, with burials dating back to the early 1700s. A low stone wall enclosed both church and churchyard. Even now, one little girl was emulating a tightrope walker on the top of it.

"Let me guess." Cal spoke from behind her, his low voice sending a pleasurable shiver down her spine. "You used to be the daring young girl walking on the wall."

"Whenever my grandmother wasn't looking." She turned toward him as Grams began talking to the pastor. "I didn't realize you attended church. Here, I mean."

"If you're not House Amish or Mennonite, this is where you worship in Churchville, isn't it?" He glanced toward her grandmother. "Katherine didn't suspect anything last night?" he asked softly.

"She didn't seem to, but it's hard to be sure. When we were kids, we thought she had eyes in the back of her head and an antenna that detected mischief."

"There was probably plenty, with three girls so close in age."

She smiled, shaking her head. "Fights, mostly, over who took what from whom. Caroline, our youngest sister, was such a good actress that she could convince almost anybody of anything. Except Grams, who always seemed to know the truth. I just hope her antenna wasn't working last night."

"She'd probably have said something, if so. She's not one to keep still where people she cares about are concerned."

She nodded, but as her gaze sought her grandmother's erect figure, the smile slipped away. Grams had changed since Grandfather's death, and she hadn't even noticed it. The strength they'd always counted on was still there, but it was muted now. Or maybe Rachel's accident had made her vulnerable.

"I see now how much this place means to her." She pitched her voice low, under the animated chatter that was going on all around them. "I don't want anything that's going on to affect that."

His hand brushed hers in a mute gesture of support. "You can't always protect people, even though you care about them."

She glanced up at him, ready to argue, but maybe he had a point. She'd protected her little sisters during those years under their mother's erratic care, but eventually they'd been on their own. The situation was reversed now with Grams. She'd always been the strong one, and now she had to be protected, preferably without her realization.

Cal raised an eyebrow, lips quirking slightly. "Not going to disagree?"

"I would, but I see one of your favorite people coming. I'm sure you'll want to talk to her."

"Not Margaret." The hunted look in his eyes amused her. "It'll be tough to keep a Sunday state of mind with Margaret spreading her version of good cheer around."

She couldn't respond, because Margaret was swooping down on them. *Swooping* actually seemed the right word—the floating handkerchief sleeves of her print dress fluttered like a butterfly's wings.

"Cal. And Andrea. How nice to see the two of you together. Again. So lovely when young people find each other." Margaret put one hand on Cal's arm, and Andrea suspected it took all of his manners to keep from pulling away.

"We weren't lost," he said shortly. "We were just talking about the inn."

In a way, she supposed they had been, since that was what concerned Grams most at the moment. "Cal's been helping us with some of the repairs," she said. To say nothing of rescuing her from dark closets.

"You are such a sweet boy, to help a neighbor who's in distress."

The expression on Cal's face at being called a sweet boy suggested she'd better intervene before he was reduced to rudeness.

"Just about everyone has been very helpful in getting the inn ready to open." Except Margaret, she supposed. "It's coming together very well."

"Is it?" Shrewdness glinted in Margaret's eyes for an instant. "I was under the impression you're nowhere near ready to open for Memorial Day weekend. Sad, to have to cancel those reservations. It doesn't give the impression of a truly professional establishment. I'd be glad to take those guests, but naturally I'm completely full for that weekend."

"I don't know what makes you think that, but we're not canceling any of our reservations." She certainly hoped that was true. "You'll be pleased to know that we expect to open on schedule."

Margaret's eyes narrowed. "That's delightful. Of course, everyone won't be as happy for you as I am. Still, one has to break eggs to make an omelet." She turned away, sleeves fluttering. "Excuse me. I must go and talk to the dear reverend about the strawberry festival."

Andrea managed to hold back words until the woman was out of earshot. "What did she mean?" she muttered. "Who won't be glad to see us open on time?"

Cal cupped her elbow with his hand. "I think your grandmother's ready to leave."

She planted her feet, frowning at him. "Answer the question, please."

A quick jerk of his hand pulled her close to him, and he lowered his head to speak so no one could hear. "A few of the old-timers don't like the idea of another inn opening, increasing the tourist traffic in town."

"Nick mentioned something about that, but he really made light of their attitude." So light, in fact, that she hadn't considered it since.

"Did he?" He was probably wondering why she hadn't said anything to him. "Well, one of those people has your grandmother cornered at the moment, so I think we'd better go to the rescue."

Grams was talking with Herbert Rush, an old friend of Grandfather's. Or rather, it looked as if he was talking at her—and not about something pleasant, to judge by the color of his face and the way his white eyebrows beetled over snapping blue eyes.

Andrea hurried over, sliding her hand through Grams's arm. "Are you about ready to leave, Grams?" She fought to produce a polite smile. "How are you, Mr. Rush?"

The elderly man transferred his glare to her. "How am I? I'm unhappy, that's how I am. The last thing this village needs is another thing to draw tourists. I wouldn't have believed it of your grandmother. Turning a fine old showplace like Unger House into a tourist trap. Someone should do something about that. Your grandfather must be turning over in his grave."

"On the contrary, I'm sure my grandfather is proud of my grandmother, as he always was." She pinned a smile in place. Grams wouldn't appreciate it if she allowed anger to erupt. She turned toward the gate, grateful for Cal's presence on Grams's other side.

Apparently this place wasn't as idyllic as she'd been thinking, and Grams was getting the full picture of its less appealing side.

He seemed to be making one excuse after another to walk over to the inn these days. Cal rounded the toolshed, checking the outbuildings automatically. Since sunset was still an hour away, he couldn't even tell himself that he was making his nightly rounds.

He wanted to see Andrea again. That was the truth

of it. A moment's sensible thought told him that pursuing a relationship with her was a huge mistake, but that didn't seem to be stopping him from finding a reason to be where he might see her.

Well, that wish was going to be disappointed, because a quick glance told him the garage was empty. She and Katherine hadn't returned from their visit to Rachel.

But someone else was around the place, judging by the late-model compact that sat on the verge of the drive. Frowning, he quickened his steps. Probably nothing, but with all the odd things happening lately, it didn't do to take anything for granted.

His muscles tightened. A woman was on the side porch, shading her eyes as she peered through the glass in the door. He shot forward.

"What are you doing?"

He reached the bottom of the steps as she spun around, her mouth forming a silent O of surprise.

"I—you startled me." She grasped the railing. "I'm looking for Andrea Hampton. I knocked, but no one answered."

"She's out just now." The adrenaline ebbed, leaving him feeling he'd been too aggressive. She was younger than he'd thought at first glance, probably no more than twenty-two or three. Blond hair in a stylish, layered cut, a trim suit that looked too dressy for a Sunday afternoon in Churchville, a pair of big brown eyes that fixed on him as if asking for help. "Can I do anything for you?"

She came down the three steps so that they stood facing one another, looking up at him as if he could solve all her problems. "Is she going to be back soon? Ms. Hampton, I mean." Then, seeming to feel something else was called for, she added, "I'm Julie Michaels, her assistant."

He couldn't help the way his eyebrows lifted. So Andrea's office was following her here. "Cal Burke." He wasn't sure what to do with the woman. Telling her to go away certainly wasn't an option, though the urge to do so was strong. "I'm not sure when—"

The sound of tires on gravel took the decision out of his hands. "Here she is now."

At the sight of them, Andrea pulled to a stop in front of the woman's car. She slid out, frowning a little.

He reached Katherine's door and opened it, his gaze on Andrea as she came around the car. "I spotted her looking in the window. Is she really your assistant?"

"She is." There was a note in her voice he couldn't quite define.

Then she walked quickly toward the young woman. "Julie. I'm surprised to see you here."

Surprised and not particularly welcoming, if he read her correctly. Now what was that about? None of his business, of course, but still… He helped Katherine out and closed the door.

"I stopped by to pick up the report."

Andrea's brows lifted. "I said I'd e-mail it in tomorrow. There was no need for you to come all this way."

"I was in the area anyway," she said. "I just thought it would be helpful. I didn't mean to be in the way." Her tone suggested a puppy that had received a swat instead of a pat.

"That was very thoughtful." Katherine stepped forward, holding out her hand. "I'm Andrea's grandmother, Katherine Unger." The glance she shot Andrea said that she was disappointed in her manners.

He was probably the only one who saw Andrea's lips tighten. "I'll get the file for you." She turned and went quickly into the house, leaving the three of them standing awkwardly.

Julie turned toward the patio, her hurt feelings, if that's what it had been, disappearing in a smile. "What a lovely place. You must be a wonderful gardener, Ms. Unger."

"I have a great deal of help. Come onto the patio where you can see the flowers."

He could go back to his workshop, but some instinct made him trail along behind them. Andrea hadn't expected this visit, and she didn't like it. Why?

"I'm sure Andrea must be a big help to you. It's great that she could take time off when you need her." Julie bent to touch the petals of a yellow rose that had just begun to open.

"Yes, yes, it is." Katherine's smile wavered a bit. "I don't know what I'd do without her at this time, with her sister in the hospital."

"I heard about the accident. I'm so sorry." The woman's words sounded sympathetic, but there was something watchful in those big eyes. "How long do you think you'll need to have Andrea stay?"

That seemed to be his cue. He spoke just as Katherine opened her mouth to respond. "Is that a Japanese beetle on the rosebush?"

Katherine turned away from the woman instantly, bending over to peer anxiously at the small leaves, brushing them with her fingers. "I don't see anything. Are you sure, Cal?"

He guided her a few steps away, keeping her focused on the flowers. "It was over here. I just caught a glimpse."

Knowing Katherine's devotion to her flowers, that

should keep her occupied for a few minutes. And off the subject of Andrea's departure. That hadn't been a casual query, and the idea of the woman trying to pump Katherine raised his hackles.

The back door swung open. Andrea strode toward them, a manila folder in her hand. She held it out to Julie.

"Here you are. Please ask Mr. Walker to call me if he has any questions."

"I will." She tucked the folder under her arm. "You have such a lovely home here, Ms. Unger. Thank you for letting me see your garden." She glanced wistfully toward the house.

He took Katherine's arm before she could issue an invitation to a tour. "Let me give you a hand up the steps. Emma sent one of the grandkids over to mention potato salad and cold ham for a late supper if you came home hungry."

"She spoils me." Katherine took his arm, leaning on it a bit more heavily than usual. "I guess I will go in, now. Goodbye, Ms. Michaels."

He shepherded her into the house and saw her settled in her favorite chair. When he got back outside, the Michaels woman was pulling out of the drive. Andrea sat on the stone wall at the edge of the patio, frowning.

"That wasn't exactly a disinterested call, was it?" He sat down next to her.

She glanced at him, eyebrows lifting. "What do you mean?"

"While you were inside, your assistant tried to pump your grandmother about how long you'd be away from work."

"I should have expected that." Her lips tightened. "Did she succeed?"

"I headed her off. How long has she been trying to look just like you?"

For an instant she stared at him, and then her face relaxed in a slight smile. "You don't miss much. Believe it or not, when I hired her, Julie was just out of college, with brown hair halfway down her back, glasses and a wardrobe that consisted of discount store polyester suits."

"She found a role model in you. I guess that's natural enough."

"At first it was flattering. It took me a while to realize that she didn't just want to emulate my style of clothing. She wants my job. And she sees my absence from the office as her golden opportunity to step right into my shoes."

"Your boss wouldn't be that stupid, would he?"

She shrugged, eyes worried. "The more days I'm gone, the easier it will be for her. If I stay too long, he may just decide he can do without me altogether." Her fingers clenched on her knees. "I can't let that happen. I can't lose everything I've worked for."

Something twisted inside him. She'd go, just like that. It was what he'd thought all along, but knowing he'd been right about her didn't make him feel any better.

"So that's it. Is your job really more important to you than your family?"

She swung toward him, anger sweeping the anxiety from her face. "I don't think you have the right to ask me that."

Matching anger rose. "Why? Because I'm an interfering outsider?"

"No." Green eyes darkened. "Because you expect me to spill my feelings and share my decisions when you're not willing to tell me a single thing about you."

Chapter 10

She shouldn't have said that. Andrea wanted to refute the words, to deny that she cared in the least about his secrets. But it was already too late. Whatever she did or said now, Cal would know that the imbalance in their relationship mattered to her.

She could feel the tension in him through the inches that separated them, could sense the pressure to shoot to his feet and walk away.

But he didn't. He sat, staring down at the edging stones along the patio, where the setting sun cast wavering shadows from the branches above. His profile was stern, the planes of his face looking as if they'd been carved from one of the planks of wood he used.

Doubt assailed her. Whatever it was that made him look that way—did she really want to know? She sensed that if he told her, that truth could change their relationship in incalculable ways.

He moved slightly, not looking at her—just the slightest shrug, as if he tried to ease the tension from his shoulders.

"You told me once I had too much of a corporate mind-set to be just a carpenter. Remember that?"

"Yes." *I don't want to know.* But she did. She did.

"I was a lawyer." He grimaced slightly. "Guess I still am, in a way, but I'll never practice again."

That was her cue to ask why, but she wasn't ready for that. She settled for an easier question. "Where? Not around here."

"Seattle." He leaned back, bracing his hands on the wall. The pose could have looked relaxed, but it didn't. "You wouldn't know the firm, but it's one of the big guns there."

"Prestigious." Her mind grappled to reconcile the informal country carpenter with a big-city lawyer. Difficult, but she'd always known there was something.

"You could say that. When I landed the position, I knew I had it made. Straight to the big leagues—not bad for an ordinary middle-class kid who didn't even know which fork to use." A thread of bitterness ran through the words. He shot her a sideways glance that questioned. "Can you understand how overwhelming that could be?"

"I think so." Cal had been young, ambitious, intelligent, and he'd gotten the break that ensured his future. She of all people knew what that felt like. "But something went wrong."

His hands clenched against the stone, the knuckles whitening. "Not for a long time. I threw everything into the job, and it paid off. I was on the fast track to partnership, and nothing else mattered."

He was circling the thing that caused him pain, getting closer and closer. She sensed it, and wanted, like a coward, to close her ears, but she couldn't.

"The senior partner called me in. Assigned me to the case of my career. One of our biggest clients was involved in a child custody dispute with his ex-wife. I was just the sort of aggressive bulldog he wanted to represent him. Win, and opportunities would open to me that I couldn't have imagined."

"You accepted." Of course he had. He wouldn't have evaded that challenge, any more than she would.

"Sure. I threw myself into the case, determined to do the best job any attorney could." He looked at her then, his brown eyes very dark. "I trusted the client. You have to believe that."

She nodded, throat tight. She thought she saw where this was going now, and already his tension infected her, so that her hands pressed tight against the stone, too.

He shrugged, mouth twisting. "I did a great job. Lived up to everyone's expectations. Demolished the opposition and won the case." He was silent for a moment, as if he had to steel himself to say the next thing. "Then I found out that my client had been lying. He really was molesting his six-year-old daughter."

She'd been prepared for it, she'd thought, but it still hit her like a blow to the heart. "The little girl—"

Dear Lord, could anything be worse?

"Yes. The child I gave back to her father."

"It wasn't just you," she said quickly. "It was a judge's decision, surely. And the mother must have had legal representation."

"I told myself that. All the arguments—that it wasn't just my responsibility, that I had a duty to represent my client, that our legal system is adversarial and everyone deserves representation. It didn't change anything. The bottom line was still the same."

"What did you do?" He'd have done something. She knew that about him.

"Went to the senior partner. He told me to forget it. I'd done my job, and it was out of my hands."

"You couldn't."

"No. Couldn't ignore it. Couldn't go to the mother without putting the whole firm in jeopardy. So I did the only thing open to me. I went to the client and told him either he relinquished custody to his ex-wife, or I blew the whistle on him. It would have meant disbarment or worse, but I'd do it."

He took a deep breath, and she had the sense he hadn't breathed in a long time. She hadn't, either.

"Did it work?"

He nodded. "Guess I was convincing enough, especially when I resigned from the firm." His voice roughened. "I saw the child back into her mother's care, but God alone knows how much damage was done to her in the meantime."

That was the guilt he carried, then. That was why he lived the way he did.

"Cal, you did everything you could. He was the criminal, not you."

He grimaced. "Nice of you to defend me. I spent months trying to tell myself that, until finally God forced me to face the truth. I'd been so ambitious, so determined to succeed, that I'd let myself get sucked into a life that didn't take into account any of the important things, like faith, honesty, other human beings. I had to stop making excuses before I could repent and begin again."

That's what he was doing here, then. Starting over.

Looking for peace in this quiet place where values still applied.

"You did the right thing." Maybe her opinion didn't matter, but she had to say it. She met his gaze. "You couldn't have done anything else."

Something in his eyes acknowledged her words. He didn't speak. They didn't touch. But they were closer than if they'd been in each other's arms. She seemed to be aware of everything about him—of every cell in his body, of the blood coursing through his veins.

She took a breath, letting the realization crystallize in her mind. She cared about him, far more than she'd known. She admired him more than she could say.

But what he'd just told her had shut out any possibility of a relationship between them, because the life she longed to keep was the very one he'd never go back to.

Emma, going up the attic steps ahead of Andrea, pushed the door open, letting a shaft of sunlight fall on the rough wooden stairs. Rough, but not dusty, Andrea noticed. Obviously Emma's cleaning fanaticism extended even to the attics of the old house.

"All of the quilts are packed away in trunks," Emma said. "It is good that they'll be useful again."

"I just hope they're still in decent shape after being in storage for so long." She emerged into the attic, which stretched out into the shadowy distance, marked by the looming shapes of discarded furniture.

Lots and lots of furniture. Cal had said the place was packed to the rafters, and he was right. Her unpracticed eye identified a dining room set that surely wasn't genuine Duncan Phyfe, was it?

Emma, weaving her way through odd pieces of furniture, let out an audible sniff. "I put them away proper. They'll just need a bit of airing, that's all."

If Emma had done it, of course it would have been done properly. She was the one who'd suggested the quilts when Andrea and Grams had been debating about drapes and bedcovers for the guest rooms.

"The English will like having Amish-made quilts in the rooms," she'd said matter-of-factly.

She was right. Their guests would come to Lancaster County to see the Amish, who ironically only wanted to be left alone, and they would be thrilled at the idea. So she and Emma were on a hunting expedition in the attic for quilts and anything else that would give the guest rooms a unique touch.

Concentrating on the decorating just might keep her mind from straying back, again and again, to that conversation with Cal the previous day. On second thought, nothing was strong enough to do that.

Cal. He'd wrung her heart with his story, and in the dark silence of the night, she'd found herself filling in all the things he hadn't said.

He'd given up everything—his career, his future, his friends—because it was the right thing to do. Plenty of people would have rationalized away their responsibility in the situation, but not Cal. He'd taken on even more than his share, and now seemed content that it was what God expected of him.

She approached that thought cautiously. Somehow it had never occurred to her, even when she was attending church regularly, that God might have a claim on one's business life. That God might require sacrifice, on occasion. That was an uncomfortable idea, but once planted, it didn't seem amenable to being dismissed.

Emma knelt in front of a carved wooden dower chest, one of several lined up near the window. Andrea hurried to join her, thinking that her jeans were more appropriate to kneeling on the wide-planked floor than Emma's dress.

Concentrate on the task at hand. The practical one was to choose the quilts for the bedrooms. The unspoken one was to use this opportunity to talk to Emma about Levi, to try and get a sense of whether he might have been the dark figure she'd seen the night of the storm.

Leave the theological considerations for later. And any thought of her feelings for Cal for later still.

Emma lifted the chest lid, exposing bundles wrapped in muslin sheets. She took out the first one, unwrapping it. Andrea grasped the sheet and spread it out so that the quilt wouldn't touch the floor.

"Squares in Bars," Emma said, naming the pattern as she unfolded it. "My mother made many quilts for your grandmother. This was one of hers."

Andrea's breath caught as the colors, rich and saturated, glowed like jewels in the sun streaming in the many-paned attic window. The quilt was bordered in a deep forest-green, with the squares done in the blues, maroons, pinks, purples and mauves of Amish clothing.

"It's beautiful." Drawn to touch, she stroked the colors. "Your mother was an artist."

Emma shook her head. "Just usual work. She was quick with the needle, I remember."

That was the closest thing to pride she'd ever heard from Emma.

"Here is one that belongs in your room." Emma pulled back the sheet on the second quilt. "Do you remember?"

Remember? She couldn't speak as the pattern came into view, myriads of diamonds expanding from the center in vivid and unexpected bursts of color. She touched it gently. How many nights had she fallen asleep trying to count the number of diamonds in the quilt?

"I remember," she said softly, her throat going tight. "Your mother made this one, too, didn't she?"

Emma nodded, her plain face softening a little at Andrea's reaction. "Sunshine and Shadow. It was her favorite pattern."

"Is that what it's called? I don't think I ever knew. I can see why—the alternating bands of dark and light are like the bands of sunlight and shadow made by the rails of a fence."

Emma traced a line of dark patches. "It's the pattern of life. Sometimes sun, sometimes shadow. Like Scripture says, 'To everything there is a season, and a time to every purpose under Heaven.' But always God is with us."

The words squeezed her heart. Would Emma consider Levi one of the dark bands? She never seemed to show disappointment or sorrow with him. Maybe this was the moment to ask, but Andrea couldn't seem to force the words out.

"I should put it in a guest room, though, not keep it for myself." But her hands clung to the quilt. Or maybe to the memory of how safe she'd felt, sleeping under it.

Emma shook her head in a decided way. "Your grandmother ordered it from my mother just for you, when she knew you were coming to live here. It made her so happy to fix that room up for you, and how she smiled when it was all finished."

The image came clear in her mind, even from those few words. A younger Emma, a younger Grams, spreading the quilt on her bed, Grams's face lit with pleasure.

"Those were happy times, when we were here," she said, hoping her voice didn't sound as choked as it felt.

"Yes." Emma seemed to be looking back, too. "It was good, all of you children together, those days when the house was so full. We are in the *daadi haus,* now, Eli and Levi and me, and Samuel and his family have the farmhouse."

Andrea sat back on her heels, her arms filled with the quilt. "Does it grieve you, that Levi won't have a family of his own?"

Emma considered for a moment. "No, not grieve. He is as God chose to make him. I accept that as God's will."

The question she had to ask stuck in her throat, and she pushed it out. "I thought I saw Levi one night from my window. Does he go out after dark by himself?"

"No." The expression on Emma's face couldn't be disguised. Fear. Stark, unreasoning fear filled her face before she bent over the chest, hiding it. "No." Her voice was muffled. "Levi does not go out after nightfall. It would not be right."

Something cold closed around Andrea's heart. The unthinkable had happened. Emma was lying to her.

Cal walked into the hallway of the inn from the kitchen and paused, looking around. He hadn't been in since the painters finished, and he let out a low whistle. Katherine should be pleased. The Three Sisters Inn was a showplace, all right, with the parlors restored to their former grandeur. He might not know much about decorating, but he knew elegant when he saw it.

He put his hand on the newel post, sturdy now since he'd finished the repairs. Emma had said that Andrea needed some help moving things up in the guest rooms. He couldn't very well say no, but he wouldn't mind a little more time elapsing before seeing her again.

He'd told her things he hadn't told anyone else. He'd like to say he didn't know why, but that wouldn't be true. He knew. He cared about her. That was why.

It wouldn't go anywhere, that caring, and she knew that as well as he did. They were too different, and the life she prized was one that he'd never return to.

He started up the stairs. Well, she'd probably be as eager as he was to restore some barriers between them.

He reached the open center hallway on the second floor and glanced around. The doors stood open to the guest rooms—four on this floor, three more upstairs. Andrea was nowhere to be seen, so he went on up the narrower staircase to the third floor.

The rooms here were smaller and didn't seem quite finished. It looked as if Andrea had been putting most of her efforts into the second floor.

A loud thud sounded somewhere over his head, startling him. He yanked open the door to the attic stairway. "Andrea?" He bolted up the stairs.

"I'm all right." Her voice reassured him as he opened the second door at the top of the stairs.

"Good thing. I thought that was you. What are you trying to do?" He picked his way through pieces of furniture to where she stood.

"I want to take this stand down to the blue bedroom." She tugged at the recalcitrant piece that lay fallen on its side, obviously the thud he'd heard. "It's heavier than it looks."

"It's solid mahogany." He bent to shift it upright, and then took a step back, looking at it. "Nice piece. What's that?" Something had fallen out when the door on the front of the stand swung open.

Andrea picked up several oversize green books. "Grandfather's ledgers." She dusted them off with the tail of her pale blue shirt and flipped one open. "Goodness, this dates back to before I was born."

"Seems like a funny place to store them."

She wrinkled her nose. "Rachel, getting the place ready to turn into an inn. Things that were in her way got stuck into the most unimaginable places. We really should do some serious sorting and organizing. These ledgers should be kept for their part in Unger house history, if nothing else."

She bent over the book. For a moment she was engrossed in her find, and he could watch her as closely as he wanted. With her blond hair pulled back in a ponytail and a streak of dirt on her cheek, she didn't look much like the sleek urban professional.

She glanced up, catching his grin before he could erase it. "What's funny?"

"Just thinking you look a little different, that's all."

"You try rummaging through this attic without getting dirty, in spite of Emma's ferocious cleaning," she said. "You certainly were right about this place. Grams could start selling things off to an antiques dealer and fund the inn for the foreseeable future."

"Your grandmother mentioned some interest from one of the local antiques dealers, but she's reluctant to part with anything. Or maybe the prospect of sorting seems overwhelming. Are you ready to start an inventory?"

"Don't tempt me." She glanced around as if she'd like

to do just that. "You wouldn't believe the stash of handmade quilts Emma and I found up here this morning."

Any potential embarrassment had evaporated in the face of Andrea's calm attitude. She'd found her way back to an easy friendliness, and that was for the best.

"Something you can use, I take it?"

She nodded, but the smile slid from her face. "I had a chance to sound her out about Levi. She insists that he's never out alone at night, so he couldn't be the person I saw."

"Did you believe her?"

She looked at him, distress filling her eyes. "I've known her most of my life. I'd have said she'd never lie. But no, I didn't believe her."

Her voice shook a little on the words, and he knew how much it hurt her.

"I'm sorry. Look, it may not mean anything. If it was Levi, he hasn't come back. Nothing's happened for a couple of days. Whoever he was, our prowler seems to be scared off."

She nodded. "And now that I've mentioned it, I'm sure Emma will make sure that Levi doesn't do any late-night wandering."

"Right." It was worth agreeing to see the concern fade from her eyes. He just hoped they were right and the prowler was a thing of the past.

He seized the stand. "Well, shall we get this downstairs?"

"Yes, thanks. I appreciate the help. Rachel's coming home in a couple of days, and the opening is in less than a week." She tried to take the other side, but he pulled it away from her.

"I've got it. Just do the doors for me."

"Macho," she said, teasing, and went to open the door.

He muscled the stand down the stairs and around the bend at the bottom. Andrea closed the door while he leaned against the wall, trying not to breathe hard.

"Let's leave it here until I have a chance to clean it."

He nodded and started down the next flight of stairs. "Anytime you want heavy moving done, you know who to call."

She followed him. "But—did you want something, before I waylaid you with the stand?"

"Emma sent me upstairs. Guess she thought you could use an extra hand."

"My thanks to both of you." She paused as they approached the landing. "That sounded like the side door." She passed him and hurried on down the stairs.

When they reached the bottom, no one was there. She glanced into the library. "Margaret." She didn't sound especially welcoming. He couldn't say he blamed her.

Margaret scurried across the room, holding out an armload of peonies. "I just brought these in for your sister. I hope you don't mind—I thought they might cheer her long recuperation. Hello, Cal. You're here again, I see."

He nodded. It was probably best to ignore the comment.

"Of course I don't mind." Andrea took the flowers. "But why did you come in the side? Wasn't the front door open?"

"I didn't." Margaret looked surprised. "I came in the front."

He'd have said the sound had been from the side door, too. Odd.

There was a rap at the front door, and James Bendick popped his head in. "Andrea—oh, there you are. And Margaret." He came in, holding a bouquet of pink roses. "I heard Rachel is coming home, so I brought her these, but someone beat me to it. Margaret, those must be straight from your beautiful borders."

Margaret batted her eyes at him. "You're such a flatterer, James."

"This was sweet of you, Uncle Nick." Andrea took the flowers, putting the ledgers down on the drop leaf table in the hallway to do so.

Bendick seemed to be determined to ignore him. Perversely, Cal leaned against the newel post, wondering how long it would take for the man to acknowledge his presence.

"Those look like some of your grandfather's old ledgers." Bendick flipped one open. "Dating back to the Dark Ages, I see."

"Cal and I found them in the attic. I thought Grams might enjoy seeing them."

Having Cal forced on his attention, Bendick nodded. "Burke. Helping out, are you?"

"Just doing the heavy moving." Cal pushed away from the post. "I'll be going, Andrea. Give me a call if you need anything else brought down."

"I will. And thank you, Cal."

If her smile was anything to go by, Andrea must have bought his suggestion that they'd seen the last of their prowler. He just hoped he was right.

He went quickly past the parlors to the side door, reached for it, and then stopped.

The side door was the only one where someone entering wasn't likely to be seen, either from the kitchen or the library. It had been locked when he'd come over. He'd tried it first before entering through the kitchen.

Now the door stood ajar. Someone had come in. Or gone out.

Chapter 11

Andrea sank down in a kitchen chair, grateful for the mug of coffee Emma set in front of her. The morning was only half over, but she'd been working nonstop. It was time to take a break.

Grams sat at the end of the table with her usual cup of tea. "Do you think the bedroom for Rachel is all right? I hate the idea of putting her in the maid's room."

"It's fine," she said quickly, before Grams could get the idea of making a change after all the work they'd already done to prepare a ground floor room for Rachel's homecoming. "She has to be on this floor because of the wheelchair, and that room is perfect. It has its own bath."

"She will be close to the kitchen," Emma added, stirring something in the large yellow mixing bowl. "She will like that, she will."

Obviously Emma was on her side in this. Neither of them wanted to start rearranging furniture at this point.

"Once she's home, we can see if there's anything else we can do to make her more comfortable," Andrea pointed out.

"I suppose you're right." Grams still looked a bit doubtful, probably over the idea of a daughter of the house being relegated to the maid's room. Rachel had certainly lived in worse when she was in culinary school, but Grams wouldn't want to hear that.

"What are you making, Emma?" A change of subject was in order.

"Rachel's favorite cake. Banana walnut." She emptied a cup of walnuts into the mixture. "Black walnuts from our own tree will make it extra good."

She inhaled the scent of bananas and walnuts. "Smells wonderful. I'd best stay away while it's baking, or I might be tempted to get into it before Rach gets home tomorrow."

Rachel home tomorrow, and the grand opening on the weekend. That would go well—it had to. Of course it would be a shame that Rachel couldn't make her special breakfasts, but Emma would serve hearty Amish meals instead and the guests would be delighted.

And once that was over, she could make plans to get back to work. They would need more help after she left, of course, but Emma's daughter-in-law seemed eager for the work, and she'd pay the salary herself, if necessary.

She glanced at Grams, wondering how she'd feel if Andrea inquired more closely into her finances. She'd opened up a little, but Andrea still didn't feel she had a good handle on how secure Grams was.

And then there was the other regret. Cal. Her mind drifted toward the night they'd kissed, and she pulled it firmly back. There was no sense in thinking about what might have been. They both recognized the attraction and the caring, but the differences between them were just too great.

Still, she couldn't ignore that sense of loss.

"I'm just relieved we've had no further problems with prowlers," Grams said. "I'd hate to have our guests upset. Those lights were a fine idea."

Grams didn't know, of course, about the other incidents, and Andrea had no intention of telling her. There were too many possibilities for troublemakers—Levi, sneak thieves, teenagers intent on vandalism, even the holdouts in the community who were opposed to the decision to open the inn. It didn't really matter who it was, as long as it stopped.

"Andrea?" Grams was looking at her questioningly.

"Yes, I'm sure you're right. There's nothing more to worry about."

Grams reached across the table to touch her hand lightly. "Thanks to you. I don't know what we'd have done without you."

Andrea clasped her grandmother's hand, the fragility of fine bones under the skin making her aware again that Grams needed taking care of. "I loved doing it."

"You have so much business sense." Grams's eyes grew misty. "Just like your grandfather."

She wasn't sure she wanted to be compared to her grandfather, but she knew that to Grams it was a high compliment. "Thank you."

"I'm thinking it's time I turned my business affairs over to you. Nick has been very helpful, of course, but he's not family. You'll do it, won't you?"

For a moment she couldn't speak. If she'd needed

anything to assure her that Grams thought of her as a competent adult, this would do it.

"Of course I will." She blinked back surprising moisture in her eyes. "I'd be honored."

"That is good." Emma used a spatula to get the last bit of batter into the pan and then smoothed the surface with a practiced swirl. "'There is a time to every purpose under Heaven.'" She quoted again the words she'd said earlier, and they seemed to resonate. "A time to turn things over to the younger generation. Eli and me, we still have plenty to do, but now it's our son's turn to manage."

"The Amish know how to do it right," Grams said, smiling. "They build the *daadi haus* for the older couple and turn the farm over to the next generation. Everyone has a role to fill."

"Ja." Emma carried the oblong pan over to the old gas range that took up half of one wall. "It is good to know where you belong."

She bent over, cake pan in one hand, and pulled open the oven door with the other.

There was a loud whooshing sound. Before Andrea could move, flames shot out of the oven, right in Emma's face.

Cal sat beside Andrea on the patio wall, waiting. The paramedics were in the kitchen with Emma. So was her husband, Eli. He and Andrea had been relegated to the outside as unnecessary.

Levi stood next to the gray buggy that was pulled up in the driveway. He'd buried his face in the horse's mane, and once in a while his shoulders shook.

"Do you think I should attempt to comfort him?" Andrea said softly.

He shook his head. "I tried, just before you came out. It seemed to make him worse, so I gave up. He'll be all right as soon as he knows his mother is fine."

"Is she?" Andrea's lips trembled, and she pressed them together in a firm line.

He covered her hand with his where it lay on the stone wall between them, and the irrelevant thought passed through his mind that when she was gone, he wouldn't be able to look at this wall in the same way.

"I'm sure she will be." He hoped he sounded positive.

Her fingers moved slightly under his. "You didn't see. It was awful. Thank goodness Grams knew what to do. She had a wet towel on Emma's face before I'd even figured out what happened."

"I don't suppose you ever saw a gas oven blow out. She probably has. It used to be a fairly common accident, years ago. Since most of the Amish cook with gas, it still happens—did while I was staying out at the Zimmerman place, but luckily no one was hurt."

What about this time? He wasn't sure what he thought, not yet. He didn't want to believe someone had tampered with the stove, but it didn't do to take anything for granted.

"Tell me what happened."

Andrea's face tightened. "I don't want to go over it again."

"I don't suppose you do, but we have to figure out what caused this."

Her eyes met his, startled. "You think it wasn't an accident?"

"I don't know what I think, yet. That's why I want to

ask you a few questions." He was surprised to hear that lawyer's voice coming out of his mouth.

She took a breath, seeming to compose herself. "Emma was baking a cake. For Rachel's homecoming. I guess she'd been preheating the oven. Yes, I'm sure she had, because I remember seeing her turn it on." She shrugged. "There isn't anything else to tell. She opened the oven door to put the cake in, and the flames came out in her face." She shivered. "I hate to sound stupid, but what made it do that?"

"The pilot light was blown out—it had to be. The gas built up in the oven, and when the door was opened, that was all it took to ignite."

"It could have happened accidentally." She sounded as if she were trying to convince herself.

"I suppose so," he agreed. "When was the last time the oven was used?"

"Last night—no, I take that back, we didn't use it last night. It would have been in the morning yesterday, when Emma baked."

Something tingled at the back of his mind. "Why did you say last night?"

"Well, it's silly, really. Grams and I were laughing about it. Emma insists on leaving something cooked for our supper, and then I put it in the oven to heat. And she always asks, so I don't even dare to heat it in the microwave. Emma doesn't hold with microwaves."

"It might have been safer, this time."

She nodded. "Anyway, neither of us was very hungry last night, so we just had sandwiches. We were joking about who had to confess to Emma." Her voice shook again, and she turned her hand so that her palm was against his, clasping it tightly. "Cal, it had to be an accident. No one would do that deliberately."

"Maybe. But too many odd things have been happening for me to write them all off as coincidence."

The back door opened. The paramedics came out, carrying their gear, and headed for their truck. Then Eli emerged, supporting Emma, who held a wet dressing to her face. Levi gave an inarticulate cry and shambled toward them.

Eli caught him before he could grasp Emma in a bear hug, talking to him softly and urgently in the low German the Amish used among themselves. Levi nodded, touched his mother's sleeve, and then went to unhitch the horse.

Andrea approached, holding her hand out tentatively. "Emma, I'm so sorry. Are you all right?"

"Ja." Eli answered for her. "The glasses protected her eyes, praise God. Her face is painful, but it will heal."

Emma came from behind the dressing for a moment, her skin red and shiny. "You take care of your grandmother, now. And my cake—"

"Don't start worrying about the cake. You can make another one for Rachel when you're completely recovered."

They watched as Eli and Levi handed her up carefully into the buggy. Levi took the reins.

"I'll come by later to see how you are," Andrea called as the buggy creaked slowly away.

She looked as if she wanted to go after them, do something to make this better. He touched her arm.

"Maybe we'd better check on Katherine."

"Yes, of course." She ran her fingers through her hair.

"I'm beginning to think I'm not very good in an emergency."

"You'll do." He followed her into the house, wondering. If this had been deliberate—but there wouldn't be any way to prove it. Still, he wanted a look at the stove.

He got his chance almost immediately, when Andrea, seeing how shaken Katherine was, took her grandmother upstairs to lie down. He waited until they'd disappeared up the steps and then opened the oven door.

When Andrea came back a few minutes later, he was still bending over the open door.

"Did you find anything?"

He shrugged. "Only how easy it would be to blow out the pilot. You'd better have someone come from the gas company to check it out, but I don't think he'll find anything wrong."

He closed the door. Andrea sagged against the kitchen counter, as if her bones had gone limp.

"Rachel comes home tomorrow. The first guests arrive on Saturday, and now Emma is out of action. What could anyone have to gain by tampering with the stove?"

He shrugged. "Someone might have thought it would delay the opening."

"Who would care?" She flung her hands out in frustration.

"Margaret cares. She doesn't want the competition. And there are those who don't want anything to draw more tourists here."

She shook her head at that. "I can't believe anyone would hurt Emma for such a reason."

He hesitated, but she had to know. "It might not have been aimed at Emma."

She blinked. “What do you mean?”

“If anyone knew that you usually heated up supper, the target might have been you.”

“But—how would they know? And even if one of us mentioned it, how could they be sure Emma wouldn’t take it into her head to bake something?”

He frowned. “That’s the thing. Yesterday afternoon, when I came in, I tried the side door, but it was locked. When we came down from the attic, Emma had already gone, but she always uses the back door. I found the side door was not only unlocked, but ajar.”

“You mean someone might have come in then and tampered with the stove.”

He couldn’t tell whether she accepted it or not. “Could have. Could have had a good idea you’d be the next to use it. Could have been a lot of things, but there’s no proof.”

“No.” Her face was pale. “There’s not remotely enough to take to the police.”

“Maybe I’m being overly suspicious. I hope so. But I don’t like it.”

“Neither do I.” She rubbed her forehead. “It has to be just an accident. There’s an innocent explanation for all of this, surely.”

“I hope so.” He wanted to say he’d protect her, but he didn’t know if he could. And he certainly didn’t have that right. He reached out to touch her cheek, the caress lingering longer than he intended.

“Take care of yourself, Andrea. Call me if anything, anything at all, strikes you as odd.”

“I will.”

But she was probably thinking the same thing he was. How did you protect yourself against something as amorphous as this?

* * *

"No, thank you, it's wonderful, but I can't eat another bite." Andrea tried to soften the refusal with a smile. Nancy Zook, wife of Eli and Emma's son Samuel, held a cherry pie in one hand and a peach pie in the other. After the huge serving of Schnitz un Knepp—ham hock, dried apples and dumplings—she'd thought she'd never eat again, but Nancy had urged a sliver of pie on her.

"Ah, it's nothing. Soon it will be time to make the strawberry preserves. We will send some over to you." Nancy put the pies down on the table and turned to offer seconds to the rest of the Zook family—Eli, Samuel, their five children and Levi.

Emma was keeping to her bed for the evening, but when Andrea had slipped over to the attached *daadi haus* to see her, she'd been insistent that she'd be back at work soon. Given the painful-looking blisters on her face, Andrea doubted it.

She'd walked over to the Zook farm late in the afternoon to bring get-well wishes and roses from her grandmother. The insistence that she stay to supper had been so strong that she couldn't have refused without insult, especially after they learned that Grams was having supper at the hospital with Rachel.

The room looked much like any farmhouse kitchen, with its wooden cabinets and linoleum floor. A wooden china closet held special dishes. One difference was that the only wall decoration was a large calendar featuring a picture of kittens in a basket. In most Old Order Amish communities, only such a useful picture could be placed on the wall.

She sipped strong coffee, glancing around the long, rectangular table with its covering of checkered oilcloth.

The children chattered amongst themselves softly, mindful of having an English guest. With their round blue eyes and blond hair, the girls in braids, the boys bowl-cut, they looked very alike.

Eli and Samuel talked about the next day's work. Levi sat silent, looking down at his pie. His clean-shaven face was unusual for an Amish adult male, but the beard was a sign of marriage. His soft round cheeks were like those of the children.

Had the figure in the rain had a beard? She wasn't sure. She didn't want to think it, but nothing that had been done would be beyond Levi's capabilities.

She glanced at the gas range. He'd know about the pilot light. But he'd never hurt his mother. That was a ridiculous thought.

A small voice at the back of her mind commented that he might have expected it to be her. All of the Zook family would know about the supper arrangements.

She wanted to reject the idea, but she couldn't. Levi seemed so uneasy with her presence at the table. He'd sent her only one startled glance when she first sat down, his blue eyes as wide as those of a frightened deer, and since then he'd kept his gaze fixed firmly on his plate, showing her only the top of his blond head.

A low rumble of thunder had all of them looking toward the windows.

"Ach, a storm is coming yet." Eli pushed his chair back. "We must get the outside chores done quickly."

The children scurried from the table, diving toward the door in their eagerness to be first out.

"I'd better leave if I don't want to get soaked on the way home." Andrea rose and held out her hand to Nancy. "Thank you so much for the wonderful meal."

"It's nothing." Nancy bobbed her head in a formal little gesture. "Would you be wanting Levi to walk you back?"

"No." That came too quickly. "I'm sure he has work to do. I'll be fine, but I'd better run."

She hurried out the back door, waving to the children as she headed for the path that went around the pond and through a small woodlot before coming out behind the barn where Cal had his shop.

Thunder rumbled again, closer now. It had been foolish not to bring a jacket, with afternoon thunderstorms forecast. Still, if she hurried, she could probably beat the rain home.

The breeze picked up, ruffling the surface of the pond and making the tall ferns that bordered it sway and dance. The scent of rain was in the air, and lightning flashed along the horizon. The distant farms, each marked by twin silos, seemed to wait for the rain.

She scurried past the pond with a fleeting memory of sailing homemade boats on it with the Zook children. The path plunged between the trees, and it was suddenly dark. She slowed, watching the path, having no desire to trip on a tree root and go sprawling.

A trailing blackberry bramble caught at her slacks, then tugged the laces of her sneakers, pulling one free of its knot. She bent, quickly retying it. Quiet—it was so quiet here. Even the birds must have taken shelter from the coming storm.

But as she rose, a sound froze her in place. Was that a footstep, somewhere behind her?

She looked back, seeing nothing, but the undergrowth was thick enough to hide a figure unless it was close. Too close.

That thought got her feet moving again. Hurry. Don't think about the possibility of someone behind you. Think about the fact that the last thing Cal told you was to be careful. Is this being careful?

Cal. She yanked out her cell phone. Better to risk feeling foolish than get into trouble. She could still feel those strong hands that pushed her into the toolshed.

Cal answered almost at once.

"It's Andrea. I'm on the path coming back from Zook's farm. Maybe I'm being silly, but I thought I heard someone behind me."

"I'm on my way." The connection clicked off.

She'd stopped long enough to make the call, and now the sound was closer. The bushes rustled as if a body forced its way through them.

Could be a deer. But even as she thought the words she started to run, feet thudding on the path, instinct telling her to flee like a frightened animal.

Around the twists in the path, careful, careful, don't trip. If you fall, he could be on you in a moment.

The sounds behind her were louder now, as if the follower had given up any need for secrecy. She didn't dare look behind her. To lose even a second could allow him to catch up.

Lightning flashed, close now, and the boom of thunder assaulted her ears. She was nearly out of the woods, just a little farther…

She spurted into the open like a cork from a bottle, and as she did the heavens opened. In an instant she was drenched and gasping as if she'd been shoved into a cold shower.

Don't stop, don't stop…

And then she saw Cal running toward her. Relief swept over her. She was safe.

Chapter 12

Cal put another small log on the fire he'd started in his fireplace and watched flames shoot up around it. Maybe the fire would warm and comfort Andrea. It was probably better than putting his arms around her, which was his instinctive reaction.

He put the poker back in the rack, glancing toward her. She sat on the sofa, wearing one of his flannel shirts, towel-drying her hair. She looked vulnerable, which made it even harder to keep his distance.

He had to find a way to help her, but he had to do it without wrecking the hard-won peace he'd found since he'd come here. Getting emotionally involved with a woman who couldn't wait to get away from this life would be a mistake. So would reverting to acting and thinking like a lawyer.

"Thanks." Andrea looked up at him, producing a faint

smile. "For the fire and the hot chocolate. I've already had enough coffee to keep me up half the night."

He sat down in the armchair, a careful distance from her. "Can you tell me about it now?"

"There's not much to tell." She frowned, absently toweling the damp hair that clung to her neck. "I'd gone over to see how Emma was, and Nancy insisted I stay for supper. When we noticed the storm coming up, they all scattered to do their chores, and I headed down the path. I'd just reached the woods when I thought I heard someone behind me."

"Back up a little. Did you see where Levi was when you left?"

"I'm not sure. Nancy offered to have him walk me back, but I said no." Her gaze met his. "I'm a little ashamed of that. I'm letting suspicion make a difference in how I treat people. That's not right."

"Maybe so, but it's probably unavoidable. So you don't know where he went at that point?"

"I think he headed for the barn with the boys, but I'm not positive, but just because I was at Zook's farm, that doesn't mean Levi was the one who followed me."

"No, but it's more probable than that someone else was hanging around, watching you."

He could see the shiver that went through her at the suggestion, and regretted it. But somehow they had to get to the bottom of this.

"So you never actually saw the person who followed you."

"No. Just heard him. At first I thought it was an animal, but once I started to run—" She wrapped her arms around her, as if comforting herself, and the too-long sleeves of the shirt flopped over her hands. "I'm sure what I heard was a person."

"I didn't see him, either." He frowned. What could anyone hope to gain by such a stunt?

Andrea shoved her hair back from her face. "That doesn't mean he wasn't there." Her voice was tart.

"I didn't mean that. I'm trying not to think like a lawyer, but old habits die hard." He'd thought he had it licked before Andrea came, involving him in her problems.

That wasn't fair. The trouble had already been here, but something about Andrea's arrival seemed to have brought it out.

"It's not that bad to think like an attorney, is it? After all, you are one."

"I'm a carpenter," he said. "Any resemblance to the person I used to be is a mistake."

A slight frown wrinkled her brows. "I can understand your grief and guilt. But do you think that necessarily means you can't be an attorney?"

His turn to frown. "You think I'm wasting my life here. Is that it? Believe me, I've gained far more than I lost in making the change. Peace. A new relationship with God." He paused, his momentary irritation dissolving. "In my old life, I'd have been embarrassed if someone brought up God in conversation. Am I embarrassing you?"

"No." Her face softened. "Maybe it's the impact of this place. I've thought more about faith since I came back than I had in the past year. Feeling—I don't know. Tugged back, I guess."

"I'm glad." He reached across the space between them to take her hand. Her fingers were cold, and he tried to warm them with his. "Even when you go away…"

He stopped. He didn't want her to leave. That was the truth, however irrational it might be. She wouldn't stay. Her life was elsewhere.

"When I leave—"

Her eyes met his, and he saw in them exactly what he felt. Longing. Tenderness. Regret.

Be careful. You're not going to kiss her again. It would be a mistake, getting entangled with someone who is determined to leave.

He rose, moving to the fireplace and leaning on the mantel. Take himself out of range.

"As far as this incident is concerned..." He frowned, trying to concentrate on the problem. "Most likely the person who followed you was Levi, simply because no one else could have known you were there. But if stopping the inn from opening is the object of all this harassment, why would he care?"

"I suppose that must be the motive—at least I can't think of any other reasonable hypothesis." She frowned. "It still seems overly dramatic to think that any of these solid, law-abiding Pennsylvania Dutchmen would resort to trying to scare me away just to eliminate another B and B."

"None of it is very logical." He had to get a handle on some aspect of the situation. He might have a better chance of doing that if his heart didn't perform such peculiar acrobatics whenever he looked at Andrea.

"There's still nothing to take to the police. I can just imagine their reaction to my story of being followed coming back from the Zook farm."

"They wouldn't be impressed, I'm afraid." They'd be polite, of course, but what could they do? It wasn't as if she'd been attacked. That thought sent a coldness settling deep inside him. The incident with the stove was an attack, but he couldn't prove it, or that she had been the target.

Andrea glanced at her watch and then shot to her feet. "Look at the time. I have to get home before Grams. I can't let her see me like this."

"You look pretty good to me." He pushed away from the mantel. "Sort of casually disheveled."

"I look as if I've been dragged through a knothole," she said tartly. She started for the door.

He followed her. "I'll walk you back."

"You don't need—"

"I'll walk you back," he repeated firmly, opening the door. "No more wandering around alone, okay?"

He thought she'd flare up at that, but she just nodded. "I'll take the dog with me everywhere I go. He might not be the brightest of creatures, but at least he'll make noise."

He wanted to offer himself instead of the dog, but that wouldn't be wise, not when just being within six feet of her made him want to kiss her. Like now.

He yanked the door open. The rain had subsided to a faint drizzle. "You're right. We'd better go."

Before he gave in to the powerful need to have her in his arms.

"Just grate the cheese." Laughter filled Rachel's voice as she sat in her wheelchair in the kitchen, the table pushed aside to give her more room. "Go on, use the grater. It won't bite you."

"I'm not so sure." Andrea gingerly lifted the metal grater, wary of its sharp teeth. Still, anything that had Rachel laughing had to be good.

Afternoon sun streamed through the kitchen windows, but she was making a breakfast frittata. At least, she was attempting to. She began grating the cheese into the earthenware bowl Rachel had chosen, trying to keep her fingers out of reach of the grater's teeth.

"You really think I can prepare a breakfast that will satisfy the guests." She frowned. "Make that three breakfasts, if Emma doesn't come back until next week."

"Look at it this way," Rachel said. "You're not so much cooking as being my hands. I'm really cooking. You're following directions."

The cheese stuck on the grater, and she gave it a shove. The bowl tipped, the grater flew up, and cheese sprinkled like snowflakes over the tile floor.

She looked at Rachel. "Your hands just made a mess."

Rachel's lips twitched. Then, as if she couldn't hold it back, she began to laugh.

Andrea glared, but an irrepressible chuckle rose in her throat.

"Go ahead, laugh. I never claimed to be able to cook. That's your department. I eat out or open a frozen dinner, and my cheese comes already grated in a bag."

"I'm sorry." Rachel's green eyes, so like her own, brimmed with laughter. "It's just that you're so competent on the computer and all thumbs in the kitchen."

"It's a good thing there's one area of my life that's under control."

But was it? The computer represented the business world to her, and how could she know what was happening back at the office when she was stuck here? E-mailing her assistant wasn't the same as being there, especially when that assistant had her eyes on Andrea's job.

"I'd be just as out of place in your office," Rachel said. "Here, hand me the bowl. Maybe I can set it in my lap and do the grating."

"No, I'm determined now. I will learn how to do this." She began again, careful to keep the bowl steady. "After all, you'll have to learn how to keep the reservations on the computer after I leave. I'll get to laugh at you then."

"Did you really get all that computerized?" Rachel shook her head. "I kept putting off trying, because it looked so hard."

"It'll be much easier once you get used to it. Much of your traffic will come from the Web site I started, especially when we get some more pictures up. Right now I just have the basics." That was one good thing accomplished, and the computer really would make running the inn easier, if she could get Rachel in the habit of using it.

"I'm astonished. You've done more in two weeks than I did in six months."

She must be getting more sensitive, because she detected immediately the note in Rachel's voice that said she was comparing herself unfavorably with her big sister.

"That's nonsense," she said firmly. "The renovations are all credited to you, and as for the garden…" She glanced out the kitchen window at the borders filled with color. "The guests will love looking at that while they have their breakfast. Always assuming I manage to make anything edible."

"You'll be fine," Rachel said. "You just have to do one main hot dish for each day. We'll serve fresh fruit cups, that special Amish-recipe granola that Grams gets from the farmer's market, and the breads and coffee cakes that Nancy offered to make. It'll be fine."

"Thank goodness for Nancy. She promised us Moravian Sugar Cakes for the first morning. I'll gain a pound just smelling them." She looked down in surprise, realizing she'd actually grated the entire block of cheese without getting any bloody knuckles. "We have to remember to bring flowers in to put on the tables, too."

Rachel nodded, turning the chair so that she could see out the screen door toward the garden. "I wish I'd been able to get the gazebo moved. That was one thing I intended that I didn't get to."

"Move the gazebo?" Andrea glanced out at the white wooden structure with its lacy gingerbread trim. "Why?"

Rachel shook her head. "You really don't have an eye for a garden, do you? It's in quite the wrong place, where it doesn't have a view. It makes the garden look crowded, instead of serving as an accent piece."

"I'll take your word for it." She wiped her hands on a tea towel. "What do I do next?"

Before Rachel could answer, the telephone rang.

Rachel picked it up. "Three Sisters Inn," she said, a note of pride in her voice. But a moment later her face had paled, and she looked at Andrea with panic in her eyes.

"Just a moment, please." She covered the receiver with her hand. "It's Mr. Elliot—has a reservation for the weekend, an anniversary surprise for his wife. He claims he received an e-mail from us, canceling, saying we aren't going to be open yet. You didn't—"

"Of course not." For a moment she stared at her sister, speculations running wildly through her mind. Then she reached for the phone. Redeem the situation first, if she could, and figure out where the blame lay later.

"Mr. Elliot?" It was her businesswoman voice, calm,

assured, in control. "I'm terribly sorry about this misunderstanding, but we certainly didn't cancel your reservation."

"You didn't send this e-mail?" He sounded suspicious.

"No, sir, we didn't. My sister has been hospitalized, and perhaps something went out without our knowledge." That made it sound as if they had a vast staff capable of making such an error.

"Seems a sloppy way to run an inn," he muttered, but the anger had gone out of his voice. "So we're still on for the weekend."

"Yes, indeed." She infused her voice with warmth, even as her mind seethed with possibilities. "And we'll provide a very special anniversary cake to surprise your wife. Don't worry about a thing."

When she finally hung up, her hand was shaking.

Rachel stared at her. "They're still coming?"

"Yes. But it's a good thing he was angry enough to want to blow up at us, or we'd never have known."

"The other guests—" Rachel's eyes darkened with concern.

"I'll get the list and call them right away." She hurried into the library, headed for the computer, hearing the wheels of Rachel's chair behind her.

"Maybe we can reach them before they have a chance to make other plans." Rachel sounded as if she were clinging hard to hope.

"Cross your fingers." Andrea paused. "The person who planned this overreached herself. If she'd waited until the last minute, we'd probably have been sitting high and dry with no guests."

"She?"

"She. I can't prove it, but I know perfectly well who did this."

"It had to be Margaret. She was in the library the other day with access to the computer. She even said something to me Sunday about hearing we wouldn't be able to open in time. But what can I do? There's no way to prove it."

Andrea had spotted Cal making his nightly rounds with a flashlight and called him in. Grams and Rachel had gone to bed early, and the house was quiet.

They sat on the sofa in the old summer kitchen that still bore remnants of the playroom it had been when she and her sisters had lived in the house. Games were stacked on the shelves to the right of the fireplace, and if she opened the closet, she'd find a few toys that Grams hadn't wanted to give away.

Cal frowned, staring absently at the cavernous fireplace. "You could bring a civil suit against her, but that would be using a bazooka to rid the house of mosquitoes."

"Not worthwhile, obviously, but I hate letting her get away with it. And the nerve of her—she just walked in the library when we were upstairs, calmly accessed the reservation records on my computer, and sent the e-mails."

He glanced at her. "The computer was on?"

"Don't remind me of how easy I made it for her. I not only had it on, it was open to the reservations. Well, it's password protected now, but it certainly got us off to a bad start."

"Did you lose any of the reservations?"

"Only one. The others consented to rebook after I'd groveled a bit."

That surprised a smile out of him. "I didn't think you knew how to do that."

"That's a lesson I learned early in my career. If there's a problem, don't waste time defending yourself. Just fix it."

"Not a bad philosophy. I'll bet you didn't know running a B and B would have so much in common with your real life."

His words were a reminder that her time here was coming to an end. She fought to ignore the hollow feeling in the pit of her stomach.

"Anyway, I'm absolutely certain Margaret's guilty of monkeying with the computer, but would she prowl around at night or dress up in Amish clothes to stand out in the rain? I don't think so."

"Anyone with such a fund of insincerity can't be trusted, but I'm inclined to agree with you about that. She'd be afraid of being caught in an embarrassing position."

"I'd like to catch her at something." She shook her head. "That sounds vengeful, doesn't it? Grams would be ashamed of me. It's just that we've all worked so hard—"

"I know." He squeezed her hand. "Are you ready for guests to arrive on Saturday?"

"I think we're in good shape, but I'm certainly glad Grams didn't tell them they could arrive Friday night. Rachel's been walking me through cooking the breakfast meals. We actually ate my artichoke and sausage frittata for supper, and it wasn't half-bad. And Nancy Zook is providing all the baked goods we need."

He nodded. "I heard from Eli that she's agreed to help out some, at least until Rachel's on her feet again."

"I expect I'll be coming back on weekends, at least through the busy season."

Did that sound as if she were asking for something—some hint of where they stood? She hated having things unresolved.

"I'm glad we'll still get to see you." His tone was as neutral and friendly as if he spoke to Eli Zook.

Maybe that answered the question in her mind. Cal recognized, as she did, that the differences between them were too fundamental. The hole in her midsection seemed to deepen.

Ridiculous. She'd only known him for weeks. But when she looked at him, she realized that wasn't true. Maybe in chronological terms they hadn't known each other long, but she'd met him at a time when her emotions were stretched to the limit and her normal barriers suspended.

And since then she'd relied on him in a way that startled her when she looked at it rationally. Did she have anyone else, even back in Philadelphia, that she would turn to for help as naturally as she'd turned to him?

No. She didn't. And that was a sad commentary on the quality of her life.

Cal apparently wasn't engaging in any deep thoughts over the prospect of her leaving. He was frowning toward the small window in the side wall.

"Shouldn't we be able to see the reflection of the garden lights from here?"

She followed the direction of his gaze, vague unease stirring. "Yes. I'm sure I could see the glow the last time I looked that way."

Cal rose, walking quickly toward the hallway and the back door. She followed. They stopped at the door, peering out at the garden, which was perfectly dark.

"Something's happened to the lights." She couldn't erase the apprehension in her voice.

"It may not be anything major." Cal opened the door, switching on his flashlight. "I connected the new lights to the fuse box in the toolshed. Could have blown a fuse, I guess. I'll go check." He stepped out onto the patio.

"Be careful."

Already at the edge of the patio, he turned to smile at her. "I always am." He lifted the flashlight in a little salute, and then stepped off the flagstones. In an instant he was swallowed up by the dark.

She clutched the door frame, hands cold. Irrational, to be worried over something so simple, but then, plenty of irrational things had been happening. She yanked open the door and stepped outside, driven by some inner compulsion.

The beam of his flashlight was the only clue to Cal's location, halfway to the toolshed. She should have gone with him. She could have held the light while he checked the fuses.

The stillness was shattered by an engine's roar. Lights blazed, slicing through the darkness. She whirled. Something barreled from behind the garage—something that surged across the grass, sound and light paralyzing her.

Cal. Cal was pinned in the powerful twin headlight beams. Before she could move the massive shape rocketed across the garden, straight toward Cal.

Screaming his name, she darted forward. The vehicle cut between them with a deafening roar. She couldn't see—the light from Cal's torch was gone. Where was he?

Chapter 13

Cal dived away from the oncoming lights, instinct taking over from thought. The roar of the motor deafened him. Something struck his head, and he slammed into the ground.

He couldn't breathe, couldn't think, facedown in the damp grass. He gasped in a gulp of cool air, shaking his head and wincing at the pain.

Think. Look. Try to identify the car.

No, truck—a four-by-four, by the sound of it. He shoved up onto his knees. The vehicle careened through the garden, ripping up flower beds, smashing the birdbath.

He forced his brain to work. It would be gone in an instant. He had to try and identify it. No license plate to be seen—the rear lights were blacked out. He fought the urge to sink back down on the grass, trying to clear his head. It didn't seem to work. Someone was shouting his name.

Andrea. She flew toward him, barreled into him. He winced and would have toppled over but for the hard grasp of her hands.

"You're all right—I thought you were hit." Her fingers clutched at him, and her voice caught on a sob.

He touched his forehead and felt the stickiness of blood, warm on his palm. He leaned on her, aware of the roar of the truck's engine. If he could get a good look at it before it disappeared around the building…

The dark shape had reached the pond. It turned, wheels spinning in the mud left from yesterday's rain. He could make out the shape, not the color. The driver would cut off down the lane….

He didn't. He spun, straightened, and bucketed straight toward them.

He clutched Andrea. Closest shelter, no time—

"Run! The patio—"

Clutching each other, stumbling a little, they ran toward the patio. He forced his feet to slog as if through quicksand, the truck was coming fast, they weren't going to make it, Andrea—

He shoved her with every bit of strength, flinging her toward the stone patio wall. Threw himself forward, the truck so close he felt the breath of the engine. Landed hard again, pain ricocheting through his body.

Metal shrieked as the truck sideswiped the patio wall, scattering stones. He struggled, trying to get to his feet, dazed, left wrist throbbing. Strength knocked out of him. If the truck came back, he was a sitting duck….

Then Andrea grabbed him, pulling him onto the patio, dragging him to safety. The truck made a last defiant pass through the flower beds, charged past the garage, clipping it, and roared off down the dark country road, disappearing into the trees.

Andrea clutched him, her breath coming in ragged gasps. "Are you hurt?"

He shook his head, wincing at the pain. "You…"

It was more important than anything to know that she was safe, but he couldn't seem to form a question.

He tried to focus on her face, white and strained in the circle of light from the door. Katherine stood in the doorway, saying something he couldn't make out, Rachel behind her in the chair.

He had to reassure them. He staggered a step toward them and collapsed onto the flagstones.

"I'm not going to the hospital. I'm fine." Cal might look pale and shaken, but his voice was as firm as always.

Andrea found she could breathe. He'd be all right. That terrible moment when she thought the truck had hit him—she could stop thinking about it now.

But she couldn't kid herself about her feelings for him any longer. That brief instant when she'd thought he was gone had been a lightning flash that seared heart and soul, showing her exactly how much she cared.

The paramedic leaned on the back of a kitchen chair, looking at him doubtfully. "Might be a good idea to let the docs check out that wrist."

"It's a sprain." He cradled his left wrist in his other hand. "The wrap is all I need."

She'd urge him to let them take him to the hospital, but she knew that was futile. She wrapped her fingers around the mug of coffee someone had thrust into her hands, wondering how long it would take for the shaking to stop.

Grams's kitchen was crowded with paramedics and police, but for the first time in her memory, Grams seemed to have given up the reins of hospitality. She sat at the end of the table, robe knotted tightly around her, her face gray and drawn.

Love and fear clutched at Andrea's heart. Grams had to be protected, and she was doing a lousy job of it.

Please, Father, show me what to do. I have to take care of them, and I'm afraid I can't.

The paramedics, apparently giving up on Cal, began packing up their kits, leaving the field to the police.

There were two of them this time. The young patrolman who'd come before stood awkwardly by the door, and the township chief sat at the table. Obviously the authorities took this seriously. As they should. Cal could have been killed.

The chief cleared his throat, gathering their attention. Zachary Burkhalter, he'd introduced himself—tall, lean, with sandy hair and a stolid, strong-boned face. He must be about Cal's age, but he wore an air that said he'd seen it all and nothing could surprise him.

"Maybe you could just go over the whole thing for me, Mr. Burke. Anything you saw or heard might help."

Cal shoved his good hand through his hair, disturbing a tuft of grass that fluttered to the table. She probably had her own share of debris, and she thought longingly of a hot shower.

"I didn't see much. Seemed like it took forever, but it probably wasn't more than a couple of minutes at most. We noticed the outside lights had gone off. I thought it was a fuse, started across toward the toolshed where the box is. The four-by-four was behind the garage, out of sight."

She nodded, agreeing, and the chief's gaze turned to her instantly. Gray eyes, cold as flint.

"You agree with that, Ms. Hampton?"

"Yes. I saw the truck come out from behind the garage. To be exact, I heard it, saw the lights. It crossed the back lawn to the pond, turned around and came back, went past the garage again and down Crossings Road. It took less than five minutes, certainly."

And they'd fought for their lives the whole time.

"Can you identify the driver?" His gaze swiveled back to Cal.

"Too dark without the security lights. As Ms. Hampton said, they'd just gone off."

"That ever happen before?"

"No." Cal's voice was level. "It hadn't."

She knew what he was thinking. Someone could have tampered with the fuse box. Would they have had time to do that and get back to the truck before she and Cal went outside? She wasn't sure, but she couldn't say how long the lights had been off.

"And the truck?" Burkhalter obviously wanted a description they couldn't give.

"The rear lights of the vehicle had been blacked out somehow. It was a four-by-four, some dark color—that's about all I could see." Cal was probably berating himself that he didn't get a better look.

Burkhalter nodded. "We've found it, as a matter of fact."

Cal's brows shot up. "That was fast work, Chief."

"Abandoned down Crossings Road, keys missing,

scrapes along the fender from hitting the wall. The back lights had been broken."

"Whose is it?" The question burst out of her mouth. If they knew who was responsible...

Burkhalter's gaze gave nothing away. "Belongs to Bob Duckett. Easy enough for someone to take it—he leaves the garage door standing open and the keys hanging on a hook."

Of course he would. Half the township did that, probably, thinking this place was as safe as it had been fifty years ago.

"Bob Duckett wouldn't do anything like this." Grams finally spoke, her voice thin and reedy.

"No, we're sure he didn't." Burkhalter's tone softened for Grams. Then he looked back at her, and the softness disappeared. "You reported an earlier incident, Ms. Hampton?"

"Yes." She glanced toward the patrolman. "We had a prowler."

"This was considerably uglier than prowling."

She glanced toward Rachel, shaken by the bereft look on her face. Rachel had expended hours of work and loving care on the garden, only to have it devastated in a matter of minutes.

"You have any idea who might want to do this?" He glanced around the table, aiming the question at all of them.

Grams straightened, clasping her hands together. "No one could possibly have anything against us, Chief Burkhalter."

Andrea moved slightly, and Burkhalter was on to it at once. "You don't agree?"

She was conscious of her grandmother's strong will,

demanding that she be silent. Well, this once, Grams wouldn't get her way.

"There are people who are opposed to another bed-and-breakfast opening here," she said carefully.

"What people?" Burkhalter wouldn't be content with evasion.

She had to ignore Grams's frown. "Margaret Allen, for one. And I understand Herbert Rush and some of the other old-timers don't like the idea."

"It's ridiculous to think they'd do this."

Grams's tone told her she'd be hearing about this for a while. Grams couldn't imagine anyone she knew stealing a four-by-four to drive it through the grounds, but someone had.

She shivered a little, her gaze meeting Cal's. *Do I say anything about Levi? Surely he couldn't be involved. He doesn't drive, for one thing.*

Cal cradled his left hand, his expression giving nothing away. A bruise was darkening on his forehead. Her heart twisted.

"Could have been teenagers," Burkhalter said. "Hearing their elders talk about the inn, deciding to do something about it. Clever enough, though, for him, or them, to put the vehicle behind the garage while they tampered with the lights. No one would see it there unless they were driving down Crossings Road, and likely enough not even then."

And no one was likely to be going down Crossings Road at this hour. It led to several Amish farms, but they were probably dark and quiet by this time.

"I trust you're not going to just dismiss this as casual vandalism." Rachel spoke for the first time.

"No, ma'am." Burkhalter's gaze lingered on Rachel

for a moment, but Andrea found it impossible to read. "We won't do that." His glance shifted, sweeping around the table. "Anyone have anything else to add?"

Someone stood outside the house one night. Someone might have pushed me into a closet. Someone probably followed me back from the Zook farm yesterday. Someone—Margaret, for choice—tampered with our reservations. There were good reasons for saying none of those things.

"We don't know anything else." Grams's voice had regained some of its command. "Thank you for coming."

Burkhalter rose. "We'll be in touch." He jerked his head to the patrolman, who followed him out the door.

Grams waited until the outer door closed behind them. She stood, pulling her dignity around her like a robe. "Cal, you must stay in the house tonight. Come along, I'll show you to a room. Andrea, please help Rachel back to bed."

She was too tired to argue. Besides, if she did have a chance to speak to Cal privately, what could she say? Her feelings were rubbed too raw to have a hope of hiding them. Maybe it was better this way.

Andrea walked into the breakfast room the next morning, wincing as the bright sunlight hit her face. The French doors stood open, and Rachel sat in her wheelchair on the patio.

She walked outside and put her hand on her sister's shoulder in mute sympathy. Rachel reached up to squeeze it.

"Stupid to cry over a garden." Rachel dashed tears away with the back of her hand. "It's just—"

"It was beautiful, and you and Grams made it." Andrea finished the thought, her stomach twisting as she looked at the damage. Dead or dying flowers lay with their roots exposed, and deep ruts cut through the lawn. The birdbath was nothing but scattered pieces, and the patio wall where she and Cal had sat bore a raw, jagged scar where stones had been knocked out. The only thing that hadn't been hit was the gazebo, probably because it stood off to one side.

"It's hard to believe that much damage could be done in a few minutes." Something quivered inside her. It could have been worse, much worse. It could have been Cal or her lying broken on the lawn.

"I am so furious." Rachel pounded her fists against the arms of the wheelchair. "If I could get my hands on the person who did this, I'd show him how it feels to be torn up by the roots."

The fury was so counter to Rachel's personality that Andrea was almost surprised into a laugh. Rachel was a nurturer, yet when something under her care was hurt, she could turn into a mother lion. "Maybe it's a good thing we don't know, then. I'd hate to see my little sister arrested for assault."

"It might be better," Rachel said darkly. "Then I wouldn't have to see the guests' faces. They'll be here the day after tomorrow, Dree. What are we going to do?" The last words came out almost as a wail.

"We're not going to waste time on anger." She had to give Rachel something to focus on other than the fury that could give way, too easily, to helplessness. "You make a list of what you want, and I'll head out to the nursery first thing. I'll spend the rest of the day putting new plants in. They'll at least last while the guests are here."

Rachel's brows lifted. "You? When was the last time you dug in the dirt?"

"Probably when I left the sandbox stage, but you'll tell me what to do. Look, I know it won't be the same—"

"What about the wall? And the lawn, and the birdbath? It would take an army to get things in shape by Saturday."

Andrea grabbed the chair and turned Rachel to face her. "Look, this is no time to give up. Now stop acting like a baby and go make that list."

"You stop being so bossy." Rachel glared at her for an instant, and then her lips began to quiver. "Um, remind me how old we are again?"

Laughter bubbled up, erasing her annoyance. "About ten and twelve, I think." She gave the chair a shove. "Go on, write the list. We'll make this work. I promise."

Smiling, Rachel wheeled herself through the doorway.

"Rach?"

She turned.

"Has anyone checked on Cal this morning?" She forced the question to sound casual.

"Grams said he was dressed and gone an hour ago," Rachel said. "I'll get some coffee started while I make up the list." At least she looked more herself as she wheeled toward the kitchen.

Andrea walked to the patio wall and surveyed the damage. She might be able to plant flowers, given enough instruction, but this she couldn't fix. Disappointment filtered through her at Cal's absence. She'd expected that today, of all times, he'd be here to help.

Well, he had a business to run. Once that would have been a guaranteed excuse, at least from her perspective. She'd changed, if all she could think was that he should be here.

Stepping over the patio wall, she began to gather the stones that were scattered across the grass. Maybe she couldn't fix the wall, but she could make the area look a little neater.

The stones proved far heavier than she expected. She straightened her back, frowning at one particularly stubborn one.

"Take it easy." Cal's voice spun her around. "I'll do that." The bag he carried in one arm thudded against the wall.

"I thought you left." Did she sound accusing?

"I went to get cement mix to repair the wall." He lifted his eyebrows. "Not very complimentary that you thought I'd desert you this morning."

She wasn't sure what to say to that. "Well, you do have a business to take care of."

"Friends come first," he said shortly.

Are we friends, Cal? What would he say if she blurted that out? She wasn't sure she even wanted to hear the answer.

Movement beyond him on the lane distracted her. "What on earth…?"

Cal turned. "Looks like the Zook family think friends come first, too."

Her breath caught, and tears welled in her eyes. Three buggies came down the lane, packed with people, and a large farm wagon bore so many flowers that it looked like a float in the homecoming parade.

She could only stand and stare for a moment. And then she bolted toward the house.

"Rachel! Rachel, come here this minute! You're not going to believe this!"

* * *

Andrea sat back on her heels, admiring the snapdragons she'd just succeeded in planting with Nancy's help.

"Looks good already." Nancy, Emma's daughter-in-law, smiled, brushing a strand of dark hair back into the neat coil under her prayer cap. "We brought enough flowers, I think."

She nodded. They'd certainly brought enough help. Eli and Cal fitted the last stone into place on the wall, while Nancy's small son stood by holding the bucket with cement. Nancy's husband and another Amish man, their red shirts a bright contrast to black trousers, used a lawn roller to smooth out the ruts. The grass seemed to spring into place in their wake. And the flowers…

"You must have gotten up at dawn to dig all of these plants to bring. We can't thank you enough for this."

"We always get up at dawn," Nancy said. "This is just being neighborly."

All along the flower border figures knelt, setting out new plants to replace the ruined ones. Children ran back and forth, fetching and carrying, the girls with bonnet strings streaming, the boys small replicas of the men.

Funny. When she'd spread the Sunshine and Shadows quilt over her bed this morning, she'd felt that they were locked into a dark stripe. Now the sun had come out. She glanced at Cal, who seemed to be keeping himself busy well away from her. Or maybe it would be more accurate to say that the dark was interwoven with the bright.

A time to plant and a time to pluck up that which is planted.

A clatter of spoon against pan sounded. Emma stood in the doorway. Her face was still red and painful-looking, but she'd arrived with the others and marched into the kitchen. "Breakfast when you are finished. The flowers must be in before the sun is high." She vanished back inside.

The comment seemed to inspire a fresh burst of industry. Nancy handed her another flat of blooms. "Impatiens," she said. "Along where it's shady."

Andrea nodded. The move brought her next to Levi, who was setting out clumps of coralbells. When he saw her, his round blue eyes became even rounder.

"Hi, Levi. Thanks for helping." In the light of day, her suspicions of him seemed silly. Levi was, as he'd always been, an innocent child at heart.

He ducked his head, coloring a little. "Help is good." He seemed to struggle with the words, and she realized he'd be far more comfortable with the language of the home. Unfortunately, she'd forgotten whatever German she'd learned as a child.

"Yes. You're good neighbors."

He stared at her, and she saw to her horror that his eyes were filling with tears. "Sorry. Sorry."

He scrambled to his feet, arms flailing awkwardly, and ran toward the barn.

She was still staring after him when Nancy knelt next to her, picking up the trowel he'd dropped and finishing the planting in a few deft movements. "It makes no trouble. Levi will be fine. One of the children will get him when it's time to eat."

"I didn't mean to upset him."

"He's been—" she paused, seeming to search for a word "—funny, just lately. He'll be all right."

"You don't know what's causing it?"

Nancy shrugged. "He doesn't talk so much. Sooner or

later he will tell his mother, and she will make it right. Some simple thing, most likely."

Nancy was probably right. She certainly knew Levi better than Andrea did.

Still, she couldn't help but wonder. Why had Levi begun to cry at the sight of her? And why had he said he was sorry?

Chapter 14

Cal pulled into the driveway and stopped close to the back garden. He'd seen Rachel mourning over the pieces of the birdbath earlier. The one he'd found at the garden store out toward Lancaster should be a decent replacement.

He got the wheelbarrow from the utility shed in the garage, struggling to manage it. Even with his wrist taped, using that hand was awkward. Lucky it wasn't the right, or he'd be out of work until it healed.

Andrea emerged onto the patio, carrying a watering can. She checked at the sight of him, then waved and began sprinkling the potted plants along the edge of the patio.

Maybe Andrea hadn't quite figured out what had changed between them last night, either. He hefted the birdbath onto the wheelbarrow with one hand. They were both trying to look busy, which probably meant they were both confused.

During those moments when they'd fought for their lives, there hadn't been time to think, only to act and feel. Trouble was, he felt too much.

Lord, does it make any sense at all for me to fall for someone like Andrea? If You've taught me anything in the past year, isn't it that this is the life that's right for me? Andrea could never be content with that. She's itching to race back to the city the minute she's free.

If he told her what he felt—but that could only lead to pain and awkwardness between them.

He was maneuvering the birdbath into place when Andrea caught the opposite side and helped him.

"This is lovely. Where did you find it?"

"Little place over toward Lancaster." If he looked at her, he might weaken, so it was better to concentrate on getting the birdbath into exactly the right spot. "I thought it would please Rachel."

"She'll be delighted." Her tone had cooled in response to his.

He hated that. But wasn't it better for both of them in the long run? Why start something that could only end badly?

Andrea touched a scalloped edge. "About last night..."

He tensed, but before she could say anything else, a buggy came down the drive, the horse driven at a fast trot. "It's Eli." He went to meet the buggy, aware of Andrea hurrying beside him.

Eli pulled up. "Have you seen our Levi since this morning?"

"No, not since we were working on the lawn." He

glanced at Andrea, and she shook her head. "Is something wrong?"

"No one has seen him all day." The lines of his face deepened. "That's not like him. He never goes far, and he always tells his mother. We are starting a search."

Cal glanced at his watch. Nearly five. Levi had been missing for something like seven hours.

"What can we do to help?" Andrea said.

"Search all your buildings. And pray."

"We'll do both," he said quickly. "If we spot him, we'll ring the bell." He nodded toward the old-fashioned dinner bell that hung next to the kitchen door.

"I must tell the other neighbors." Eli was already turning the buggy, and he rolled off without another word. The Amish habit of leaving off the niceties of conversation could seem abrupt, but it was certainly understandable now.

Andrea glanced toward the house. "Grams and Rachel are resting, and they wouldn't be much help in any event."

He headed for the garage. "They don't need to know yet. We can start at this end and work our way out toward the barn."

While he checked the cars and the garage loft, Andrea opened the door to the attached utility shed.

By the time he came back down, she was dusting her hands off. "Nothing in there but a lot of spiderwebs." She hesitated a moment, as if something was on her mind. "You know, Levi was a little odd this morning."

"Odd in what way?" He headed for the old brooder coop, which stood next in the line of outbuildings.

"He was upset when he realized I was working next to him." She seemed to be choosing her words carefully.

"I tried to talk to him, but all he'd say was that he was sorry. Then he ran off, almost in tears."

"You didn't get a sense of what it was all about?"

She shook her head. "When I mentioned it to Nancy, she said he'd been withdrawn lately, but she didn't take it seriously."

"What could he have been sorry for? For what happened last night?"

"I don't know." She brushed her hair free of the collar of her shirt with an irritated movement. "Does that seem very likely? He doesn't know how to drive, does he?"

He flung open the door of the brooder coop. It was packed solidly with furniture. "A mouse couldn't hide in here." He closed the door again. "I wouldn't think Levi could drive, but a surprising number of Amish people can. Learn when they are teens, most of them. What direction did Levi head when he ran off?"

"Toward the barn—yours, not the old one. But wouldn't you have seen him if he were there?"

"I haven't been in all day. Too much else to do. Maybe we'd better check there next."

She nodded, trotting beside him as he quickened his pace. It wasn't the first time Levi had wandered off, but he didn't generally go farther than the Unger place. Levi could have decided to take refuge in the barn, he supposed, hiding from some imagined misdeed.

They hurried up the earthen ramp, and he pulled the door open.

"Levi! Levi, are you in here?" The words echoed in the barn's lofty spaces.

Andrea grabbed his arm. "The trapdoor to the lower level. It's open."

He swung around, following the direction of her

pointing finger. The hatch, used long ago to throw hay down to the stalls in the lower level, was always kept closed and bolted. Now it yawned open.

He was there in an instant, bending to peer down into the shadowy depths. His heart jolted into overtime.

Levi lay on the floor below, arms outstretched, blood darkening the straw beneath his head. His hands were open, palm up, and next to his right hand, glinting in the shaft of sunlight that pierced the dimness, lay a ring of car keys.

Andrea sat on the plastic chair in the hospital waiting room. She glanced at her watch. How much longer? Surely the doctors knew something by now. At least they'd been given this secluded room in which to wait, rather than sitting out in the open where others could stare at the quaintly dressed Amish.

Grams sat bolt upright on her chair, as if to show any sign of weakness would be a betrayal. She had her arm around Emma, who wept softly into a handkerchief. Nancy sat on Emma's other side, having left the children with Rachel, who'd been quick to say she'd be more trouble than she was worth at the hospital.

Men clustered in a group in the far corner, drinking coffee and talking in low voices. Every now and then the door opened and more Amish appeared, quickly segregating themselves by sexes. A carryover from their separation in church or simply a male desire to be as far away as possible from female tears.

The men's black jackets, the women's black bonnets seemed almost a sign of mourning. She shook off that thought. Levi would be all right. He'd been breathing on his own when they brought him in. That was a good sign, wasn't it?

Each time the door opened, all eyes went to it. Each time, Emma sobbed a bit more.

"I don't understand." Emma's wail was loud enough to startle even the men. "Why did Levi go to the barn? How did he fall?"

Grams took the twisting hands in hers. "We'll know when he's well enough to tell you," she said firmly.

Eli came to his wife and patted her awkwardly on the shoulder. "We must accept," he said. "It is God's will."

Was it? The questions that had hovered at the back of Andrea's mind since she and Cal found Levi forced their way to the front. Her eyes sought out Cal. He was filling his foam cup at the coffee urn, but, as if he felt her gaze on him, he looked up and brought the cup to her.

"Have some. I know it's awful, but at least it's hot."

She took the cup, rising and moving toward the window, where they had the illusion of privacy. "Do you really believe Levi could have driven that truck?" She kept her voice low.

He glanced toward the group around Eli before answering. "It's starting to look that way. Samuel admits that Levi was fascinated by cars. He thinks some of the local teenagers might have thought it was funny to show him." He shook his head. "I just can't figure out how he'd get away from home last night. Emma has been keeping pretty close tabs on him."

"She has, but she was probably exhausted. I don't see how he'd have gotten the keys if he didn't do it. Unless the driver dropped them someplace and he picked them up. And assuming they're the keys to the truck."

"Maybe we're going to find out."

The door had swung open again. This time it was Chief Burkhalter. He glanced around the room, seeming surprised to find it so crowded.

"Any word yet on the boy's condition?" He directed the question to Eli.

Eli shook his head. His normally ruddy face was gray with pain. "The doctor will come when they've finished, he said."

"In that case..." His gaze singled out the two of them. "Maybe you'd step outside so we can have a word, since you found him."

She was grateful for Cal's hand on her back as they followed Burkhalter out into the hallway, knowing everyone watched them go. In the corridor, he gestured them into a room a few doors away.

It was a replica of the other waiting room with its pale green walls and generic landscapes. The chairs looked just as uncomfortable. Burkhalter jerked three of them into a circle. At his commanding look, they sat.

She had nothing to feel guilty about, did she? So why did she feel as if she wanted to look anywhere except into Burkhalter's face?

"Tell me about finding him."

Cal nodded. "Eli came over to tell us he was missing and asked us to search the property. Ms. Hampton and I happened to be out in the garden at the time. We started searching the outbuildings."

"It didn't occur to you to look in the inn first?"

Andrea blinked. "I suppose I knew it was unlikely Levi would go inside. He's—well, skittish around strangers." She thought of the rabbits that looked askance when she came out onto the lawn and hopped quickly away.

"So you started searching. What took you to the barn?"

"I remembered that he had gone that way when he left the group that was repairing the damage from last night." She closed her mouth, reluctant to say anything that might contribute to his suspicion.

"Did you talk to him at all this morning?" The man seemed to have radar for evasions.

"Yes, a little. He seemed upset." She darted a glance toward Cal, but he couldn't help her. "He said he was sorry."

"Sorry about what?" Burkhalter's response was like the crack of a whip.

"He didn't say. He ran off." She shook her head to forestall any questions. "There's no point in asking me anything else. That's all I know. I remembered he went toward the barn, so we went there. We saw the trapdoor open." Her voice shook a little, and Cal's hand closed hard over hers. "We found him."

Burkhalter transferred his gaze to Cal. "That trap-door. You always leave it open?"

"No. I always keep it closed and bolted."

"What did you do after you spotted him?"

"Called the paramedics. Went down to see if we could help him." Cal had apparently decided he could be as laconic as Burkhalter.

"I ran back to the house to ring the dinner bell," she said. "We'd agreed that's what we'd do if we found him."

Burkhalter nodded, his gaze fixed on her face. "You know, Ms. Hampton, whenever the police get called in, people get choosy about what they say. Mostly it's innocent enough, but they don't want to say more than they have to. Wouldn't you agree, Counselor?"

If Cal was surprised that the chief knew about his past, he didn't betray it. "Maybe so, if they think it's unimportant."

"Cops get so they have a sense when someone's hiding something." He turned on Andrea. "How about it, Ms. Hampton? What aren't you telling me?"

She blinked. He really did have radar. "It's nothing."

"Tell me anyway, and let me decide if it's nothing."

She brushed the hair back from her face. She had no choice, and surely nothing she said could make matters any worse now.

"There was another incident, after the prowler call. I was locked in the downstairs pantry. I thought it was an accident—maybe I bumped the door myself."

"And what else?"

"One night when it was storming, I went to close the windows. I saw someone standing out on the lawn, watching the house." She hesitated. "It appeared to be a man in Amish clothing. I couldn't identify him any further."

"She called me," Cal said. "I came over—didn't catch him, but I found the place where he'd been standing. Judging by the way the grass was trampled, he'd been there for quite a while."

Burkhalter made a show of consulting a small notebook. "I understand your housekeeper had an accident with the stove."

"Yes." Levi wouldn't do anything to hurt his own mother. Surely Burkhalter could see that. "The repairman couldn't say whether someone had tampered with it or not. It could have been an accident."

"Quite a string of bad luck you folks have been having," he observed.

She waited for him to probe more deeply, but to her surprise, he rose.

"You can join the others, if you like."

"Chief." Cal's voice stopped him at the doorway. "Those keys—were they the keys to the stolen truck?"

He didn't move for a moment. Would he answer?

"Yes," he said. "They were."

The stack of green ledgers in the middle of the library desk gave Andrea pause. Rachel, searching in the lower kitchen cabinets for a bundt cake pan, had unearthed yet another batch of Grandfather's records that she'd put away in an unlikely place. Andrea had delivered a lecture on organization, but doubted whether it would do any good.

Andrea pushed the ledgers to one side and switched on the computer, feeling too tired to deal with much of anything this morning. The doctors had come out at last and announced that Levi had a severe concussion and several broken ribs, but would mend. Emma's tears had turned to rejoicing, and the bishop, a local farmer named Christian Lapp, led a lengthy prayer of thanksgiving.

Finally she'd persuaded Grams to come home. It had been nearly one before the house was quiet, and then she'd lain awake, unable to turn off the questions in her mind.

They'd all come down to one, in the end. Why? Why would Levi do such a thing? Until he told them, no one would know.

Guests were arriving tomorrow. She shoved her hair back and called up the reservations on the computer screen. Were they ready? Aside from a sense that all of them would have difficulty playing the genial host, she thought so.

The front door opened. “Hello?”

“In the library.” She shoved her chair back, but the visitor came in even as she rose.

Betty. For a moment it seemed odd, seeing the woman anywhere but behind her desk at Unger and Bendick.

“Betty.” She gave what she hoped was a welcoming smile. “What brings you to see us?”

There was no returning smile. Betty marched to the desk and set down a stack of file folders and several computer disks. “Mr. Bendick asked me to bring these to you.”

Andrea stared at them blankly. “I’m sorry?”

Betty’s lips pressed together in an offended line. “Mrs. Unger informed him that you would be handling all her finances in the future.”

With everything else that had been happening, she’d forgotten that vote of confidence from Grams. “I see. I didn’t intend for you to bring those over. I’d have come in to talk with Uncle Nick.”

“He thought this would be best.” Even Betty’s hair, piled in some sort of complicated knot on her head, seemed to quiver with indignation.

It looked as if she’d have to mend some fences. “My grandmother didn’t intend any lack of confidence in Uncle Nick. She appreciates everything he’s done, but she thought she’d have me do it rather than to take advantage of him, as busy as he is.”

Betty leaned over to flip open the top folder. “There are forms here that Mrs. Unger must sign. Please have her do so.”

Obviously Betty was offended on Nick’s behalf. She

found it hard to believe that Nick cared all that much. Surely managing Grams's affairs was an extra burden he didn't need.

"I'll have her sign them when she gets back from the hospital."

Betty paused, and Andrea could see her need to hold on to the grudge battling her curiosity. The curiosity won.

"Is she visiting that Zook boy who caused all the trouble?" Incredulity filled her voice.

"My grandmother is good friends with the Zook family." Andrea stood. "Thank you for dropping these off. I'll take care of them."

Betty glared at her for a moment. Then she turned and stalked out. The front door slammed.

"She isn't too happy with you." Cal walked in from the kitchen as she sat down.

She felt the little jolt to her heart that seemed to come with his presence. "Did you bring my grandmother back from the hospital?"

"She wanted to stay a while longer, so Emma arranged for someone to pick them both up. I told Katherine I'd stop by and update you."

"How is Levi?"

He came and perched on the corner of the desk. "The doctors seem satisfied. He should come home in a few days, if all continues to go well."

That was good news, but where did they go from there? "Has he said anything? Explained?"

He shook his head. "He's conscious, but he doesn't seem to remember much about his injury. Burkhalter tried to question him, but Levi got so upset he gave up." He shrugged, clearly not happy with the situation. "Levi had the vehicle keys, so there doesn't seem to be much doubt that he did it."

"Why?" She shoved the desk chair back. "That's what kept me up half the night. What could Levi possibly have against us?"

"Emma was afraid she had the answer to that. It seems the Zooks got worried that if the inn was successful, your grandmother might decide she wanted to use the property they lease from her. She thinks Levi heard them talking and misunderstood. Got some foolish idea he was helping them. And Emma finally said that he does get out at night sometimes."

Her throat tightened. "Poor Emma. It would be hard for her to admit that."

"Well, your grandmother assured her the land is theirs to use as long as they want it, and when I left they were holding each other and crying, so I think they're going to be all right."

He shifted position, not looking at her. "You know, I have an offer to go out to the Zimmerman farm and work on a cabinetry job. I kept putting it off because of everything that's been going on here, but now that it's resolved, I should go."

"I see." She sensed he was saying more than the words indicated. "When will you leave?"

"This afternoon. It'll take a few days, so I suppose you'll be gone by the time I get back."

For a moment she couldn't speak. This was it, then. Cal was letting her know, in the nicest possible way, that he didn't want a relationship with her.

Well, that was for the best, wasn't it? They were committed to completely different values. This wasn't about the distance between Churchville and Philadelphia. It was a question of what they wanted from life. Since that couldn't be reconciled, it was better to make a clear break before anyone got hurt.

She managed to smile, forced herself to hold out her hand. "Thank you again for everything you've done to help us get under way. I'm sure I'll see you when I come back from time to time."

He nodded, holding her hand for a moment as if there was something else he wanted to say. Then he turned quickly and was gone.

She sank back in the chair. She'd been wrong about one thing. It was already too late to keep from getting hurt.

Chapter 15

Barney whined, lifting his head from the library carpet to look at Andrea. He probably wondered why she was still at the computer when everyone else in the house was asleep. Over the past week, she'd gotten into the habit of keeping the dog downstairs with her after Grams went to bed, letting him out for one last time and then putting him into Grams's room when she went up.

"It's all right, boy." She leaned back in the desk chair, covering her eyes with her hands for a moment. The figures on the computer screen had begun to blur, particularly when she tried to compare them with the cramped writing in Grandfather's last couple of ledgers.

Maybe it would be better to take all of the financial records back to the city with her on Monday, so that she could go over them at her leisure. She'd begun to find discrepancies. It looked as if Grandfather had been failing more than she'd imagined in his final years.

She studied the portrait above the mantel, her grandfather's painted features staring back at her. Was that what happened? Had he really lost that sharp business sense of his and been too proud to admit it? She was startled to realize it hurt to think of him that way.

Aware of the dog whining again, she closed down the program and stacked the ledgers on the edge of the desk. "All right, Barney. You can go out, and then we'd both better get some sleep."

Barney, understanding the words *go out,* trotted toward the back door. When she opened it, he darted outside with a sharp woof.

She leaned against the door, trying not to look in the direction of the barn. Of Cal's empty apartment.

Working on the financial records had, for a few hours, absorbed her mind completely. She could get lost in the rows of figures as easily as other people got lost in a good book.

Now the pain came rushing back. Cal had shut the door on whatever might have been between them. She understood his reasons, but he could have given her some say in the matter. At least, he could have if he felt what she did.

Maybe she was wrong about that. Maybe those close moments between them, those kisses, had been merely attraction to him, with nothing more solid behind it.

Her mind fumbled with an unaccustomed prayer. *I'm trying to find my way back to You, Lord. For a while, I thought Cal was going to be part of that, but I was wrong. Still, no matter how much it hurts to lose him, knowing him has helped me look at things more clearly. Please, guide me to live the way You want.*

No lightning flashed. She didn't have a burst of insight. But peace seeped into her heart, easing the pain and giving her comfort.

Barney barked, the sound muted. Frowning, she stepped outside and called, “Barney! Here, boy!”

Nothing moved anywhere in the lighted area of the yard. He must have gone farther afield while she stood there lost in thought.

Everything looked perfectly peaceful, but somewhere beyond the fringe of outbuildings, the dog yipped.

She reached back inside to slip the flashlight off its hook. She’d have to get him—if she went up to bed without him, Grams would have a fit. And he’d probably wake the house with his barking.

At least, with Levi in the hospital, she didn’t have to worry about encountering any prowlers. Poor Levi. Would charges be brought against him? Surely not, if Grams had anything to say about it.

She crossed to the toolshed, shining the light around. Beyond the range of the security lights it was pitch-black, the sliver of a new moon providing little illumination.

She called again, her voice sharp. This time the answer was a whining cry that sounded distressed, and her fingers tightened on the flashlight. Was Barney hurt? Trapped in some way? She hurried toward the sound, behind the row of outbuildings, into the blackness.

Yards ahead of her, across the overgrown lane, loomed the dark bulk of the old barn. A shiver went down her spine. The sound seemed to be coming from there.

The building had been kept in repair, but it hadn’t been used for anything in years. Still, there might be something that Barney’s collar could have become hooked on.

That must be it.

She trotted toward the earthen ramp to the upper level, flicking the flashlight around as she went, hoping she wouldn't spot any night creatures larger than a mouse. But the dog's presence had probably frightened away any other animals.

One of the big double doors stood ajar just enough for Barney to get through. She'd have to see that it was secured—something else to add to her to-do list. They couldn't have inn guests wandering around where they might get hurt.

She entered, swinging the light. The space was empty, an oil mark on the floor mute testimony to the farm vehicle that had once been parked there. Grandfather must have had the barn cleared out when it was no longer in use.

Her flashlight beam picked up a small door opposite the entrance. The dog's now-frantic barking came from there.

She hurried across the dusty floorboards and grabbed the door, yanking it open. A foul, metallic aroma rushed out at her. Memory stirred. They'd kept fertilizers and pesticides in here long ago. Her light bounced off floor-to-ceiling shelves, still laden with rusty cans. The place looked like a toxic waste dump. Her grandfather's care of the building hadn't extended to clearing this out, apparently.

Barney's eyes shone in the light, and he wiggled with impatience. "Barney." She was embarrassed at the slight tremor in her voice, even though there was no one but the dog to hear. "What happened, baby? Are you stuck?"

Sure enough, the dog's collar was caught in the prongs of an old harrow that lay on the floor. She hurried to kneel beside him. When she patted him, she had to try to quiet his excited leaps and attempts to lick her face.

"Hold still, you silly thing. I can't release you when you're doing that." She put the flashlight down, fumbling with the collar, the dog's jumps nearly knocking her over. The flashlight rolled, illuminating what lay in the corner.

Nick Bendick. Uncle Nick. He sprawled against the wall, unconscious. Alive? Her heart seemed to stop.

"Uncle Nick?" She hurried to him, dropping to her knees next to the inert form.

She groped for his wrist, breathing again when she felt a pulse—weak, but at least he was alive. She grabbed the flashlight, trying to focus with hands that were shaking. It looked as if he'd stumbled on the harrow, hitting his head against the wall. But what on earth was he doing here?

The circle of light wavered, and she forced herself to steady it. It touched Nick's hand, lying lax on the barn floor. Her breath caught, and the world seemed to spin.

In Nick's hand was a dog leash, next to it a torn paper bag, dog biscuits spilling from it.

She couldn't seem to move. Barney hadn't gotten tangled up on his own. Nick had been waiting, knowing she always let the dog out the last thing at night. Had trapped Barney, apparently intending to use him to lure her here.

Her mind struggled to the obvious conclusion. The financial records. Anger swept through her. This was about her interest in the financial records. Grandfather hadn't been losing his touch. Nick had been cheating him.

She had to get help. Run to the house, call the paramedics and the police, let them sort it out. She hurried back to the dog, struggled with the collar for another moment, and finally got it free.

Uncle Nick. It was impossible to believe. Could he really have intended to hurt her? Surely he'd never hurt anyone in his life.

Except Levi. Her mind seemed to leap from one understanding to another. Levi, lying on the floor with the keys planted next to him. How much of what had been happening had been caused by Nick's frantic efforts to keep her from looking into the financial records? He must have realized she was the one person who would understand what he'd done.

The authorities would figure it out. Barney beside her, she hurried toward the door. Cool night air hit her like a slap in the face. Get help. That was all she could do now.

She darted toward the distant house, the circle of light bouncing ahead of her, and Barney woofed at the unexpected excitement. If Grams heard him, came out—well, she'd have to know the truth about the man she'd trusted soon, in any event.

If Cal were at the barn, she'd call on him for help. But he wasn't. He'd left. Ridiculous, to feel that she needed him.

She rounded the corner of the toolshed and flew straight into someone.

She stumbled back, gasping. The security light showed her Betty, of all people. Another surprise in a night of surprises. She grasped the woman's arm.

"You have to help me. It's Nick—he's hurt. He—"

"I'll help."

Betty patted her reassuringly with one hand. The other lifted something. Light reflected from a long, silvery shaft. It swung down, pain exploded in her head, and the ground came up to meet her.

Andrea struggled to open her eyes, but her head spun and ached. She'd just lie here another minute…

Then consciousness came rolling back. Nick. And Betty. Betty had hit her with a golf club. Impossible, but it had happened. Nick and Betty must be doing this together.

A warm, furry body next to her, a rough wet tongue washing her face. "Barney," she whispered, coughing on the word.

She moved, aware of hard wooden boards beneath her, of the acrid smell that made her want to gag. She was back in the tiny storage room in the old barn. Barney was with her.

Something hard poked into her ribs. She rolled, feeling for it, and pulled out the flashlight. Fumbled for the switch, thinking if she had to stay in the dark another instant she'd start screaming…

The light came on. Maybe this was worse. She could see the tall shelves on either side of her, enclosing her with their load of poison. She sucked in a breath and was instantly sorry when the air burned her throat.

Then she saw what still lay against the wall. Nick.

Her mind spun.

Get out. She had to get out. She stumbled to the door, groping for the handle. Locked. Incredibly, Betty had locked her in here. Betty. How could she even have gotten her here? It was impossible.

Then she identified the sound that rumbled from beyond the door. A car's engine. Betty must have driven up the overgrown lane behind the outbuildings and hauled her in here.

She pounded on the door. “Betty! Let me out of here. You can’t get away with this.”

“Can’t I?” Betty’s voice was muffled by the thick door, but she must be standing close to it on the other side. “I think I can. You’ve always underestimated me, all of you. My plans have been made for a long time, my money safely salted away under another name. I knew Nick would break down at some point. He always had such a soft spot for your grandmother.”

She sounded like an indulgent mother, admitting a failing in her child.

“You were stealing from the firm.” Hard to think it through, with the fumes fogging her brain. “But Nick—was he in it with you? Is that what this was all about?”

“Nick had a little gambling problem, you see. Borrowed some money from the accounts. He wasn’t very good at it. Your grandfather would have found him out in a week if it hadn’t been for me.” There was a trace of pride in her voice.

“Betty, think about what you’re doing.” She forced herself to be calm. Rational. One of them should be. “Just let me out, and we’ll go to the police together. I’ll get you a lawyer—”

Betty chuckled. “Dear Andrea, always so sure you know what’s best. I have no intention of going to the police. You and Nick are going to have an unfortunate accident, and I’m going to be far away by the time it’s sorted out and they start to look for me.”

“Accident…” She tried to move, but her muscles didn’t obey. She could lie down, just rest for a moment; it would be all right….

Shock sent her upright. Her mental fog wasn't just from the closed room and the cans of chemicals. The car was running because Betty was pumping carbon monoxide into the room.

She dropped to her knees, fingers fumbling along the bottom of the door. Yes, there was the mouth of a hose, thrust under the corner of the door.

Please, Lord, please, Lord, help me know what to do. If I can just block it...

She swung the light around, picking up an old feed sack shoved onto a shelf. Grab it, twist a piece small enough to fit into the hose, stuff it in, coughing and choking, prayng it blocked enough to give them a few more precious moments to live....

A few moments. Not enough. No one would look for her until morning, probably. How long would it take until they searched here?

She slumped back, trying to force her numbed wits to move. The walls were closing in. She couldn't stop them, and she felt the familiar panic, blurred by her fogged mind, but there, creeping in, loosening her control.

Father, help me hold on. If I panic, I'll die. Forgive me for drifting away from You. Hold me in Your hands, living or dying.

Hands. Hands reaching out to her, pulling her free. She shook her head, knowing it was a memory, but a memory of what?

It wouldn't come. Think. What else could she do?

Noises outside the door. A car door opening and closing. The car driving away. Betty was gone.

She was still alive, and so was Nick from what she could tell. But not for long unless she could think of something. She swung the light around. Metal shone for an instant on the shelf—she reached, hand closing on a bar about the size of a tire iron.

Excitement flooded her, clearing her mind. If she could get the door open…

But a moment's effort showed her that was impossible. The door was solid, resisting her feeble efforts to open it.

Think. Think. If you can't get out, maybe you can get air in. The wall behind her was solid stone, the end wall of the barn. Nothing there, but the wall to her right must be an outside wall.

She crawled over to it, dragging the bar. Barney, whimpering a little, struggled to her side. Was it her imagination, or was the air a little better here? The dog seemed to think so. He put his nose at the base of the wall, right where the siding boards came down to meet the floor.

Nick. She crawled back to him, grabbed his arms, and dragged him toward the wall. No time now to worry that she was injuring him further. If she didn't get them some air, they would die.

Adrenaline pulsing, she ran her hand along the joint, feeling the slightest crack between the boards. Big enough to wedge the bar in? Her fingers seemed to have grown stupid along with her brain. It took three tries before she forced the bar in.

Wiggle it, shove it, find something to hit it with—but there she ran out of luck. There was nothing loose in the room sturdy enough to hit the bar. She'd have to keep wiggling it, trying to force it through to the outside, but her mind was fogging again.

Ironic. She'd filled up the slight crack with the pry bar, cutting off whatever air might come through.

Give me strength, Lord. Help me. I know You're here with me. I know whatever You intend is right. But I can't stop trying, can't stop fighting....

"To everything there is a season, and a time for every purpose under Heaven. A time to live and a time to die..."

Barney slumped to the floor. Poor boy. He'd go first. She and Nick were bigger, so they'd last longer. Push, keep pushing, a little farther...

"A little farther, Drea." Her grandfather's voice. He was the only one who'd ever called her that. "Just a little farther. Don't stop now. Another inch, and you'll reach my hands."

Another inch. A vague dream of Grandfather's strong hands, tight on hers, lifting her out into the cool air, holding her close. Safe. She'd always been safe with him.

Safe in God's hands. Living or dying...

Another inch. She pushed the bar, felt the resistance give way as it slid through. Befuddled. Taking a moment to realize she had to pull the bar back out.

Feel the cool air on her face, rushing in through the hole she'd made. Drinking in long gasps of it. Drag Nick's limp form, then Barney, up to the opening, feeling the dog stir.

But tired. So tired. She slumped down, head on Barney's fur.

Chapter 16

Cal eased off on the accelerator when he hit the outskirts of Churchville. He was making a fool of himself, rushing back at this hour, but the urge to see Andrea again, to clear the air between them, had been too strong to ignore.

He'd tried hiding from life, and it hadn't worked. He couldn't hide. Life kept finding him.

And beneath that urge to see Andrea had been something he couldn't explain, a sense that all was not right. An urgent feeling that he was needed.

Well, he was here, and how he'd explain arriving at this late hour, he didn't know. They'd all be asleep, probably, and he'd have to wait until morning to see Andrea anyway.

But as he turned into the drive at the inn, he saw the glow of lights in the library. It had to be Andrea, sitting up late at the computer. Relief flooded through him, making him realize just how tense he'd been.

A glimpse of movement drew his attention. From beyond the outbuildings, a dark car spurted out, hit the winding country road and raced away.

Cal jammed on the brakes and slid out, leaving the motor running, all his instincts crying out. That was wrong, very wrong. He ran toward the back door, and the minute he saw it, he knew his instincts were on target. The door stood open, light pooling out onto the patio, and no one was there.

His feet thudded across the patio. None of them would go off and leave the door standing open at this hour. He bolted inside and ran for the library. Lights on, computer on, desk chair pushed back. It looked as if Andrea had just walked away.

Some rational part of his mind kept insisting that there could be a logical explanation, but he didn't believe it. Rachel—Rachel was sleeping on this floor now, in the little room off the kitchen.

He saw the light go on as he ran to it. He was probably scaring her to death.

"Rachel, it's Cal. Is Andrea with you?"

"No. What's happening?" Fear laced her voice.

He flung open the door. Rachel sat up in bed, pulling a robe around her.

"The back door is standing open, and I can't find Andrea."

"If she took the dog out—"

He felt as if he'd been doused with cold water. "That must be it. Sorry. I'll just check."

Logical explanation, see? But the fear drove him back out to the patio. "Andrea! Andrea, are you out here?"

A light went on overhead, and he heard footsteps on the stairs. Katherine. She hurried toward him.

"Cal, what are you doing back? Why are you calling for Andrea?"

"Is she upstairs?"

"No." She glanced toward the library and paled. "She and Barney were still down here. She must have taken him out. But why didn't she hear you call?"

"I'll look for her. Where's a flashlight?"

She pulled a drawer open and thrust a heavy torch into his hand. "I'm calling the police."

He jerked a nod and hurried out the door. Better a false alarm than a tragedy. He'd never been one to go on instinct, but this sense was stronger than he'd ever experienced.

Is it You, Lord? If it is, help me to listen. Show me where to go. Please, keep her safe.

He ran across the lawn toward the outbuildings. The car that had no possible reason for being there—it had come from behind the outbuildings. He swung the light around.

"Andrea! Where are you?"

Nothing. The buildings were dark and silent, the security lights reflecting from them, mocking him. They hadn't kept Andrea safe.

And the dog—the dog must be with her. "Barney!" he yelled. "Here, boy. Barney!"

Not even an answering woof. He paused by the toolshed, the urgency pounding along his veins like a power in his blood, telling him to hurry, hurry. But where?

Lord, help me. If this is from You, help me.

He took a breath. Think. The car came down the disused lane behind the outbuildings—the lane that led only to the old barn. He ran, heart thudding in his ears. Behind him, from the house, the bell began clanging insistently. Katherine, trying to rouse the Zook family to come and help.

The circle of light bounced. He rounded the corner, saw the barn doors, and knew the instinct that drove him was right. Both doors stood open, and the grass leading to them was bent down from the passage of a car.

He thudded inside. A car had been in here—he could smell the fumes. Strong, too strong. He swung the light around. Empty, nothing…

The light flashed on a door—solid as the barn, the old-fashioned latch dropped down into its pocket, securing it. He ran toward it, stumbling on a length of hose, righting himself, reaching the door.

Flung it open and staggered back from the fumes. Andrea. He took a deep breath and threw himself through the door. Woman and dog lay together against the outer wall. Another figure—a man. Bendick. Still, too still.

He grabbed Andrea, stumbled back out, through the barn, out into the cold night air. Think, remember your CPR training, but even as he thought it she coughed, choked and gasped in a gulp of air.

Tears filled his eyes. *Please, God, please, God.* He knelt in the damp grass, holding her against him. "Andrea, wake up. Say something. Breathe."

She stirred, murmured something, then sank limply against him. But she was breathing. Her eyelids fluttered.

"I've found her!" he shouted at the top of his lungs. "Call the paramedics." Poor Katherine must be terrified, but he couldn't do anything else. He'd have to go back in for Bendick….

Lights bobbing toward him—Eli, his son and the oldest grandson with him, running with trousers pulled on over nightshirts.

"In the barn, the back room. Bendick and the dog. Mind the fumes." Samuel nodded and pelted into the barn with the boy, while Eli knelt beside him.

"Will she be all right, then?"

"She's breathing." He looked at the older man, not ashamed of the tears that spilled over. "She's alive."

"Thank the Lord," Eli said.

The wail of a siren split the night.

Yes, thank You, Father. Thank You.

Andrea toyed with the piece of dry toast that was all she thought she could get down. They sat around the breakfast table in various stages of exhaustion. Emma kept pressing food on people, as if that were the only cure for the night they'd been through.

Since she'd missed most of it, either through being unconscious or at the hospital, she tried to concentrate on what Chief Burkhalter was saying, but her gaze kept straying to Cal.

His face was drawn, the skin pulled tight against the bone, as if he'd been in battle and wasn't sure it was over. She'd had no chance to talk with him alone, and still didn't know what had brought him back. She only knew he'd come in time to save her. That was enough.

Barney padded around the table from Grams to her, sighed, and thudded heavily to the floor next to her, as if he'd decided that she needed his protection.

"…caught up with the woman on the other side of Harrisburg," Burkhalter was saying. "She tried to bluff it out. Might have gotten away if Burke hadn't gotten to you in time." He eyed her soberly. "Just glad you're okay."

She nodded, not sure she trusted herself to speak. The memory was too fresh.

"I don't understand." Grams seemed to have aged overnight. "I'd believe anything of Betty, but Nick—we've known him and trusted him for thirty years."

"Are they talking?" Cal asked.

Burkhalter shrugged. "The woman clammed up tight and asked for a lawyer. Bendick is still in the hospital, but he's babbling like Conestoga Creek." He turned to Grams. "Might make you feel a little better to know that apparently Bendick never intended to steal from the company. He had gambling losses he was ashamed to admit to your husband, took money to pay them off intending to replace it, he says, but the secretary found out and started blackmailing him. I imagine a thorough look into the books will prove she helped herself to quite a bit. Whether you'll ever get it back again is another question. The lawyers will have to sort that out."

"I still don't understand," Rachel said. "What was the point of all of the tricks they pulled? Was that Uncle Nick or Betty?"

"According to Bendick, they figured Andrea was the one person who might make sense of their doctored records, especially if she got hold of her grandfather's ledgers. The secretary was pulling the strings, blackmailing him to try and scare Andrea away. He claims he couldn't take it anymore, was coming here to tell you the truth when she attacked him."

The timing suddenly made sense. "I had the ledgers on my desk in the afternoon, when Betty stopped in. She must have thought I was on to them."

"We found the ledgers in her car," Burkhalter said. "Looks like they had some hope of locating them before you did. And he thought if Mrs. Unger gave up the idea of the inn, you'd go back to the city and leave things alone."

"Levi saw him." Emma spoke unexpectedly, her hands holding tight to the back of Grams's chair. "He finally told us. He saw Mr. Bendick here when he shouldn't of been. He wanted to tell Andrea, but he was too shy. Mr. Bendick said to meet him in Cal's place, so he could explain. Instead he pushed him."

"Levi—he was trying to tell me that night when he stood outside the house. And he followed me when I left the farm."

Emma nodded. "He meant to help. He didn't know how."

It was all starting to fall into place. "What about Rachel, the hit-and-run? Did they do that?"

"Bendick claims not," Burkhalter said. "We'll keep looking, but we may never know the truth about that."

Grams reached up to clasp Emma's hand. "At least Levi and Rachel are going to be all right."

"And Ms. Hampton," Burkhalter added. "The secretary hoped we'd think Bendick was guilty, at least long enough to let her get away." He shifted his gaze to Cal. "What made you come back, Burke? Did you suspect it was something to do with the books?"

Her breath stopped. *Why, Cal? How did you know?*

"No, not at all." He looked as if he were blaming himself. "I just..." He hesitated. "I just had a feeling."

Grams glanced at the clock and got to her feet. "Goodness, we'll be having guests here before you know it. We have to get ready." She bustled around the table, making shooing motions with her hands. "Andrea, you go and rest before you fall over. We'll take care of everything. Go on now."

People began to scatter. If Cal intended to tell her anything, it would have to wait.

The final guests left on Monday afternoon, heaping delighted praise on Three Sisters Inn. Andrea looked at Grams and Rachel. They wore grins just as goofy as hers probably was.

"We actually did it," she said. "I'm not sure I believed it would work."

"I did." Rachel patted her arm. "Thanks to you, and Grams, and Emma, and Nancy, and everyone else who helped out."

"They all said they'd be back." Grams sounded a little surprised. "Two couples have already booked for a second visit."

"You know, Grams, if you're able to recover the money Betty stole, you might not have to run the inn." She was fairly certain she knew the answer to that, but they may as well get it out in the open.

Grams looked astonished. "Not run the inn? Of course we will. This is the most fun I've had in years."

Andrea hugged her. It looked as if she'd been wrong about a lot of things, but this was one time when she didn't mind that.

Grams patted her. "You should go and rest. You both should."

"Sounds good." Rachel stifled a yawn.

"I think I'll go out back and get some fresh air first." Andrea whistled to Barney, who scurried to her side. She patted his head. "You're my self-appointed watchdog, aren't you?" So maybe he wasn't the brightest dog in the world, but he was loyal.

Afternoon sun slanted across the lawn, filtering through the trees to touch the brilliant colors of the flowers. The sandstone patio wall glowed golden. Cal sat, just where she thought she might find him.

The dog padded quietly at her heels as she stepped off the patio and went to sit beside him.

He gave her a questioning look. "You're not turned off by the view out here after what happened to you?"

That was a nice, safe way to start what they had to say to each other. "It's still beautiful." She managed to look at the dark bulk of the old barn where it lifted above the outbuildings. "I guess there's something about nearly dying that makes you appreciate life."

"I should have been here," he said abruptly, emotion roughening his voice. "I shouldn't have left until I was sure everything was all right."

Sorrow deepened. It would have been better if he'd said he shouldn't have left at all, but he hadn't. She'd have to accept that.

"You came back in time, that's all that counts." It took an effort to keep her voice even. "What made you come back, Cal? I need to know."

He touched her hand lightly, and that touch seemed to reverberate through her. "I kept thinking I'd been unfair, leaving the way I did without talking to you. I tried telling myself I'd done it for the best, but I wasn't very convincing." He looked at her then. "I'm sorry."

She nodded, trying to dispel the lump in her throat. "That's why you came back last night? Because you'd been wrong to leave without talking to me?"

"Not exactly." His brow furrowed. "I don't know

if I can explain. I just felt an overwhelming pressure to come, not to wait for morning, not to delay, just to come." His fingers wrapped around hers. "I think God was giving me the push I needed. That's the only explanation I have."

"It's all you need." The feelings she'd had when she was trapped came flooding back—the assurance of God's presence, the half-remembered dream about Grandfather. "Remember when you asked me what brought on my claustrophobia?"

He looked startled by the change of subject, but nodded.

"I found out. Some of it I remembered, some Grams told me. When I was five, I fell into an abandoned well behind the old barn."

"That would certainly do it."

She nodded. "Grandfather was out in the field with Eli and some of the men. They heard me cry. My grandfather had the men hold his legs and lower him down so that I could reach his hands. He pulled me out."

"And you didn't remember it?"

"No. I asked Grams why they didn't tell me, but apparently they thought it was better forgotten. Last night—last night I remembered, some of it at least. When I was digging the airhole, I could feel God's presence with me. Somehow I'd lost that certainty of His presence, but now it's back. And I remembered my grandfather's voice, telling me to reach farther so I could take his hand. It kept me going."

Cal held her hand between his palms, and his touch comforted her. "You feel differently about your grandfather than you did when you came."

She nodded, wanting to articulate it. He needed to understand how she'd changed. "I can see him more clearly now, and look at the situation like an adult instead of a child. He was a strong, stubborn, fallible human being, not a superhero. He loved and he made mistakes, like we all do. But the loving—that was the important part."

"I'm glad," he said simply.

She turned to face him. "Understanding that made me see that I want things to be straight between us. No long silences or things left unsaid."

"That's asking a lot. I'm not sure I'm brave enough for that."

"I think you are." She had to give him the choice. Either they could take the risk of loving each other, or he could go back to hiding from the world in his safe, peaceful sanctuary.

He looked down at their clasped hands. "You know why I left. I'd started to care about you too much. I knew the kind of life you want, and I couldn't ask you to change. It seemed better—safer, I guess—if we parted before it became too difficult." The corner of his lips curled slightly. "I was wrong. It was more than difficult. It was impossible. Andrea, I know that hiding isn't the answer for me. I choose this life because it's right for me, but I don't want it to come between us."

Something lifted inside her, and she wanted to laugh. They'd been so foolish, trying to protect themselves from falling in love. God had known better than they had.

"Funny thing about that." She couldn't help the lilt to her voice. "Being here with family again, seeing how unreasonable my boss is and how cutthroat my colleagues, made me take a serious look at what I want out of life. Maybe that security I was looking for doesn't mean I have to have the biggest office, or make the most money."

He was looking at her with so much love shining in his eyes that she didn't know whether she should laugh or cry.

"I was thinking I might start a little bookkeeping business of my own, where I could be my own boss. You know any small towns that might need a business like that?"

He slid his arm around her and drew her close. "I think we might be able to find the right place. And I know a carpenter who'll give you a good price on office furniture."

She leaned into him, feeling his strength, knowing his character and his faith. She'd been looking for security in the wrong place, just as Cal had been looking for peace in the wrong place. God was calling them to love and to dare, not to hide and be safe.

She lifted her face, meeting his lips, and knew this time she was home to stay.

* * * * *

SPECIAL EXCERPT FROM

Love Inspired®

Discovering he has a two-year-old son is a huge surprise for veterinarian Wyatt Harrow. But so are his lingering feelings for the boy's pretty mom...

Read on for a sneak preview of the fifth book in the ***LONE STAR COWBOY LEAGUE: BOYS RANCH*** *miniseries, THE DOCTOR'S TEXAS BABY* by Deb Kastner.

Wyatt glanced at Carolina, but she wouldn't meet his eyes.

Was she feeling guilty over all Matty's firsts that she'd denied Wyatt? First breath, first word, the first step Matty took?

He couldn't say he felt sorry for her. She should be feeling guilty. She'd made the decision to walk away. She'd created these consequences for herself, and for Wyatt, and most of all, for Matty.

But today wasn't a day for anger. Today was about spending time with his son.

"What do you say, little man?" he asked, scooping Matty into his arms and leading Carolina to his truck. "Do you want to play ball?"

Not knowing what Matty would like, he'd pretty much loaded up every kind of sports ball imaginable—a football, a baseball, a soccer ball and a basketball.

Carolina flashed him half a smile and shrugged apologetically. "I'm afraid I don't know much about these games beyond being able to identify which ball goes with which sport."

"That's what Matty's got a dad for."

He didn't really think about what he was saying until the words had already left his lips.

Their gazes met and locked. She was silently challenging him, but he didn't know about what. Still, he kept his gaze firmly on hers. His words might not have been premeditated, but that didn't make them any less true. He was sorry if he'd hurt her feelings, though. He wanted to keep things friendly between them.

"There's plenty of room on the green for three. What do you say? Do you want to play soccer with us?"

Shock registered in her face, but it was no more than what he was feeling. This was all so new. Untested waters.

Somehow, they had to work things out, but kicking a ball around together at the park?

Why, that almost felt as if they were a family.

And although in a sense that was technically true, Wyatt didn't even want to go down that road.

He had every intention of being the best father he could to Matty. And in so doing, he would establish some sort of a working relationship with Carolina, some way they could both be comfortable without it getting awkward. He just couldn't bring himself to think about that right now.

Or maybe he just didn't want to.

SPECIAL EXCERPT FROM

Love Inspired SUSPENSE

Paige Olson's five-year-old daughter may have witnessed her father's murder, but she won't talk about it—and now a gunman's hunting them down. Homicide detective Miles Callahan will do anything to protect Paige and her little girl...even if it means breaking police protocol.

Read on for a sneak preview of
THE ONLY WITNESS
by Laura Scott, *available February 2017*
from Love Inspired Suspense!

"I looked up the license plate of the black sedan from the restaurant," Miles said, his expression grim. "The sedan is registered to Sci-Tech."

"They sent gunmen after us?" Paige asked in a strained whisper.

"Yeah, that's what it looks like."

"They're after me because of my ex-husband, aren't they?"

"I think so, yes." Miles reached over and cradled her icy hands in his. "I'm sorry."

Paige gripped his hands tightly. "You have to find Travis before it's too late."

He didn't want to point out that it might already be too late. Whatever Abby had seen on the tablet had frightened her to the point she wouldn't speak. Had Travis told her to keep quiet? Or had she seen something horrible? He found himself hoping for the first option, but feared the latter.

LISEXP0117

"I'm not sure where to look for Travis," he admitted. "There's no way to know where he'd go to hide if he thought he was in danger."

"Did you give the police the list of names I gave you?" Paige asked. "I know they're only a few names, but…"

"I've been searching on their names, but I haven't found anything yet. At least we have another link to Sci-Tech. No wonder they were stonewalling me."

"I might be able to get inside the building," Paige offered.

"No." His knee-jerk reaction surprised him, and he tried to backpedal. "I mean, if they're the ones behind this, then it's not safe for you to go there. Besides, how would you get in?"

She lifted her uncertain gaze to his. "I know a couple of the security guards pretty well. If I waited until after-hours, when there's only one security guard manning the desk, I might be able to convince them to let me in."

"I know you want to help, but it's not worth the risk." He couldn't stand the idea of Paige walking into the equivalent of the lion's den. "You don't know for sure which security guard would be on duty. And besides, if anything happened—Abby would be lost without you."

She blinked, and he thought he saw the glint of tears. "Logically, I know you're right, but it's hard to sit back and do nothing, not even trying."

"I'll find a way to do something while keeping you and Abby safe." He couldn't stand the thought of her worrying about things she couldn't change. He'd protect her, no matter what.

LISEXP0117